Rebecca's Journey

by

Winona Bennett Cross

Cover Art by *The Wild Rose Press, Inc.*

The Wild Rose Press, Inc.
PO Box 708
Adams Basin, NY 14410-0708
Visit us at www.thewildrosepress.com

Publishing History
First Edition, 2024
Trade Paperback ISBN 978-1-5092-5575-7
Digital ISBN 978-1-5092-5576-4

Published in the United States of America

Dedication

With the greatest gratitude and love I dedicate this book to my husband, sons, and granddaughters. They believed in me even when I didn't.

I posthumously dedicate Rebecca's Journey to Mr. Jerald Haynes my Junior year American History teacher who presented the Oregon Trail and the Westward Expansion in such a way it took up residence inside my heart in 1968.

Chapter 1

Leaving Day

Dawn broke through the clear Missouri sky as eighteen-year-old Rebecca Pierce and her mother, Sarah, stepped off the porch of the boarding house into the crowded noisy street. Rebecca's dog, Bolo, barked and ran circles around her. "Everything feels so alive today, so exciting. Calm down, Bolo."

"It's chaotic. I wonder if we've made the right decision to leave. This journey was the dream you and your father shared. Not mine. Not after your brother passed."

"It will take a great deal of stamina, but we will make it and in the long run be thankful." Distracted by a young boy chasing a ball in the street, Rebecca watched as his mother grabbed him by the back straps of his overalls and turned him around to face her. The boy tucked his chin to his chest, wiped his nose on his sleeve, and whispered something she couldn't hear.

Laughing, Rebecca elbowed her way through the crowd of excited emigrants offering polite apologies that could barely be heard over bellowing oxen, neighing horses, and braying mules.

The air buzzed with excitement and anticipation as the road filled with families leaving kith and kin behind in their quest for the land of promise.

Today was leaving day.

Surely, you have more coffee.

Did you pack the basket for today's meals?

Snatches of conversation carried on the wind like colorful ribbons flying from a maypole.

Is everything tied down?

I'm afraid I'll never see you again.

Rebecca wiped tears from her face. When did she start crying? Tears had come unexpectedly and at the oddest moments since yesterday at the cemetery while saying goodbye to her father and brother.

She pointed to a group of people hovering around the general store, clamoring for extra supplies. "I imagine every seller has long since run out of necessities."

"Probably. Peppermint sounds good."

The open door of the store that had belonged to her family caught Rebecca's attention. "It seems strange to see new proprietors here."

"I agree. Doors close for new ones to open."

A short while later as she and her mother left the mercantile, Rebecca carried a parcel containing two pounds of peppermint sticks, two tins of peaches, and a large tin of soda crackers.

"Hey, watch where you're going."

A hand on her arm kept Rebecca from falling or dropping her package. She glanced up into the green eyes of a stranger who sported double dimples. For a second, only a second, she couldn't breathe. *What is wrong with me?* "I, well, I'm sorry. I wasn't paying attention. Excuse me."

"Not a problem, ma'am." The young man tipped his

hat. "Name's Zachary Miller. You headed for the wagon train? I'm gathering up a few things to ride with them myself."

"Yes, we are. If you'll pardon me, my mother and I need to check the oxen and horses."

"Take care. Reckon I'll see you again." Zachary tipped his hat again and walked away.

Rebecca watched him leave, flushing when he glanced back at her once more. What was she thinking? Why would a handsome stranger fluster her? She was always in control. The memory of a time when she allowed her impetuous behavior to control her surfaced. Though really not that long ago, she felt like the incident occurred a lifetime before, but still caused heat to fill her cheeks. She took her mother's arm. "Do you remember the time I galloped Glory bareback down Main Street? My skirts were tucked, but they kept rising up, flapping in the wind, and showing my legs all the way to my knees."

Sarah chuckled. "How could I forget? I was mortified. Your father laughed until his sides hurt. He loved your independence. Where on earth did these thoughts come from?"

"I've changed. I'm changing. I understand the need to be more serious and responsible."

The line of wagons came into sight. Each one gleamed with a bright white cover. The two wagons Rebecca and Sarah owned were near the front of the line.

Their teams had been yoked. Her two finest horses—Glory, her bay mare, and her black stallion, Patriot, were tied to the back. The best hopes she and her father shared for their dream depended on the valuable horses. Four brown oxen stood at the front of each wagon. Heads bowed, they chewed cud as if it was a delicacy and slept on their feet.

Shielding her eyes from the morning sun with her hand, Rebecca greeted Jodie Smith. "Hello, Mrs. Smith. Your face seems to have gained some color. You just may be on the mend. A little rest and good food work wonders, don't they?"

"It's just Jodie. Remember? Thank you for all you've done." Jodie glanced northward and commenced to fidgeting.

Rebecca followed Jodie's gaze and saw Silas Smith striding their way. In the short time since they met, she'd heard Silas ordering Jodie and their twelve-year-old son, Aaron, around with harsh words and threats. He treated them with disrespect, jerking Jodie by the arm and cuffing Aaron on the side of his head. Maybe he was anxious about the trip, but the sense of potential trouble settled in Rebecca's stomach like a weighted rock. The Smith family had lost their farm, and illness killed three of their children. Rebecca and Sarah wanted to help them. Meeting them had seemed providential, as they needed someone to drive their second wagon, which carried supplies for the general store her aunt had opened.

Silas tipped his hat to Rebecca and Sarah. "Mornin', ladies."

"Silas," Sarah greeted Silas.

Rebecca did the same.

He ignored Jodie and walked past Rebecca, brushing her shoulder. He stopped, arched an eyebrow, and laughed before stalking away toward the back of the wagon.

The way he watched her soured her stomach and

made her skin itch and crawl as if ants had found their way under her sleeves. She pulled her shawl tighter and crossed her arms over her chest. Rebecca heard Misty whinny and hurried to check on the horse. She found Silas tugging on the halter with a coil of rope around his arm. Misty kept backing away from him, but she could only go as far as the rope allowed. Ears flat, eyes wide and white, she pawed the ground. "What are you doing? This is a gentle mare. She was treated cruelly before my family got her. She's afraid of you. Let go of her rope."

"Where did this nag come from?" Silas moved into Rebecca's space forcing her to step back.

Jodie rushed around the wagon and ducked her head. "Rebecca gave her to me because I told her about Pudding and how much I missed her. I'll be taking care of her."

Silas dropped the rope then slugged the mare beside the eye. He spit on the ground. "I don't give a damn where you got her. Don't expect me to take care of a damn horse."

Jodie rushed to Misty. She checked her eye which thankfully, although swelling rapidly, wasn't bleeding. "I'm going to get a cool wet cloth to put over her eye. Stay away from my horse, Silas."

"Just what are you going to do if I don't? You're just a weak woman with no brains to speak of. I'll hit who or what I think needs it."

Jodie gasped and covered her mouth.

Rebecca moved in, standing toe to toe with Silas. "If I catch you treating anyone or any animal with cruelty you'll be dismissed on the spot. I'll see to it. Now, go finish getting the wagon ready to leave."

"I am the man in this group. Don't forget it. Women.

You're all worthless and only good for one thing. That horse is nothing but a nag. Aaron is a useless boy." Silas spun, heading toward a group of men watching the lead wagon, slapping Aaron on the head as he passed.

Rebecca glanced to the side and saw Aaron's face turn red and his head all but disappear into his shoulders. She and Jodie stood on each side of Misty, scratching her ears. They shared a glance, realizing a friendship had been forged. A bond that began with a horse.

"Misty was my brother's horse. He got her from a man who mistreated her. Joseph died in an accident a few months ago. He was fifteen."

"I'm sorry about your brother. I knew about your father. I'm sorry for that, too. Silas is edgy. Leaving Independence was a sudden decision. I hope you understand. I'll take care of her." Jodie's words tumbled out fast.

"I know you will."

****

Rebecca checked the oxen one last time. The milk cow tied to the side stood chewing her cud. Rebecca scratched its head and whispered to it. She climbed onto the wagon seat beside her mother. Excitement built and bubbled inside her. Eagerness kept her from sitting still. She had waited to leave for a full year. Despite her being eager, the loss of her father and brother weighed heavy as a stone. Shouldn't she feel guilty about being excited? Her dog, Bolo, wedged himself between Rebecca and Sarah. He whined and scratched at his collar.

"Stop it. You need to wear it."

"It's important to check on this often." Sarah warned and leaned over to do so herself.

Rebecca sighed. How many times would she have

to be reminded of the secrets?

Sarah straightened her back and shoulders and reached up to stroke the tortoiseshell comb holding her auburn hair in a loose twist at the nape of her neck. She brushed horse and dog hair from Rebecca's skirt. "I believe your father and brother are with us today."

Sadness and determination waged war on her mother's face, and Rebecca didn't trust herself to speak. She pulled her shawl together in the front, tied the fabric in a loose knot, and rubbed a corner of the deerskin bag she carried. The bag held her favorite possessions—the rock she picked up at the cemetery yesterday, two pencils, a blank journal, several willow branches to keep her teeth clean, a letter from her father, a knife, and a tortoiseshell hairbrush.

Voices rose along the wagon line. Rebecca stood on the seat to see Colonel Wilson standing on the tongue of his rig. She nudged her mother and pointed. Her nerves built like fire taking hold, moving from her belly, flipping up to her racing heart and the breath she held. Images of her family discussing the trek blossomed in her mind. She closed her eyes and smelled the fried chicken, tasted the sweet cream in her coffee, and felt the work-roughened loving hands of her father squeezing her own. They'd sat around the table talking all at once. Raising horses and cattle, farming, and helping Aunt Emma with the general store had been their combined dream.

Chapter 2

Wagons Ho

The shrill sound of a whistle vibrated through the air. Everyone stopped what they were doing and watched their leader.

Rebecca clasped her hands together. Shivers of excitement danced from her head all the way to her toes.

A resigned and mournful sigh escaped Sarah's lips. She ran her fingers over the embroidered red roses on the collar of her dress. "It is time."

"Ladies and gentlemen. We'll be leaving Independence soon. This train is the first to leave. Follow my rules." Colonel Wilson stopped speaking long enough to spit a stream of brown tobacco to the ground. He presented an imposing figure dressed in buckskin from head to toe. His dark beard was shot with gray. A leather strip held his long brown hair in place. Rebecca had met him and knew his eyes were sapphire with lighter rims. She fanned through a book her father had written notes in, as he planned the trek.

"Listen to me without question. Despite my suggestions, some of you may find you've overloaded your wagon and will be forced to leave things on the trail. If you think there is anything unnecessary, get rid of it now. You'll soon realize you packed too much when the oxen and mules become footsore and can't pull a load. Supplies will be available in the Oregon Territory and maybe at forts along the way." Colonel Wilson stopped speaking long enough to glance at the eager emigrants.

"The most important possessions you have are your wagon teams and any livestock you have in the herd. Care for your animals and they will serve you well. We are fortunate to have grain wagons. Give your wagon teams and saddle horses a measure of feed each morning. Groom them, check their hooves, and water them."

"How far will we travel each day, Colonel?" a man shouted.

"About fifteen miles if the weather and conditions are good. We will break fast and hitch up one hour before dawn. Expect a two or three-hour nooning when we make good time. We camp at dusk. It will take five to six months to reach Oregon. That's a long time, folks. Much of the land will be in territory with little water or forage for the stock. You'll get dirty, sick, and tired. You'll need guts and grit.

"Men are expected to participate in hunting parties and guard duty. I will not tolerate fighting, drinking to excess, profanity, laziness, or cruelty." Colonel Wilson gazed from man to man.

Rebecca leaned in and whispered to Sarah. "This may benefit us. It will give Silas direction."

"We're coming to realize Silas wasn't our best choice, but it is too late to do anything about it. Jodie and Aaron will work hard."

Colonel Wilson's voice interrupted their conversation. "Fill your water barrels, canteens, and other containers every chance you get. Doc Randolph said to boil any water not coming from running creeks or rivers to prevent illness. Cleanliness is important."

Another dirty stream of tobacco hit the ground.

A small group of men, a woman, and a little child stood beside the colonel's wagon.

"I wonder who those people are?"

Sarah leaned forward to see where Rebecca pointed.

A tall horse—deep red sorrel, almost mahogany colored—arched its neck and pranced in place. The man she ran into in front of the general store sat in its saddle. *Handsome and knows how to sit a horse. Tall and straight. Loose reins.*

Rebecca rubbed the corner of her bag to feel the rock she picked up at the cemetery, reminding her this journey was meant to honor her father and fulfill the dream they shared. She promised him when he lay dying that she would make their dream come to pass. Anything causing her to lose sight of that vow couldn't be allowed. The mere thought of veering away from that promise for any reason brought her back to reality. Most girls her age had married and were having children. She was often pressured to do the same. Even her best friend, Evie, didn't understand why she refused to seek a husband. Shaking the thoughts from her mind, she turned her attention back to Colonel Wilson.

"One last thing. We have a rider and four walkers joining us. They will need your help along the way." Colonel Wilson pointed to a young couple. "Especially, these folks, the Granger family."

A young man with no hat, patched britches, a gray shirt, and suspenders put his arm over the shoulder of a slight young woman holding a thin toddler. She wore a mended, faded calico blouse, and tan homespun skirt. Two long brown braids lay like frayed ropes across her shoulders. She'd wrapped her shawl around herself and the child. They waved without making eye contact. A nanny goat tied to the side of a handcart bleated.

"In exchange for a meal, water, or a place under your wagon at night, they will help with your chores. Our other walker is Edward Thatcher, and our rider is Zachary Miller." The Colonel motioned to each person as he introduced them.

Rebecca stood to catch a better glimpse of the walkers and riders. Her gaze landed on Zachary. She caught him glancing her way. Blushing, she sent him a closed mouth, one-cornered smile. He rewarded her with a dimpled grin. Her heart plummeted to the bottom of her belly, then began beating as fast as a shooting star. She rationalized her feelings. *It's his horse I noticed. What is wrong with me?*

"My own team consists of Doc Randolph who you met at your health checks. Red O'Reilly is our cook. Brent Henry is our scout and back in the rear is Jack, our farrier and all-around hand. Questions?"

"Will the wagons always be in this order, Colonel?" A woman dressed in a silk emerald dress boasting ribbons, lace, and several petticoats twirled a lace parasol in her hands. Her wagon was near the back and was hitched to four matched horses.

"No, Mrs. Garson. We will rotate each day. The first wagon behind mine will move to the rear." Colonel Wilson coughed. "Does that answer your question?"

Mrs. Garson tilted her chin. "I suppose it does, sir. However, I had imagined we would be stationed ahead of these poorer emigrants. After all, my husband is from the New York City Garsons."

Colonel Wilson pulled a fresh plug of tobacco from

his pocket, plucked the used wad from his cheek, and threw it to the ground before sticking the new chew in his mouth. He stood with his hands on his hips, legs apart, and continued. "Madam, every family on this train has paid the same price for passage, including the walkers and riders. Didn't I tell you to trade those show horses for oxen or mules? They won't make it a week pulling that wagon. You and your husband will be the first to find it necessary to lighten your load if you don't do something about those horses."

"Well, I never!" Mrs. Garson folded the parasol and tightened the wide green satin ribbons of her bonnet. Her blonde curls bounced on her shoulders when she plopped down with a flounce.

Sarah turned toward the rear of the wagons. "Mr. Garson is bringing in a team of oxen."

"Good. Those horses are beautiful and not meant to pull a heavy load. They need to sell them before we leave."

A buzz of conversation, the sounds of nervous animals and crying children added to the rattling of harnesses and yokes, and excited voices of the emigrants. Anticipation buzzed through the air.

Rebecca grinned. The tiny hairs on her arms rose and her skin tingled. She leaned across Bolo and grasped her mother's hand. "Ready?"

Her mother glanced at the rifle and bullwhip next to her, tied her gray bonnet, and pulled on a pair of black leather gloves. "I am as ready as possible."

Colonel Wilson loped his buckskin gelding down the wagon line. Back at the front he stood in the stirrups, pulled his hat low, spat, and waved forward. "Wagons, ho!" His voice reverberated and echoed. The wind blew the fringe on his chaps toward the west.

A burst of activity broke the peace of dawn. Bullwhips cracked. Oxen leaned into their yokes, straining against the weight of their burdens. One by one, twenty-five wagons moved past family and friends standing on the side of the rutted dirt road. Many of them ran toward the travelers, throwing last minute gifts of bread, cheese, dried fruit, meat, and trinkets to the pioneers.

Chapter 3

Skirt Circles

The sun rose higher in a sky decorated with fluffy white clouds. Rebecca sighed in awe at the dewdrops sparkling on the grass as if diamonds had been tossed indiscriminately by an unseen hand. A chilly breeze from the north added a freshness to the clean, clear air. Two hours after leaving Independence, the wagon train was well into the young spring grasses on the outskirts of town. The sweet scent of crushed wildflowers and new grass relaxed her as everyone settled into the beginnings of a routine.

Rebecca couldn't sit still. She wiggled, turned to tighten the ropes on the front closure of the wagon cover, hugged Sarah, and scratched Bolo's ears. "Goodness. Imagine all the wonders we will see. I have my journal and will fill it with words, sketches, plant specimens, and anything else I want to remember. What are you the most excited about, Mother?"

Sarah sat silently before answering. "I wouldn't say I'm excited. More anxious, but I can't wait to reach the end of the trek and see Emma again."

"This wagon is so rough. I'm going to jump down and walk." Rebecca pulled her skirt together and leapt gracefully from the seat. Bolo joined her. She stretched then matched her stride with the speed of the turning wheels. "Ahh, this is much better. Join me, Mother. I'll have Aaron guide our oxen."

Her mother frowned. "I'm sure it is smoother, but I can't jump from the seat."

"Of course, you can. I'll catch you."

For the first time since losing her husband and son, Sarah genuinely laughed out loud. "All right. Catch me."

Rebecca stretched her arms out to catch her mother when she vaulted, and then the two settled into a brisk pace.

"You are correct, my dear, this is much nicer. I may walk every mile. Call Bolo back before he wanders off too far."

Rebecca stuck her fingers in her mouth and whistled.

"Rebecca! Please don't whistle. It isn't ladylike."

Rebecca laughed and tucked her arm into her mother's. "We'll soon be on a long trek. No need to be a lady. Let's have Jodie and Evie join us."

"Certainly."

Rebecca flashed Jodie a wink and a dare when they reached the wagon on which she rode. "Good morning, Jodie. Would you like to walk with us? It's much smoother."

Jodie looked toward the head of the oxen. Her husband urged the team forward with loud cursing and the guide stick. "I don't know."

"Aaron is walking with our team." Rebecca stretched out her arms. "Come on, I'll catch you. I caught Mother."

"No need to catch me." Jodie took a deep breath and jumped. She fell to one knee but quickly found her balance and was on her feet.

Rebecca rushed to help but Jodie waved her away and brushed dirt from her brown skirt. "I'm fine. It is farther than I figured. At least I didn't tear my new skirt."

"It's probably at least two hours before we stop for nooning." Rebecca stood moving from foot to foot. "Mother, could we walk away from the wagons for a short while?"

"I'm sure it would be fine. Jodie, please join us."

"I'll get Evie. She and Hans are six wagons down." Rebecca walked faster and headed for her friend. When she reached the Shuler wagon, she called out, "Evie, will you join us for a walk?"

"Sure. There is a young couple behind us. You remember Annie? Her parents own the boarding house. Let's ask her, she seems quite distraught."

"Of course. We'll wait while you ask her."

Evie returned with a woman who resembled a young girl. "Jodie, this is Annie Murphy. She and her husband are seeking the same new life we are. Annie, you remember Rebecca and Sarah Pierce?"

Annie mumbled, "Yes."

"We are going to get away for some privacy."

The five women walked toward a small stand of trees.

Jodie glanced over her shoulder. She frowned, her forehead wrinkling.

"Is something wrong, Jodie?" Sarah pushed her bonnet back, letting it fall. The ribbons pulled tight. She reached up and loosened them.

"Nothing is wrong. Silas doesn't like it when I'm with others. Lately, he's become easy to anger." Jodie walked, her head down, hands clasped across her stomach.

"It will be all right. We're walking away for privacy. My aunt went to the Oregon Territory last year. She wrote it was important to organize a group of women for these times. We will stand with our backs to the center, holding our skirts out to form a circle. This allows the woman in the middle complete privacy. Aunt Emma called them skirt circles."

"I was worried about that."

Rebecca craned her neck to watch white clouds drifting along at a slow pace while she held her skirt out to the sides. "The sky is bluer than I believe I've ever seen it. The wagons look majestic, all in a perfect line. Everything is almost unbelievable. Evie, how is Hans with all of this?"

"He's fine. He has such big dreams. A little nervous, I guess. He still has trouble speaking English instead of German when he gets nervous or frightened. I think he and Annie's husband, Jacob, will be a big help to each other." Evie tucked a strand of white-blonde hair behind her ear.

The women chattered, plucked wildflowers, and talked about their personal dreams for the Oregon Trail. The earliest hours of the trek were better than Rebecca could have imagined. She heard the nicker of a horse, turned, and saw a rider coming toward them. She stopped. "Who is that coming toward us?"

Evie followed Rebecca's gaze. "Isn't it one of the riders the colonel introduced this morning? The one named Zachary."

"Maybe." Where did this feeling of tightness in her chest and rolling in her stomach come from?

"Good morning, ladies." Zachary tipped his hat to

each of them, but his attention lingered on Rebecca. "My name is Zachary Miller. I noticed you walking out here alone and wanted to make sure all is well."

Sarah acknowledged Zachary. "We're fine, Mr. Miller. Just out for privacy and a short walk. My name is Sarah Pierce. This is my daughter, Rebecca. The young ladies beside her are Jodie Smith, Evie Shuler, and Annie Murphy."

The temperature rose several degrees in Rebecca's mind. She began to sweat. Even without a looking glass, she realized her face was a most unflattering shade of red. She shook her head and wiped her brow with a handkerchief. "You have a beautiful horse, Mr. Miller. What's his name?"

"Name's Zachary. Horse's name is Red."

"Pleased to meet you," Rebecca and Sarah said in unison.

"Colonel Wilson suggested I check with you about helping on the trail. He said you were traveling alone." Zachary made eye contact with Rebecca.

Evie giggled.

Rebecca shushed her with a sideways glance and an elbow jab. "Any help you can offer will be greatly appreciated. My mother and I have prepared well for the trip, but I imagine obstacles might occur that require assistance."

"Sounds fine. I'll stop by at nooning if that isn't a problem." Zachary stood until Sarah nodded her approval, then reined Red around and returned to the wagons.

"Well, Rebecca. Someone seems smitten with you," Evie teased making Rebecca laugh.

"Not true. He just met me. Besides, you know about

my vow to Father." Rebecca narrowed her eyes at Evie, daring her to say another word.

Time passed quickly. A rhythm formed along the line. The men and women walking with the oxen set the pace behind the lead wagon. Rebecca chose to move among the people. Meeting as many folks as possible became an important goal even though her mother had admonished her not to be nosy. She jotted down the names with short descriptions in her journal.

"Halt. We'll stop for two hours for a noon meal." Colonel Wilson's deep voice forced Rebecca's daydreams to vanish like dew evaporating from grass when the sun rose.

Teams of oxen stopped abruptly, some coming within inches of running into the wagon in front of them. Men shouted and stood in front of the oxen pushing against the yoke. The women gathered supplies for a light lunch and a short rest. No fires were lit.

A blood-curdling scream came from behind them. Rebecca tossed biscuits wrapped in a red bandana to the ground and ran toward the sound, expecting the worst. A familiar young boy dressed in overalls and a red shirt had fallen beneath a wagon. His mother sobbed and disciplined him at the same time.

"Didn't I tell you to stay away from the wagon when we start or stop? Didn't I tell you to stay away from the wheels at all times? Will you ever learn to listen?"

"Yes, ma'am." The boy shuddered in his mother's arms. "I won't do it again. I promise."

Rebecca gently touched the mother's shoulder. It was the woman whose sons had argued over a ball in the busy road of Independence before leaving day. "Mrs. Slaton? I'm Rebecca Pierce. Can I help?"

"No, thank you, Miss Pierce. Oh, I don't know. He frightened me. Jeb here has promised not to jump from the wagon when it's moving. He fell directly under it a moment ago. Thank God it stopped when it did."

Rebecca leaned over and tousled Jeb's unruly brown hair. "Listen, Jeb, we're the first wagon today. Would you like to play with my dog? His name is Bolo."

Jeb wiped his nose with the back of his hand.

"Well, he would love it if you and your brother would come play ball with him. Can you do that?"

The boy pleaded. "Can I, Ma? Can I?"

"All right. Come back when I call you. I'll keep Obed here with me."

Rebecca and Jeb walked side by side. Bolo ran back and forth between them. "I don't know what my mother has planned, but I'm ready to eat. I'm starving."

"My ma is fixing biscuits and bacon left from breakfast. She said me and Obed could even have some jam." Jeb puffed out his chest, proud to be having jam for lunch.

"That sounds delicious." Rebecca retrieved Bolo's ball from a box and gave a hearty toss, which sent both boy and dog running after it.

"Who is the little boy?" Sarah asked.

"Jeb Slaton. He was almost hurt a while ago jumping from the wagon. He came to play with Bolo while his mother makes dinner." Rebecca motioned for Jeb to sit on the quilt she had laid on the soft grass.

Aaron came to help with the animals. He loosened the yokes on the oxen enough that they could graze before hobbling the horses and the cow in a grassy spot. "Guess I should help Pa. He might have trouble getting the oxen settled."

Rebecca gently straightened the corners of a beloved quilt sewn by her grandmother while her mother retrieved cheese, bread, butter, and raisins from the cook box. The thick grass made a comfortable and clean-scented table for dining. She touched a specific pink calico square. "I remember wearing a dress made from this fabric."

A swift glimpse of nostalgia softened her mother's features.

"Jeb, you and Bolo settle in."

"Yes, ma'am. Why does your dog have to wear this itchy collar, Miss Rebecca? He don't seem to like it." Jeb scratched Bolo under the leather strap around his neck.

"I just didn't want him to run away." Rebecca explained as Jodie walked toward them. "Allow me to introduce Jeb Slaton. This is Mrs. Smith and her son Aaron. They're driving our second wagon."

Jeb kicked a pebble and said hello. His shyness evaporated quickly when Aaron reached for a biscuit. "Biscuits!"

Rebecca heard someone come up behind her. *Silas.* He made a move to sit beside her. She stood and moved to a far corner on the quilt. Why would he pay so much outrageous attention to her?

Silas murmured swear words under his breath. He snatched a biscuit from the wrapping and plopped down to eat.

Suddenly Bolo barked and Glory whinnied. Rebecca turned to find herself staring at the long legs of a sorrel horse. Taking a deep breath, she lifted her gaze into the eyes of Zachary Miller.

Zachary tipped his hat. "Good to see you ladies again."

Rebecca's face turned to fire. Clearing her throat, she spoke up. "We're glad you came. Why don't you put Red over there with my horses? You met Jodie this morning. This is her husband, Silas, and son, Aaron. The young man is Jeb Slaton joining us for dinner and to play ball with my dog." *Stop babbling, Rebecca!* she chided herself.

"Good to meet you all." Zachary hobbled his horse.

Silas grumbled but didn't speak to Zachary.

Rebecca shifted her bread from one hand to the other. A quick glance confirmed what she knew—her mother was watching the exchange with Zachary.

Sarah wiped her mouth with a napkin. "Zachary, find a corner and join us."

Zachary removed his hat and spoke to her mother, but his gaze kept returning to Rebecca. "Thanks, I will. Most women would have stayed after the losses you suffered, not taken the risk. I admire your courage."

"Thank you. I'm not sure courageous is the word I would use. Rebecca and I decided it would be best to follow through with our plans when my husband passed away. I have a sister and brother-in-law who traveled west last year. We're joining them to help with their general store. It is likely you will be able to help us at times, so thank you for the offer. It's just us plus the Smith family."

Jeb's mother called, and he jumped up. "I have to go. Thanks for the biscuit and raisins, Mrs. Pierce. Can I play with Bolo again, Miss Rebecca?" He was gone in a dead run before anyone could answer him.

"Of course," Rebecca shook her head while speaking to the retreating back of the five-year-old.

"That boy can run, can't he? I bet he's a handful."

Zachary chuckled. His eyes followed the blur left by the active child.

Rebecca laughed. "Yeah, I love his enthusiasm." She finished her meal and stood to stretch her back. This strange new feeling like butterflies fluttering in her stomach with Zachary nearby confused her. "Zachary, why have you chosen to go to the Oregon Territory?"

"I guess I'm going west for the same reason most of us are, to start a new life in a new land. I want some of the land for farming and ranching. Next year I hope I can afford to send for my family."

Rebecca inhaled and held her breath. *He has a family. I wonder if he's married. Why do I care? I'm not at all interested in marrying or becoming beholden to anyone but mother and myself.* "Where are you from?" The question carried on the breath she had been holding.

"I'm from Caledonia, Virginia. My parents and sisters stayed on our farm. I hope they're doing well." He dropped his chin, took a deep breath, and rubbed his left eye with a knuckle.

Rebecca glanced away. No words were spoken. The understanding that every person on the journey left something or someone behind was tangible.

Silas suddenly stood up, spilling his coffee on the heirloom quilt and jerked Jodie up by the arm. "Let's go. I can't take any more of this sentimental garbage. Bunch of uppity cowards."

Jodie pulled her arm loose and rubbed her shoulder. She followed her husband but glanced back at the others. Aaron wrapped his arms around himself and walked next to his mother, staring at the ground.

"Rebecca, you stay away from him." Sarah leaned over and blotted the coffee with a dry cloth.

"I can handle him." Rebecca cleared the dishes and leftover food.

They watched Silas return to the other wagon and saw when he slapped his son on the head and ordered him to prepare the oxen, every word embellished with cursing.

Zachary's jaw muscle throbbed, and a dark flush covered his cheeks. From temper no doubt, Rebecca thought.

"I'll watch him. I can't tolerate a man who treats women and children like he does. He won't hurt any of you." He strode off.

Rebecca watched, ready for the confrontation sure to occur.

"Leave the boy alone," Zachary told Silas.

Silas turned and stared at Rebecca before grinning at Zachary. "Or, what?"

"You don't want to know," Zachary spat the words out, turned, and stomped away.

Rebecca met Zachary at the front of her wagon. "Thank you. I am beginning to wonder what he is capable of. We needed the help. Jodie and Aaron were sick when we met them."

"Yeah. I can believe it."

He took a breath and hesitated as though he wanted to say more, then continued. "Time for me to check in with Colonel Wilson."

"Wait," Rebecca halted his steps and handed him a package wrapped in cloth. "Take this food to the Granger family. They must be hungry."

"Sure. See you later. Watch yourselves, ladies."

"We hope to see you for supper," Sarah called out.

Rebecca tucked her chin and lowered her lashes.

Zachary walked away, and she sighed. What was this strange tightness building in her chest? Why on earth could anyone cause her to think beyond the end of the trail and fulfilling the dream she shared with her father?

Chapter 4

Dancing Under the Stars

The train of pioneers moved forward with each creaky turn of the wheels. Rebecca climbed to the back of the wagon and checked the cream that had risen to the top of a crock. She skimmed the yellow fatty blend and put it in a pottery bowl, hoping to find a plump mound of butter at the end of the day. Leaning out, she said, "We'll see if the wagon motion turns it to butter."

Mother chuckled. "It will be nice with supper tonight."

****

The sun began a slow descent on the horizon. Shadows lengthened. Excitement rolled through the wagons as their first day ended.

Colonel Wilson whistled. "Halt! Circle the wagons. Leave only a few inches between the tongue of one and the rear of the one behind yours. Corral the teams inside the wagons. Feed your animals, water them, and brush them down before you eat."

Rebecca removed the yokes and rubbed the oxen with a large rag. She scratched them where the heavy yoke had rubbed throughout the day and cooed to them. "I think I'll put something between your shoulders and the yoke tomorrow. Make it softer for you. How about a little walk to the stream?"

Rebecca placed ropes around the necks of the oxen, the cow, and Patriot before mounting Glory to lead them to water. The animals lined up to drink their fill, grabbing bites of grass along the bank. Other pioneers gathered around her with their teams. Most of the emigrants chatted and offered introductions. Silas hadn't shown up with the other team. She headed back with her livestock.

A man threatened to "beat you if everything isn't done."

Rebecca recognized Silas's voice. She glanced up to see Aaron struggling to lead the team and his mother's horse with nothing but a single rope while Silas walked behind him shaking a stick, taunting the animals and his son. The oxen remained yoked.

Streaks from recent tears marred the boy's face.

Rebecca ordered Bolo to stay and ran toward Aaron. She stopped just before running into Smith. "What are you doing?"

Silas grabbed her by the shoulders. He leered at her heaving chest as she tried to catch her breath. "Well, I'm just making sure the animals are cared for like you insisted."

Rebecca jerked her shoulders away. "Remove your hands. Leave Aaron alone. Stay away from me."

"Sure, miss. I'll stay away from you. But I won't leave the boy alone. He is my son and don't forget it." Silas pivoted on his heel and strode to the wagons.

Rebecca went to Aaron and took the stiff new rope he held and draped it over the horse's neck. She helped him guide the team toward the water. As the animals drank, Rebecca lifted her apron, spit on the corner, and wiped drying blood from a cut over Aaron's left eye.

"How did this happen? I'll put something on that when we get back to the wagon, but first let's take care of your animals. Bolo will keep my team near the stream. Supper is waiting."

"I'm not really hungry." Aaron avoided answering her question. He glanced at Rebecca and whispered, "Will my father be there?"

"I'm not sure, but I doubt it. Your mother will join us, though. I will make sure he has food if that's worrying you." Rebecca whistled for Bolo and heard his high-pitched bark.

"I don't worry about him. He used to be nice and a good pa. He even cried when we had to sell our mule. He gets angry more often. I used to help him around the farm before we lost it." Aaron took the rope as his team drank, leaned over, and cupped some cold water into his mouth.

Coming over a small rise on their way back, Rebecca stopped. The beauty of nature never failed to fill her with thanksgiving. She inhaled deeply, memorizing, and appreciating the pungent smell of clean grass, clear water, dusty animals, and sweet wildflowers. The peaceful scene before her brought unexpected tears to her eyes. She pointed to the distance. "What a beautiful sight. What do you think, Aaron?"

Below them, Sarah knelt before a campfire stirring something in the pot. The young Granger family sat nearby with bowls at their feet. Their toddler stood, stumbled, fell, and got up laughing. Zachary stood between her father's stallion and Red, giving them treats from the palm of his hand. The first day on the trail was coming to an end without any major incidents. She whistled and waved to get their attention. Zachary waved back.

"There's Ma. She's coming from our wagon. Pa isn't with her." Aaron sighed.

"Go ahead and eat. I'll feed the animals, then join you. Show your mother the cut over your eye." Rebecca led Aaron and the animals to her wagon. She released the eight oxen into the corral made from the circled wagons and rubbed her hand over her belly hoping to stop the growl announcing her hunger. Next, she put Glory in the circle and removed her halter. When she turned to leave, she ran headlong into Zachary, causing him to stumble. His horse jerked back, trying to rear up, but he held fast onto the lead rope.

Her hands splayed across Zachary's taut, muscular chest. Rebecca sucked in a deep breath. "I am so sorry. I didn't hear you. Are you all right?"

"Never better." Zachary put his hands over hers and laughed.

Rebecca stepped back. "Thanks for helping."

"Shall we eat?"

"Sure." Rebecca followed him to where her mother dished up food for everyone. Her hands shook when she took the bowl of hot stew and a biscuit. She dipped the bread into the liquid until most of it was soaked up. The first bite was warm and welcome. "Guess I was hungrier than I thought."

Sarah laughed. "Hard work does that."

Later, after everyone had left, Rebecca helped her mother clean up. Sarah whispered, "Why were your hands shaking? Does it have anything to do with Zachary Miller?"

"Mother! Of course not."

****

Lanterns twinkled from the front of the line.

Rebecca put the last of the supplies in the cook box and set a pot of beans on the floor to soak for the next day. She leaned against a wheel to rest. A few minutes later she noticed several people walking toward the front of the line and heard lively music.

She brushed her hair and put on a clean white apron. "Mother, I'm going with Evie and Hans so we can listen to the music and dance. Do you want to go?"

"No, dear, I think I'll settle in and work on the tablecloth I'm embroidering. I told Emma I would have at least one finished by the time we reached Oregon. Do you want to sleep out here or in the wagon tonight?"

"Out here. It's so beautiful."

Rebecca walked toward the sound of music with Hans between her and Evie. Several young people from the train walked along with them, mostly the younger ones. The preacher's two oldest daughters met them on the path.

"Good evening, ladies. It's good to see you here. How do you feel about the first day?" Rebecca asked.

"It's been a learning experience, to be sure. Father gave us his blessing to come away tonight for dancing. Isn't it what we all hoped for?" Sally, the eldest daughter, had bright eyes that sparkled like jewels. She took her sister's hand and rushed away.

Rebecca's heart tried to keep rhythm with the fast-paced fiddling she heard. Her feet itched to be moving. This is exactly how she'd imagined the trip would be. The first day was nearly perfect. When they rounded the front of Colonel Wilson's wagon, she stopped and sucked in a deep breath. Zachary sat on the wooden boxes with two other men. He played the guitar and had his head back in an exhilarating laugh. Anxiety tightened her stomach, she wanted to turn and run. "I think I need to check on Mother."

"What? Why?" Evie followed Rebecca's gaze to Zachary. "Oh no, you don't. Just stay with me and Hans."

Rebecca went along but tried to stay in the shadows. When the music stopped, she saw Zachary staring at her. He put his guitar to the side, said something to another man, and stepped down. She watched, still as a statue, as he walked toward her with that double-dimpled, heart-stopping smile of his. He had changed into a bright white shirt and tied a blue bandana around his neck. Why were her hands sweating?

Zachary reached her. "How are you tonight, Rebecca? Would you like to dance?"

Rebecca wiped her sweaty palms on her skirt and patted her hair. "Yes."

Zachary escorted her to the center of the clearing, put his arm around her, grasped her hand, and pulled her close. The fiddlers played a slow waltz. Zachary led her in the dance. When the music ended, he bowed but continued to hold her hand. "You dance well. We'll have to do it again, but I have to get back on the box."

Rebecca felt the despised beet-red blush rise from her neck to her face to her scalp. *Will I ever outgrow this thing?* She reached up and felt her cheek. "Thank you for the dance."

Brent Henry came up behind her and asked for a dance. "May I have this next one?"

"Surely." They went round and round in a fast reel that left her breathless but exhilarated. Her braid loosened, allowing tresses of curls to fly with each turn. She felt wild and free.

Brent bowed. "I'm leaving on a scouting mission tomorrow. Would you dance with me when I return?"

"Of course. I don't know if I could handle another one that fast." She held her side and laughed.

"Sure, you could. I've seen you running between the wagons." Brent wiped his forehead with his sleeve.

"Yes, but that's what I have to do."

Rebecca accepted an offer to dance from the colonel. She laughed when she saw Brent asking Sally for the honor of a dance. "Thank you, Colonel, for having this wonderful evening planned. So much fun! I've met some wonderful people today."

"I do this on purpose. Socializing gives strangers an opportunity to mingle and relax before the rigors of the trail set in, allows others an opportunity to know who will be helpful if the need arises and often starts romance in bloom among the emigrants. I noticed Brent and the preacher's girl."

Two hours later Rebecca sighed and leaned against a water barrel. "Evie, thanks for making me stay. This was wonderful."

"Are you ready to head back?"

The musicians put their instruments away and jumped from the boxes serving as a stage.

Zachary walked over and stood beside Rebecca. "I'll walk you back if that's okay."

Rebecca didn't know how to respond. Uncomfortable, she finally spoke up. "Thank you for the dances. I had a good time. I am sure Mother would appreciate it if you walked me back."

Zachary hooked his arm through Rebecca's and sighed. "Such a beautiful night. Clear, bright moon and more stars than I could ever count."

Rebecca glanced over to see him gazing at the sky. His sigh touched her heart. "Stars never fail to enchant me."

Rebecca felt queasy when they neared her wagon. What was she supposed to do now? What if he tried to kiss her? She had never been kissed. "Mother is waiting for me. Thank you for everything, I don't believe I'll ever forget it."

Zachary lifted her hand and kissed the back.

Rebecca watched him walk away before moving to the front of the wagon. She twisted her hands together, cracking her knuckles. Confusion rocked her thoughts. The journey had begun only that morning, and here she was, breaking her self-imposed promise to fulfill her father's dream. Her plan had been to help her father raise horses in Oregon from the day her family began setting up the trek. That plan did not include any man. Not Zachary Miller or Brent Henry.

She clambered into the wagon and changed into a nightshift. Taking her journal and a pencil from her bag, she climbed back down, hoping she didn't disturb her mother.

"Come lie down, Rebecca. The bed isn't as soft as that feather mattress in the back, but the scenery isn't as beautiful either." Sarah patted the bed beside her.

Rebecca kneeled beside her mother and kissed her on the forehead before lying down. She pillowed her head on her arms. "I thought you were sleeping. Mother, have you ever seen stars so bright or a moon so big?"

"Only once dear, I'll tell you about it sometime. Very special, much like your evening. Tell me, did you dance?"

"Yes. I waltzed with Zachary twice and did a reel

with Brent Henry. That dance left me breathless. It made me uncomfortable when they were standing near me. What does that mean?"

"Only that you're growing up, and two young men find you attractive."

"That can't happen. I will not break my vow to Father."

"You didn't make the vow to your father, you made it to yourself. Let things go where they will."

"Yes, ma'am. Sleep well." Rebecca sat up to write in her journal. She moved the lantern closer and lowered the wick.

April 12, 1845

Day one is coming to an end. It will take a few days for everyone to settle in. Some are having trouble working with the animals. One of the walkers, Mr. Thatcher, is helping the Garson family from New York. It is becoming apparent that Silas Smith was a poor choice for our second wagon. His wife and son cringe and change when he comes near. I like them, but he frightens me. I'm confused about the feelings I have about a rider named Zachary. Today was beautiful. Tonight, most of the members of the wagon train went to Colonel Wilson's wagon to dance. I danced many times. Mother has fallen asleep beside me. We are beneath the stars. Two are extra bright. I believe they are Father and Joseph.

Chapter 5

Another Day on the Trail

A crowing rooster awakened Rebecca. Twenty-six days had passed since they left Independence. She sat up and stretched, moving her neck from side to side to work the kinks out. The cracking of her bones seemed loud where she lay on the ground. Noises of another day on the trail increased: creaking leather, the rattle of cooking supplies, the thud of firewood being stacked, and the hushed tones of husbands and wives trying not to wake their children echoed. She inhaled deeply, smelled coffee and bacon.

The calm amidst the noises of the awakening camp comforted Rebecca. Closing her eyes, she visualized a rustic log cabin on a rise with a creek running past a kitchen garden and more horses than she could count grazing in knee high grass. A tear fell from her eye. *This is what it will be like. Just as we dreamed.* She rose to greet her mother. "Good morning. This day promises to be special."

"Yes, it will be a fine day. I confess I still feel uneasy. There are so many unknowns facing us."

"We will trudge forward. I'll get the buckets and canteens. Let's meet Jodie and Evie and walk to the water's edge." Rebecca crooked her elbow and offered it to her mother.

"Yes, let's begin the day."

Rebecca turned away and moved to pick a bunch of orange, purple, and white wildflowers peeking high over the grasses. She plucked them, tied them together with a long leaf, and handed them to her mother with an exaggerated curtsy followed by an impish grin. Sarah took the flowers and put them to her nose, inhaling the mingled scents of earth and sweetness.

"They're lovely. Thank you."

The sound of men laughing captured Rebecca's attention. She turned to see Zachary enjoying morning coffee with the colonel and Brent Henry. Their jovial actions made her laugh. "They're happy this morning, aren't they?"

"Yes."

Rebecca's mind circled to the promise she made her father. Why on this earth did those two men turn her head? Zachary and Brent. Both tall, good horsemen, and funny. She shook her head to get the men out of her mind. "I'll start the coffee. It won't be long before the colonel is ready to head out for the day."

Rebecca stoked the coals she had banked before retiring. She hung the coffee pot on the iron hook, hoping it would boil quickly. The sound of whistling and horse hooves forced her to whirl around. Zachary walked toward her with a grin, his horse in tow.

"Good morning, Rebecca. Coffee ready?"

"The same to you. It will be in just a few moments."

Zachary pushed a stray curl from her face. "I'm going on a scouting trip with Brent. We're leaving this morning to find a water source so everyone can have some rest and replenish before we hit the first difficult area of the journey. I don't know how long we will be gone."

"That sounds exciting. I wish women could go on scouting expeditions. I would love it."

"Perhaps one day. Here comes your mother with the makings for breakfast."

"Will you join us?" Rebecca glanced at him.

"I ate with the colonel, but I will take some coffee." Zachary took the tin cup she held toward him, slurped the hot drink, and handed it back before mounting Red and riding away.

The skin on her cheek where he had tucked her hair behind her ear tingled. She reached up and touched it before waving at him.

Chapter 6

The Storm

Six days later Rebecca saddled Glory. Urging the horse into a trot, she crossed a grassy bluff. The warmth of the spring sun on her shoulders reminded her of rides she took near Independence. A breath she hadn't known she was holding escaped her lips. Her arms and legs relaxed. A tall tree filling out with new leaves in varying shades of green compelled her to sit and think, plan and dream. She dismounted and tied Glory to the trunk. Dark green feathery ferns surrounded its base creating an earthy, scented rug.

She settled against the rough bark and wiggled her shoulders until she found a semi-comfortable position, then took her knife and journal from her bag. She cut several sprigs of the plant, made a note describing the area, and put the delicate leaves between two pages of the book, holding the covers tight. She ran her fingers over her name burned into the leather, treasuring the gift from her father. Sitting cross-legged, Rebecca wrote down her thoughts and made sketches in the book. Finishing the day's entry, she opened to the first page and read the note her father had penned.

Darling Daughter, it is my wish that you follow your dreams. Not just for Oregon but for the rest of your life.

I believe you have a God-given ability to work with horses and other animals. It is what you love, so do it. Our ranch in the new land will be among the best because of you. I know you miss Joseph and sometimes try to be a son to me. Just be my daughter. Never forget that your mother and I love you, Papa.

Her father's words reminded her of his belief in her ability to achieve the dream they shared. She shivered when the sun hid behind a bank of darkening clouds, leaving a chill in the air. Rebecca moved from beneath the tree. Thick, ominous black clouds began boiling on the distant horizon. Taking a deep breath of the heavy, oppressive air, Rebecca pulled her shawl tighter across her chest. Bolo whined and inched closer to her. "What is it, boy?"

Glory pawed the ground and tossed her head. Rebecca moved in front of the mare, patted her on the neck, and talked quietly to calm her. A strike of lightning slashed through the sky, slamming into the horizon. Seconds later a roar of thunder shook the ground. Rebecca felt Glory's haunches tighten. She grabbed a handful of mane with one fist and the reins with the other, bounded to the horse's back, and leaned into her neck.

Glory raced off in a full gallop, heading away from the storm toward the wagons, which circled without releasing the teams. People ran back and forth trying to secure their belongings and animals. Colonel Wilson's bellowed commands carried on the wind.

Rebecca jerked on the reins and jumped from Glory's back. Her hair blew around her face, impairing her vision. Her skirt, pushed tight against her legs, made moving forward feel like pushing a barrow filled with grain up the hill to the barn. The thick air and howling wind made breathing difficult.

"Mother, take Bolo! Get inside the wagon! I'll check on the Smiths." Rebecca pulled a lid off of the water barrel as she ran past.

The sky opened with a vengeance, and heavy drops of rain fell in sheets, pelting everybody and everything. Rebecca placed her hands around the corners of her mouth, screaming for Jodie and Aaron to get inside their wagon. Cursing and beating the oxen with the bullwhip, Silas attempted to hold the oxen.

Rebecca grabbed it from him. "Get in the wagon with your family!" She stood with the oxen for a moment, hoping to calm them and to catch her breath.

Lightning struck time after time like streams of fire aimed for destruction. Thunder roared and shook the earth. Water gushed from the sky, stinging like nettles. The riders working with the loose livestock were manhandling their frightened mounts into circles to keep a stampede at bay. Bullwhips snapped, lassoes slapped against thighs, and cowboys shouted at the animals.

"Be careful!" Rebecca screamed to one rider who was bucked off his horse just after a lightning strike. He rolled to his feet and grabbed the reins of the frightened animal before it could stomp him. She hesitated, not knowing whether she should help the wrangler or run to the wagon. He waved her away with an exaggerated motion.

Rebecca hurried through the wind and rain, vaulted onto the wagon seat, and dove through the opening into the folds of a patchwork quilt held by her mother. Her body shook so hard her teeth rattled, causing her to stutter. "I-I've n-never seen a s-storm come out of nnowhere with such fierceness." She took a breath and crinkled her nose. "It smells like brimstone, not like the sweet spring rains at home."

"Everyone is frightened. You must remove those wet clothes."

"Help! Help us! Please, we need help!" a woman outside the wagon screamed.

Rebecca glanced out to see Ginny Granger carrying her toddler. They were soaked to the skin. Ginny was screaming and sobbing. Rebecca reached out. "Give me the baby and climb in. Hurry."

Rebecca took the baby. The fear that he was dead nearly stopped her heart. "He's not moving."

Sarah took the toddler and peeled off his clothes. She wrapped him in two quilts then held him close to her chest. "He will be fine when I get him warmed up. Rebecca, you take care of Ginny."

"Here, let me help you." Rebecca aided Ginny out of her clothes, pulled a dry chemise over her head, and wrapped her in a quilt. She rubbed her hands up and down the woman's arms, trying to infuse warmth into her cold body.

"My husband! I think he's dead." Ginny sucked in a ragged breath, fainted, and collapsed.

"Mother, I need your help. Hurry, put the baby on the mattress." Rebecca turned the stricken woman onto her side, grabbed the smelling salts from her medical kit, and waved the bottle beneath Ginny's nose, then laid it to the side. She dried her hair and rubbed her arms and legs until Ginny moaned and opened her eyes.

Wrinkles formed on Ginny's forehead. Within seconds she tried to sit up. Her voice was choked and hoarse with tears. "My husband? I think lightning hit him. He was trying to get to us. Is my baby alive? He turned blue when I was running with him. Children are not supposed to be blue. Are they?"

Rebecca rubbed Ginny's shoulder. "He's fine. Just cold. Mother removed his wet clothes and wrapped him up. You'll be fine as well. I'll go check on your husband when I can, but you and the baby need to rest. For now, I'll fix you some honey water and give the baby some milk."

"Thank you, Miss Rebecca."

The storm rumbled for hours. Puddles and small rivers of rapidly running water snaked through the wagon yard. Rebecca crawled to look out the cover every few minutes. Helplessness rose and fell as she watched those with her and wondered about the well-being of the other emigrants. She was restless. She needed to get out and help others. It was her job, her goal, to be a leader.

The baby slept peacefully snuggled against his mother wrapped together like in a cocoon.

Rebecca's mother's eyes became wide and wild each time lightning and thunder rocked the wagon, and Sarah stared at the baby. Silent tears fell without stopping.

Rebecca took her mother's hand and squeezed it. "Everything will be fine. The last time I checked, the sky was beginning to clear. This will be over soon. When it is, I'll start a fire for hot tea and coffee. We didn't get much water inside the wagon. Everything will dry when the sun comes out."

"Darling Rebecca, I hope you're correct. However, it isn't right that you try to take on the welfare of everybody. You're strong, but don't push your limits."

"I will do all I can. But I won't let myself become

too tired or ill to continue at a healthy pace. I promise, but I must check on Mr. Granger and the Smiths first." Rebecca tried to reassure her mother.

As the storm moved on, the emigrants crawled from their wagons. Rebecca greeted those near her with nods and forced smiles. The truth of the damage shocked her. She unyoked the oxen, dried them with rags, and moved them inside the circle.

Step by muddy step, she made her way to Colonel Wilson. The wet soil sucked at her boots. Her skirt was soaked and splattered. Doc Randolph leaned over a thin man laid across two barrels. She watched, and unexpected tears spilled as the doctor pulled a thin sheet over the body. "Doctor Randolph, is that Mr. Granger?"

"Yes. He was struck by lightning. Do you know where his family is?"

"His wife and son are in our wagon. They're sleeping now but the baby was cold and blue when Mrs. Granger brought him to us. I wonder if you would find time to check on them?" Rebecca bowed her head and whispered a prayer for this man and his family.

Doctor Randolph grasped her cold hands. "And, your mother, how is she?"

"She seems to be fine. I believe having someone to take care of is helping her."

Colonel Wilson walked up behind Rebecca. "What will happen to his family?"

"I'm sure Mother will take them in. We have plenty of food and water. We will manage. I'll tell Mrs. Granger about her husband."

Colonel Wilson took Rebecca's elbow. "I'll go with you. I need to be the one to tell her. I will offer to return the money she and her husband paid when we reach journey's end. The handcart will have to be dismantled for firewood."

"Yes, sir."

When Rebecca and the colonel reached the wagon, she peeked inside and whispered, "Mother?"

"Yes, dear."

"The colonel needs to speak to Mrs. Granger." Rebecca rubbed her temples.

Sarah covered her mouth and turned to get Ginny's attention. "Ginny, Colonel Wilson needs to speak to you."

Ginny slowly climbed out. When she saw Colonel Wilson's somber face, she dropped to the ground in a sodden heap.

Rebecca reached to help her up.

"He's dead, isn't he?"

Colonel Wilson's voice was thick and shaky. "Yes, ma'am. Hit by lightning. When we reach the end of the trail, I will repay your deposit. It's the right thing to do."

All remaining color in Mrs. Granger's face drained away leaving a pale, waxen image. Her voice was a mere whisper. "Thank you for telling me. Miss Rebecca, will you help me back into the wagon?"

****

After tending to the others, Rebecca took a deep breath. Everyone in the wagon slept. Except for an occasional shout from the outside, all was quiet. She rubbed her hands on the sides of her skirt and felt mud drying. She held them in front of her and saw they were almost the same color as the dirty water standing in puddles outside the wagon. The cold-to-the-bone need for a warm bath overcame her. With no fire, a tepid wash would have to suffice. The water bucket in the wagon was almost full and would have to do. She sliced a small piece of lavender-scented soap from a bar, stripped, left dirty clothes in a pile at her feet, and washed herself from the top of her head to her toes. Being clean, or relatively so, left her feeling more human.

Twisting her still dirty tangled hair in the back, Rebecca secured it with a blue ribbon. A small bit of buckskin peeked from beneath her mother's clothing in the chest. Puzzled, she tugged on the soft, tan fabric until it was in sight *A pair of Joseph's britches!* Confusion and an unexpected sense of bitter betrayal knotted in her throat. Her father had allowed her to wear britches when she worked with horses, but her mother forbade her to ever don them again after he died. *And she lied to me!* The day she asked about taking some of the britches on the trail, her mother told her she had given every pair to a man in the general store. Why would she lie? A volcano of anger erupted in Rebecca's chest. She shook her head to banish the emotions. Her job was to be the strong one, to take care of others. How could she do that if the only person left in her life she trusted turned around and betrayed her? What else had Mother lied about?

Her mother cleared her throat. Rebecca turned to face her. She shook the folds from the britches and held them at arm's length. "Mother, I found these when I was changing."

"I see. I couldn't make myself leave them behind."

"You lied. You told me you weren't bringing any of their clothing. Not Father's or Joseph's. Why did you lie? Why did you bring them?" Rebecca's voice, controlled at first, increased in volume and disbelief with each word.

"I told you. I couldn't leave them. I don't like it

when you wear britches. I never have. You are a young lady, and ladies do not wear trousers. I don't know why your father ever allowed you to wear them in the first place. I hoped you wouldn't find them."

Rebecca stepped back when her mother stretched out her arms and attempted to come to her. The claustrophobic confines of the wagon didn't allow her to get far enough away. The shaking hand of her mother brushed hers. Rebecca jerked back and held up her palm. "No, Mother. Don't touch me right now. I am angry and sad, and I feel betrayed. You have never lied to me. I do want to wear the britches. And I will. I'm the one who takes care of the horses, the teams, the cow, and other work usually done by men. Playing the role of a lady isn't necessary. Not out here. This storm today should be proof enough of that."

Rebecca swiped the tears from her face with the clean dress hanging from her arm and pointed to the pile of clothes she hadn't picked up. "See that torn, wet, muddy dress on the floor, Mother? I could hardly walk much less ride or run when it was soaked, and the wind blew so hard against me."

Her mother's sad, stricken, and ashen face frightened Rebecca. "All right. You may wear Joseph's britches. Three more pairs are in the chest. However, my dear, when you go dancing in the evenings or to worship services you will wear a skirt. Dear God, what will people say?"

"I imagine everyone will be shocked." She was too upset to be forgiving. Not yet.

Her mother turned away.

Rebecca tucked the dress away, grabbed one of her brother's shirts, and began to dress. She rolled the chemise toward her waist from the hem before tucking it inside the waistband of the soft britches. Twirling, bending, and stretching with ease, she relished the freedom the garment afforded her. She squatted, knelt, jumped, and took a few steps forward and back. The chaos and confusion of the day diminished.

Sarah turned back to face Rebecca. "I realize you enjoyed wearing your brother's britches. I didn't understand it then nor do I understand it now. I do not like it. It seems you are trying to take on the roles of your father and brother."

"I have no notion of replacing Father or Joseph. Although it falls to me to do the tasks they would have done. There are times I revel in that role and others when I would like nothing more than to just be a girl, even though I have no intention of marrying. At least not for a long time."

Sarah covered her mouth with one hand and wiped tears from her eyes with the other. "I understand."

"I need to find dry firewood. We need hot water for tea and bathing." Rebecca climbed out of the back of the wagon. Bolo jumped from the seat in the front and came toward her, shaking with his tail tucked beneath his legs. She hugged him and checked the soggy collar.

Enough dry wood to start a fire lay beneath the corners of a canvas tarp. Rebecca retrieved it. She cleared out the fire pit and started a good-sized blaze, then set the kettle on to boil. Sighing, she held her hands out to the golden warmth. Soon, the water in the pot bubbled. Hot tea with honey seemed perfect.

Someone chuckled. Rebecca turned. Silas stood leering at her. Rebecca couldn't stop the shudder of revulsion his nearness caused. "Can I help you? I'll prepare some tea for you and your family. Is everything well with the wagon?"

"Jodie and Aaron are fine. They're both unsettled since they're scared of damn near everything. Cowards. I must say you ain't much like a lady in those pants."

Rebecca narrowed her eyes. "I am comfortable. Now, tell your family I have a fire and hot water. Then, you and I will clean up this mess and check on others. Keep your lecherous opinions to yourself."

Smith tipped his hat without removing the leer from his face.

Climbing back into the wagon, Rebecca glanced around inside. She gathered wet clothing, quilts, and shawls in her arms. "Mother, I'm going to lay these things over the top of the wagon to dry. Is there anything else I need to take?"

****

Small campfires lit the dusky surroundings. Clothing, bedding, and supplies had been tossed over the bows, tongues, and seats of every wagon. The smell of bitter coffee and musky animals mingled. The sound of saddles and voices from the outer edges of the circle intruded into the somber cleanup. Rebecca walked toward the sound of Zachary's voice. *They're back.*

Almost a week had passed since Brent and Zachary left to find water. They arrived as sodden as the rest of them. Both men had their hats down, shoulders hunched. The horses could barely walk, and held their heads low, often allowing their noses to touch the ground. She watched from the shadows as Zachary removed Red's tack before rubbing him down and giving him a bucket of grain. He lifted his eyes and made direct eye contact with her.

She turned away, confused about why she was so relieved to see him. The tension in her shoulders diminished. She didn't feel alone. Sucking in a deep breath, she urged herself to control her emotions. Being strong and true to herself was the only way she could achieve her goal. She had to make it to the Oregon Territory. That's all, just get there. Father counted on her. Zachary couldn't become part of her life.

"Rebecca?"

Rebecca forgot about her vow and moved toward him when he called her name. "I'm glad you and Brent made it back safely. Seems like you were caught up in the same storm we were." She touched his scruffy, bearded cheek with two fingers before pulling them away as if they had been burned.

"Yeah, the rain hit us hard. Sure, could use some coffee. I noticed a fire at your wagon. We lost our pack horse. He ran off. Couldn't catch him. He'll show up." Zachary's voice was soft and sounded too tired for description.

"Come along, I can make you coffee and get you some dry clothes. Are you hungry? We have leftovers from last night."

Taking her hand, Zachary brought it to his lips. "Sounds good."

Rebecca didn't pull her hand away despite the urge to do so. His hand was rough where he'd held the reins.

"When did you start wearing pants?" He chuckled and kept walking.

"Father used to let me wear them when we worked the horses. Mother hated it and still does. Today, I almost got hurt trying to ride and run in my skirts. I found these in the chest. They belonged to my brother. Does it bother

49

you?" She glanced up trying to gauge his reaction. All she saw was acceptance.

"No, it doesn't bother me. You might hear some hateful whispers, maybe even some jealous comments from narrow-minded folks, but I think they are practical."

"Mother lied to me. She said she didn't bring any of Joseph's or Father's britches because she didn't want me wearing them." Her throat tightened. "She said they aren't ladylike."

"She'll get over it, and the others don't matter." Zachary raised his head. "Your mother is coming from the other side."

Rebecca tugged on his arm to keep him from stepping away. "Wait, there is something you need to know. Mr. Granger died today. He was struck by lightning. His wife and baby are going to be riding with us. I thought they were going to die. The baby was limp and blue. Mrs. Granger fainted. I've never been so frightened in my life."

"Died? Mr. Granger? Isn't he the man who was walking with only a handcart?"

"Yes." Rebecca stopped in front of the fire.

Rebecca looked away when her mother reached to shake Zachary's hand. "I'm happy to have you back. Did you find the water source you were searching for?"

"Yes, ma'am. It's about three days ride from here. Maybe longer because of this mud."

"Mother, would you like some coffee?"

"No, my dear. I am going back to check on Mrs. Granger and lie down."

Rebecca chose two cups and poured coffee to the brims. She and Zachary sat side by side on a supply box.

Their shoulders, hips, and thighs touched, but neither of them moved. Fatigue stifled their conversation, yet the silence wasn't uncomfortable. Rebecca finally relaxed at the conclusion of an extraordinary day.

"Thanks for the coffee. I needed it, and your company. Now, it's time to rest. The colonel is allowing some of us to sleep in the grain wagon."

Rebecca glanced at Zachary. "That will be more comfortable than the muddy ground, I'm sure."

He took her hand, kissed it, and stood. "See you tomorrow."

Rebecca stayed on the box. The touch of his lips on the back of her hand lingered warm and welcome. She rubbed the area with the first two fingers of her other hand.

May 13, 1845

I am exhausted. Today began perfectly with a lone ride. A dangerous storm came out of nowhere. Lightning. Thunder. Wind. Horizontal rain. Mr. Granger died after being struck by lightning. His family will stay with us. Mother lied about bringing Joseph's britches (which I now wear). Forgiveness will come, likely after rest. Zachary returned. Lost their pack horse. There is water about three days from here. Seeing Zachary calmed me. He is steady.

****

Jodie unfolded Aaron's patchwork pallet under the wagon seat and laid a faded, frayed quilt and pillow on it. "Aaron, it's time to bed down."

"I'm too tall to fit there anymore." Aaron yawned.

"I know. I wish you would stop doing that. Growing I mean. However, it's too wet for you to sleep under the wagon or the moon." Jodie kissed her fingertips and touched them to Aaron's cheek.

The unwavering and familiar sadness cocooned her, filling Jodie's throat with lumps, and her eyes with tears she should shed. She climbed into the back of the wagon and unrolled the musty straw mattress she shared with her husband. "The bed is ready," she told Silas who waited on the flour barrel.

Silas huffed. "'Bout damn time. God, I hope I don't have to listen to you sobbing again tonight. 'Bout time for you to realize we had to accept this job."

Jodie turned around to make sure her back was to him, splashed water into the basin, and washed her face. Silas didn't realize it yet, but the dangers of the day had strengthened her spine and removed the ever-present cowardice. At least for the time being. Silas shifted, making the bows creak.

"This opportunity to travel west with Sarah and Rebecca fell into our lap. Pure luck, I tell you. Pure luck."

Soft, gentle snores from Aaron comforted Jodie. She could talk to Silas without waking him. If Silas kept his voice down. For the first time in her life, she would be brave. Without a word, she slid beneath the bedding. Her heart was beating too fast to count. She positioned herself on her side and propped on her elbow and watched her husband. "Listen to me, Silas. I have something to say. I expect you to hear what I say and be silent until I've finished. There is little respect left in our relationship, but I believe love remains at some level."

"Is that so? Just what would you do that could fix that?"

Jodie sat up straight and looked him in the eyes. The back light from the lantern illuminated his face, including the sneer and narrowed eyes. "I can try. I have more backbone than you know."

"Hell, all you do is cry and walk or ride east every chance you get." Silas hissed, each word escaping between clenched teeth, stabbing Jodie in the heart.

Jodie put a finger to her lips. "Of course, I cry. I'm surprised you don't. In the last six years we've buried three children. Only a few months ago, we lost our farm and home. We lost everything. I ride east to think of the children, to pray for them, to gather my soul into some form of normal in this chaos."

"Why can't you move forward? Going west is an opportunity to make a new life. Every man gets land." Silas rested his hand on Jodie's hip, but she pushed it away.

"We aren't guaranteed any land because we didn't pay for passage on the wagon train."

"Sarah and Rebecca are guaranteed land. I saw a letter in their wagon. You must be wrong. If women can get land, so can I. I am a man." Silas snickered in the dark.

"Rebecca's uncle is signing in their stead. Why were you prowling in their wagon?"

"Goddammit. Why can't you be strong and smart like them?"

Jodie pulled a handkerchief from beneath her pillow and blew her nose. "I am. You've just never noticed. Our life has been one of poverty and heartbreak."

She picked up a quilt and went out the back cover. She wouldn't stay next to him even if it meant sleeping on the muddy ground. Luckily, she found a tiny slice of dry tarp and spread her blanket upon it *Lord, help me.*

Chapter 7

Lay-By

Five days later, the sound of water dancing and dripping over and around stones in the stream provided a welcome rest and natural music. Deep green low-lying bushes dotted the banks of the stream. The flight of startled birds brought laughter. The early colors of dusk announced that the wagons would soon circle for the night.

Colonel Wilson had promised two days plus the current half-day to recuperate, catch up on chores, and socialize despite losing time because of the storm.

Rebecca placed one fatigued foot in front of the other as she plodded beside the oxen. "Trudging" was the word Mother used. Appropriately so. Glancing up, she saw Sarah sitting on the wagon seat, her shoulders hunched, arms folded across her abdomen. The storm and their argument, had taken heavy tolls on them. Sarah had developed a mild cough that left her lethargic. Rebecca ran her hand down her buckskin clad leg. A twinge of guilt nicked the edges of her heart. She would please her mother and wear a skirt tonight. After a real honest-to-goodness bath in the clear and welcoming water.

"Halt!"

Rebecca grabbed the yoke when Colonel Wilson shouted the order. Bolo bolted from the wagon, hurrying to sit at her feet. She scratched him behind the ears. "Now, sweet boy, we rest. You probably don't need to rest. After all, you sleep under the wagon seat all day."

Outriders working the livestock broke off and began stringing rope around the herd for a makeshift corral downstream from the camp. Grass and water were abundant. The rope fence and the presence of riders would deter stampeding unless something spooked the animals.

Everyone moved upstream to prepare for the respite. Livestock was herded to the corral. Rebecca met Zachary at the rope line and handed him the leads for their animals. She gave each animal a measure of grain in a wooden feed bucket before brushing dried mud from their coats. "Have you spoken to Colonel Wilson about his plans while we lay by?"

Zachary took her hands in his. Their eyes met and held for a long moment. "We will repair wagons and other equipment. Cook up a few meals. Wash clothing. Hunt for large game to be shared. The farrier is planning to make new shoes for the oxen and horses if necessary. Some folks had him make spare sets for their teams and horses before we left. Said he prefers that because he doesn't have to haul out the anvil or start a fire. Plus, we can't forget the dance tomorrow evening. I'll take you for a ride away from here for a spell before the dance. How does a picnic sound?"

She laughed and squeezed his hands. "Of course, I will go with you. Two full days might sound like a long time, but it's bound to pass quickly."

"In time we'll be entering some of the harshest

terrain on the trail. It's clear that many of us depend on you to pay attention to the health needs of the others. It would probably be a good idea if you made note of those who are most likely to suffer to the extreme, or even succumb, in the months ahead."

Rebecca took her lower lip between her teeth and narrowed her eyes as she began a mental review about who might be in jeopardy. "I know. I should ask Doc Randolph what herbs and plants to gather while we're here. He has asked for my help if illness breaks out."

"He's concerned about cholera." Leaning down to pat Bolo on the head, Zachary continued, "Poor dog, even he is tired. Have you had any more problems with Silas?"

Rebecca glanced at Bolo and chuckled. "That dog isn't tired. I stay away from Silas."

"Good. That's for the best."

Rebecca stood and wiped a weary hand across her face. "I need to help Mother. Join us for supper?"

"Sure."

Rebecca sucked in a deep breath when Zachary kissed the back of her hand.

After pulling cooking supplies from the wagon, she prepared potatoes to be fried with an onion over the open fire in the iron skillet—one of her favorite meals. Rebecca's mouth watered at the thought. There would also be flapjacks made with milk and an egg. Bolo gave a single warning woof.

Rebecca turned to see a barely recognizable Mrs. Garson from New York City approaching from the rear of the wagon. Dirt stained her fine silk skirt. Thorns on the deceptively beautiful yellow flowers that grew wild had ripped tears in the hem. Her blonde curls lay limp on her shoulders. Quite a change from the pretentious well-dressed lady at the beginning of the journey. She was pale. Her shoulders were stooped. And she shuffled her feet. "Miss Rebecca."

"Mrs. Garson, how are you? Can I help you?"

"I am as well as can be expected. I came to ask about Mrs. Granger. I heard she was widowed in the storm. Do you think she would be interested in cooking for us and helping with chores around the wagon?" Mrs. Garson had a difficult time catching her breath.

"I'm not sure, but I imagine she would be thankful. Let's ask her." Rebecca turned and called out, "Ginny, Mrs. Garson would like to speak to you."

Ginny stood up after assisting her toddler. "Yes, ma'am."

Mrs. Garson extended her hand. "Mrs. Granger, my husband and I need help. Would you consider cooking for us and helping with the chores? We would provide food for you and your son. We could pay you a tidy sum when we reach Oregon. There isn't room in our wagon for you and your son to sleep, but if you could continue staying with Mrs. Pierce it would work out well. I have come to realize I wasn't prepared for the journey."

Rebecca watched Mrs. Garson's face redden. It was difficult for the over-proud woman to admit such a thing.

Ginny cleared her throat and murmured, "It might be good for us. Can I talk to Sarah and get back to you?"

"Of course. Do you think you could find out before morning?" Mrs. Garson pushed.

"I will let you know. Thank you for thinking of me."

"You are most welcome. By the way, Mr. Thatcher, the walker, works with our teams and wagon for food and water. You would need to cook enough for him as well."

****

Suppertime filled the air with the smells of coffee and cooking. It had been weeks since the energy in the camp had been alive with the promise of rest and comfort. There were no hurried endeavors to clean up or rushed preparations to leave for the next day when they finished eating. The silence that generally settled over the camp due to duty and fatigue had been replaced with hope, conversation, and spurts of laughter.

Rebecca joined Sarah and several women walking to bathe upstream. The colonel had divided bathing areas in sections for men and women. She removed the stiff and dirty buckskin pants and blouse then waded into the water carrying floral scented soap for cleansing. Gasping, she ducked beneath the cold surface. Giggles and sighs lifted above the splashes. Bolo barked and romped in and out around the women. Rebecca handed the sliver of soap and rag to her mother. "Please, wash my hair and back?"

The smile that brightened her mother's face filled Rebecca's heart with an overwhelming surge of love. "Sure, if you return the favor."

The long-awaited bath seemed downright luxurious after so many weeks of dust, dirt, endless walking, and working. Rebecca dressed in the blue dress she had draped over some bushes and went back to the wagon. The reflection in the mirror pleased her. The lantern's glow captured the shine of the long dark curls twisting down her back. Needing to be alone with her thoughts, she walked away from the campsite. Settling on the cool, damp grass, she retrieved her journal from her bag.

May 16, 1845

We've stopped for a blessed three days of rest. I'm finally clean again.

Bolo growled and crouched low to the ground. The hair on the back of his neck stiffened in a crest over his shoulders. He sniffed the air.

"What do you hear? It's nothing, I'm sure. Settle down." Rebecca put her hand in Bolo's collar and patted the ground beside her. "Lie down."

Zachary says the colonel plans to stay for two full days. It will be nice. I will prepare as much as is possible for the remainder of the trip. I feel confused about my growing feelings for Zachary, but I don't know how he feels, nor do I know if I can honor Father as I wish any longer. Mother is better but tires easily. She was too tired for my comfort even before the storm. I am afraid she is getting sick. Bolo is lying beside me, but he continues to growl low in his throat. I can't see anything. Perhaps it is the new mood and energy in camp that has him on edge. Evie announced that she and Hans will be having a baby about the time we arrive in Oregon. What a blessing that will be. Silas Smith continues to watch me. He makes me uncomfortable. He even scares me, but I do my best to keep those feelings hidden or else they— and he—may gain control over me. He seems to show up wherever I wander. When Jodie and I ride away from the wagons, he follows even though we are on horses, and he walks.

Rebecca leaned over to pet Bolo. She ran her fingers over his neck. The knowledge of the valuables hidden within his collar kept her on edge. A feeling of dread and fear increased her breathing, and she willed herself to slow it. Something or someone was out there. Just out of sight.

Bolo crawled toward the unseen threat near a stand of bushes.

Silas stood from behind the brush. He towered over Rebecca and Bolo. "I've wondered about that collar you and your mother are so protective of. What secrets are hidden there? The dog don't like it. Unhook the damn thing and let me see." He reached toward her, but hesitated when Bolo bared his teeth and snarled. "Keep that mangy cur away from me."

"There is nothing remarkable about his collar. It's made of horsehair and probably itches." Rebecca stood and whispered, "Go."

Bolo lunged. Smith stumbled backward. The dog leapt up and locked onto part of Smith's upper arm. He held on with a lockjaw grip. Blood spattered man and dog each time Bolo shook the arm.

Rebecca called him back. "Release."

Bolo let go.

Silas clutched his arm and pulled a handkerchief from a shirt pocket to stop the bleeding. A twisted grimace of pain contorted his features, making him the image of the monster some believed him to be. "That damn dog needs to be shot. He ain't nothing but trouble around here."

Hiding her shaking hands behind her, Rebecca straightened, threw her shoulders back, and spoke clearly. "What you mean is that he protects me. My dog is loyal. Better than some people I could name. He has the ability to figure out who bears watching, as you've just learned. Because of him, and my own instincts, I know you are nothing more than a beaten man who believes bullying others is the way to make yourself feel important. You like to scare people. It doesn't work on me. Or my mother."

"You don't know a damn thing about me. You have no idea what I will do to get where I want to be. Or, how far I'm willing to go." Silas picked up the hat that had fallen to the ground when Bolo attacked, turned, and stomped away.

Rebecca wrapped her arms across herself in a protective hug. She needed to regain control of her thoughts and stop the shudders racking her body and mind. Her heart quivered, rather than beat. Her stomach curled into knots with such intense cramping she had to double over, holding her arms against her belly. Breathing all but stopped. She intended for the deep breath she forced down her tight throat and lungs, to decrease her fear. It didn't work. She had to calm down before going back to the camp. Picking up the journal from where she'd dropped it, she jotted down the incident.

Silas showed up. He confronted me about Bolo's collar. Maybe I should take it off and hide our gemstones elsewhere. I had to sic Bolo on Silas. Bolo bit him on the arm. I do not believe it to be as bad as Smith tried to make out. Should I tell Zachary about it? He is always telling me to be careful. The day is done. There is little doubt that my sleep will be restless, even on the feather mattress tonight. If only I can calm my nerves about Silas. Tomorrow comes soon. Not to mention dancing.

Chapter 8

Gemstones and Kisses

The lovely sound of her mother humming awakened Rebecca. She recognized the melody as one she had sung to her and Joseph when they were young. The lullaby spoke of hope and happiness. Tears sprang into her eyes, she listened for a moment and climbed out of the wagon. "Mother, it's been a long while since I heard you sing. I've missed it. What are you doing up this early?"

An affectionate look crossed her face, warming Rebecca's heart. "I'm making a cake for tonight. And preparing as many meals as I can before we head back out on the trail. What are your plans?"

"Taking Patriot to the farrier. Something has been bothering me, though. Remember when I told you about Bolo biting Silas? And about him wanting to know more about Bolo's collar?" Rebecca stopped speaking until she got the half-nod to continue. "He suspects that we have something of value in there, so I removed the gemstones. What would be a safer hiding place? The lining of your heavy cloak?" Rebecca swiped a finger through the bowl of cake batter and popped the sweet mixture in her mouth.

Sarah gave Rebecca a playful slap on the hand. "Stay out of that. You've always tried to lick the bowl clean before I cooked the cake. Perhaps we should put each gem in a different place. I have another collar for Bolo without anything in it. If Silas manages to get hold of it, he will find it to be nothing but horsehair."

Rebecca chuckled and shrugged. "Is there a way we could remove a board from the hollow space on the back of the wagon seat where the money is hidden?"

Sarah put a finger to her lips. "I don't want others to overhear our conversation. I fear others would notice if we tried to do that. The boards are nailed in place."

"We'll figure it out. After breakfast I have a busy but quiet day. Colonel Wilson has asked me to take the children out to gather grass while we are taking this break from traveling. I don't expect any problems from them. Young Jeb won't give the others a choice. I also want to gather plants for medicinal use."

"Do you and Zachary have plans to go to the dance together?"

Heat rose from the back of Rebecca's neck, flooding into her cheeks. Would she ever feel comfortable about these growing feelings for Zachary? Would she ever not feel guilty about wanting something for herself? "Yes, but so is everyone else on the trail. It is nothing special. Just part of the evening Colonel Wilson wants for everyone. Zachary and I are going on a ride before the dance."

Sarah handed her the bowl and spoon to scrape and lick as a knowing look crossed her face, making her eyes twinkle. "Really? Nothing special?"

****

What made getting dressed for a simple horseback ride so nerve-racking? Rebecca changed dresses twice before settling on a green one with flowers embroidered on the collar for the picnic and dance later. She pulled her hair back into a loose bun. A quick glimpse in the mirror reflected the unruly tendrils near her temples that kept curling this way and that rather than staying in front of her ears as she wished. *Reminds me of that female creature from mythology with snakes for hair.* With a harrumph of surrender, she turned and climbed out of the wagon.

Bolo yipped once and wagged his tail so hard it made his backside twist. "You are something else, dog. What are you excited about?"

"Probably about going for a run while we're out for our ride."

Startled, Rebecca glanced behind her and saw Zachary mounted on Red. He held Glory's reins. She rubbed Glory's nose. "Ready? I'm ready to get away, especially since we hit the trail again tomorrow."

Zachary handed her Glory's reins, and Rebecca climbed onto the saddle.

"I thought we would head north. How does that sound?"

"Lead the way. I'm all yours. I mean, I mean...." Rebecca dropped her chin and laughed nervously.

Zachary glanced at her and grinned. "I'll take you being all mine anytime."

The mid-afternoon sun warmed them without being too hot. Rebecca removed her shawl and tied it to the back of her saddle. "It's been nice not having to worry about putting a certain number of miles behind us or if the oxen can make it any further. Have you noticed how everyone is more relaxed with these two days of rest?"

"I have, but everyone's fatigue and fear will return soon enough. Brent said after we pass Scott's Bluff and

Chimney Rock, things get rougher. I think we'll be hitting that landmark within the week."

"What makes it so much worse?"

"Rocks, mountains, less forage, diminished water supplies, along with the usual monotony. He said something about a pass through the mountains. We may see Indians, but they won't bother us if we don't bother them. Colonel Wilson said they love to trade with the pioneers on the trail."

Rebecca shifted in the saddle and turned to Zachary. "Mother and I brought along sewing needles, beads, calico fabric, and a variety of teas. My aunt told us to have goods to trade. What will the Indians trade?"

"I heard they will gladly barter dried meat, berries, bison hides, and their own medicines for our goods. It's all about want and need, isn't it?"

Zachary reached across and took her hand. She adjusted the reins but didn't remove her hand from his. "Seems to be. Is it true they will try to steal our horses?"

"Most likely. But we'll set up extra wranglers as we pass through Indian Territory. I know I'll help with that duty. We'll keep the best horses inside the circle. Can't have anyone trying to take Red, can I?" Zachary patted his horse on the neck.

Bolo took off chasing something in the grass that caught his attention. Rebecca watched him and laughed. "I see the trees, it's a perfect time to stop. I have bread and cheese in my saddle bag."

"Sounds good to me. Race you to that little rise over there!" Zachary pointed out the small hill, released Rebecca's hand, kicked Red, gave him free rein, and galloped toward the trees.

Within three long strides, Glory passed Red.

Rebecca whooped and waved back in Zachary's general direction. "See you there!"

Rebecca leapt from Glory's back when she reached the trees. She bent at the waist, catching her breath while laughing, and peering sideways with a teasing grin at Zachary as he rode up. "I figured Red could outrun Glory any day with those long legs of his. Guess I was wrong."

"What makes you think I didn't let you win? After all, a gentleman would have done just that." Zachary slid off the saddle, loosened the cinch, and replaced Red's bridle with a rope halter.

"Most women—most ladies, would never be caught riding astride with skirts flying in a race with a man. But I am different. Always have been, I suppose." Rebecca's usually confident voice trailed off to a whisper. "Mother doesn't like it, that's for sure."

Zachary took Rebecca's hands in his. "You're right. It's your uniqueness and willingness to bend the rules that draws me to you. Like those fireflies we see around the campfires."

Rebecca allowed him to pull her so close she could feel his heartbeat. She wanted to close every gap between them.

"Have you ever been kissed, Rebecca?"

Zachary's fingers on her cheek tingled in a pleasant but different, way, leaving unexpected warmth. She opened her mouth to speak, but the words wouldn't come. Shaking her head, she confirmed that she had never been kissed.

Zachary chuckled. "Let me fix that."

When Rebecca first felt the soft, tentative touch of his lips, she knew kissing him was the right thing to do. He kissed her lips, her cheeks, her eyelids, and her lips again. The kiss deepened yet remained soft. She kissed him back without worry, shame, or guilt. Everything about Zachary felt comfortable. She didn't know what to do or say when the kiss ended, so she got her shawl from the saddle and spread it on the grass. She glanced up. "Hungry?"

Zachary sat down beside her and bumped Rebecca's shoulder. "Yes, I am. Starved."

Rebecca took the knife from her bag and cut thick slices of cheese from the slab. She piled the cheese on two pieces of bread and handed one to Zachary. "Enjoy."

A guttural sound of pleasure escaped him when Zachary took the first bite of the soft, fresh bread and sharp cheese. "Will you tell me something? It's a delicate question. Personal."

"Depends on the question, I imagine. What is it?" Rebecca set her meal on the shawl and turned to give him her full attention.

"When we've talked about our dreams for the future in the Oregon Territory, you've often mentioned a vow to your father. Each time you do, you become distant. At first, I wondered if I had done or said something to upset you."

"The vow?" Rebecca stood, paced three long strides, returned, and stopped in front of Zachary. She knelt, taking his hands in hers. "It's one I made to my father when he became ill. Before he died, I promised to make his dream of a horse ranch come true. I promised I wouldn't let anyone or anything get in my way. It was the dream we shared. Horses were our plan for happiness and the future. Glory and Patriot along with the other horses we have in the herd are seed stock for making that dream to come true." Unexpected tears trickled down her cheeks. Zachary leaned forward and wiped them away.

"Could any part of your promise include me?"

"Yes. Possibly. I don't know. I imagine so, but the fear of failing remains."

"I don't understand. My dream is the same as yours. To raise horses, cattle, and have a small farm."

Rebecca cleared her throat. She wrung her hands just as she did when twisting excess soap and water from the laundry. "It's just that …well, you know, for women doing anything independent of a man is frowned upon. I am afraid if I become betrothed or marry, I will have to give up my own dream and give up the parcel of land my uncle has agreed to sign for on my behalf. As a woman, I can't even have land in my own name. It may sound ridiculous, but I am determined to fulfill the vow and show others that I can build a dream just as surely as any man."

"I have four sisters. I understand what you mean. My oldest sister, Katie, is eighteen and is set on teaching school in the Oregon Territory. I don't think teachers are allowed to be married. My parents want her to marry. Be like everyone else. But, my sweet Rebecca, you need to know I would never keep you from achieving your dream. I need you to believe in that. I would just share in it and help you make it happen." Zachary moved to her side, pulled her close, and kissed the top of her head.

Sighing, Rebecca leaned into him and took his hand in her own. She didn't feel a need to make conversation or twitter about like a coquette. With each passing day, she allowed him more space in her heart. The feeling of trust followed by a pleasant ripple of something unfamiliar glided through her as smooth and comforting as silk on skin.

"Tell me a little more about your family. I know you miss them terribly," she asked as they resumed the meal.

Zachary squeezed her hand and took a deep breath. "Let's see. Where to begin. I have four younger sisters. Katie, Hazel, Helen, and Ruth. I told you about Katie. Hazel wants nothing more than to be married and have about fifty kids. She's seventeen. Helen is a romantic and dreams of prince charming. She's sixteen. Ruth fourteen. She changes her mind like the wind. My parents are coming west next spring.

"My great grandparents came to America from Scotland. It was a brutal time there according to the family stories my mother has told me. She was a MacGregor." Zachary glanced over as if to gauge her reaction to the introduction of his family.

"That's interesting. You seem to have a loyal and loving family. I can't wait to meet them. We'll have our homesteads up and running by next September, don't you think?"

"I sure hope so." Zachary stood and helped her to her feet.

Rebecca crossed her arms over her stomach. "I had more than enough to eat. Besides, tonight we will feast."

"I'll get the horses."

Rebecca met Zachary as he brought the horses from the grazing area. She placed her hands on each side of the horse's faces one at a time, kissing them, and scratching their ears. She bent down to pet Bolo and kiss him on the head. He licked back, forcing her to laugh aloud. "Silly dog."

"You sure do love those animals, don't you?" Zachary took her hand.

"I do." Rebecca stood on tiptoe and kissed Zachary

on the cheek. "I may like you more, though."

"We'll see about that. I don't usually care for second-hand kisses." A deep-throated chuckle rumbled in his throat.

Rebecca stepped back. What on earth could he mean? "What? Second-hand kisses? What does that mean?"

"Just that I get my kisses after you've kissed the horses and dog. What's a man to do?"

Rebecca covered her mouth to smother a giggle. Her audacity surprised her, yet it left a sense of power building within her inner being. "Hush. I'll kiss you first next time. Let's get back. Mother needs help preparing supper."

Zachary saluted her. "Yes, ma'am." He bent his head low, wrapped his arms around her, and kissed her deeply and with intense longing.

She leaned into the kiss, returning it with the fervor awakened in her heart. Beneath her hands his chest felt solid, strong, and safe.

Rather than hurrying back, the two held hands and walked the horses down the hill. A scene filled with serenity lay before them. Livestock grazed, their tails switching at insects. Fires danced near each wagon. Children ran around playing a game of tag. Their whoops of laughter carried on the wind. The aroma of meat, stews, cakes, and bread mingled. Groups of women huddled together laughing at private conversations. Chords of music brought dancing to Rebecca's mind. "I expect a dance every chance you get."

Zachary tipped his hat and bowed. "Yes, ma'am. I'll come by and pick you up in a couple of hours."

Chapter 9

Betrayal

Zachary couldn't recall a day that had given him such joy and hope. The feelings he had for Rebecca made him think of love. Breathing became difficult. His heart bounced around in his chest. A simple glimpse dampened his palms, forcing him to wipe them on his pants. Her laugh pulled every intelligent thought from his mind, leaving him as tongue-tied as a child caught stealing sweets. This must be what love feels like. He chuckled, thinking about the way his sisters swooned over boys and the teasing he knew they would dish out to him. He missed them.

The night ahead promised a shared meal, music, dancing, and conversation. A night tailor-made for professing love and desire. A desire to last a lifetime. Zachary felt his way into the deepest corner of his saddle bag and removed his grandmother's ruby necklace safely wrapped in a pink floral-embroidered silk handkerchief. He held the cloth to his nose and breathed deeply the sweet rose scent of his mother. Light from a nearby lantern bounced from the facets of the gemstone. Tears sprang to his eyes as a memory flashed of his mother removing the chain from her neck the morning he left on this trek, admonishing him to use it for survival, if necessary, or betrothal if he was so blessed.

A cornucopia of scents teased the travelers in the campsite—slabs of meat roasting on spits, baked bread, vegetable soups, and sweets. The coming feast had Zachary hurrying along in anticipation. His mouth watered and stomach complained with rumbles loud enough for those around him to hear. Such aromatic and tasty meals were rare on the trail. The melody of Rebecca's laughter tantalized his ears. He all but skipped like a joy-filled child heading toward the sound.

Eager to see her, Zachary headed toward the front of the wagon line. He was probably grinning like an idiot schoolboy, but he couldn't erase the smile from his face. It must have been infectious because everyone he passed shared glimpses of true joy with him, not merely the half-glances of polite society.

He drew closer to the lilt of Rebecca's laugh. He rounded a wagon and stopped, skidding to a heels-grinding-the-dirt abrupt halt which left ruts in its wake. The image before him stunned him. *Unbelievable!* What could this mean? He sidled behind the wheels of a wagon and stooped low to watch and listen.

Rebecca stood face-to-face with Brent, who was holding a bouquet of wildflowers toward her. She sniffed them, laughed, and said something near Brent's ear. Zachary moved closer and tilted his head in hopes of hearing the conversation. Anger and frustration warred with disbelief at the scene in front of him. *What is going on?* Was his heart breaking? He couldn't catch his breath. His chest was so tight it hurt. Just a few hours earlier Rebecca had been in his arms. Now, she was standing too close to Brent. She kissed him on the cheek, pulled her skirt out to the sides and dipped in a deep, exaggerated curtsy, then turned away with a fanciful wave.

This was too much for him to bear. He left. Someone, one of the wranglers perhaps, asked where he was headed. Zachary lied and mumbled something about helping with the horses. Anger, frustration, and confusion fought for the rights to his heart. *Surely, I misunderstood. Is Rebecca playing me for a fool?* He leapt onto Red and galloped off in the direction of the herd of horses. He didn't know what he was going to do or where he was headed.

****

Rebecca laughed, raised her arms to the sky, and twirled around. She had successfully talked Brent into swallowing his fear and telling Sally he loved her and wanted to make her his bride. Brent had rushed away following their conversation to ask the preacher, Sally's father, for her hand. Zachary would be delighted for his friend. She walked with a bounce in her rapid pace to find him. No one had seen him around the chuckwagon. She asked several people if they had seen Zachary. No one had.

Approaching her own wagon, she called out, "Mother, have you seen Zachary? I can't find him and have some very good news for him."

Sarah came from the other side of the wagon carrying a tray with food on it. "Not lately, my dear. Only when the two of you came back from your picnic."

"I'm worried. He said he would meet me here to go to the dance. I've been talking to Brent. I wonder if I just missed him?" Rebecca rubbed her forehead with her index finger and thumb. Confusion, along with an unsettling sense of dread, rose from deep in her abdomen and settled in her chest, next to her heart.

"I'm sure all is well. Wait here. He'll show up." Sarah repositioned the tray, balancing it on her hip, and squeezed Rebecca's shoulder.

"No, I'm going to find him. Something is wrong. I can feel it. I'll meet you at the dance."

Rebecca walked from family to family asking after Zachary. Nobody had seen him or Red. They had disappeared. A wrangler passed her on his way to the herd of cattle and oxen. She held up her hand, signaling him to stop.

"Hello, I can't find Zachary anywhere. Have you seen him?"

The wrangler pointed toward the other herd. "I saw him while ago, riding out toward the horses. Said he was going to stand guard tonight for someone. He didn't seem like himself, though. Didn't make any jokes or ask how I was."

"Thank you." The news stunned Rebecca. Fear stole her breath and caused her heart to tighten in her chest. Tears filled her eyes, she shook them away, pulled a handkerchief decorated with embroidered blue birds from the sleeve of her dress and wiped the salty moisture from her face. *What is wrong? Something has happened. Where are you, Zachary? I need to find you.*

Rebecca hiked her skirt up and ran back to the wagon. She clambered onto the seat and into the back to change into her brother's pants and a warmer shirt. She tossed some food into her bag, grabbed two canteens, and saddled Glory. "Come on, girl, we're going for a ride."

She whistled for Bolo and rode out in the direction the wrangler had suggested. Though it wasn't yet dark, streaks of pink covered the horizon as the sun began its descent. Darkness had never frightened her. It wouldn't start now.

Except for a few large hoofprints in the softer soil, there was no evidence of Zachary. Rebecca reined Glory to a stop, thanked the Lord for a clear, moonlit sky and kept the North Star on her right. An hour had probably passed since she left the train. She stopped occasionally checking for any signs of Red. When it became too dark for her to make out any tracks, she relied on Glory and Bolo to lead the way with their keener senses of hearing and vision.

Time moved like sap escaping through the bark of a maple tree during winter. She wanted to kick Glory into a full gallop but was afraid she would miss Zachary. Leaning into the horse's neck she whispered, "I am truly frightened. He didn't give me any hint that anything was wrong. Maybe I shouldn't have let him kiss me. Does he think I'm a harlot?"

****

Brent Henry saddled up as soon as Sarah reported Rebecca missing. Her shaking voice, pale color, tear-filled eyes, and wringing hands would likely never leave his memory. His heart sped up just hearing the words "Rebecca's missing." Why in hell would she head off alone before dark? Where could she be going? He was worried as well.

Brent found Sally waiting for him near the area set aside for dancing and feasting. She blushed when she saw him. He loved the way her blushes began on her neck and creeped up to her forehead. He dismounted and went to her. "Zachary has gone missing, and Rebecca left to find him. Colonel Wilson ordered me to head out and find them."

The blush he aroused and loved and the welcoming sparkle in her eyes disappeared. He didn't care who was around, he took Sally in his arms, pulled her to him, and kissed her on the mouth then the forehead. "I'll probably be back before morning. We'll get our dancing done. I promise."

"I know. Be careful." Sally stroked his cheek with the back of her hand.

"You go ahead and have a good time, my love." Brent leaned in for one last kiss. Heading west seemed his best option. The colonel had mentioned Zachary had gone missing before Rebecca. Why would he just up and leave? *Damn, I hate puzzles and mysteries. I don't have a good feeling about this.* A long night lay ahead of him. Here he was, out to find two friends, when he should be dancing and eating and talking to Sally about their own dreams for the Oregon Territory. A flash of irritation struck his heart. *Not fair! He had finally chosen a path of action towards a future with Sally. Now, this gets in the way. Just wait until I get my hands on them.* Brent shook his head at the ridiculous vision of him throttling his friends.

After several hours Brent stopped long enough to grab a piece of bread and some meat from his saddlebag to put an end to the gnawing hunger growing in his belly The temperature dropped. Brent tugged his vest tighter. Standing in the stirrups he surveyed the starlit area. A bright glow, which could only be a campfire, a few hundred yards away caught his attention. A sigh of pure relief escaped his lips, surely Rebecca or Zachary or both warmed their hands nearby. His instinct was to gallop, but he chose to move slowly and carefully.

****

Rebecca sat with her knees pulled to her chest. Her chin and tear-stained face rested on them, and she stared into the flames of her small fire. Her shawl and warm shirt did little to break the chill from the gusts of wind. Finding Zachary continued to elude her. Glory grazed nearby and Bolo slept with his nose tucked beneath his curled body. Never had she felt so lonely. Never had she felt so confused. Questions bounced around in her mind, but none had answers. Was this a test? She could almost always think her way through any problem. Was her vow to her father being tested? She knew, at some level, that every question would be answered. A new stronger promise grew in her soul. She would find Zachary, she would figure out what happened, and if he was still inclined, she would agree to meet him halfway if she could fulfill her father's dream. If. If. If. "If" suddenly seemed like the most frightening word in her vocabulary.

Bolo sat up, sniffed the air, and wagged his tail. "What is it, boy? Is someone out there?"

Rebecca heard the creak of a saddle and the measured steps of a cautious horse. Turning, she saw Brent riding up. She stood to greet him. Hope and fear clamored in her heart. "Have you found Zachary? What are you doing out here?"

"Sorry, if I scared you. No, I haven't seen Zachary. Not yet. The colonel sent me out to find both of you. What's going on, Rebecca?" Brent dismounted, leaving the reins loose so his horse could graze. He stepped close to her and put his hands on top of her shoulders.

Rebecca searched the darkening horizon searching for an answer. "I don't know. I just don't know. Zachary and I went on a picnic. He never showed up to take me to supper and the dance. I talked to one wrangler who had seen him. I fear something is very wrong and I can't even imagine what it might be." Rebecca covered her face with both hands.

"Everything will be fine. You'll get your answers when Zachary shows up," Brent reassured her.

"Did I frighten him off? Was I too assertive? Too independent? What do you think?" Rebecca's ragged breath, sucked in through pursed lips, sounded like fabric being ripped from a bolt of cloth.

Brent took over the situation. "Well, there isn't much we can do about any of that right now. Get some rest. At sunrise we'll head out and find him. I bet everything is fine. He may be a little confused about something, likely resting by a fire. Let me take care of the horses and add more wood to this fire so it won't go out in the night."

"Tell me about Sally. Was she upset because you had to leave?" Rebecca poured Brent a cup of coffee.

"Sally is one of a kind. She was disappointed but understanding. She's worried about you. She stuffed my saddlebag with food. You hungry?"

Rebecca dropped her chin to her chest. "No."

Brent put his hand on her upper arm and squeezed.

There were no answers to the questions and doubts circling like a top with a new string through Rebecca's mind. She couldn't imagine how Brent could be so certain that Zachary wasn't leaving her behind. After all, he disappeared after being with her.

****

Zachary moaned. During the longest night of his life—stiff, sore, and sleepless—he made the decision to return to the train. Facing Rebecca would be the first thing he would have to do. She would be upset. Hell, he was upset. She betrayed him. He shook his head, unable to place Rebecca in any situation where she would knowingly hurt anyone. Especially him.

Red nickered and pawed the ground when Zachary reached into the saddlebag. "Hey, boy, you ready for some breakfast?"

While Red munched oats from Zachary's flattened palms, the gentleness of this horse cleared his mind. Acceptance, no judgment, is what mattered. The future may not meet the dream he desired, but he could and would fulfill the one he had when he set out on this trail. Get to Oregon and bring his family next year.

Satisfied, he saddled Red and reined him toward the train.

Not long after heading back he heard a dog barking. *Bolo?* Did Rebecca come after him alone? Heading toward the sound, he prepared himself to see Rebecca sooner than he anticipated. What would she do? What would he do? Straightening in the saddle he rode ahead. The smell of smoke wafted in the air. Voices? The voices of a man and a woman. Hell, was Rebecca with Brent?

Zachary saw them before they spotted him. Rebecca poured water on the fire and kicked dirt on the ashes to put it out while Brent saddled the horses. He reined in and watched from behind some trees. Seemed like they were planning to head out soon. Rebecca's eyes were swollen and red. Had she been crying? Brent led the horses to her while Bolo raced from one to the other. She took the reins, leaned in, and kissed Glory on the nose.

Moving on, he rode up to where they stood. A knot in his throat kept him from speaking.

"Zachary," Rebecca whispered. Her eyes filled with

tears, but she rubbed them away before they could fall.

"Good morning."

"Mornin' Zachary. Good of you to join us." Brent chuckled, obviously trying to ease the shockwaves of tension among the three of them.

Zachary dismounted and faced Brent. Anger built in his chest, tight and explosive. He looked directly at Rebecca. "Well, what do you two have to say about last night? The least you could do, Rebecca, is not lead me on."

Rebecca stood as tall as possible, planted her legs, and put her hands on her hips. "What on earth are you talking about? When you didn't show up for the dance, I got worried and came to find you. The colonel made Brent come for me."

Brent moved between them. "I'm beginning to think there's been a misunderstanding. Zachary. It's time for you to explain yourself."

"Why should I explain?" Zachary huffed.

"Because I need to know why you left." Rebecca sat on a rock. Her shoulders drooped with defeat.

Weak and exhausted, Zachary allowed the anger to drain out of him. "I saw you with Brent at the colonel's wagon when I was coming to pick you up for the dance. You were holding a bouquet of flowers, whispering, laughing, and carrying on. Hell, you even curtsied. I knew then you weren't as serious about me as I am, was, about you. So, I left."

Brent shook his head and mounted his horse. "Time for me to go back to the wagon. I'll tell everyone you're safe."

****

Rebecca's face heated. She stifled the burning

anger. Her chest tightened with frustration and unshed tears. *I'll be damned if I cry in front of him. I've been independent all of my life, thanks to my father. He never wanted me to sit around sewing and cooking. I will not give up my independence for anyone.*

She gestured to a rock then sat, straight and stiff with her arms crossed over her chest. "Sit down. You've got it all wrong. Now, listen. What you saw was a very nervous Brent asking me if those flowers were suitable for Sally. He wanted to know how to tell her he loves her. I told him. And, by the way, she agreed to marry him last night."

Zachary hung his head. "God. I am so sorry, Rebecca. I didn't think. I simply misjudged and jumped to conclusions."

"Obviously. I'm done talking for now. Mother will be worried. We should get back." Her words were clipped, tight, and strangled by the knot in her throat. Now that she knew he was safe, she wasn't going to be as forgiving as she'd normally be.

Rebecca stood and moved to mount Glory. She kicked her into a trot leaving Zachary behind. She glanced back to see him standing where she left him, staring at the ground. Bolo watched her and twisted his head to see Zachary. She whistled. Bolo barked once and bounded to her.

What was she going to do? Several more months of travel lay before them. She would have to see him every day. After a while, heavy dread, haunting fear, and helpless uncertainty replaced her anger. Was he so easily led to jealousy?

She knew Zachary was within calling distance when she stopped to rest. He had been following at a respectful distance. She took a piece of cheese and some dried apples from her saddlebag and tossed the cheese to her dog. Bolo caught the treat in mid-air and took off running.

She settled on the ground, sitting cross-legged among a patch of yellow and blue flowers. Munching on an apple, she absently picked a handful of the blue ones and pulled the petals off one at a time. When the sweet-scented vibrant petals filled her lap, she gathered them in her fist and squeezed them until they were bruised and discolored. She opened her hand and let the flowers fall to the ground. A scratching sound got her attention. She watched a small brown mouse scamper away, zig-zagging a path through the tall grass and flowers.

The scents, sounds, and sights of the small area relaxed her. Watching the little mouse cleared her head for a moment. She wondered what she would have thought if she had seen Zachary interacting with another girl like she had been with Brent. Would she have jumped to conclusions? Shouldn't trust be present even in the earliest stages of a relationship? Was she involved in a romance with Zachary? Shaking her head, she realized she would have to at least confront him to reach an understanding.

****

Close enough to smell the flowers where Rebecca sat, Zachary stayed on Red, still as a church mouse. Did she realize her expressions spoke as clearly as her voice? The creased, puzzled brow. The downturned mouth. Even the tender way she plucked petals from the flowers before crushing them showed her feelings. She was the most fascinating woman he'd ever known. Gentle, independent, caring, stubborn, courageous, loyal, curious, and loving. Sadness overcame Zachary when he realized, due to his own fault, she was probably wondering about his ability to be trustworthy and questioning a possible place for him in her life.

He clicked his tongue, urging his horse forward. He tried to smile at Rebecca when she lifted her eyes to him, but it felt tight and forced. She didn't return the gesture or even a true acknowledgment, and her green eyes were dull. "Rebecca, may I join you?"

She waved her hand in a "be my guest" motion.

He dismounted and sat on a downed tree trunk. Silence as thick as heavy morning fog hung between them. Zachary cleared his throat and spoke. "I usually don't respond so irrationally. When I saw you with Brent after the picnic and at the exact time I was coming to take you to the dance, the situation struck me wrong. I was mistaken and rash. You didn't do anything to deserve what I did. I shouldn't have taken off. I regret it and I apologize from the core my soul."

Rebecca finally raised her eyes to his. Would she accept his apology?

"I do accept your apology, but it has made me wonder if jealousy is a part of you that I didn't know existed. I would think the afternoon we spent together answered any questions you might have had about how I feel about you. Instead, you took off without any explanation to anyone."

"You're right, but—"

Rebecca held her hand out with her palm facing him. "No, don't interrupt. Your actions concerned me. My mother is probably sick with worry, and Brent missed the opportunity to share the evening with his newly betrothed. It was selfish. I am puzzled and need some time to think about everything. Perhaps I acted just as you did when I took off to find you, forcing Colonel Wilson to order Brent to go after me."

Zachary rubbed his chin. "I understand. It is probably best if we get back to the wagons."

"Yes. We should show up together." Rebecca stood and called Bolo, who loped out of the brush with a rabbit in his mouth. He sat in front of her, dropped the bloodied animal and waited for the pat on the head she freely bestowed.

Zachary grinned and picked up the carcass. "Good boy, Bolo. Guess we, I mean you, will be having rabbit for supper. I'll clean it for you."

Chapter 10

The Return

Every eye turned to Rebecca and Zachary when they rode back to the wagon line. What are they thinking? The heat of embarrassment and shame scorched her face and sent her heart plummeting to her stomach. She shook her emotions away and straightened in the saddle. She had nothing to be ashamed of. Neither did Zachary to be honest. *We are both guilty of poor judgment.*

Zachary rode to the colonel's wagon, leaving Rebecca to ride to her own. Which was fine because she didn't want to see anyone. Confusion overwhelmed her. All she knew about couples was the example her parents and a few others demonstrated. Their relationship had been a visual representation of love, cooperation, communication, courtesy, and laughter despite what happened in life. Good or bad. She sighed, knowing her mother would have answers. She arrived at their campsite where she met her mother with open arms and free-falling tears. She left Glory for Aaron to care for and climbed into the wagon with Sarah.

Throwing herself across the feather mattress, Rebecca pulled a pillow to her chest and hugged it. "Mother, what should I do? Have you heard why Zachary left?"

"I don't know what to tell you. Yes, I know about Zachary, but I think he merely overreacted. He had special plans last night as well. I think you should get some rest. We won't be stopping for at least two hours." Sarah pushed stray curls from Rebecca's face and covered her with a light quilt.

"I think you're right, as usual." Rebecca offered a lopsided but sincere grin.

"Give him time and space. When he gathers the courage to come see you, greet him with a welcome and a willingness to sit down and talk things through."

"Can I trust him?" Rebecca sat up, crossed her legs, and reached for her mother's hand.

"I think so. Yes, I do. You rest. I need to check on Aaron." She climbed to the wagon seat and jumped down.

Rebecca tugged her bag from beneath the quilt and took out the journal.

June 16, 1845

Last night I was supposed to be at the dance with Zachary to celebrate before rolling out again after two and a half days of rest. The colonel said we would have to travel maintaining a strict schedule.

Zachary left last night without a word to me. It frightened me. I rode out to find him. Brent showed up—he had been sent to find me and Zachary. I had no idea why he left until he showed up this morning. He was angry. He saw me talking to Brent about Sally before the dance and thought I was betraying him.

How can I know if I can trust him not to question every little thing I do? I explained. He apologized. I am confused. I don't know what to do, but I do know my heart feels something for him. Is he a jealous man? Until last night I would never have thought such a thing about him. Mother says he probably just didn't understand what he saw.

Later today or tonight I will try to talk to him. I don't know what will become of our relationship. Do we have a relationship? I will honor the vow to Father. That has been my plan since his death.

****

Hat in hand, Zachary made his way to the colonel. Embarrassment slowed his steps and shortened his stride. "Sir. I owe you an apology. I am sorry for riding away half-cocked. It caused a great deal of worry for everyone. I wasn't thinking."

"No, you weren't thinking. Yes, you did cause concern. Rebecca rode off without a second thought. You put her in danger. I had to send Brent after her. While you were away, three lives were in danger. I think you should take care of your horse, find something to eat, and get to work.

"By the way, you owe everyone on this train an apology. We waited two hours after dawn to head out. Time we needed. I would begin with Sarah, then move on to Sally. Don't forget Rebecca and Brent." Colonel Wilson spit on the ground.

Zachary lowered his eyes. "Yes, sir."

The sight of Red tied to a wagon with his head hanging and still wearing his tack brought a lump to Zachary's throat. This was the first time he had ever neglected his horse. Zachary quickly removed the saddle, replaced the bridle and bit with a halter, and brushed him down until he gleamed. "Sorry, Red, for riding you so hard. I think I love Rebecca, and I am afraid I've ruined the chance to have her in my life. What do you think, old boy?"

Red nickered and put his head on Zachary's shoulder. Shame scratched its way through his thoughts. His actions weighed on his heart and mind like a heavy anvil farriers use. "You're hungry. Be right back with grain."

Zachary saw Brent at the feed wagon. The two of them stood facing each other. Silent, but staring hard. "Brent, I'm sorry for causing so much trouble. For forcing you to miss the dance with Sally. I saw you with Rebecca. Both of you seemed to be flirting with each other. I thought...I thought the two of you—"

"You thought the two of us were what? What did you think?" Brent stepped closer to Zachary. Toe-to-toe and in his face.

Zachary tilted his head away from Brent. "I thought she was two-timing me and that you weren't as true a friend as I'd hoped. Rebecca and I had just spent a special afternoon together. I believed we shared something. Then I saw you. Got mad and took off."

"How much of an imbecile can you be, man? That girl is smitten beyond reason with you. She was helping me figure out how to ask Sally to marry me. And I'll tell you another thing, the tears in her stubborn eyes almost did *me* in. I ought to belt you for that if nothing else!"

"Rebecca told me after you rode off this morning about you proposing to Sally, and I'm sure I damaged our friendship." Heartbreaking heaviness weighed him down and prevented eye contact. Zachary kicked at a small rock on the ground and rubbed the center of his chest with a fist. The only thing he wanted to feel was Rebecca in his arms.

"Yep, you caused some damage, but it doesn't have

to be permanent. You can make this right. Be patient. Be available, friend."

"Thanks. I need to make my apologies to some others before any more time passes."

Zachary reluctantly made his way to Rebecca and Sarah's wagon. Nerves writhed in his stomach like tangled snakes around rocks in a cave. His mouth dried up as he approached Sarah. Rebecca was nowhere to be seen.

"Sarah, may I speak to you about last night?" He turned his hat around in his hands to hide the shaking and walked beside the oxen with Sarah.

Sarah offered him an understanding and sympathetic look. "Of course."

"I am genuinely sorry for overreacting yesterday. It was wrong of me," he whispered.

"Thank you for the apology. I hope you will understand and give Rebecca some space for a few days. She is confused." Sarah's words were sharp but gentle.

"Do you think Rebecca will talk to me?"

"Now isn't a good time. She's worn out and is asleep. Give her some time." Sarah's dismissal was clear.

****

Rebecca lay snuggled on the feather mattress listening as Zachary apologized to Sarah. The vow to her father was her most important goal. That notion slipped when Zachary came along. Not again. Never again, she thought as sleep overcame her.

Stopping for the noon meal jostled some items, causing them to shift and fall. Rebecca sat up. Her bag had fallen between two barrels. She reached for it, tugged on the strap, and watched as the journal fell out.

Her father's last letter to her fell into a crevice. The mere sight of it loosened the tight hold she had on her emotions. Sobs rose in constricting waves through her chest.

"Rebecca?" Sarah threw back the canvas opening and crawled over the wagon seat.

"I thought I lost my journal. I can't lose it. I don't know what to do about Zachary. What would you do?" Rebecca fell into the outstretched arms of her mother.

"Shhh. I have no answers for you. The choices you and Zachary make require communication and consideration. You will have to talk to him, but not today. He stopped by to apologize and speak to you. I sent him on his way. Time for you to eat something." She handed Rebecca a biscuit with butter and jam.

"Thank you."

Chapter 11

Chimney Rock

Zachary couldn't bear the thought of speaking to anyone. He made his way to Red tied beside a grain wagon and slid down the side of a wheel to eat. Surely, Rebecca would talk to him again. Probably tomorrow. He decided to lie low and stay away for at least a day.

Pulling his hat down to cover his eyes, Zachary tried to sleep. Moving took concentration and purpose. The frustrating sadness of being heartsick dragged him to a depth he didn't know existed.

A low-throated chuckle and kick on the sole of his boot awakened him. He lifted his hat to see Silas's smirk. "Seems to me like you've lost your girl. She may never have anything to do with you again."

Zachary leapt up and slugged Silas with a fist to the chin that knocked him to the ground and left him bleeding in the dirt. "You son of a bitch, don't you ever talk about Rebecca. Don't even say her name in my presence. She's a fine woman with a heart of gold and an independent courage you could never understand." He spun on his heel and stalked off.

"You'll regret that, you little bastard. I swear to God. You'll be sorry."

Zachary ignored the threat Silas screamed at him

and walked away. His thoughts moved from one memory to another. Rebecca's soft gaze. Her kisses. The way she petted that silly dog. The depth of the love he felt but tried to ignore. Yet, his impulsive actions may have finished that blooming feeling before it had a chance to unfold. When had he ever been jealous? Or that angry? Never. He shook his head in disbelief. He'd never been in love either.

"Zachary, walk with me," Colonel Wilson ordered.

"Yes, sir."

"Well, boy, how are you doing since you returned this morning?"

The colonel's arm crossed Zachary's shoulders. The touch of forgiveness tightened his throat. "I feel like I've lost my best friend. I'm angry at myself. Do you think Rebecca will listen to me? Will she let me back in her life?" Zachary stopped and turned to the man who'd become his friend as well as leader.

"You need to decide what you're going to say when she does let you near her again. Tomorrow would be good, I imagine. Help with the herd today, it'll give you time to think."

A sudden ripple of excitement moved along the wagons. People walked away, pointing to the northwest. Men gathered round each other laughing and patting one another on the back. Women took the hands of their children and bent down to their level, pointing to show them the large outcropping of rock in the distance.

"What do they see?" Zachary asked.

"It's Chimney Rock. The first major landmark on the trail. Most folks see it as proof of a measure of success because we've completed one-third of our journey. We are a few days from it. Problem with

Chimney Rock is, we start running into areas of alkaline water that will kill the teams if they drink it. Brent will ride ahead scouting for problem areas. We will have to take on as much water as possible tonight when we stop." Colonel Wilson spat and climbed on the seat of his wagon.

"I have noticed more rocks and dust. Less grass and water, too." Zachary acknowledged.

"I plan to make an announcement tonight. Make sure the teams and horses are given opportunities to graze and drink. Ask the wranglers to check their hooves for signs of breakdown. We may need to stop to shoe the horses and oxen."

Zachary put his hand above his eyes to block the sun. "Yes, sir." *I am thankful to this leader.*

"I will try to allow a brief time to stop when we get closer to Chimney Rock. Betrothals tend to take place there, by the way." Colonel Wilson winked, chuckled, and slapped Zachary on the shoulder.

Zachary stared wistfully at the distant red stone outcropping with a narrow, tall point atop it. "I doubt if I will be able to make any kind of announcement."

"Try not to dwell on it. Let Red walk behind my wagon and rest. Use my horse to help the wranglers. Stay busy. It will take your mind off everything." Colonel Wilson gestured over his shoulder to indicate the buckskin horse tied behind the wagon.

"Yes, sir. I think it will be good for me to be out among the herd. Will you watch after Rebecca? Silas has been sniffing around. I don't trust him." Zachary sensed Rebecca's presence and saw her stepping onto the wagon seat. Their eyes met. Zachary waved at her. Rebecca lifted one hand and returned to the inside. *Don't worry,*

Rebecca. I will watch Silas. He won't bother you.
****

The colonel's horse was eager to be untied and ridden. Zachary turned it toward the herd. He neighed, tossed his head, and loped away. Leaning forward, Zachary patted and praised the beautiful buckskin. "You aren't as special as Red, but you have a smooth gait."

The wrangler he had spoken to yesterday intercepted him. "Why are you on the colonel's horse?"

"He sent me out to work with the extra livestock until tomorrow. My horse needs rest. Everybody seems excited about coming near Chimney Rock."

"Yeah. Brent says we may be visited by some Indians as we get closer to the rock and Scott's Bluff. So, watch for that. He said they will probably just want to trade, but they may try to steal the horses."

"Indians? Friendly, you say?" Worry crept up Zachary's back making him shiver like he was trying to shake off a demon. Rebecca would stand in front of Glory or Patriot and threaten anyone trying to get to them.

Horses and other livestock of every breed and color grazed and rested on the peaceful plains. They had such deep souls. Some lay down and ate the grasses near them. He walked among them allowing his horse to graze. Tomorrow he would have to go back to help his friends. This was the life he wanted. Except he wanted to share it with a wife. He wanted to share it with Rebecca.

Chapter 12

Murder

Silas watched things more closely than anyone realized. Zachary had been sent to the herd of livestock. Rebecca went back inside the wagon after she saw Zachary. Jodie had gone off on one of her typical lone rides to the east.

He approached Aaron and Sarah as they sat eating. Leaning his gun against the wagon he growled. "Give me a couple of those biscuits and bacon. I'm goin' hunting. Try to nab some fresh meat."

Sarah wrapped some food in a red bandana for him. "I hope you can bring back a rabbit."

"Yep. I'll do it." Silas turned and headed west at a fast pace.

When he was out of sight of the wagons, he tracked back to the east. He had plans for Jodie. Just the thought drew a barking, black laugh gurgling from the depths of his heart. It was time. Hell, it was past time.

****

Jodie rode away from the wagon train. The tightness in her shoulders eased, anxiety lifted, and she felt safe with each long, loping stride. God, how she hated leaving Missouri and going on this journey. How she had grown to fear, and hate, Silas with each passing day. She worried about Aaron's safety as well as her own. The demands her husband made became more demeaning and dangerous by the day.

A fully leafed tree stood alone in a field. Wildflowers dotted the ground. *Perfect.* She urged the palomino mare forward. Dismounting, she led the horse toward the tree and anchored one of the reins with a large stone to keep her from wandering off while allowing her to graze.

Sixty-five days had passed since they left Independence. A lifetime ago. She leaned against the tree and slid to the ground letting the rough bark scratch her back before sighing and closing her eyes. A few minutes of rest would revive her.

An unusual noise roused her. Misty stomped and whinnied. Jodie's heart raced. She pressed her palm against her chest, held her breath, and listened. Glancing around, she saw Silas striding toward her and stood to greet him. He carried a brace of two prairie chickens and a rabbit. Blood dripped from the rabbit's neck. *Why was he here? How did he know where to find me?* "Silas, you frightened me. How did you know where I would be?"

Jodie watched as Silas held up the dead animals. A thin-lipped sneer sliced across his face. "You ain't as clever as you think, woman. I always have an idea about where you go on your rides. Always east, but you ain't ever going back. I've been doing a little hunting. Thought stew would be good."

Jodie released a breath. Dark dread continued to wrestle with reason in her mind. Her stomach quivered at the thought of eating anything. "Stew does sounds delicious. I thought I heard gunshots earlier. Must have been you hunting. Would you like to ride back with me?"

Silas stepped forward. He reached over and pushed one side of Jodie's hair behind her ear. "That won't be necessary. I'll walk."

"Oh, that's fine, if it's what you want." Jodie twisted toward Misty. "I'll ride back now. I imagine Rebecca and Sarah will welcome the fresh meat. I know Aaron will. He's taken to growing again."

Silas followed her gaze. He walked to the mare in three long strides, bent down to pick up the rock holding the reins in place, turned, and glared at Jodie with narrowed eyes. "You think this rock on your nag's rein will keep her from running off? You've never been overly smart."

Jodie's mouth dried up. She couldn't take a meaningful breath. Her head spun. Her knees weakened. She lifted her eyes to his. Stepping back, she whispered, "What are you doing with the rock, Silas? Misty will wander away. You are frightening me. Put it down, please."

Silas laughed from a deep guttural place in his throat. "You'll find out soon enough. Lightening the load, as Colonel Wilson would say."

"Step away from me. Now! Let me on my horse." In that moment Jodie knew exactly what Silas planned to do. Everything came into sharp focus—the rich tang of the damp earth, the blue of the sky, the metallic taste of fear, the erratic beating of her heart. The knowledge she would never see Aaron again broke her heart, then almost stopped it.

"Aaron needs me. Please think of him." Jodie hated the sound of her shaky begging voice.

"Don't think so." Silas grabbed Jodie by the back of her neck with one hand, spun her around, and bashed the back of her head in with two hard blows. Laughing, he slapped the mare on the rump and sent her galloping away with reins flying.

He positioned Jodie's body so her bloodied and battered head lay on the rock. Bits of gray brain tissue and clotting blood smeared the ground and the sides of the rock. Satisfied that the murder seemed accidental, he gathered the dead animals and ambled back in the direction of the wagons. He practiced grieving as well as plotting to get everything from the Pierce women.

****

Misty galloped into the wagon yard covered in frothy sweat on her neck and flanks. Two men grabbed the reins and tried to calm her down.

Colonel Wilson rushed over. "Isn't this Jodie's horse? Where is she?"

A man spoke up. "Yes, sir. It's her mare, but she's not with it. Horse sure is skittish."

"Anybody seen Silas?" the colonel snarled.

Sarah ran toward the scene with Rebecca behind her. "Silas came by a few hours ago and said he wanted some food because he was going hunting. He walked off to the west."

Rebecca took the reins from the man holding Misty. She gave the mare a dried apple, then unsaddled her and searched for wounds. She didn't see any. Something had happened. Something terrible. Jodie was nowhere to be found.

"Where's my ma, Rebecca?" Aaron asked with a flat, emotionless tone.

Rebecca knew he couldn't help but notice the somber faces surrounding him. She shook her head, opened her arms, and hugged him. Her heart went out to the boy as he fought to keep his sobs in check. After all, he was twelve. Almost a man.

"What's going on here?" Silas demanded. He tossed his gun and the fresh kills to the ground.

Aaron jerked from Rebecca's grasp and stood directly in front of his father. "What did you do to my mother?"

Silas pushed him to the side. "Nothing. Now, go clean those animals."

****

Colonel Wilson organized a small group of men to search for Jodie. He had to force Rebecca to stay behind with Aaron. *Everyone on this train thinks Silas killed Jodie. I hope we're all wrong.* He stood in the stirrups and pointed east. Jodie always rode east. "I imagine we'll find her out there somewhere. She couldn't be far. Bet that horse got spooked and threw her."

"We'll have that damn horse for supper if it caused any harm to my wife," Silas spouted off, posturing for the gathering crowd.

"Horseshit, Silas. That horse is gentle as a lamb. She wouldn't throw anyone without reason. Now, shut up and help us find your wife." Colonel Wilson's words were loud enough for everyone to hear, but the ice in his voice, the tight set of his jaw and the grim, straight line of his mouth spoke louder than any words.

The riders in the search party were silent, staying attentive to the surroundings.

"There's a large tree over there. It's where I would go to rest." One of the searchers shouted and kicked his horse into a gallop. The others followed.

The first man to the tree found Jodie lying in a pool of her own blood and brains. "Looks like she got thrown and hit her head on a rock."

Silas wailed. "Let me through, goddamn it. Oh, my Lord, Jodie. What happened to you?" He picked up her body, dropped to his knees, and rocked back and forth.

Colonel Wilson unfolded his bedroll and laid it flat on the ground. He had to swallow a lump in his throat before speaking. Jodie was one of his favorite emigrants. "Bring her over here, Silas. We have to wrap her up and get her back so we can properly bury her."

"No, I can't let go."

Something about the man's distress seemed false to the colonel, but he gave Silas the benefit of the doubt. "You have to. I'll do it for you. You need to figure out what to tell Aaron."

Colonel Wilson wrapped Jodie's body and tied it to the back of the horse Silas had ridden. The men rode slowly back into camp. Aaron ran to the horse bearing his father and dead mother. He tried to scream, but sobs tore from his throat instead. "Did you kill her?"

Silas dismounted and put his hands on Aaron's shoulders. "Of course not. Why would you even think such a thing? I reckon Misty got spooked and threw her. We have to bury her. Get me the shovel."

Aaron shook, shrugged Silas's hands off, and stepped away.

"Stop, Aaron. Ask Rebecca and Sarah to dress her in the blue dress wrapped in muslin. She was saving it for when we reached Oregon. Go on now."

****

Rebecca and Sarah washed Jodie's body, dressed her, and hid the shattered skull beneath a lace bonnet.

"Jodie's body is ready, Silas." Rebecca stepped down from the wagon and spoke quietly.

"Thank you. Come on, Aaron, we need to get your mother."

Silas carried the body to the dark hole in the ground. Dust slowly settled and filled the air. He laid Jodie in the earth. Aaron threw a fistful of dirt over his mother. His sobs echoed and bounced throughout the camp. Silas threw more dirt in the grave which landed on her waxy, ashen face.

Almost every member of the wagon train gathered for the somber burial. The preacher spoke words meant to comfort, but few heard him. People were on edge, wondering how many more would die on the journey. This was the second loss since the train headed out. When the preacher cited the twenty-third psalm and said amen, every man, woman, and child responded likewise.

Rebecca held a limp bouquet of wildflowers. She felt Zachary's presence the moment he entered the circle of grief but didn't acknowledge him. Loneliness and a hollow feeling weakened her resilience and resolve. She staggered while laying the flowers on the grave. Turning to Zachary she reached for his hand. "Give me some time. I want to talk, but not today."

Zachary squeezed her hand. "I'll come by tomorrow at nooning."

"No. Let's wait until evening. We'll have more time then." Rebecca joined several other men and women picking up stones and carefully arranging them on top of Jodie's grave, making a cairn to protect it from hungry predators.

****

Silas picked up a large gray stone and placed it near Jodie's head, proud of himself for his act. *If only these people knew that a rock like the ones meant to protect her is what I used to kill her. It's perfect that I didn't find her. Rebecca will be mine. Zachary is next.*

****

Sarah made stew with the rabbit and prairie hens. The rich broth and vegetables smelled tantalizing, but none of the group around her had an appetite except the Granger toddler and Silas, who both ate with mumbled appreciation for the tasty meal.

"Aaron, please try to eat something. You need your strength." Sarah insisted and handed him a bowl.

Silas spoke up. "You have to eat something. Soon we'll be on the trail again. I need your help."

Aaron managed to force down a few bites before jumping up from the quilt and running behind the wagon. The sound of his retching resurrected feelings of intense sadness Sarah hadn't felt in weeks. She hadn't been able to eat properly for days when she lost her son and husband. Neither had Rebecca. Sometimes life, in its joys and sorrows, brought about a deeper understanding of the importance of moving forward and having faith.

"I'm going to share the stew with the wranglers." Sarah gathered up the remainder of the stew. She wanted to make sure Zachary had something to eat. The walk cleared her mind, allowing her time to think. Jodie's death didn't add up. Misty would never have thrown her. Jodie was a good rider. Silas rarely went hunting, and if he did, he wasn't usually successful. *I wonder if Silas killed her. Aaron asked him twice if he did it. Why would a boy ask his father that?*

The twisted knot in her stomach gripped tight, forcing her to stop walking. A certainty settled over her that Silas did indeed kill Jodie. But, why? She tried to breathe but couldn't get a deep breath. Fear rose from the pit of her stomach, inching its way to her throat. She choked when she realized the reason Silas killed Jodie. *Rebecca.* Silas saw the falling-out between Zachary and Rebecca as an opportunity.

Chapter 13

Prairie Preparations

Colonel Wilson rode down the wagon line, stopping often to talk to the emigrants. Pastor Hendricks, the Garsons, and Hans and Evie walked beside their wagons. "I need you men to walk with me."

"Certainly, Colonel." Mr. Garson stood near the colonel's horse, waiting with his hands in his pockets as the others ambled over.

"Gentlemen, I'm sure you've noticed we are nearing Chimney Rock. Tonight, we'll be stopping at a nice water source. I know you've filled your barrels, but now I want every possible container filled with fresh water. Once we pass that landmark, water will be less accessible and may carry disease or be alkaline. Questions?"

"Just one. What do you think really happened to Jodie? Folks are saying Silas hurt her. God rest her soul," Pastor Hendricks remarked.

"Looking like an accident. Have to ride along now." Colonel Wilson spoke rapidly, without conviction.

****

Rebecca walked beside the oxen, lost in thought. Despite what happened with Zachary, she couldn't stay inside the wagon. She would have to think about what to say to him tomorrow. Yet for now, she enjoyed the sunny day and soft breeze. Plenty of grass still grew on the trail, but there wasn't as much, and the ground was rockier. The beauty of the trail took her mind off Jodie's death for a moment...so sudden, so violent. Sadness and despair overcame her. Jodie had been her friend.

Sarah told Rebecca to be watchful around Silas. She believed he murdered Jodie. Even without proof. Rebecca whispered to the lead ox. "I think Mother is right. I believe Silas murdered Jodie. Maybe in an argument. His temper is well known. I can't imagine he would do such a thing because of me. What do you think?"

The ox didn't answer but lumbered on.

"Rebecca." Colonel Wilson rode up beside her and dismounted.

"Good afternoon, Colonel. It's a beautiful day despite Jodie's death and...well, you know."

"Agreed. I'm ordering everyone to fill their water containers tonight."

"We just filled our barrels. Ours are hardly empty." Rebecca's puzzled response furrowed her brow.

"We need them to be as full as possible and fill every available vessel you have. Zachary can help."

"The two of us will talk tomorrow. I don't know what will happen."

Colonel Wilson took her hand. "Listen to him with an open mind and heart."

"Yes, sir." Rebecca crossed her arms over her chest, hoping the colonel wouldn't insist on discussing Zachary, relieved when he rode away.

Rebecca waved to Sarah. "Mother, can you join me?"

"What do you need, my dear?" Sarah tucked her hair

behind an ear and laid a cooking pot aside.

"Colonel Wilson has ordered that we fill as many vessels as possible with water tonight. Do you think it would be wise if I had Silas and Aaron help? After all, they just buried Jodie."

"I'm sure they will be able to help. We need them. Don't allow yourself to be alone with Silas. Colonel Wilson is motioning for us to circle the wagons. It seems earlier than usual."

Once they stopped, Rebecca hitched an ox to a sled-like contraption her father had made. She loaded it down with buckets, pitchers, a coffee pot, bladders, and jars. Bolo zig-zagged between her and anything else that caught his attention on the way to the river. She laughed at him despite the tension and sadness of the past two days. A small part of her felt guilty for allowing herself even the tiniest pleasure. The self-confidence she felt in Independence had diminished, but was still there, and she wouldn't lose that part of herself. With that thought, she walked away with a lengthened proud stride.

She saw Silas at the riverbank watering the oxen and faltered. He was grieving. She had to show him respect for that at the very least. "Good evening, Silas. How are you?"

"Fine. Just doing my job."

"Did you bring any containers for water?"

"No. Aaron is going to bring some later."

Rebecca glanced away when Silas watched her. She reached for two pails. Silas moved to her side.

"Here, let me help." Silas put his hand over hers to grab the rope handles on the buckets.

Rebecca jerked away. "No. I'm fine."

Bolo nosed in between them. His warning growl

stopped Silas from trying to touch her again.

"Can't you teach that damn dog to behave? He better not bite me again," Silas snarled.

Rebecca watched Bolo's brows move as his eyes watched Silas and her. "He is obeying his training. Doing what I taught him. You may use this sled later."

"Yeah. I'll have Aaron get the containers." Silas strode off muttering and cursing under his breath.

Rebecca watched Silas leave. He seemed more angry than sad. He wasn't concerned about Aaron. She turned to the task at hand. The water was cool, clean, and calming. Sighing, she filled the last bucket and led the ox back to the camp. She would return later to bathe and wash clothes. With that thought, she went back to the wagons with Bolo nipping around her feet.

Chapter 14

Aaron's Grief

Silas watched Rebecca from a copse of trees near the stream. *I'll kill that damn dog next. When I get Rebecca away from Zachary.*

He called for Aaron and got no reply. He searched for him in the wagon and at Sarah's. Hearing muffled crying, he followed the sound. Aaron sat beneath Misty's belly with his head on his knees and his arms holding them so tight he resembled a ball. The boy's grief caused a moment of sadness to rise in his chest and had his throat closing. He coughed to clear it. "Aaron, son. What are you doing under that horse? If she gets spooked, she might kick you."

Aaron flinched and lifted his head just enough for Silas to see his swollen eyes and the snot running from his nose. "Don't touch me. I don't want anyone to ever touch me again, especially you. You know this mare would never hurt me or anyone else for that matter."

Silas stretched out his arm and held out his hand with the palm up. "Come into the wagon with me. I bet Rebecca has something she could give you to help you calm down and rest."

Aaron refused to take his hand. He sniffled and unfolded. He had grown since leaving Independence.

Damn, the boy's as tall as I am, Silas thought with a hint of unease.

His stature and tone of voice indicated Aaron realized that too when he said, "I want to talk to Rebecca. Ask her to bring Bolo, please."

"I'll get her. And that damn dog. Be careful of him. He always barks and growls at me. Even bit me once."

Aaron lifted his chin and glared. "He's never threatened me in any way. I'll wait for Rebecca in the wagon. I probably need to pack some of Ma's things away or give them to some of the other ladies. I bet Mrs. Granger could use some aprons and dresses. Will you ask around? Mother didn't have much, but there is no need for us to keep it."

Silas was amazed at the kind thoughts of his son. Thinking of others at such a time. *So much like his mother.* For a moment he was proud.

Silas wasn't in a big hurry to find Rebecca. He went to the Garsons' wagon to talk to Ginny Granger. Mr. Garson and Edward Thatcher were adding hot tar to their wagon bed. "Excuse me, gentlemen. As you know I lost my wife today. We are gathering her things together and wondered if Mrs. Granger might like to have her clothes."

Edward stepped forward. "She's on the other side of the wagon cooking supper. I'll ask her to come talk to you."

Silas shook Mr. Garson's hand and couldn't help but notice his clothes. Even on the trail it was evident they were fine and expensive despite the wear and tear. Envy slithered as cold and dangerous as a snake up his back. He deserved to have the best, and he would get it. He wiped his hand on the side of his threadbare homespun

109

pants.

"Say, man, I am truly sorry about the horrible accident that killed your wife. She was such a gentle woman. Is there anything we can do for you?" Mr. Garson asked.

"What did you say? My apologies, I was thinking of something else."

"I was offering our sympathies and asking if you need anything. Is anyone preparing you a meal?" Mr. Garson took Silas by the elbow and led him to his wife and Ginny.

"Thank you for the offer of a meal. Sarah is preparing supper for me and Aaron. Did you want Jodie's clothes, Ginny?"

"I could surely use them. I am sorry for your loss, Silas. Such a tragedy." Ginny didn't make eye contact and spoke softly.

There was no doubt she needed the clothes. But accepting items from a woman who recently passed surely led to shame and embarrassment. Two emotions Silas knew all too well.

"Thanks. Rebecca will bring the clothes to you as soon as possible." Silas turned and walked away. A smug hint of satisfaction crossed his face at how well his deception worked. No one except Aaron suspected he had anything to do with Jodie's death. They would all be eating out of his hand soon.

He found Rebecca at the wagon. "Rebecca, Aaron needs you. He's inconsolable and asked that I get you. His stomach is gripping him. Can you go to him?"

Rebecca wiped her hands on a rag and tossed it over her shoulder. "I'll take some peppermint and chamomile tea for his stomach and to help him rest. Losing a parent is such a heartbreaking ordeal."

"Aaron asked that you bring that mutt of yours."

****

Rebecca didn't respond. She took peppermint oil and chamomile from her medicinal box, poured a cup of hot water over the tea, and covered it with a cloth to steep. She slapped her thigh. "Bolo, come."

The trek to the other wagon was only a few feet away, but the walk felt like an eternity. Her heart ached for Aaron, but the thought of Silas made it clench with fear. "Aaron, it's Rebecca. I've come with some tea and the company of a very friendly dog."

A shaky sob invited her in.

Rebecca lifted the flap at the back of the wagon and climbed in. She forced a smile and leaned over Aaron. "Here, this will help you feel better and get some sleep. This has been a horrible day, hasn't it?"

"Yes. Ma is gone. Forever." Aaron sipped the bitter tea.

Rebecca laughed at the grimace he made and the sounds of distaste. "It's bad, I know. Drink it anyway."

A tiny chuckle eased Rebecca's worry. She whistled for Bolo. He bounded in with a yip, lolling tongue, and licks of love covering Aaron's face.

Aaron laughed and wrapped his arms around the dog he loved so much.

"Perhaps, I should allow Bolo to stay with you tonight. What do you think?"

"That would be nice. I have something to tell you. It's secret. Will you stay and listen?"

Aaron clutched her hand.

"Of course, what is it?" Cold dread settled over her shoulders like a shroud. She didn't want to hear the words she feared Aaron was going to say.

"Rebecca, I am pretty sure Pa murdered my ma."

"What do you mean?" Rebecca held Aaron's hand and squeezed, hoping to offer him a measure of courage and comfort.

"I've listened to my folks talk at night when they thought I was asleep. Ma cries almost every night. She didn't want to come on this trip. Pa made fun of her and got angry with her. One night she was feeling sadder than usual because she missed my dead brothers and sister."

"I didn't know. I'm sorry."

"Pa told her he wanted her dead so he could have you and get your money and land. Now she's dead. He wants Zachary 'out of the way.' What does that mean?" Aaron choked on the last words and erupted in coughs and sobs. He made himself as small as possible curling into a ball.

"We must make sure you're safe. Stay in your wagon with Bolo. Don't worry about me. I'll stay aware." Rebecca stayed with the upset and frightened boy until he fell asleep. Her heart raced. The news stunned her and left her thinking of ways to protect the people she cared about. Taking a deep breath, she ran her hand over Aaron's head and made the decision to fight fire with fire if it came to that.

Rebecca startled when Silas climbed into the wagon. "How's my boy?"

She willed herself to be calm, smoothed her skirts, and answered. "He's sleeping. It will take time for him to accept this loss."

"Did he talk to you about anything?" Silas rubbed his bearded chin with one hand.

"Not really. He's upset about losing his mother, but

that is to be expected. If you'll excuse me, I need to get back to my wagon." Rebecca left. It took every bit of courage she could muster not to rush to Zachary.

Waterproof cloths lay on the ground with blankets and pillows beneath the sleeping tent she'd made by stretching a blanket over a rope tied to two notched sticks pushed into the ground. Emotional and physical fatigue felt heavy. Moving her arms and legs took effort. Fear tightened her throat and numbed her mind from thinking clearly. Stars and a waxing moon lit the cloudless sky. Rebecca studied them, trying to find the constellations Zachary had shown her. With a deep sigh, she allowed herself to cry for the first time since Jodie's death. She would tell Sarah what Aaron told her. Tomorrow. After resting. But first, she needed to catch up her journal.

June 16, 1845

Zachary is with the wranglers. Tomorrow we will talk about the misunderstanding.

Jodie died today. Silas said it was an accident. He was convincing. Aaron says she was murdered by his father. He told me to be careful, Silas wants to marry me—for my money and land. Should I tell Zachary?

Chimney Rock is near.

God bless us all.

Rebecca awakened, startled by someone calling her name and patting her shoulder. She drew the knife from beneath her pillow and sat up quickly. Aaron stood beside her tent.

"What is it? You frightened me. I could have hurt you." Rebecca put the knife away and patted the mat beside her. "Sit down and tell me what's wrong."

Aaron dropped his chin to his chest. "I couldn't sleep. I had a bad dream. Can I stay with you?"

"Of course, you can stay. I'll get some quilts to make you a pallet. How about that?"

"I'm sorry to bother you, but I'm scared. What is going to happen to me? Can Bolo stay with me?" Aaron rubbed the back of his hand under his nose.

"I don't think we could keep him away from you. He seems to think you belong to him."

Rebecca stayed with the boy until he was asleep with both arms wrapped around Bolo.

Chapter 15

Trading With Indians

Screams awakened Rebecca just as the sky became streaked with pink before sunrise. She rushed to pull her clothes on and jumped out of the wagon. Aaron followed her. Bolo barked and leapt out, landing on all four feet with the fur on the back of his neck standing on end. "Bring Misty to me, then take Bolo inside with you."

Rebecca tied the horses beside the inner front wheel. They were skittish, pawing the ground, and wild-eyed. She cooed and stroked the animals. "Calm down. It is nothing. The noise is just too much for you. I'll have grain as soon as I can."

Colonel Wilson galloped up and down the line ordering the emigrants to protect their animals, arm themselves, and get inside their wagons or inside the circle. He stopped beside Rebecca as she stepped over the wagon tongue. "Get back in there, Rebecca."

"What's going on?"

"There's a raiding party on the bluff. Two of the braves tried to take horses from the herd but were run off. Be safe. If they're friendly, prepare to trade. Get your rifle, but don't put it in sight. I have to keep moving."

Rebecca rushed into the wagon. "We need to gather some of the things we brought to trade. Aaron will help you. I'll wait on the wagon seat or with the horses and oxen."

Sarah wrapped her hands over her stomach before a coughing fit took over.

Keeping low and to the sides of the wagons, Rebecca ran head-long into Silas who just stood there leering at her with a rifle thrown over his shoulder. "I hear we have some Injuns out there. I've been hankerin' for a fight."

Rebecca glared at him without flinching. When she spoke, her voice, delivered with acidic hate, rang with force and confidence. "There will be no fighting unless we receive orders. Colonel Wilson said it is likely they only want to trade or that they are curious."

"Only good Injun is a dead Injun."

"Stay out of sight. Keep that rifle down." Rebecca shoved past him.

****

Two hours later, twelve Indians, including five females, made their way down the bluff. The women dragged things wrapped in blankets. The braves rode straight, holding their bows across the withers of their bony horses.

"They don't seem to be armed for a fight. Colonel Wilson is right; they probably want to trade. What do we have?" Rebecca asked.

"Sewing supplies, cloth, tea, and peppermint oil. I also have biscuits and honey left from yesterday." Her mother sat on a barrel of flour with her head low. She coughed and wiped her mouth with a handkerchief.

A large blot of blood stained the handkerchief. Rebecca wasn't surprised because Sarah's skin was often pale and dotted with beads of sweat. She had been coughing and tired since the storm. Rebecca put the back of her hand on Sarah's hot forehead. Why hadn't she noticed sooner? "You're sick. I will make you some tea and put you to bed."

"I'll be fine. We need to do this trade, don't you agree?"

With the colonel and Brent beside them, Rebecca and Sarah stepped up to meet the women and motioned for them to sit on a bearskin rug they had laid out.

Rebecca sat first and patted the blanket. Sarah sat next to Rebecca. A beautiful Indian woman with a baby motioned for the others to lay out some trade goods. Sharpened rocks for skinning animals, root vegetables, dried meat, and moccasins.

Rebecca laid out the calico fabric, needles, pins, teas, and a vial of peppermint oil.

One of the women reached for the cloth, held it by the edge and watched Rebecca with a question in her eyes that reflected intense curiosity.

Rebecca stood and showed off her calico dress then pretended to sew with the needles and pins.

Laughter passed between the women who couldn't speak a word of each other's language. Rebecca admired the softness of the buckskin dresses they wore. She motioned to see if it would be acceptable to touch it. Each of the women gave a hand signal that gave her permission. Rebecca stroked the garments. "So soft. I wish I could learn to tan hides to be this beautiful."

One of the women reached to touch Rebecca's knitted shawl.

Rebecca turned with a broad, triumphant smile. "Colonel, will you please bring us a kettle of hot water and a few cups. I want to make tea."

When she had hot water, Rebecca made chamomile tea and shared it. She mimicked yawning and being sleepy.

The women giggled and made the same motions. One pointed at the small vial.

Rebecca doubled over at the stomach and made groaning noises. She put one drop of oil in the tea and pretended to feel better.

The trade took place with new friendships made and no hostility. Until Silas came from behind the wagon holding his rifle and pointing it toward the braves.

"Get back, Silas. You are not needed," Rebecca ordered and watched as the braves nocked their arrows and pulled back on the bow strings.

"I came to protect you from these savages."

"If you would pay attention, you'd see that I don't need protection. Especially not from the likes of you." Rebecca spit the angry words out.

Colonel Wilson moved to Silas and tried to grab the gun, but it went off. The blast didn't hit anyone, but the frightened women grabbed their new goods and the items they brought to trade and ran toward the braves.

An arrow was loosed and hit the cover of a wagon. No one was hurt, but fear took over, causing several emigrants to scream, take up their guns, and make threats.

"Get in your wagons! Put your damn guns down. This trading party does not mean us any harm. You, Silas Smith, are under seclusion in the farrier's wagon until I say otherwise. You are a hothead and almost got us all killed. Brent, take Silas to Jack's wagon. Tell him I said to work this asshole into the ground."

Silas stepped in close to the colonel and poked him

in the chest. "You have no right to do that, Colonel. I ain't done nothin' wrong."

Colonel Wilson wiped the spittle Silas spewed in his face. "You did *everything* wrong. I ordered that no weapons be visible, and no one antagonize the trading party. You will be sent to the back wagon, and you'll stay there. Now, I have to get some horses to give those braves as a peace offering."

Colonel Wilson's bright red face and harsh, loud voice indicated his temper was near the breaking point. He pulled the tobacco from his mouth and tossed it at Silas's feet, where it landed on the toe of his boot.

Rebecca helped Sarah into their wagon and went back to talk to the colonel. "May I help you choose some horses? I will give two."

"Yeah." Colonel Wilson put more tobacco in his mouth, held out a hand, and helped her mount behind him.

****

Zachary and another wrangler had herded the horses into a tight circle. They rode outside the perimeter with ropes ready and rifles in the scabbards. The attempt to steal horses had failed but went wrong so easily that he didn't think the attempt had been serious. He worried about Rebeca. *Hell, probably no need to worry. That girl can take care of herself.* Her independent spirit made his heart race. He wondered if she knew how pretty she was.

"Here comes the colonel," a wrangler shouted.

Zachary saw the colonel heading their way. Rebecca rode behind him. What the hell is that about? He tipped his hat at them. "I've been worried, heard a gunshot."

"Everything is fine. Rebecca, Sarah, and a few other women were trading with some of the Indian women.

Silas came barreling from behind a wagon pointing his rifle at them. The gun went off when I tried to grab it. One arrow was loosed, but no damage done. Now, because of that arrogant hothead, I have to give them at least four horses as a peace offering. Rebecca offered two of hers. I'll give two from the herd." Colonel Wilson spit on the ground, dismounted, and helped Rebecca down.

They picked from the best of the herd. Zachary took Rebecca back to meet her mother while the colonel and the other wrangler prepared the animals for trade.

****

The four horses were tied in a stringline led by Colonel Wilson. Several of the braves remained on the bluff. He left his rifle behind but had a handgun. A wrangler accompanied him. "Stay with me and don't make any aggressive moves. You won't need that pistol so keep it hidden. Follow my lead."

"Yes, sir. I am jittery. I heard you know some of their talk. Is that true?" The wrangler settled in the saddle. He filled his cheek with air and exhaled with so much force, the bandana around his neck ruffled.

"Mostly all I know is sign language, but I manage. Show respect, let them lead the conversation, and check the horses. I guarantee they'll be impressed with the animals. Those horses are sounder than any they've likely ever seen. You ready?"

Riding slowly and deliberately to the bluff, the colonel kept his eye on the braves. They stayed on their horses, sitting straight and proud. The other members of the trading party weren't in sight. "When we get about halfway there, I'll take the horses and ride to them. Alone. You stay back and don't make any moves unless

I motion for you."

The elder brave rode to them. He had a leather band around his forehead with three feathers fanning out at the back. One was an eagle feather, indicating a position of leadership in the tribe. His long braids hung over his shoulders. He wore a breechcloth over buckskin pants and no shirt. He motioned for Colonel Wilson to come forward.

Colonel Wilson made eye contact with the brave, whose eyes were obsidian and without emotion. He made the signs for peace and apology. He led the four horses to the brave. "I am giving you the horses in apology for the actions of the man with the gun." He knew his words meant nothing.

The brave took the rope from the colonel and inspected the horses from their teeth to their tails. He ran his hands down their legs. He finally showed his satisfaction with a fist to his heart and a flash of white teeth. He left the colonel standing beside his own horse.

The completed trade relieved Wilson, yet the anger burning in his chest toward Silas had been stoked and fanned back into flames as he rode back to meet the wrangler who'd accompanied him. *Something more had to happen to that idiot.* He needed to have a meeting with his team and maybe Rebecca and Sarah. If he could prove Silas killed Jodie, he could leave him at Fort Laramie or have a trial within the wagon train.

"Let's get back. You return to the herd. I need to check on Rebecca and Sarah before I get back to my wagon. We're minus four nice horses thanks to Silas." Wilson dismounted and kicked at a tuft of brown grass. The grasses grew in clumps rather than in a blanket on the ground. It wouldn't be long before he would have to order the emigrants to ration their food supplies. The country was still beautiful, and would continue to be so, but it would be a different kind of beautiful.

The wrangler eyed him, a hint of worry creasing his brow. "Listen, Colonel. I may be stepping out of line, but you should know that most of us think Silas murdered Jodie. There's talk that he wants to force Rebecca to marry him. May just be talk."

"I know. Don't concern yourself. You aren't out of line. I've heard the same rumors, and it is something I need to address. I am watching him. Jack Farris will keep him busy. Thank you, however, for going with me. I didn't think there would be any problems, but I'm glad things went smoothly."

Chapter 16

Sarah's Illness

Several hours had passed since the incident with the Indians. Colonel Wilson ordered everyone to head out.

"Aaron, please get the teams ready. Give them and the horses their grain." Rebecca reached over and took Aaron's hand. She squeezed it, hoping the boy would be comforted. He was still unsure of himself and afraid of his own father.

Rebecca encouraged Aaron to eat despite his protests that he wasn't hungry. She handed him a warm biscuit with a golden-brown crust and melted honey butter dripping over the edges. One biscuit led to three and a cup of milk. "Hungry, were you?"

"Yeah, reckon I was." Aaron's shy chuckle relieved her. Aaron would be all right given time. She reached over and mussed his shaggy hair.

Conversations around the fires had focused on Jodie's death and the anticipation of reaching Chimney Rock. Rebecca hoped those things pushed the gossip about her and Zachary to the backs of their minds. She had seen the glances of curiosity and smugness from many of the women. Men mostly ignored her, but they gave Zachary a hard time for causing unnecessary worry on the trail.

Step-by-weary-step the emigrants trudged forward when the colonel shouted the order to head out.

Rebecca led the oxen without paying attention. Her mind moved back and forth about seeing Zachary later. She knew it was important to find out more about him. About why he would be so impulsive and the jealousy he showed. She cared about him and her feelings went deeper than she could ever have imagined.

She motioned for Aaron to meet her in front of her team. "Let's tie a rope to the yoke of the team you're with to the back of my wagon and you can walk with it so I can do some things inside and prepare for supper."

"Yes, ma'am."

Rebecca sat on the floor of the wagon with her mother and sorted through the things they still had for bartering after losing the items in the trade earlier that day. Nothing more than busy work. They had plenty because of the preparations her father insisted they make. She was nervous about talking to Zachary. The day's journey had been interrupted, but every mile added up and was important.

"Mother, I need to walk away for a bit. Do you want to go with me? Evie has to go all the time now that she's expecting a baby." She waited for a response. Hoarse coughing and labored breathing stopped her in her tracks. Sarah clutched her stomach with one hand and the center of her chest with the other, she doubled over, and coughed into her fist. Her face turned red with blue undertones. Rebecca rushed to pat her mother on the back. Fear stiffened her arms and pulled every logical thought from her brain. *What do I do? She's been getting sicker but denies it.* "Mother, what's wrong?"

When Sarah stopped coughing, she could only

manage to grimace and shake her head. The linen handkerchief had blood on it when she pulled it away from her mouth. She tried to stuff it in the pocket of her apron, but Rebecca saw it.

"That's blood. Lie down, I'm getting Doc Randolph." Rebecca jumped out of the wagon as it slowly rolled along and shouted at Aaron to keep moving. She hiked her skirt up and ran as fast as she could to the line.

When she reached the doctor she was breathless, tears had streaked down her face leaving salty, dirty tracks. "Doc! Mother is ill. She's coughing up blood. Come with me."

"Let me get my bag." The doctor hurried to follow, carrying his black leather bag.

****

"Wait out here, Rebecca. Pull your teams out of line. I need to examine your mother without movement." Doc Randolph climbed in and sat next to Sarah.

"How come you haven't said anything to Rebecca about being so ill? She said you were coughing up blood. That's a new development." Doc Randolph held Sarah's wrist and felt for the sign of a strong heartbeat with his fingers. Her pulse was regular, but weak. He pulled an instrument from his bag and listened to Sarah's heart. Putting his finger to his lips, he motioned for her to be quiet and lie still. He listened. Concern etched furrows in his brow.

"I'll be fine. I need rest is all. Don't want to bother Rebecca." Sarah stuttered the words, the effort to breathe much less talk reduced her voice to a breathless whisper.

"You are not fine. You have something wrong with your lungs. Consumption. I'm going to give you some medicine to help you sleep. You are not to get out of this wagon until you feel stronger. Sarah, you are quite ill. What shall I tell Rebecca?" Doc Randolph caressed Sarah's hot, dry brow. He had grown attached to this beautiful widow.

Rebecca came in through the back. "What is it? What's wrong?"

Sarah's eyes searched his, silently begging him to tread lightly in what he tells Rebecca.

"I…am ill…" Sarah coughed and gasped. "But…I—" She cleared her throat. "—will…be fine."

The determination in Sarah's voice belied what Doc Randolph knew to be true. He put his hands on Rebecca's shoulders, forcing her to make eye contact with him. "Listen, Rebecca. Here is what I want you to do. Boil some beef bones and give your mother sips of broth every few minutes. Mix some chamomile tea with willow bark in it to help her rest. I have some mentholated salve for you to rub on her chest. She is to rest. When the wagons are stopped for the night, raise the sides of the canvas for fresh air. When we're traveling, keep them down so excess dust doesn't get inside. Keep her clean. Keep her bedding clean and dry. And keep her as comfortable as possible. You can do this."

Rebecca shook her head. "She's very sick, isn't she? Will she die?"

"No, she won't die. I won't let that happen." He climbed out and strode away.

****

More frightened than she had ever been, Rebecca turned at Aaron's sharp intake of breath when he saw Sarah lying on the mattress practically gasping for air. "It will be fine. We just have to watch after her and make sure she's comfortable. Stay here. I need to boil some beef bones before we get back in line."

She hurried to do as Doc had ordered. Once she'd settled her mother into the bed with broth and cool cloths handy, she relieved Aaron, and he led the oxen back into the procession.

When the colonel called to stop for the evening, Rebecca gathered things for a cold meal. She tied it in a cloth and handed it to Aaron along with a quick kiss on the cheek. "I'm going to the grain wagon to meet Zachary. I won't be gone long. Don't forget to give Mother sips of broth every few minutes."

Distraught but determined, Rebecca took on the tasks she felt were hers and hers alone. Nervousness about seeing Zachary made her clumsy. She dropped some of the food she carried, tripped over a stick, fell, and spilled a full canteen of water. *Pull yourself together. You can do this!* Standing, she wiped her sweaty hands on her clothes and walked to the first grain wagon.

She saw him before he noticed her. Running his fingers through his hair and leaving it tousled, he paced back and forth. She could see his mouth moving as though talking. Taking a deep breath, she called out, "Zachary, it's me. I brought a small meal."

"I'm glad you came. I was afraid you wouldn't. How is Sarah?" Zachary motioned for her to take a seat on a chair.

"Aaron is taking care of her. He's being so brave. Where did you find this chair?"

"The colonel let me use it. I hope all will be well. Thank you for bringing the food. Honestly, I might not be able to eat a bite. I have so much to say to you."

"My appetite isn't what it usually is either." Rebecca

unwrapped the food and served it.

Zachary took her hand and squeezed it. He seemed pleased when she didn't pull away.

Each of them nibbled without speaking. Silence was so loud it overwhelmed. Rebecca couldn't hold back her thoughts another moment. "We do need to talk about what happened. About Mother. About Silas. And, not just about the miscommunication, but about Jodie and the trade with the Indians. I need to know if you habitually misinterpret things and run away without confirming what you think you see. I need to know if you have problems with jealousy and anger."

****

Zachary laid the biscuit in his lap. He moved closer to Rebecca, placed his hands on her cheeks, and lost himself in her brilliant green eyes. They were always more vivid when she had been crying. "No. I swear to you. That was the first time I've ever behaved that way. Believe me, I'm as surprised as you. I didn't, I don't, understand why I reacted that way. The only thing I can figure is, since this is the first time I've ever loved anyone, I didn't know what to do or how to do it. I am truly sorry. I wish I could turn back time and fix this mess."

"I have thought about everything, and I can understand how what you saw could be misconstrued as something more than what it was. Surely you know I would never do anything like that. Neither would Brent. The two of you are friends. He told me you knew he was interested in Sally. Didn't you think about that?" Rebecca's words rushed out of her mouth. She took a deep breath and pulled the braid from her shoulder, tossing it to the back.

"Do you think we can begin again? Put this behind us?" Zachary's voice dropped to a whisper. He broke eye contact with her.

"I think we should stay apart for a few more days. Continue thinking. I will say this, and I mean it—I think I love you. I think you love me. I hope it will all work out, but I need some time. Can you accept that? There is so much going on with Mother being sick. Jodie was killed, maybe murdered. Aaron is staying in our wagon and needs support. Will you give me until Chimney Rock to consider and try to get my thoughts together?"

Zachary stood and gave Rebecca a hand to help her up until they were face-to-face. Tears filled her eyes. He wiped them away with his index finger. "Yes. I can wait. I will respect your wishes. The colonel wants me to help the wranglers for a few days. There is something else bothering you, isn't there? I can see it in your eyes."

"I'm not sure I should say anything. It might cause someone, especially you, to be harmed." The last word escaped through Rebecca's pursed lips along with a long breath.

"What? Are you in danger?" Zachary put both his hands on her shoulders and squeezed them.

****

Tears had always been a sign of weakness to Rebecca, and here she was shaking and fighting to keep from sobbing and screaming. Words had never been difficult for her. She struggled with how much to tell him especially since she was on the verge of deciding if she could trust him anymore. Taking a leap of faith, she told him. "It's Aaron. He's terrified. He told me he believes Silas killed Jodie. He overheard Silas talking to Jodie one night. Silas told her he wanted to marry me for my land

and money. We don't have much money. I don't know where he got that notion. He told Jodie that he had to get rid of you and her. A few days later Jodie died. I have to keep the people I care about safe." Rebecca knuckled a tear off her cheek.

Zachary moved his hands from her shoulders and clenched them into tight fists forcing the knuckles to turn white. "That son-of-a-bitch needs killing. I can't, I won't, stay away from you. I will tell you this, I don't know if you're aware, but the colonel has sent Silas to the farrier's wagon and ordered him not to come near any of us until he can learn to do his share and respect others. He did that because of that stunt when we were trading with the Indians."

"I know about it. Do you think Silas is capable of murder?" Rebecca closed her eyes to rid herself of the vision of Jodie lying dead in the wagon. She noticed Zachary's face had reddened and the muscles in his jaw clenched. He narrowed his eyes and clenched and unclenched his fisted hands at his sides.

Zachary cleared his throat and spoke up. "Yes. I think Silas is capable of anything to get what he believes he wants or deserves. Including murder."

Rebecca knew, at that moment, without any doubt that she had to stay away from Silas. She had to keep Aaron away from him. He murdered Jodie. Silas would never stay confined to the farrier's wagon. It would be too easy for him to just walk away and go wherever he wanted. He would obey the colonel's orders for a few days and give others time to forget. They would lapse back into the routine of walking day in and day out.

"I need to get back to the wagon. I need to be with Mother and keep Aaron safe. Come by and share our meals; you don't have to stay away. I imagine Aaron will be grateful for your help. That is, if you want to. Good night, Zachary." She kissed him on the cheek. Just maybe everything would work out.

As soon as she returned to the wagon, Rebecca checked on her mother. Her breathing seemed easier, and she slept soundly. Aaron sat next to Sarah, holding her hand. His head lolled to the side, and he snored quietly. "Wake up, Aaron. You can go lie down in your wagon. I can see that you've done an excellent job. Take Bolo. Thank you."

The air was warm. Rebecca lifted the sides just as Doc had ordered her to do. She took the lantern from a hook and held it near her mother. Although she remained pale and oh, so still, some color had returned to her face. She caressed her mother's forehead, relieved to find it wasn't as hot.

"Mother. I need you to wake up and take some of this broth. Then, I'll clean you up and change your bedding and chemise. I'll even use some of your rose-scented soap. That will bring you around for sure." Rebecca tried to keep her voice light and not let the heavy worry tint her words.

Sarah moaned but opened her eyes and propped up on an elbow to sip the broth. "Mmm, good."

Rebecca chattered away while she fed and bathed her. "I saw Zachary. I'm sure all will be well. He will be around to help with the wagons and teams every day."

"Knew it would be fine." Sarah's words were almost too faint to hear.

"Now, do you feel better? If it's all right with you, I think I'll go check on the horses and the team. I don't know if the cow got milked. I want to make sure Aaron is settled in. Bolo is with him." Rebecca tucked the top sheet around Sarah's shoulders and inhaled the sweet scent of rose oil.

"I'm fine. Go ahead." Sarah sighed and fell back to sleep.

Rebecca made her usual rounds, ensuring everything was as it should be. *Bless Aaron. He remembered to milk the cow.* She sat on the wagon seat, watched the stars lighting and sparkling the black sky, and felt in her soul that everything would be fine. It was a feeling so deep she couldn't touch or define it.

Chapter 17

Sunflowers

Sunrise cloaked the sky in colors most of the travelers had never seen. The sun, round and red, seemed hot and close enough to touch. Orange bled into yellow while the blue sky behind it all enhanced the view of the towering reddish-brown outcropping of rocks making up Chimney Rock and Scott's Bluff. They would end the day at the base of the landmark. The usual creak of wagon wheels, bellows of oxen, and shouted words of the emigrants set the day in motion.

Colonel Wilson rode to the end of the line to check with the farrier, Jack Farris, to find out how he was handling Silas. Jack was working on a horse's hooves when he arrived. "Mornin'. How's it going?"

"Damn you, Colonel, for sending that lazy sack of worthless to stay with me. I ain't no babysitter. I want to know the story. From you, not him." Jack dropped the horse's leg, crossed his broad, muscular arms over his chest, and stood to his full six-foot, five-inch height. He had an old scar caused from a knife fight in a saloon that ran from his left eyebrow to his chin and stretched into a grimace when he talked.

"You know the story. His wife died. I think he murdered her but don't have no proof. Then he threatened the trading party, waving that damn rifle around. Almost led to an attack. I'm worried about his thoughts toward Rebecca. I sent him to you, hoping you might scare or work some sense into him."

"He has to be told to feed the animals. He ain't a friend of them. As you know, I have a team of eight since my wagon is so heavy. He don't know how to clean hooves on oxen or mules or horses. He'll damn well learn. You know I take care of the teams for some wagons every morning before I head out and follow the rest of you. Silas thinks it's an unnecessary inconvenience. Of course, the men aren't happy when it's their turn to get a late start because I'm working on their teams."

Silas sauntered over to the colonel and Jack, carrying his tin cup of coffee. "Talkin' about me, I imagine. This situation won't work out. I need to be near my boy. He just lost his mother."

"Well, your boy ain't missing you much. Matter of fact, he asked me not to let you come back." Wilson narrowed his eyes. "My advice to you is to keep busy and stop trying to be someone you ain't."

Jack interrupted. "Didn't I tell you to start making hoof covers for the working livestock and horses out of those rabbit skins and cow hides? I showed you how to run a leather drawstring through them. How many have you done? It's so easy, you can walk and do them. We'll be needing them soon."

"I ain't done none. That's woman's work." Silas slung the cold dregs of his coffee on the ground, splattering the colonel's trousers.

"The hell you say," Wilson roared. "You'll do whatever I say and whatever Jack says, or I'll arrest you for not following rules and turn you over to the cavalry at Fort Laramie."

"You can't do that." Silas sputtered and backed away.

"You didn't pay attention to my rules, did you? I can and I will. And if you try to leave this wagon and go to the Pierces' or to your boy, I'll send you packing before we even get to Fort Laramie."

Jack laughed so hard he had to hold his sides. His deep bass voice boomed and vibrated.

****

Silas stomped off. He grabbed a sling bag filled with rabbit hides, leather strips, and an awl and threw it over his shoulder. He felt like he was going to explode like them volcanoes he heard about. His ears were hot, and his chest was so tight he couldn't suck in a deep breath. The only thing he could think of was getting even. At this point, he wanted to kill anyone who got in his way. He had to calm down, or he would lose any chance he had of having his way with Rebecca.

He stayed with Jack pretending to listen to the things the farrier showed him about hoof care while mindlessly poking holes in the fur with an awl and working the string around the top to make a pouch. Rubbing his hand over one of the rabbit pelts, he couldn't help but feel jealous of the oxen who would be wearing them, fur side in, for protection. He wished his socks were this soft. *Hell, even the animals around here are treated better than me.*

"That's the last one. Get Mr. Garson, and tell him his oxen are ready. I'll get this team yoked up. We should catch up quickly this morning." Jack motioned for Silas to get going.

Silas didn't acknowledge him. He walked away to fetch Garson. An idea came to him. He puffed out his chest, acknowledging his brilliance, and hummed a mindless tune. He would get what he wanted. Just walk away pretending to do something for Jack. He would wait a few days and suffer through that man's endless nattering on about nothing.

****

Sarah awoke to the jostling of the wagon. Her mouth was so dry, her tongue stuck to the roof. She tried to lick her lips. Glancing around, she saw the chamber pot sitting near the mattress. Her crystal bell sat on an upturned bucket. She scooted to the edge, took the bell with both hands, and rang it.

"I'm here." Rebecca climbed in carrying a canteen and a cup of tea. "Here, let me help you. I'm sure you need the pot."

Sarah lifted one corner of her mouth. She was so weak she could barely move. How long had she been in the back of the wagon? Was it days? "How long have I been sick?" she rasped.

"I don't know for sure. Doc Randolph told me you've been having trouble breathing and that something is wrong with your lungs. He asked me to feed you beef broth and tea every few minutes. I'll sit you up so you can wash and use the chamber pot. I'll straighten your bed linens while you clean up."

Sarah used the chamber pot and gratefully accepted a warm washcloth from Rebecca. "I would love to clean my mouth. Do you have any twigs in your bag?"

"Oh, Mother, the fact that you want clean teeth makes me want to dance, sing, and shout! Does the sun rise in the east?" Rebecca hugged her, though not as tightly as Sarah would have liked.

"Speaking of that, let me open the back cover for you. The sun and sky this morning are putting on quite a show. We'll be stopping at the base of Chimney Rock tonight. One-third of the way there."

Sarah squinted her eyes and wrinkled her brow. "Are we in front of the other wagons? Weren't we in the middle?"

"Doc Randolph has ordered that we be the first wagon behind his and the colonel's for the remainder of the journey. We need to minimize the amount of dust you're exposed to. I will keep the sides of the canvas down during the day, but if you want to see out, I can lift them and stretch cheesecloth around the sides. Doc probably won't object to that if the cloth is tight enough."

"Just the back and this side will be fine. Being confined to this wagon isn't likely to help me. I will go stir crazy."

"Doc was clear about his expectations. He wouldn't take kindly to any of us not obeying his orders."

Mid-way through the afternoon Doc Randolph visited Sarah. "Good afternoon, how do you feel? You have more color in your cheeks. Rebecca took good care of you. I see she came up with an ingenious way to keep dust out of the wagon and still let you see the trail."

He put the back of his hand on Sarah's forehead. "The fever has lifted. May I listen to that heart of yours?"

Heat rush to her cheeks. "Of course."

The doctor listened to her heart and lungs. "Sounds better, but still not what I would like to hear. We'll keep up with the broth and salve, but I want you to eat something solid today. If you're still improving, I'll take you for a short walk this evening."

"That sounds lovely."

****

Chimney Rock loomed larger than life with each mile, appearing as though it reached Heaven. Rebecca led the oxen and gawked while Aaron played games of tag with Bolo and some children. Tension in camp since Jodie died and the Indian trade made the children restless. Children shouldn't be expected to put one foot in front of the other for hours on end without playing.

Big yellow flowers with brown, almost black centers waved in the breeze. Some were taller than a grown man. They grew in lines and clumps and seemed to raise their faces to the sun. Rebecca cut one for her journal. The brown centers held seeds. She plucked one, sniffed, licked, then ate the crunchy and sort of sweet kernel. She ate another and another. All from one flower. Excited, she called the children to her. "Come here. See what I found."

As usual Jeb led the way. "What? Let me see. I got here first."

Rebecca handed the precocious boy a few seeds. "Try these. They're pretty tasty."

Jeb figured he was being tricked. "No. You first."

Rebecca ate another seed and made sounds of delight. "It's good. Try it."

Aaron and the others circled around Jeb daring him to eat.

"Fine, then." Jeb tossed the seeds into his mouth, chewed on them, spit out a woody part, and swallowed.

Sadie Lawson elbowed Jeb out of her way. "Give me some. I'm not afraid to eat them."

Rebecca put her hands on her hips. "Well, what do you think?"

"Good, they're good."

With Jeb's acknowledgement the other children gathered flowers and seeds of their own. A spitting contest resulted. Girls against boys. As the wagons continued to roll, the children played, frolicked in the prairie grass, and laughed louder than they had in days.

"Take a few flowers to your mothers and show them what we've found."

Rebecca turned to scratch an ox behind the ear. Things were going well. Sarah was better. Silas was down at the far end of the wagon line. Aaron was laughing again. She couldn't wait to see Zachary.

****

Sarah sat up and gathered pillows around her so she could see out. She felt stronger and could breathe better sitting up. Reaching for a brush and hand mirror. She was a mess. *Lord, I need to make myself presentable.* She bent over at the waist, letting her long auburn hair fall onto her lap, and began brushing, one patient stroke at a time. Detangling the snarled tresses was an effort, and she had to rest often. She twisted her hair into a bun and secured it with a comb. Rebecca had left the ewer and bowl close so she could wash up. She rubbed a sliver of scented soap on a cloth until it made a small mountain of fragrant suds, then washed her face and body. She pulled on a clean chemise. Fatigue washed over her from her shoulders to her toes. She leaned back against the pillows and fell fast asleep.

The sounds of the wagons circling, and the animals being taken from their yokes awakened her a while later. She felt her forehead—no fever. Needing fresh air and to see what was going on, she scooted around and climbed onto the wagon seat and breathed deeply the clean air. A cough began to rise in her chest, but she squelched it. "Rebecca, do you need any help?"

"What? Of course not. Aaron and I have this. He's taking care of the animals. Why are you out of bed? Doc Randolph won't be happy." Rebecca talked so fast the words ran together.

"On the contrary, he is coming to take me for a short walk. What will we be having for supper? Do we have any sweets left?"

"I started a fire as soon as we stopped. I'm making vegetable soup and corn cakes. We don't have many more sweets, but let me show you what I found today." Rebecca reached into the pocket of her apron and pulled out a handkerchief folded up with several seeds. "Taste these."

Sarah took a few seeds and put them in her mouth one at a time. "These are good, but it sure is a lot of trouble to get to the nut inside the shell. I imagine they would be nice mixed in with a bread. What do you think?"

"Maybe. I'll harvest some more later. The prairie is full of the brilliant yellow flower I discovered that these come from." Rebecca pointed to the east. "That's Chimney Rock."

"Goodness, it's so tall! And the setting sun makes it seem like it's on fire. How many colors do you figure are streaking through the sky?"

Rebecca grinned at her and counted on her fingers. "Orange, red, yellow, pink, blue. I don't know, but I will document this in my journal. I think I'll put some of these seeds in the corn cakes. It's good to see you feeling better. Rest here while I get supper going and make some tea. Do you want a cup?"

"Yes, do you think I could have two lumps of sugar?"

The sound of Rebecca's laughter raised Sarah's spirits.

****

Zachary walked with Doc Randolph toward the Pierces' wagon. "I'll check on Sarah. If she's up to it, I'll take her for a short walk to get some fresh air. I confess, I am still concerned. She's sicker than she or Rebecca realizes."

Zachary acknowledged Doc Randolph, allowing a haphazard, crooked grin to cross his face. "She's tough. I know she couldn't be getting better medical attention than from you and Rebecca. I hope to see Rebecca tonight. Any suggestions?"

"You two will be fine."

"I hope so. Sarah's on the wagon seat. I don't see Rebecca. I do smell coffee and soup. She must be fixing supper." He left Doc Randolph, followed his nose, and saw Rebecca before she knew he was near. He stopped to watch her in the glow of sunset. *Damn, she's beautiful. How come I hadn't noticed her hair had red in it? What's that song she's humming? It's familiar, but I can't figure what it is.* The ruby necklace that had belonged to his grandmother and mother was burning in his pocket. He wanted to see it around Rebecca's slender neck. "Want to share some of that coffee I smell?"

****

Rebecca twisted around to see Zachary standing there with that perfect dimpled charming grin on his face. The one that squeezed her heart, released it, and set it to galloping as fast as Glory through her chest. "Sure. I'll pour you a cup. I'm making Mother some tea. With two

141

lumps of sugar at her request. I think she's excited about taking a short walk with Doc. Do you think he's sweet on her?"

"I know he is." Zachary smothered a girlish giggle with his hand.

Rebecca laughed out loud. "I'm not sure how I feel about that. Mother was always so dependent on my father and so in love. I do want to see her happy, though. Be right back."

Zachary acknowledged her with an incline of his chin and that smile she loved so much. "I'll be waiting."

Rebecca took the tea to her mother and came back carrying two bowls of stew and two corn cakes. "You hungry? I've got a surprise, but I won't tell you what it is. You have to figure it out."

"Smells good. I'm starving. Let me take one of those bowls from you."

"I took some to Aaron. He's feeling melancholy. I'm worried about him. He seems fine one minute, then he is fighting tears. I hardly know what to say to him because he's a child, basically an orphan. I told him I would check on him again later."

Butter dripped over the edge of the warm corn cake onto his hands when Zachary took half of the treat in one bite. She saw the moment he noticed there was something different in it. He turned it over. "What is this? Is it a bug? I've never had anything like it."

"It's a seed I found today. Those tall yellow flowers contain hundreds of them in the center. The children and I discovered them." Rebecca bit into the corn cake and crunched on a seed. "They really do taste better in the bread."

She handed him some seeds from her apron. His

fingers touched her palm when he took them, and a lightning-fast shock ran up her arm and into her heart.

Rebecca wanted to hold his hand for a lifetime but jerked away. The promise she made to her father surfaced. Would falling in love prevent that vow from happening? She reached over and touched his cheek. "Sometimes I feel like we've settled the misunderstanding between us, and at others, I feel we should talk more. I don't want to keep hashing this out, so I'm going to say I think everything is fine, and let's move forward. I want to see you. I still fear you might get angry or impatient with me. My dream is making it safely to the Oregon Territory and starting the ranch my father had his heart set on."

Zachary splayed his fingers and brushed the hair that had fallen in his face to the side. "I understand. I love you and will honor whatever choices you make. I have never been quick to anger or impatience. Well, except for my recent mistake. The whole incident still bothers me, but trust me when I say I've learned my lesson. Brent and I have made amends, too."

"Good. I knew you would."

Zachary pointed to Chimney Rock. "I wish we had time to explore. Colonel Wilson wouldn't give permission because it's getting dark, and we're leaving earlier than usual tomorrow. I hope we can see it at sunrise. I can't imagine it could exceed this majestic sunset. Time for me to get back and check on Red." He stood and cupped her face in both hands, leaned down, and gently kissed her.

"Come early tomorrow morning for coffee. We can watch the sunrise." Rebecca kissed him on the cheek and watched him amble away.

****

Sarah strolled arm in arm with Doc Randolph. She was weaker than she would admit, but being away from the wagon did her good. She suspected the tall gentleman she walked beside had feelings for her and felt as if she could easily fall in love with him also.

"How are you doing, my dear?"

"I'm tired, but fine. I confess that I am ready to lie down though." She adored his gentle, caring acceptance which was as comforting as any embrace, kiss, or touch.

"Well, then let's get you back. Rebecca will wonder what I've done with you."

When they arrived at the campsite, Rebecca was waiting for them. "I need to check on Aaron. How was your walk? Can I help you get settled in before I go?"

Sarah waved her hand. "No need. Go ahead. Doc will help me."

After Rebecca turned to go to the other wagon, Sarah stood on her tiptoes and reached up to kiss Randolph on the cheek. "Thank you for taking me for a walk and for caring. You are a remarkable man."

Doc tipped his hat. "You are most welcome, my dear. May I help you into the wagon?"

Sarah took his hand. Butterflies twisted her stomach into knots. She hadn't felt such pleasant flights of fancy in years. All caused by attraction. "Good night. I hope to see you tomorrow."

"Sleep well."

Chapter 18

Threats

Silas delivered a recently shod mule to a family and quietly made his way to the wagon where Aaron was with that damn dog. He knew Rebecca would be there, checking on the boy before bedding down. He drew a knife from the shaft of his boot, hid it behind him, then climbed into the wagon. Surely, no one had seen him. He sneered at the two of them. Aaron lay on the mattress. Rebecca sat on the flour barrel, which was covered with a lace cloth and white ewer and bowl with painted violets on it. It had been one of Jodie's prized possessions. Silas wanted to shatter it. "Well, well. Thought I would check on my son."

Aaron sat up and scooted back to the edge. "I don't want you to visit. I'm fine."

Bolo growled and bared his teeth. Rebecca raised her hand with the palm facing her dog. "Sit. Stay."

"What do you want, Silas?" Rebecca edged between him and Aaron.

"I have a deal to make with you."

****

The suggestive laugh Silas tossed her way sent shivers of unreasonable fear up and down her spine before settling in the pit of her stomach. Rebecca

145

breathed in, breathed out, and willed herself to sound strong and unafraid. "Why would I deal with you about anything? You can't even be trusted to stay in the back wagon with Jack Farris as the colonel ordered."

"Because if you don't do what I say, I'll kill your boyfriend and, maybe, even Aaron." Silas showed the knife to them. The blade glinted from the lantern light when he lunged to press the sharp edge against Aaron's heart.

Aaron gasped. Large, fat teardrops clung to his lashes before falling one at a time down his cheeks. He held his breath.

Bolo growled but didn't move.

Rebecca tried to understand what was happening. She couldn't move. Paralysis threatened to keep her from reacting and protecting Aaron. She had a knife in her boot. "What do you have in mind?"

"Tell that do-gooder Zachary that you've decided not to let him back in your life. Tell Colonel Wilson you need my help around these wagons. You'll be my woman. That, or they die."

Silas detailed his ultimatum with a flat voice and sharp threats hidden in the words uttered between clenched teeth. Rebecca knew he meant it. She had to think. If she tried to rush him with her own weapon, he would hurt Aaron. Bolo wouldn't stand a chance if that deranged man threw the knife in the confines of the wagon. She decided to take a chance. She pretended to move toward him and pulled her knife from her boot. "I'll never give in to you. I think you're a coward and wouldn't do a thing."

"Really? Tell her, Aaron. Tell her I killed your ma. Good riddance." Silas pressed the sharp edge of his weapon to Aaron's chest until drops of blood seeped through his nightshirt.

"Pa. Don't do this." Aaron sobbed.

"I don't want to hurt you, son, but I need to have my life in the Oregon Territory make me an important man. Rebecca can make that happen."

Rebecca dropped the knife from her shaking hands. She felt a scream building in her core and swallowed over and over to squelch it. "All right, Silas. Let's talk. Outside of the wagon. You leave Aaron and Zachary alone."

Silas grinned and raked his eyes up and down in a way that made her skin crawl. "You are pretty. And, you have some money and will have land in a few months. Just what I want. A rich woman with land."

She refused the hand Silas offered. "I can manage. Do not touch me unless you are given permission. Understood?"

"We'll see." He growled in the back of his throat.

"I understand. But you will allow Aaron to stay in my wagon. He will not be permitted to be alone with you. Ever. I will be given the opportunity to talk to Zachary by myself. For now, don't you think it would be a good idea for you to go back before the colonel finds you. After all, you want me to talk to him." Rebecca was thankful her voice sounded firm and unafraid, not shaky. How did she manage that? On the inside, her breath grew tight while her heart stopped and every inch of her trembled. More afraid than she had ever been in her life, she clenched her teeth together to keep them from rattling and swallowed over and over to keep from vomiting. She stared at the hulking shadow of Chimney Rock to keep from panicking.

"Yeah, Jack might be a big man, but he whines about keeping the damn wagons and oxen in proper shape. You have two days to get rid of Zachary."

Silas offered her a limp salute, a suggestive leer, and walked off. Rebecca clutched her stomach and vomited. *What will I do? Do I say anything to Mother? I need to check on Aaron and let Bolo out.* "Aaron, can I come back in the wagon? Your pa is gone."

Aaron peeked out of the cover and motioned for Rebecca. "He's really gone?"

The tear-stained tracks on his cheeks and red-rimmed blue eyes broke her heart. How much more could he stand? He was just a boy. "Yes. I think you and I should go to my wagon with Bolo. Gather up a few things. I want you to stay near Mother and me. We'll manage the oxen."

"I can't. Pa will kill Zachary. He really will. I don't care what he does to me." Aaron choked on his own tears.

"Don't say that. I told him to stay away for two days and give me time to think about what to say to everyone. He agreed. I will think of something." Rebecca stroked Aaron's cheek. "Now, let's go. I might even find something sweet for you."

Aaron wiped his nose on his sleeve. Sweets always sounded good to a youngster. He stepped out of the wagon and clutched Rebecca's hand as if his life depended on it.

"For tonight I'll move a few things around so I can make you a pallet. Tomorrow we'll shift some things around and make you more comfortable. I'm going to have a cup of tea with Mother. You rest." Rebecca handed him a handful of raisins and a sugar cube.

148

"Yes, ma'am."

Aaron stuffed the raisins in his mouth and put the sugar on his tongue to melt. He moved to the pallet on the other side of the wagon bed, covered up with a soft quilt, and fell asleep within seconds, evidence to Rebecca he felt safe there. With them.

****

Sarah waited for Rebecca. "Rebecca, what is going on?"

"I don't know if I should tell you yet. Something serious. Do you feel like sitting on the seat and talking for a few minutes?" Rebecca's voice shook.

"Of course." Sarah handed her daughter a cup of tea, wrapped herself in a night robe, and joined her on the quilt she had laid out for watching the stars.

"I hardly know where to begin."

Fear skittered up Sarah's back. Her heart quivered. Her breathing all but stopped. "What is it? You must tell me everything."

"What I have to say has to be kept quiet for now. Can you do that?" Rebecca grabbed both of Sarah's hands.

Sarah's heart was beating too fast. She pressed her hand against her chest. She couldn't stand the fear on her daughter's pleading face. "Just tell me."

Rebecca sucked in a ragged breath. "Silas showed up in the wagon when I was with Aaron. He pulled a knife on us and cut Aaron. Just a prick—"

"What? Why on earth did he do that? Is he insane?" Sarah couldn't believe what she heard.

"I think he is mad. He is insisting I end my relationship with Zachary and become his wife or he will kill both of them. He even threatened to kill Bolo. He said I could make him important because we have money and will have land. He admitted to killing Jodie. If I say anything to Colonel Wilson or Zachary, he will kill them. I don't know what to do." Rebecca dropped her chin to her chest. Her shoulders drooped. She suddenly seemed too tired to sit up.

Sarah sat quietly, too stunned to think, or speak. Finally, she pulled Rebecca close. "I hardly know what to say. What are you going to do? You can't be alone. Neither can Aaron. Yet we have to keep the oxen moving and cared for."

"Don't worry about the wagons or oxen. I'll tie the back wagon team to ours when we travel. Aaron will stay in our wagon. I promise, I won't be alone. We could move Ginny and Sean to the second wagon. I think she would be relieved. I don't know what to say or do about the colonel. Should I tell him? Silas will kill again. That is the one thing I know for sure. I probably shouldn't have said anything. I need to write in my journal before I lie down."

Sarah hugged her daughter. "Sounds like you've already figured out what you need to do but maybe writing in your journal will help bring your thoughts into focus. Just be careful, Rebecca. Stay aware of your surroundings, especially until you know exactly what is happening. And don't be alone. At all. Ever."

"I promise."

They went back inside, and Rebecca pulled out her journal...

June 18, 1845

The last two days have been eventful and frightening. When we were trading with the Indians everything was fine until Silas tried to shoot at them.

Colonel Wilson sent Silas to work with Jack Farris. He threatened to kill Aaron and Zachary unless I became his woman. He drew blood with his knife on Aaron's chest. He confessed to killing Jodie. I am terrified. He wants to marry me. Never, not ever. I don't know how to handle this. I talked to Mother. She has been ill with her lungs. She is better, but I'm afraid she'll die.

Zachary and I have talked. I think things will work out, but he agreed to give me more time. But now I'm not sure I even have time. Should I tell him about Silas? Should I talk to Colonel Wilson? I don't know what to do! I know guidance will come if I just stay calm enough to hear it....

On a lighter note, I found some tall flowers that have nice seeds in them. They're tall, yellow, and filled with the nuts in their center. The children enjoyed gathering them. They're tasty in corn cakes.

Chimney Rock is imposing. Tall, beautiful colors. Brownish-red, gold, tan, and surrounded by wildflowers. It is one of the sights on the trail I will never forget. Wish I could have been closer to it.

Chapter 19

Living in Fear

Two long days had passed since Zachary agreed to give Rebecca time and space. He saw her for most meals, even talked to her about everyday things like the weather, but there was something on her mind. Something she wasn't telling him. Something that was causing a great deal of worry. When he asked her what was wrong, she claimed to be tired or concerned about Sarah and Aaron. Her ever-present joy had been replaced by an almost permanent frown and a furrowed brow.

She had agreed to go for a walk and talk to him tonight after supper. He shouldn't be nervous, yet he was. He rehearsed his words time and time again. Love should solve every problem, shouldn't it? He reached into his inner pocket and twisted the gold chain of the ruby necklace between his fingers. He hoped it would soon lie over Rebecca's long lovely neck.

He spent the morning repairing a wheel for a family, tedious time-consuming work that put him behind the wagon line. A fleeting feeling of satisfaction crossed his mind when he thought about the people he had met on the journey. He was blessed to be one of the riders helping others. He had earned the trust of Colonel Wilson and many of the travelers.

****

Rebecca decided to ride Glory out to find more flowers and berries. She needed to be alone. Her mother wouldn't like it. Neither would anyone else. She would be alert. A stand of tall plants with sharp-edged leaves and a tower of creamy flowers caught her attention. She cut one with her knife and rubbed the strong, tightly woven, fibrous stem between her fingers, inhaling the clean, musty scent. The waxy residue on her fingers reminded her of soap. Could this be the plant she had heard of that Indians used for washing and soaking up blood in deep wounds? She gathered several more as an addition to her medical supplies.

She had little to do but think. She hadn't figured out how to handle the situation with Silas. Or Zachary, for that matter. She wanted to scream and run and get away from everyone.

The sound of a horse alarmed her. Her nerves left goosebumps rising on her arms. She stood straight and tall, looking for the rider. What if Silas had found her? She grabbed Glory's reins and prepared to run. Looking up she saw Zachary. The breath she didn't realize held escaped on a sigh. He waved and smiled wide enough for her to see his double dimples.

She waved back still holding the plants. What was she going to say to him? She was afraid Silas would learn that they were together and hurt him.

"What are you doing out this way?" Rebecca asked.

"I helped the preacher fix a broken wheel. What are you doing?" Zachary took her hand.

Rebecca sucked in a deep breath and jerked her hand away. The desire his touch left lingering on her fingertips distracted her. "You frightened me."

"I'm sorry. Didn't mean to. What is wrong? I can tell something's going on."

She couldn't breathe. She couldn't speak. She couldn't think. Her throat tightened, threatening to choke her. She lifted her head and met his eyes. "We need to talk."

"Let's sit over there." He took her hand and led her to the grassy space. "Tell me what has had you upset to the point of withdrawing from everyone. I'll listen without judgment."

Rebecca wrung her hands then wiped them on her skirt. "I can't say."

"Why? I can tell something's wrong. If it's me, I deserve to know."

"It isn't you. It's... Well, it's just... I am frightened... Mother has been so ill. Jodie's death has affected my very soul." Rebecca choked on her words. Her throat closed. She shut her eyes and took several deep breaths, willing herself to relax, then opened them to see the flash of fear crossed Zachary's face.

"Tell me what's wrong. I don't think it's just Sarah or Jodie."

Rebecca had peeled the leaves, fibers, and flowers from one of the plants she'd cut for her journal. Its remains lay in shreds on her lap. "I need to have time to consider my own future and to get Mother safely to the end of this journey." She grasped a handful of the plants remnants and twisted them as if wringing water from them. "The vow to my father feels like it's slipping away."

Zachary leaned forward and picked up the plant's guts from her lap. "What else is it?"

His insistence stiffened Rebecca's resolve. She

didn't like anyone pushing her to talk or digging into her private thoughts. "Will you listen without interrupting me?"

Zachary hesitated, then took a deep breath. A corner of his mouth lifted on one side. That cheek dimpled and distracted Rebecca for one beat of her heart. Her words rushed out, tumbling over each other. "I don't know what to do, where to go, or who to trust. Two days ago, Silas showed up when I was sitting with Aaron in the back of the wagon . . ."

She stopped herself, tucked the shreds of the plant into her apron pocket, stood, and paced. Dust lifted from her heels as she pivoted and continued her nervous steps. "I have to be careful about everything I say. The safety of those I love the most could be at risk." *Including yours.*

"You can trust me." Zachary picked up a handful of pebbles and shifted them from hand to hand. He sat quietly giving her the time to gather the courage to keep talking.

Rebecca stopped her pacing, stood still in front of Zachary, and took one of his hands. "You have to understand and agree that I can't be involved right now. I care deeply about you. Never doubt that. Please, just give me a bit more time."

"All right. Now, sit down and let's talk." Zachary patted the ground beside him.

Just as Rebecca gathered her skirts to sit down, she saw Silas walking with a team of oxen toward a wagon. Her mouth became dry. Her heart stopped beating. She reached out to take his other hand. "Zachary, I can't talk right now, but I promise we will talk about this after we ford the river tomorrow. I'm sorry, but I just can't take the time to tell you what I need to right now."

"I understand. I see him, too. I won't let you out of my sight tonight. I'll check with the colonel. He said he wanted to talk to me about the fording. You should get on Glory and ride back to the wagon." Zachary squeezed Rebecca's hand, scrambled to his feet, and leaned in to kiss her on the cheek.

Rebecca mounted her horse and watched Zachary walk to the colonel's wagon. She could feel Silas staring at her. She knew he wouldn't do anything at this time of day. She allowed the fear and hate she harbored for him to settle in her core being for a moment. Only a moment.

She tied Glory to the wagon and walked to the oxen team. She talked to the lead ox as if it understood her and could offer advice. "I don't know what to do about this horrible situation with Silas. Pretend, I guess. I've never been one to fake anything or give in to threats or fear. I'm losing myself, the independent person I have always been. I hate it. The truth is, I want to be Zachary's wife, raise horses, and build a comfortable home on our own land."

The ox never answered her but nudged her bag, hoping to get a treat. Laughing, she fed him a handful of grain.

Sarah came over and put her arm around Rebecca's waist. "Those animals love you so much. Your father and I knew from the time you were a baby that the connection you have with animals is a gift to be cherished. One time we found you curled up in the corner of a stall with a mare and her new foal. I believe they sense your trust and return it one hundred percent."

"I need to talk to you, but I don't want anyone to suspect we're discussing anything more than what we plan for supper." Rebecca took her mother's hand.

"Certainly. It's about Silas, isn't it?"

Rebecca considered her words before speaking. She didn't want to frighten her mother, yet she had to be clear. She rubbed her temples and pinched the bridge of her nose. "I saw Zachary this afternoon. We haven't talked about Silas. I need to protect him."

"I understand. I am as frightened as you. Are you getting one of your sick headaches?"

Worry wrinkled her mother's forehead.

"This headache isn't the kind that makes me sick. I think Zachary and I will work things out. Tonight, at some point, Silas will show up. He told me to expect him. I need to be ready and have Aaron out of the way. Good Lord, I don't think I can do this." Rebecca suddenly clutched her stomach, ran around the wagon, and suffered through a round of dry heaves.

Sarah stood beside Rebecca and offered a damp cloth to wipe her face and mouth. "You can do anything you set your mind to, Rebecca Pierce. You are your father's daughter. You share his compassion and ability to face whatever comes your way with courage."

****

Zachary rode past the farrier's wagon. Silas had made his way back to where he belonged and was making protective fur shoes for the oxen. Anger so extreme it made him want to break something rushed through him. He sucked down deep breaths in an unsuccessful attempt to squelch it. He knew in his core that Silas was up to no good. *I'll kill the bastard if he tries to talk to me. Stay calm.*

Silas swaggered over to Zachary with his long-legged stride. "Well, if it ain't the lover boy. You and

Rebecca still on the outs? I reckon you'll find that Rebecca will soon belong to me."

Zachary stayed in the saddle. He wanted to beat Silas Smith. He wanted him dead. "Rebecca is not your business. But if you hurt Rebecca or Aaron or anyone else I care about, I will personally put a bullet in your head."

Silas laughed.

Zachary rode away.

****

Silas showed up when everyone was bedding down. Not wanting him to see Aaron, Rebecca waited on the wagon seat. "I know you're here, Silas. Show yourself," she whispered toward the sound Silas made while he tried to sneak around.

"Evenin'. Do you have any news for me? I ran into Zachary this afternoon. He didn't seem happy to see me when I mentioned I had plans to see you. I told him you're mine. Don't that sound nice?"

"Leave him out of any conversation. Do not ever call me yours again. I am not, nor will I ever willingly be, yours." Rebecca spat the sharp, clear, tense words directly to Silas.

Silas leaned forward, closing the gap between them to mere inches. "I thought we had a deal. Am I going to have to hurt or kill someone?"

"I didn't say that. We don't have a deal of any kind. I will protect Aaron and Zachary from you no matter what. Go away. I'm tired. Tomorrow will be a rough day when we ford the river. Maybe you should be helping Mr. Farris." She dismissed him with a wave of her hand.

"Damn you, girl. I've never been around a woman who was so mouthy." Silas stomped away.

Rebecca fell to her knees in the wagon. The bravado she had was gone. Sobs exploded from her core. "I can't do this. Why is he so evil?"

"I don't know why he is like that. I do know I was proud of how you handled him. I heard every word. So did Aaron. We all need to get some rest." Sarah patted the feather mattress.

Rebecca crawled to the other side of the wagon. "Aaron, it is going to be fine. I talked to Zachary today. He doesn't know everything. I have to tell him about your pa. I think he's bedding down under the wagon later to watch over us."

"I just want everyone to be safe. I was afraid for you. I hate my pa." Aaron's voice was tight as though his words became strangled on a knot in his throat.

"I understand. Now, let's get some rest." Rebecca removed her dress, put her knife under her pillow, and snuggled beneath the quilts beside her mother.

Chapter 20

River Crossing

Rebecca dressed as quickly as possible. Today they would be crossing the shifting sands of the North Platte River. It was early. The rifle report to awaken the emigrants hadn't yet vibrated through the air.

"Mother, it's time to wake." Rebecca stroked the loose auburn curls from Sarah's face.

She moved to where Aaron slept and shook his shoulder. The glow of the lantern she carried cast a shadow over his face making him seem younger. "Time to cross the river."

She climbed out of the wagon. The hot coals remaining from the evening before smelled of ash. Bright orange streaks slashed through the embers. Rebecca stirred the fire to life and added more wood. She watched, mesmerized by the reds, oranges, blues, and yellows as the sparks caught, and heard the roar when the fire came to life. She held her hands over the flames to warm them. The early morning magic was her favorite time of day. Everything seemed new. Full of promise. She sighed and began the chores, starting with coffee. The rich, warm aroma made her stomach growl and roll. Excitement filled her heart when she considered the new adventure today. She hoped it would distract her from

Silas but that was unlikely. He haunted her day and night. She worried to the point of illness but tried to continue as if nothing was wrong. It was the only option she had. She wanted to run to Colonel Wilson with Zachary and tell him everything.

The light, sweet scent of rose water announced Sarah's presence. "I've brought bacon, things to fix biscuits, butter, honey, and jelly. I figure we need a hearty breakfast. What have you heard about crossing the river?"

"Colonel Wilson said it isn't too deep, but it's sandy and has places like quicksand. Brent has found the best course. Zachary is helping with the livestock. He suggested we let Aaron ride Misty and guide a team. I'll do the same. You and Ginny will need to stay on the wagon seats. The teams might need the encouragement of a cracking bullwhip." Rebecca poured two cups of coffee and handed one to her mother.

In a matter of minutes, biscuits were baking in the Dutch oven, and bacon sizzled in the iron skillet. Just like any other day, breakfast was served and eaten on a quilt. Rebecca bit off the end of a thick, crisp slice of bacon. "This is good. I think we need to put the bedding and important papers up as high as possible before we leave."

Aaron joined Sarah and Rebecca. He yawned, scratched his head, and filled a plate. "I can do that in both wagons." He ate half of a biscuit in a single bite, then licked the honey and butter dripping over his fingers and wiped his greasy hands on the front of his shirt.

Rebecca mimicked a cough to stifle a chuckle. "I think it would be best if you help me with the oxen and livestock. Mother and Mrs. Granger can take care of things inside. By the way, have you milked the cow?"

Aaron shook his head and started to push himself up. "No. But I will."

Sarah grasped Aaron's hand and gave it an affectionate squeeze. "Finish eating. Rebecca was just giving you a hard time."

Getting Aaron's goat with a little teasing never failed to leave her laughing. Even though it had only been a few days since the seemingly endless parade of troubles began, she felt her heart beating with the love for a younger brother when Aaron was nearby. Rebecca missed Joseph, but sometimes felt twinges of guilt at how much she enjoyed Aaron. He kept his promises and worked harder than most men. Much harder than his worthless father. A shudder worked its way through her core at the thought of Silas. One negative thought diminished the moment of levity.

"Good morning, everyone." Ginny settled Sean on the quilt.

"It's going to be a busy day." Rebecca handed Ginny a plate piled high with food.

****

Zachary and Brent rode up. Both horses were wet. Zachary tipped his hat before dismounting to gather up a couple of biscuits. "Hey, Baby Boy, give me that bacon."

Ginny's son, Sean, loved the game of give and take Zachary played with him. He squealed and laughed, grabbed his bacon-stuffed biscuit, and toddled off, still laughing at his own cleverness.

The simple bit of fun had become the best part of beginning the day for the small group since Ginny and her baby started staying with them. Each morning, they shared a simple breakfast before Ginny and Sean left to work with the Garsons.

Rebecca handed a cup of coffee and a biscuit to Brent while Zachary played with Sean. "They're something, always teasing each other. How is Sally?"

Brent bit into the biscuit. "Biscuits are good, better than Red's, the cook up front. Sally's doing well, just trying to help with everything. I tell you, it's difficult finding any time to be alone with her. How are you and Zachary? Are things better?"

Rebecca laughed. "Zachary and I have talked things over. I think everything will be fine. We're going to talk again tonight."

"That's good. You two belong together. Sally and I believe that." Brent reached for another biscuit.

Rebecca didn't reply right away but she allowed her thoughts to wander. "Thanks, Brent. Be careful out there."

Brent stuffed the last of the biscuit into his mouth and stood to leave. "See you later. Thanks for the coffee and food."

"You're always welcome at our fire."

Rebecca caught Zachary's eye. "Are you about ready to ford this river?" She flushed when his dimples winked at her.

"I'm ready. Brent and I are spreading the word that Colonel Wilson wants everyone to put the wagons in a loose circle after crossing. The wranglers will come along and put rope lines between the each one to serve as a corral for the oxen. We're making sure the animals rest and eat before we head out tomorrow morning."

"What about the last ones across? They won't get as much rest." Rebecca stood next to Zachary, needing the comfort his presence gave her.

"I reckon they'll rest while they're waiting to cross.

They won't be yoked until it's their turn to go." Zachary grabbed Rebecca's hand, rubbed his thumb over the back of it, and lingered a moment before letting it go.

Rebecca glanced at him and mouthed a silent thank-you. He had taken up for her when she begged Colonel Wilson to let her help when the animals swam across. He was reluctant at first, but Zachary reminded him of how hard she worked and how the animals trusted her.

Ginny came up behind Rebecca, interrupting her thoughts. "Rebecca, how deep is the water?" Her voice quivered despite the brave attitude she tried to maintain.

"It isn't too deep. Zachary said it might reach the bellies of the oxen at the most." Rebecca moved closer to Ginny. Her face was white, and her hands shook in the folds of her apron. "Are you all right?"

"I'll be fine. I'm just frightened of water. I had a bad experience and almost drowned when I was a girl. Water terrifies me. My older sister did drown. I couldn't save her. The memory has never left my mind. Fording the river is scary." Ginny pulled the ties on her apron tighter and tucked a handful of raisins in the pocket, undoubtedly for Sean.

Rebecca took Ginny's hand and gave it a comforting squeeze. "If it makes you feel any better, you won't be in the water. You'll be on the wagon seat guiding the oxen with the bullwhip if necessary. I'll ride alongside my wagon, and Aaron will be with this one."

"Thank you. It's time for me to fix breakfast for the Garsons. Edward is going to be hungrier than usual."

"You seem to have made a lasting friendship with Edward."

"I have. He has learned to take care of the wagon and teams for Mr. Garson. I think he would be a good husband and father. He enjoys playing with Sean." Ginny's cheeks reddened. One at a time she touched them with the back of her hand.

Rebecca took one of Ginny's hands, grinned, and winked at her. "Is that right?"

"I'm a recently widowed mother. I must consider the future. Don't you think?"

"You should consider the future. Not only that, but you and Sean deserve to be happy. Never forget that. We'll see you back over here when the fording begins."

****

Horses and livestock were herded near the river. The North Platte flowed slowly. The herds would swim across before the emigrants with their wagons, teams, and belongings. Rebecca rode Glory to the spot Brent identified as the best place to begin. Her job was to keep the animals from running to the side. Bolo stood beside Glory. He panted and his ears pointed in the direction of the activity. The bellows of oxen and cattle mingled with the shrill whinnies of horses and drowned out most other sounds.

Brent led the way for the first group of animals crossing. Zachary and other wranglers rode to the sides and rear. The squeal of lassoes in the air and against their thighs and shouted commands kept the herd moving. The river was shallow enough that most of the animals were able to trudge through with the water at their bellies. Foals and calves had to swim.

A newborn calf was separated from its mother and went under. Rebecca rode over, threw a rope around its neck, and brought it up. She dismounted, picked up the calf, threw it across the saddle, and mounted Glory. The calf bawled, shivered, and shook. Rebecca untied the shawl around her shoulders and tossed it over the calf. She rubbed its neck and hummed to calm it. For the first time in too long she felt the joy of working toward her dream. This was something she would do when the journey ended. She looked to the bright blue sky with clouds streaking across it and whispered a prayer of thanksgiving. Difficulties would never force her to give up. Not even Silas Smith could deter her.

Water churned around the legs of the wild-eyed animals. Some floundered and had to be pulled back to their feet. Rebecca watched helplessly as a horse fell and trapped its leg. She heard a bone snap followed by the shrill scream of the doomed animal. Her instinct was to ride over and check on it, but she couldn't leave her place. It had been hard enough to convince Colonel Wilson she would do as ordered. The loud, ear-shattering report of a rifle made her stomach lurch. She tried to swallow the bile that rose to her throat but ended up spewing vomit into the muddy water.

The shot frightened the animals, and they tried to run. The wranglers pushed them back into a cohesive group using horses, lassoes, and whips. The herd continued to lumber and splash to the other side. Rebecca couldn't take her tear-filled eyes away from the sight when Colonel Wilson roped the dead horse and dragged it out of the water

Time seemed to pass quickly, but Rebecca wasn't sure how long it really took to herd the animals across to the safety of a rope corral on the opposite bank. When Glory stepped onto the grass, Rebecca lifted the calf and gently helped it down. He wobbled and cried. Within seconds his mother ran over, sniffed, nudged him toward her udder, and licked him dry. The happy ending brought relieved tears to her eyes.

Rebecca reined Glory into the river to return to the bank on the other side. They would be in the first group to ford. "Just two more times for us to cross today, girl. Then, you can rest and graze."

"Rebecca! Wait." Zachary rode toward her.

She waited. He could make her feel like the most beautiful girl in the world despite being soaked. He leaned forward and touched her face. "I'll accompany you back. I think we need to talk some more about Silas tonight. He'll be across the river from us. What do you think?"

She put her hand over his and held it for a moment. "I would love nothing more than spending time with you. I'm not sure I want to talk about Silas. But I'm glad that, tonight at least, he won't be a threat."

"I've been standing by, keeping quiet, and watching you slowly fall apart. I know you care about me. I love you." Zachary grinned.

The concern and love on his face relieved Rebecca's fear. "I believe I love you as well. I know Silas will do something to you or Aaron if he gets a chance."

"Silas is serious. He has made you feel like you're stuck with no way out. You're in danger. It seems he has the upper hand in your mind. My thought is that you can tell me more while we're crossing. Help me understand. We can come up with a way to keep him away from you."

For the first time in days, Rebecca's heart was at ease. She stopped in the middle of the river, reached over, and kissed Zachary. She didn't care who saw. She didn't care what anyone thought. "Thank you. We'll get through this."

"I know. Have I told you how beautiful your green eyes are when they flash?" Zachary pulled her closer for another kiss. The horses stood still and patient until he clucked for Red to move on. Glory followed.

Crossing the river without having to watch animals moved quickly and seemed like an adventure. Rebecca felt carefree, if only for the time it took to cross. She wanted to be with Zachary without the fear of Silas hanging over her like the sword of Damocles. "I'm ready to enjoy an evening without worry."

"We'll have to be careful because of Silas. More so when he realizes we aren't going to be swayed by his threats." Zachary grabbed Glory's reins and stopped both horses. He ran his hand through his hair, tilted his head to the side, and watched her relax.

"This river crossing—just the two of us—is special. It's been a while since I could relax even a little. Now I can. I just want to enjoy the ride and your company. Do you understand?"

Zachary cupped her cheek in his hand for a moment, then urged the horses forward.

As soon as the horses stepped onto the riverbank, they shook the water from their coats, sending sprays in every direction, including on Rebecca and Zachary. They laughed, dismounted, and wiped their faces. Holding hands, they walked to the wagons.

Bolo barked in his happy and excited high-pitched yip. His tail wagged so hard he fell over before bounding across the ground and jumping straight into Rebecca's arms. She laughed and fell backward, almost losing her balance. "Goodness, Bolo. I love you, but you stink like a wet dog. Get down."

Zachary leaned against a tree. "Well, someone's

happy to see you."

****

Activity around the campsites reminded Rebecca of a disturbed bed of ants. Each of them scurrying from job to job. Women wrapped bedding and clothing in waterproof tarps. Barrels of food were rearranged in the beds to balance the wagons. Tools that usually hung outside were moved inside. Horses, cattle, and goats were tied near the front so they could be released easily if anything went wrong.

Rebecca turned at the sound of her name to see several children sitting in a semi-circle with Evie watching over them. Evie waved at her and motioned for her to join them.

Rebecca turned to Zachary. "I'll be back as soon as I talk to Evie."

"Sounds fair." Zachary kissed her on the cheek.

The children stayed seated, but they wiggled and waved as Rebecca approached. She winked. "What has Miss Evie got you sitting here for?"

The cacophony of young voices shouted, each one saying something different.

Jeb stood and pointed at Sadie Lawson. "I'm the boss, but Sadie says she is because she's seven and I'm five. Girls can't be a boss."

Sadie jumped up and stood toe-to-toe with Jeb. "Who says? Girls are just as good as boys."

Evie stepped into the center of the semi-circle and raised her hand for silence. "Sadie, you and Jeb sit down and listen. Miss Rebecca and I are the bosses. They're waiting to get instructions on how to behave when we cross the river. I was going to tell them, but you arrived just in time."

"All of you seem to be doing well. Are any of you afraid to cross the river?" Every young hand, except brave and stubborn Jeb's, went up.

"A little fear will make you safer because you will think about your actions. You little ones will be asked to sit on the wagon seat with your mother or whoever is driving. Some of you may be asked to sit inside, but I would rather you sit on the seat because things inside can fall. Babies will be on pallets or in baskets under or on the seat. Older children, you will be asked to help others. You'll either be riding double with someone or be on the wagon." Rebecca paused. Most of the children were calm, but curious.

"I might not be tall, but I can swim." Jeb stood as tall as possible with his shoulders back and his arms crossed over his chest.

"Don't you think your mother would rather you help with Obed? Your father will be riding alongside, he may let you ride with him. You can't swim across the river."

Jeb huffed. "I'm five years old. I'm a big boy."

Rebecca glanced at Evie. She covered her mouth to keep from laughing out loud. The other children elbowed each other and grinned. "Of course, you're a big boy, Jeb. That's exactly why I insist you stay with your mother."

"Yes, ma'am Whatever you say."

"All right. Go back to your wagons and get settled. It won't be long until we begin moving again."

She turned to talk to Evie while the children milled around and chattered. Evie sat on the ground with her knees to her chest and rocked back and forth.

"Is something wrong? You're pale." Rebecca feared something she couldn't identify.

"I'm just anxious. My stomach is cramping. I may vomit. Truth be told, I'm nervous about crossing." Evie covered her mouth with her palm and swallowed several times.

Rebecca pulled a canteen from her shoulder and handed it to Evie. "See if this helps. I'll make peppermint tea for you as soon as possible."

"I need to help Hans finish preparing our things. I'll be fine." The tight-lipped grimace Evie offered emphasized her pale color, flat eyes, and green-around-the-gills face.

"Are you sure? How much more do you and Hans have to get done?" Rebecca needed to go back to her own family, but Evie was like family. *I'll check on things. Make sure Evie is settled and talk to Zachary.*

"Not much. He borrowed a horse and is riding with the team. I have everything settled inside. I need to make sure Hans eats something before we cross over." Evie grinned and crossed her heart with the first two fingers of her right hand.

"Fine. But, let me know if you need anything." Rebecca turned to walk to the wagons. She had a few moments to reflect on the future as she sidestepped some short thorny bushes. Things were finally falling into place. She hoped. The excitement and hope at the beginning of the trail sat at the back of her mind covered with worried thoughts of Evie, fatigue, Silas and his treachery, her mother's illness, the soaring of her heart when she was near Zachary, and her first kiss. Bolo bounced around Glory's hooves and followed with his head down. When Glory heard Patriot whinnying, she trotted toward him. Rebecca gave the horse her head and followed. "Mother, are you ready?"

Sarah's arms were laden with quilts. "Aaron and I have done everything. He's nervous about riding Misty and guiding the oxen, but he can do it. Ginny has set up a wooden box under the seat with a quilt at the bottom in hopes of containing Sean. I wished her luck."

Rebecca laughed and hugged her mother. "That boy can be a handful. Zachary and I have decided to discuss what's going on with Silas tonight since he will be with the farrier wagon on this side of the river."

Rebecca glanced over Sarah's shoulder and saw Aaron hugging his horse. She waved, turned around, and went about the business of removing Glory's saddle and bridle. Aaron paced and acted nervous. Rebecca gave him time alone. He trusted her and knew she would never ask him to do anything that might cause harm. *He's had to endure so much. From people he trusted or should have been able to trust. He is just a boy on the verge of becoming a man sooner than he should have to.*

When Rebecca released Glory, the mare lay on the ground and rolled with her legs in the air kicking and snorting while Rebecca retrieved Patriot and tacked him up. His black coat picked up the light, making it seem dark blue as he eagerly pranced side to side tugging on the reins. She pulled his face to her own, scratched his ears, and whispered. "Calm down. I need to take care of Glory as you well know."

Rebecca rubbed the bay mare down and tied her to the lead ox. She could quickly loosen the knot leaving her to swim if necessary.

A shrill whistle from Colonel Wilson stopped the emigrants. A surge of anxiety mixed with eagerness moved through the wagon line and hummed in the air. This crossing would be the longest since leaving day.

Rebecca understood problems could occur, but knew it wasn't as dangerous as some feared.

The colonel addressed the crowd. "We're going to cross five wagons at a time. Keep two wagon lengths between each one. I have guides on horseback to help anyone if necessary. My wagon and the chuck wagon will go first. Stay in line. See you on the other side."

Rebecca helped Sarah onto the wagon seat, patted it, and told Bolo to jump. She made sure the oxen were properly yoked, checked Glory and the cow. She mounted Patriot and rode to the wagon handled by Aaron and Ginny. "Aaron, are you ready? Remember all you need to do is ride near the lead ox. It will follow you. What did you do with the goat? I don't see her."

Aaron grinned and pointed at Ginny. "She insisted on putting her inside the wagon."

Rebecca chuckled. "Well, that's a first. Make sure the goat isn't tied too tightly. She will need to swim if something happens."

"I understand." Aaron straightened his shoulders, made sure his boots were heels down in the stirrups, and took the reins. A flash of fear crossed his face. He stood in the stirrups and turned to the farrier wagon at the end of the line.

"You won't have to face your pa. He can't hurt you from this side of the river. They won't cross until tomorrow." Rebecca gave him a thumbs-up to boost his confidence. Misty arched her neck and chewed on the bit. Aaron leaned forward and rubbed her sleek golden neck.

Rebecca had seen signs of increasing self-esteem in Aaron and wondered if he had ever been praised or offered tasks that would give him the feeling of worth. "I know you can do it. I wouldn't have asked you otherwise."

She rode the few yards to Ginny, who was as pale as the wagon cover. She clenched the handle of the bullwhip so tightly. Her right hand was white and her left visibly shook on Sean's shoulder.

"You'll be fine. The crossing won't take long. About an hour. Just think, on the other side we will have the rest of the day and part of tomorrow to get our thoughts and supplies together."

Ginny cleared her throat and blinked away tears. "I am truly frightened."

Rebecca leaned out of the saddle and squeezed Ginny's hand. "I'm sure you are. I do remember that you lost your sister. It's our turn. The colonel has moved forward."

Rebecca moved to the front of their wagons, guiding the oxen into the shallows of the river. Patriot pawed at the water splashing it to his belly. Rebecca encouraged the team to enter the water. They followed with full trust but bellowed their dislike. She watched her mother. "Ready? It may get rough in a few places."

"I'm fine. The most difficult thing for me right now is keeping Bolo from jumping in after you. He isn't happy."

The river bottom was stirred up. Sand and silt turned the water brown. Pebbles and small stones caught in the axles. The wheels rolled through, leaving muddy paths covering the tracks of the teams and horses. The water got deeper as they neared the middle of the crossing, hitting the bellies of the oxen and the bottom boards of the wagon. Rebecca rode to the rear and leaned in to see if there were any leaks. "The wagon is dry. I'm glad I put extra tar on the slats."

"How are Ginny and Aaron?" Sarah asked.

"Fine. Aaron is staying with the team and doing a good job."

Screams from a man and woman broke the conversation. Rebecca turned to see the wagon belonging to the Slaton family turned on its side, spilling its contents into the water. Mr. Slaton struggled with the yokes, trying to release the team before the weight drowned them. She reined Patriot around and saw Jeb and Obed clinging to a chair in the water.

"Ma! Help us." Jeb screamed and held Obed's arm which bled profusely, staining the water red. Both boys shivered, their teeth clicked together, and they clung to each other.

Rebecca rode to Mrs. Slaton as she dived into the water. Her skirts billowed and pulled her under. She got her footing and swam to the boys just as Rebecca reached them. "Hand me the boys. Hold onto to my horse's tail. The water isn't over your head, but it is deep enough to keep you from walking. I'll get you to our wagon. The others will retrieve as many of your things as they can."

Mrs. Slaton's teeth chattered, preventing her from speaking. Rebeca lifted three-year-old Obed up first. The deep cut on his arm would likely require stitching, but for now, all she could do was wrap a bandana around it. "Obed, you're being so brave. This will help keep your arm from hurting. Jeb did a good job of protecting you like a big brother should. Jeb, I'm going to give you a boost up into the seat with my mother. She might need some help. Will you check in the back for quilts for your brother and mother, then help keep Bolo settled?"

"You know I can. I can do anything. Are you going

to help Pa with our stuff?" Jeb asked.

"I see several men helping your pa. They will try to pull your wagon to the riverbank if it isn't too damaged. I'll be back soon, but we must keep the wagons moving."

A wooden cage of drowned chickens floated past Rebecca. *If only someone had been able to open the gate.* The gravity of every loss stung. If they weren't on the endless trail and at home, the loss of a few chickens wouldn't be given a second thought.

Relief flooded Rebecca when Patriot lunged out of the water. She dismounted and rushed to check on the Slaton family. Jeb crowed that he had kept Obed from bleeding to death. "I'm sure you did, but I need to take care of his arm. Will you help my mother lead the oxen and other animals to the proper place in the circle?"

"Yes, ma'am. I can do that."

Rebecca picked Obed up, then lowered him to the bed. He was pale and cried for his mother. "She's coming with us. Let me see your arm."

The bandana was soaked in blood. Some had dried. When Rebecca pulled the cloth from his thin arm, the wound began bleeding again. She pressed her hand hard on the cut, causing Obed to scream out in pain. "Mrs. Slaton, will you get me some clean rags from that small chest beneath the pitcher? I need the medical kit tucked beneath the mattress I need to sew this cut up."

Rebecca took the items from Mrs. Slaton's shaking hands. "Will you get the vial of laudanum, the curved needle, and about four inches of the catgut in the clear vial? Obed, your ma is helping me so much. I want to give you a few drops of this medicine. It tastes bad, but don't spit it out."

Obed's big blue eyes filled with tears again and

widened when Rebecca placed the drops in his mouth. He tightened his lips together and grimaced.

"You are such a brave boy." Rebecca washed her hands and threaded the needle. When Obed's eyes grew too heavy to keep open, she cleaned the wound and sutured it closed. A small noise caught her attention. Tears rolled silently down his cheeks as Jeb watched from the wagon seat.

"He'll be fine and will sleep for several hours. Do you want anything?"

"Can I have some of that hard peppermint candy you keep in your bag?" Jeb sniffled and wiped his nose on the sleeve of his shirt.

Rebecca made eye contact with Mrs. Slaton. She reached into her bag and pulled out the cloth wrapped around the candy. "Of course, you can have a piece. I need to help my mother and Ginny. Mrs. Slaton, I'll make you a cup of tea when we start a fire. I'll try to find out about your wagon and belongings."

The animals had been brushed and released into the makeshift corral by the time Rebecca joined her family. She found her mother, Ginny, and Aaron in the second wagon straightening the belongings. "Everything seems to be under control. I'll make a fire and put on some coffee and water for tea."

Sarah stopped folding the bedding. "How is the boy?"

"He'll be fine. I had to stitch up his arm. He won't be able to use it for a few days. How do you tell a three-year-old not to use his arm?"

The sound of unfamiliar footsteps startled Rebecca. She felt for the knife in her bag and stood, relieved to find Mr. Slaton there. She covered the place in her chest that reminded her of a galloping horse and wished her heart would stop beating so fast. "Mr. Slaton. How are your things?"

"Can you tell me where my family is? Are they hurt?"

"Obed cut his arm, and I had to sew it up. Your wife and Jeb are fine. You can find them in my wagon."

"Thank you. We released the team. They're frightened but should calm down soon. We lost bed linens and food that wasn't secured. Thankfully, the lids on the flour and meal barrels stayed put. The tar kept much of the water out. Will you excuse me?"

Rebecca held up her hand. "Certainly, but can you wait a moment while I finish preparing calming tea for your wife? Would you like coffee?"

"I could use some strong hot coffee. Thank you."

Rebecca placed the cups on a tray and handed them to Mr. Slaton, who all but ran to the wagon where his family sought shelter.

Fatigue overtook Rebecca as her adrenaline-fueled energy level hit bottom. The day had been a success despite the accidents. No people were lost. Only one horse was lost. No wagons were totally lost. Young Obed suffered the only injury.

Rebecca carried a bucket of hot water to the wagon and poured it into the ewer so she could wash up. Feeling clean erased some of the tiredness. Cleanliness was one of the virtues that made sense. Bathing, whether it was in a tub, a river, or splashed from a pitcher never failed to make her feel as if she washed away more than grime.

She chose a neatly folded red-and-white-checked blouse and brown homespun skirt from the chest. Her hair had escaped the braid. She worked for several minutes untangling the mess. Brushing it smooth, she chose to leave it down and tied it back with a ribbon. She knew it was important to tell Zachary how she felt about him. The subject of Silas would come up. How could it not? Talking about him and, saying the words aloud, would make his threats real. She wished she could just forget and shake the situation off like a bad dream. She was certain Zachary would help. She was just as sure she would never feel as safe as she should.

****

Dusk glowed around the camp. Conversations and laughter offered comfort and an awareness that everyone was well. Rebecca sat on a stool and waited for Zachary. She was ready to see him without the specter of Silas hovering over her. She had heard Zachary's laughter mingled with the sounds of men talking and joking around the fire beside the cook's wagon. The livestock grazed in the grass. They had natural access to water. All was well.

Rebecca stood when Zachary ambled toward her. She ducked her chin to her chest and realized she had met the one man in the world she could love and dream and build a life with. She continued to safeguard her heart with caution because of the vow, and if she was honest, a part of her was still gun-shy about the way he got angry and ran off. But knowing she'd told him how his actions bothered her, and his acceptance of her feelings brought a measure of comfort. When she lifted her head, she saw his hand outstretched for her. She accepted the gesture and looked into his blue eyes sparkling with humor. Trust and love replaced caution. "Is everything settled for the night with Colonel Wilson?"

He reached down and tucked a loose strand of hair behind her ear. "Everything is fine. He told me to visit you and catch up on what we missed when I went off half-cocked. He knows about Silas."

"What? How? Has Silas hurt someone else?" Sensations like spiders crawled up her back, bit her, and left venom in every muscle of her body. Rebecca shook her shoulders trying to shed the feeling of eight-legged creatures attacking her. Would the fear ever go away?

"I really don't know how he knows. It doesn't matter."

Tiny pestering flying insects assaulted the two of them when they reached the water's edge. Zachary tried waving them away with his handkerchief.

Rebecca pulled her shawl over her head and waved her hand in front of her face. "Why do these bugs attack everyone? They must be some sort of water creatures. We should find a place that isn't so full of them. The buzzing is driving me to distraction."

"You're right." Zachary grabbed her hand, laughed, and took off running. Rebecca struggled to keep up.

She tugged on his hand, forcing him to adjust his pace. "Slow down. Not everyone has legs as long as yours."

"Just trying to help you get away from the tiny flying dragons, my lady. I will be your knight in shining armor if you will have me." Zachary bent at the waist in a deep bow.

Rebecca giggled and stood on tiptoe to kiss him on the cheek. "It seems your armor has a few chinks in it. However, I will allow you to safeguard me."

They returned to the wagon where the fire burned bright, but no one was nearby. Rebecca reached inside and pulled out a quilt, unfolded it, and laid it on the ground. Sitting in the middle, she patted the space beside her, inviting Zachary to join her.

Zachary knelt beside her and took both of her hands in his. He leaned forward, kissed her on the top of the head, and whispered. "I do love you. I will never lie to you or give you reason to doubt me again. I will keep my temper in check."

"I care deeply for you. I do. But I continue to be afraid of what Silas can or will do. He has the capacity for murder, as you know. We won't worry about him tonight. He's across the river now, but…" Rebecca pointed to the shadows of the barge and wagon illuminated by the campfire where Silas was with Jack Farris. Tomorrow Jack and Silas would float across and join the others. "I wish to God I never had to see Silas Smith again."

"No worries. Not this night. It's just us." Zachary glanced at his saddlebags thrown across the tongue of the wagon. He thought about giving Rebecca his grandmother's necklace. *I'll wait. The timing isn't right. Not tonight.*

The sound of boots and swishing skirts drew Rebecca's attention away from Zachary. She dropped his hand and turned to identify the source of the sound. Brent and Sally ambled out of the shadows. "It's Brent and Sally." She stood and welcomed their friends.

Brent led Sally into the circle of light. "Sally and I were out for a walk and saw you two settling in. Thought we would join you."

Zachary stood and reached to shake Brent's hand. "You're more than welcome to join us."

"Getting some rest?" Brent asked.

Zachary grinned. "Haven't had much chance to rest yet. But soon."

"Have a seat, there is plenty of space on the quilt. I made some coffee. Let me pour you a cup." Rebecca busied herself pouring the brew. She handed Sally a cup and reached across her to give Brent one. "What did you think about fording today? I thought it was exhilarating."

"It was exciting. Except when the Slatons' wagon tipped over. How is their boy? I heard he got hurt." Sally laid her hands in her lap, balancing the cup between them.

"He's fine. Just a cut. It seems with every sunset I am more energized to move forward despite being bone tired. I just want to make it to Oregon, get the land, and settle down. Do you have any specific plans?" Rebecca asked.

Brent glanced at Sally and winked at her. "The first thing we want to do is get married. I told the colonel I wouldn't ride scout for him next time around. He was disappointed but understood."

Rebecca settled beside Zachary once more. "Congratulations. It makes the time pass more quickly when we can talk about things and make plans. Are you going to wait to get married? I thought you might be the first couple to get married on the trail."

"Truth is, we have considered getting married while we're on the trail. We may try to purchase a wagon at Fort Laramie." Brent cleared his throat. His voice, rich with awe, squeaked. "I'm amazed at how I can be so deeply in love with Sally after such a short period of time."

Zachary grinned. "Rebecca and I haven't talked about marriage, but it is a conversation I hope we'll soon have."

Rebecca heard him suck in a breath. He glanced out of the corner of his eye to see her reaction. Her heartbeat escalated when she realized he hadn't meant to say the words that were spoken. Relief flooded his face when he realized she wasn't upset. She chuckled and took his hand. "We'll see."

Sally sipped from the blue enamel-ware cup. "Rebecca, what are you wanting to do when we reach the Oregon Territory?"

"My father and I dreamed of settling on a piece of land with water and healthy forage to raise well-bred horses and cattle. We wanted a ranch. I want that life. I want the dream. I want the vow I made to come true. Mother wants a home with a kitchen garden and flowers. She would prefer living in town. We will be staying with my aunt and uncle above their general store until our new home is built.

"My father died just a few weeks before leaving day. I will make this happen for my entire family. It is my goal, my promise. I am thankful that my uncle, who went west last year, agreed to sign for the land for Mother and me. It's that simple, and that complicated."

Zachary caught her gaze and winked. "Maybe, just maybe, we'll have adjoining sections of land. Truth is, Rebecca and I share the same dream of ranching and farming. My parents and sisters are coming west next year. I miss them and can't wait to have them here. I hope to have a home waiting for them."

Sally hooked her arm through Brent's. "I am thankful to have my family with me. A church with a home next door is waiting for my parents. I can't imagine not seeing them or sharing every step with them. I am thankful that my family has grown to love Brent as much as I do in such a short time also. It sometimes astounds me how we are all on this trip together and share so many of the same dreams, yet we are all such different people in so many ways."

Rebecca's thoughts turned to Silas and the fear his evil thoughts and actions brought about in her circle of friends and family. She thought of the wealthy Garsons and how they struggled to do the physical work required on the trail. They owed their survival to Ginny and Edward Thatcher, a walker, who'd sought his place on the trail with nothing but the clothes on his back. Her heart swelled with love for her best friend, Evie, and the baby she would soon have. The new relationship developing between her mother and Doc Randolph seemed unbelievable, but it brought her joy to know her mother was feeling some degree of happiness. Finally, her mind turned to the fact that she had fallen in love despite the promise to not let anyone into her heart. "You're right. I imagine most groups who choose to travel west experience some of the same feelings we do."

Brent stood up and held out a hand for Sally. "I need to get Sally back to her father before he sends out a search party for us. It's been a nice evening. Thanks for the coffee. I'll see you in the morning, Zachary. Colonel Wilson wants us to ride across and help Jack and Silas get the farrier wagon over here."

"Yeah. He said something to me. I would rather do anything than help Silas Smith, but I do what the colonel asks." Zachary shook hands with Brent, then folded Sally's hands between his own. "Have a good rest."

****

Late June, 1845

It's been an exciting day. Fording the river. Young Obed got a bad cut when his family's wagon capsized. Jeb was brave of course. The Slatons lost many of their possessions. Zachary and I talked about the impact of Silas in our lives. The man frightens me. Brent and Sally came by late tonight. I have started thinking about marriage myself. I can't forget about the vow. Tiny flying insects bite and darken the sky. Zachary said he would vanquish them and be my knight in shining armor. He makes me laugh.

****

Silas watched as campfires on the other side of the river were banked, leaving the flames to smolder enough to keep the emigrants warm. He knew which wagons belonged to Rebecca and Sarah. He knew where his son slept. He had a plan. A sneer slashed an evil scar across his face.

Jack Farris checked on the oxen and his horses. He pulled a bedroll from the back of his wagon and settled with it beneath a tree. "Silas, I'm going to bed down now. Make sure the fire is controlled before you turn in for the night. I want to get up before sunrise and prepare to ford the river."

"Yeah. I'll take care of it. I think I'll eat first." Silas rummaged through the food box. He pulled out a few strips of beef jerky and walked around the wagon before settling next to a wheel. His thoughts were on taking Rebecca and his son.

Within moments, Jack, a creature of habit, was snoring. He'd pulled his hat low over his face. His hand rested on the butt of his pistol, and his feet were crossed at the ankle.

Silas decided Jack was sleeping soundly when his

hand fell away from the gun and dropped to his side. He didn't move for a few more moments, then rose slowly, leaving his blanket piled to seem like he lay beneath it. He had gathered three rocks and stacked them beside the wagon within easy reach. Silas picked up one stone at a time. He walked away from Jack just in case he'd heard him. A few steps later, Silas came up behind Jack and with a single, strong blow hit him on the head with the largest rock.

Jack struggled to rise bellowing like a bear. The second rock hit him on the back of his head, knocking him down and rendering him unconscious.

Silas used the third rock to make sure the damage was done. He tied Jack's hands to his knees and left him lying on the ground, leaving a bloody mess beneath the man. He didn't know for sure if Jack was dead but chuckled at his clever use of stones. He felt like David slaying Goliath. Invincible. Strong.

Within moments, Silas had saddled one horse and lashed supplies to the other. He took a lantern, food, three full canteens, a blanket, clothes, and Jack's handgun, rifle, and knife. Leading both horses quietly away from the camp, Silas headed south and east, the opposite direction of the wagon train. His plan was to backtrack, stay out of sight, and follow closely enough to know what was going on. Time was on his side. He doubted the colonel would waste much time on him. They were nearing Fort Laramie and the Snake River, and the colonel would have to be alert for any unusual activity or danger along that stretch of the trail.

The weather grew colder each night, so there was no time for dawdling. He would get to Rebecca and Aaron when they least expected it. And Jack Farris, well, he would be dead by morning if he wasn't already. Silas turned and smirked at the disappearing sight of Jack lying helpless, or dead, on the ground.

Chapter 21

Hans and Evie's Great Loss

Something awakened Rebecca. A dream? A noise? She didn't know. Her skin crawled and itched. Climbing out of the wagon, she wrapped herself in a quilt, and settled on a stool beside the fire's ashes. She saw shadows cast by the moon over the circled wagons and resting emigrants. Across the river she saw the glow of the fire where Silas waited with Jack.

It's too quiet.

You're just restless.

The idea of marriage to Zachary brought joy to her heart, but an uneasy sense of the unknown wrapped around her like the tentacles of a sea creature. How did couples know if they should get married? How many got married for convenience like Ginny Granger and Edward Thatcher were planning to do? How many were like Brent and Sally, completely sure of their love and the future?

Someone came running and shouting toward where Rebecca sat. He stopped in front of her, his breath hitching on sobs. "*Mein* baby. It's Evie. She is bleeding and hurting. I don't know what to do."

"What? When did this begin?" Rebecca hurried to retrieve her bag, medicine kit, and a robe. She tried to remain calm, but her voice screeched on the upswing of a scream. She grabbed Hans by the elbow, forcing him to stay with her rather than run ahead. "We can talk and run together."

"I don't know what is wrong. Evie, *mein frau*, my wife was telling me she didn't feel like eating or cooking. She told me to get some cold biscuits. Then, she grabbed my arm and screamed. Blood flooded out of her. She fainted. I came for you."

"Run ahead of me and boil water. I will need it." Rebecca spoke in a calm, measured manner even though her heart broke into shards of glass and her insides felt as though they ripped away from the walls of her body. *Evie is losing this baby. What can I do?*

Slick, clotted blood lay on the wagon bed. Rebecca drew in a deep breath. The metallic tang and stench of human waste, blood, and tissue assaulted her senses. She grabbed a lantern and put it on a flour barrel. The sight of Evie lying there moaning and gripping the sheet in clenched fists caused her breath to falter, but she forced herself to speak up and touch her friend. "Evie. I'm here. Let me check you. I think you may have lost the baby."

"Rebecca, you came." Evie's voice cracked. Pain and the beginning of grief showed in her trembling chin, clenched eyes, and raspy breath.

Rebecca took Evie's face and held it between her palms. She coughed to keep from sobbing. "I'm here. You've lost the baby. I won't leave. Hans, I need that hot water now."

"I have the water. What do I do? What do I do? Rebecca, what do I do?" Hans pushed his way inside and plunked the bucket of water on the floor with a splash.

"Evie needs you." The fear in his eyes and his white

pallor caused Rebecca to worry about him. He stared at the body of his baby. Rebecca moved to make room for Hans to kneel beside Evie.

Evie stroked Hans's cheek. "Calm down, Hans."

"What's going on here?" Colonel Wilson shouted from outside.

Rebecca moved to where she could speak to him calmly. Glancing down, she noticed that Evie's blood covered her hands and arms and soaked the front of her blouse. She crossed her arms over her chest and tucked her hands into the crooks of her elbows. "Evie has lost the baby. She is losing blood. I need help. Please ask my mother to come back with you and to bring some clean rags."

"I'll be back. Doc Randolph will be with me. Take care of her." He spun around and ran to where the doctor lay sleeping.

Rebecca took one of Evie's aprons, lovingly picked up the remains of the baby boy and wrapped him tightly. How could anything so small be so perfect? Her own tears dampened the apron. "Evie, I have the baby. Do you want to see him? He's very small."

"Boy." The word escaped from Hans in a whimper. He pulled Evie closer.

"Let me see him. Just for a moment. We have to bury him well, so wild animals won't get him." Evie whispered and held out her arms.

Rebecca handed the baby to his mother.

Sarah joined Rebecca. Tears filled her eyes, but she wiped them away and handed Rebecca a handful of rags. "Do you think it's a good idea to let her see the baby? He's not much of anything. He was too small to live."

"He's everything to her and she is going to leave

him in this cold unfamiliar place. Forever. She wanted to see him."

Doc Randolph came into the small space. "I must focus on delivering the afterbirth."

Rebecca stepped away. How could she sound so calm and collected when she wanted cry out loud at the injustice? She wanted Zachary. This was the hardest thing she had ever done. Even worse than burying her father and brother.

The sound of Zachary's boots calmed her in a profound way. Rebecca took a deep breath and tried to swallow the tears trapped in the back of her throat. Instead, a wounded wail came from her. *My, God, he looks like a savior.* "Zachary, I'm glad you are here. Will you help Hans dig a grave? They need to bury their baby."

"Of course." Zachary gathered her to him. "Of course, I will. It will be fine, but not for a while. Together we'll help them."

For just a moment Rebecca allowed herself to bury her face in the crook of Zachary's shoulder.

****

Zachary pulled away from her and moved to put his arm around Hans's shoulder. "Let's prepare a comfortable resting place for your son," Zachary urged, his voice firm, but heavy and deep with sorrow.

Hans took a spade from the tool hook on which it hung. "Yes. We should prepare a resting place for my boy."

"There is a small tree over there." Zachary pointed to one of the few trees in the area. It seemed comforting but lonely in the desolation of the prairie. He waited and watched as Hans came closer, his head so deeply bowed his chin met his chest, his shoulders slumped forward. Hans held the shovel handle in a loose fist as if it was burning his hand. He dragged it behind him, leaving a gouge in the ground.

Zachary reached for the shovel. "Here, let me carry that for you."

Hans raised it, ready to hand it to Zachary, but pulled the tool back to his side and jerked it away. "No. I have to do this, but thank you for offering."

"I understand. This place feels nicer, safer even, than any other place around here." Zachary leaned against the tree. He turned his head away, wiped tears from his face, and raised his eyes to the sky. A full moon and galaxy of stars lit the way for mourning. If things weren't so sad, he would have felt elated at the beauty of the night.

Zachary watched Hans rub his eyes, strangle the handle of the shovel, and stab the point into the dirt. He lifted his foot, rested it on the beveled edge, and shoved. When the dirt broke, and the moist soil turned over, his knees refused to hold his weight. Hans sobbed and wailed.

Zachary rushed to him. Bending over, he grasped Hans's hands and pulled him to his feet. "Listen, this is the worst thing to ever happen. I can't imagine your pain. Or Evie's. Rebecca and I are here for both of you."

"I know. Thank you. Will you finish the grave?" Hans whispered. His flat voice held no strength. No emotion. No change in tone.

Zachary picked up the shovel and turned to finish preparing the small grave. The chore only took a few moments. "It is finished. Let's check on Evie. Do you think you could manage some coffee? I'm certain we can find some."

"Yeah. Coffee might be good." Hans lifted one corner of his mouth. "I hear Evie crying. Someone else is in there with Evie and Rebecca. Do you hear him?"

"Sounds like Doc Randolph."

Hans took a deep breath, held it for a moment, pulled himself up on the wagon and crawled inside.

Zachary wasn't surprised to see Sarah tending the fire and pouring coffee before he could even say hello. He took the cups careful not to spill a drop. "How is she?"

"Not well. It is all so heartbreaking. I am glad to have you back. Evie is asking for Hans." Sarah rubbed her arms. Her words sounded hollow.

"Has the bleeding stopped? Hans has been beside himself with worry about that."

Sarah sat on a three-legged stool beside the fire. "Yes. Doc managed to stop it when he delivered the afterbirth. Evie's grief is profound. She isn't aware of much and won't let go of the baby."

She pulled a handkerchief from the pocket of her apron and blew her nose. "I apologize for such unladylike behavior."

Raised with sisters, Zachary knew women weren't supposed to talk to men about such delicate things with a man. They surely never blew their noses in front of anyone. Therefore, Sarah's apology didn't surprise him. "It's fine."

Doc and Rebecca joined them. Zachary opened his arms and held Rebecca as she sobbed. Her tears and the blood on her clothes stained his shirt. He reached around Rebecca and shook Doc Randolph's hand. "How is Evie?"

"Evie will be fine physically, but she is distraught beyond any measure I ever recall seeing. We can't wait much longer for the burial. The longer we put it off, the harder it'll be on them." Doc put his arm around Sarah's waist, wiped a trail of tears from her cheeks, and kissed the top of her head. He handed her a square of yellow flannel embroidered with flowers in the corner. "Sarah, my dear, will you warm this blanket over the fire, please. Having a warm blanket to wrap the baby in will be comforting for Evie and Hans."

"Certainly." Sarah took the blanket and held it close to the flames then handed it to Doc.

Doc folded it tight and put it inside his jacket. "Rebecca, are you ready? It is time."

Rebecca didn't answer but followed him to Evie and Hans's side. "Hans. Evie. It is time."

Zachary and Sarah cringed when Evie shrieked and screamed. "No! You will not take my baby."

****

Hans moved closer to Evie, lying on the blood-stained mattress. He saw the afterbirth in the chamber pot. Vomit and bile built up pressure in his core, threatening to erupt. He swallowed hard. "Evie, let me hold him. Plea—"

"Not yet." The devastation in his beloved wife's eyes ripped at Hans's heart. "Doc Randolph brought a warm blanket for him. What are we going to name him?"

A weak, choking sound came from Evie. "Just as we decided. Hans Joseph Shuler."

Hans turned his attention to the doctor. "Can she get out of bed?"

"She needs to remain in bed for a few days. But if you're able, you can carry her for the burial."

Hans stood as tall as he could in the confines of the wagon. "I will carry her, and she will carry the baby."

Rebecca scooted to the head of the mattress. "Let me help you clean up."

Hans reached for his son once more and held him close while Rebecca washed Evie's face and the blood from her body and brushed her hair before helping her into a pair of bloomers with protective rags in them, then slipped a clean night shirt over her head.

Hans moved back to Evie's side. "Rebecca, will you give us a moment. We'll be out soon."

Rebecca squeezed his arm in a gesture of support and left them alone in the wagon to say their good-byes. Within moments Hans climbed down carrying his wife and son. He refused offers of help. The sounds of livestock bellowing and emigrants talking caught his attention. He turned to see Colonel Wilson watching from the gravesite, holding a white-washed cross in one hand and his lantern in the other.

Hans lifted his hand in a weak wave at the colonel, but it took all he could muster from deep within to attempt such a simple thing. Life, in general, made him happy. Evie sure as hell made him happy. Would happiness elude him for the rest of his life? No, he wouldn't allow it. *Evie will be happy again and if she is happy, I am, too.*

Zachary, Rebecca, Doc Randolph, and Sarah joined him as he walked the longest distance of his life carrying his whimpering wife and forever sleeping son. At the gravesite Hans sat Evie in a straight-backed chair Zachary provided. "Thank you for thinking to bring a chair for Evie."

"It's the least I can do. You'll never truly be ready

for this, but it is time to bury your baby. Let him rest in peace. Do you want me to place him in the grave?"

Hans turned from one grief-stricken face to the other. "Yeah. I can't do this. I'll stay beside Evie." He took the baby from Evie and whispered something only she could hear. His words elicited a muffled sob and a searching glance. Turning, without allowing his hand to leave Evie's shoulder, he kissed his son and handed him to Zachary.

Evie took Hans's hand when he stood behind her. Her tears had dried up. She just stared ahead at the hole in the ground. "Hans, is it deep enough? Will he be warm?"

"Yes, he is in a warm blanket. Predators will not be able to get to him when we place rocks over the grave. Little Hans will be safe forevermore."

"Colonel, will you say some words?" Evie croaked, her voice tight with grief.

"I will." Colonel Wilson pulled a small Bible from his pocket and turned to the twenty-third psalm. He read it slowly, letting the words land on the hearts of the others. When he finished the prayer, Colonel Wilson paid his condolences to Hans and Evie, mounted his horse, and galloped away to catch up with the wagons that had pulled out as he'd commanded.

Hans and Evie watched as Zachary gently laid their baby in his grave. When the sound of clods and small rocks caught up in the loose soil landed in the grave, Hans lifted Evie into his arms and carried her back to their wagon.

****

Using the light of lanterns, Rebecca and Sarah began picking up rocks to lay on the grave, while Zachary and

Doc Randolph found larger, heavier stones to build a cairn.

When every stone was wedged in place, Zachary took the white-washed cross and set it at the head of the grave and built up a sturdy anchor for the cross with extra stones. Walking to where Rebecca stood, he allowed himself to cry and grieve. "Rebecca, I don't think I could stand losing a child. How will they go on?"

Rebecca squeezed his arm and wiped her own tears with the sleeve of her dress. "I can't imagine it, but we could do it together. Don't you think?"

"Yeah. Together." Zachary pulled Rebecca to him. He whispered in her ear, "I do love you."

Rebecca wiped his tears. "I love you, too. Evie and Hans are strong. They will be fine, but I imagine the remainder of our journey will be sad for them. I've known Evie all my life. She is stronger than she appears tonight."

They walked to Hans and Evie's wagon and arrived to find everything prepared for leaving. Someone had thrown out the ruined items, scrubbed the floor with vinegar, replaced the mattress with a thick feather cushion and clean bedding, and refilled the water pitcher.

"Who could have done such a nice thing? Who do we thank?" Hans hugged Evie closer to him.

"I don't know. For now, both of you rest. Zachary and I will walk with your team."

****

I don't know what today is, but it's one Evie nor Hans will ever forget. There are times when profound loss enters our hearts. It can't be shaken off, but can never be forgotten. Evie lost her baby tonight. I can still smell blood. Little Hans was so small, so perfect. We buried him beneath a tree, wrapped in a warm blanket. Some kind soul cleaned the floor of their wagon and replaced the mattress. I suspect Ginny and a couple of the other women. That quality of mattress could only have come from the Garsons. Morning will come, and we will move forward just like any other day. I will write more later. I am so sad.

Chapter 21

Finding Jack

Colonel Wilson stretched, yawned, and pulled on a clean undershirt. He removed a woolen cloth and picked up the shiny, dark mahogany wooden box beneath it. He rubbed a hand over the surface and opened the box that had once belonged to his wife. She had kept trinkets and sewing supplies in it. His favorite cigars were nestled inside on a bed of cotton batting. He picked up a half-smoked cigar, closed the lid, covered it, and left the wagon. Striking a match on the bottom of his boot, he lit the cigar and sucked in two deep drags. The smell relaxed him. His thoughts turned to his duty and the emigrants. It had been a long night with the tragedy that befell the Schuler couple.

As expected, the cook had coffee waiting for him. "Mornin', Red. You ready for the day?"

"Yeah. Brent saddled the horses. The two of you are ready to cross the river and help Jack come back with Silas. He said to tell you he was going to check on his bride-to-be before heading out."

Wilson grunted and expelled a long stream of smoke. "That's fine. I want you and Zachary to get the wagons rolling. We'll catch up." Standing, he put his hands on his hips, arched his back, and stretched again, allowing his bones to settle into alignment. He snubbed the remaining bit of his cigar on a wagon wheel and put it in his pocket. It would last one more morning. He took a plug of tobacco, stuck it in his cheek, and began chewing.

Riding to the river's edge, he and Brent were silent except to acknowledge greetings and questions from emigrants. Urging the horses into the water, they forded the river. Reaching the other side Wilson called out to Jack. "Where are you?"

Dismounting, the colonel and Brent allowed the horses to shake the water off. The barge was empty except for the stomping and bellowing of oxen tied to the ropes on the floating corral. "He's not here. Neither is Silas. Don't feel right, just don't feel right. The campfire hasn't been banked. It's still glowing. Best place to start."

"Right." Brent rubbed his freshly shaved face, tied his horse to a nearby bush and strode toward the fire. They spied Jack lying on his back in a pool of blood and Brent took off running. "Colonel, he's over here! Maybe dead. Silas isn't near, but that doesn't mean he's gone. Horses are missing."

Brent reached Jack first. "He's alive, but unconscious. He was hit in the head with rocks. He's been tied up."

Wilson spit a stream of tobacco to the ground and shouted. "Damn son of a bitch. That bastard has done it again. I'll kill him, swear to God, I'll kill the son of a bitch. Try to wake him up. We need to get him to Doc Randolph. Help him to his feet while I check on things before we hit the river."

"Will do." Brent removed the binding from Jack's

hands and feet as Wilson moved toward the wagon. "Wake up, we have to get you across the river."

****

Jack groaned, clenched his hands into fists, and punched Brent in the arm. His eyes widened when he realized who he'd slugged. "Sorry, Brent. Where's that damn SOB?"

Brent cursed under his breath. "Bastard ain't here. Neither are the horses. But we need to get you to the barge."

Struggling to rise, Jack pushed himself to a kneeling position, then reeled unsteadily. He inhaled a deep breath, tightened his lips, and struggled to his feet. Pressing a hand against the back of his head, he took short slow, steady steps to the barge. He stopped often to clear his head. His blood boiled with murderous desire. Murder. He had done time for that. Colonel Wilson had believed in him and hired him on as farrier and general hand on the wagon train. He was a man who believed in second chances. *Damned if I won't help the colonel in any way I can, but I can't murder again. I won't unless it's in self-defense. That could work.*

Jack allowed the colonel to help him onto the barge.

Wilson spit another stream of tobacco into the river and addressed Brent. "Take off and get the doc so he can be waiting for us. I can handle the barge with the oar. The water is calm."

"It would be faster if two of us were able to pole it over. Let me help you push it into the river."

"Do as I say. I can get across the river."

****

Brent saluted, mounted his horse, and splashed into the river. The tops of the wagons were visible beyond a nearby mesa. Curious emigrants jumped out of his way when he kicked his horse into a gallop before it was completely out of the water, in a hurry to reach Doc Randolph, yelling for him the whole time.

Randolph called a halt to the entire train. He grabbed the reins of Brent's horse when it skidded to a stop. "What's wrong? Where's Colonel Wilson?"

Brent jumped from the saddle and faced the doctor. "Get your bag. We're going to the riverbank. The colonel is bringing the barge across with Jack. Damn Silas beat him over the head, knocked him out, stole his two horses and most of the food and took off in the night."

"Was he conscious when you rode over? Did he know anything? Could he talk to you? I need to know everything."

"His head is a bloody mess and cut up. He tried to get up, seemed unsteady. Kind of like he couldn't get his footing. The colonel and I got him on the barge and Colonel insisted I ride across beforehand so you could meet them." Brent stood with his hands on his hips, staring at the barge, and swallowed the curse words raising bile from his gut. He wanted to vomit.

He felt Doc's hand on his shoulder. "Listen, son, you couldn't have made a difference. Silas Smith is a mean viper of a man. Problem is, he thinks everything he does, everyone he hurts, everything he steals is fine because he wants it. He has no morals, no conscience. He'll end up in jail somewhere. Or dead."

"Think I'll pray for dead." Brent realized several people, including Sally, Zachary, Rebecca, and Sarah had joined him. Even Bolo sat on his haunches next to Rebecca, wagging his tail in lazy arcs across the dirt. Sally strode to him and stood by his side. When she took his hand, he relaxed. Some of the explosive anger that had been building to dangerous levels settled into a slow simmer. He pulled her closer and breathed in the scent of the peppermint candy she had in her mouth, then kissed the top of her head.

"Head back to your wagons and keep rolling. Zachary, stay with Brent and me. Build a fire and boil some water." Doc Randolph spoke with the authority of a revered member of the train. He picked up his bag and waded into the water to climb on the barge before it came to shore, assessing Jack as they moved toward him. "Pale, unfocused eyes. Bandage stained with blood." He shook his head and mumbled, "Head injuries are sneaky and often worsen before they begin to heal. Morning, Jack. Looks like you've been through several rounds with a bear."

Jack rubbed his temples. "Yeah, goddamn Silas ambushed me in my sleep…." Confusion wrinkled his brow. His words were shaky and slurred.

"Relax. Let me check your head. Might hurt when I take off the bandage." Randolph slowly peeled the bloody rags from Jack's head. There was one deep cut surrounded by several smaller lacerations, and three knots, all at the back of his head. He pointed at Brent. "Bring me some of that hot water. Zachary, heat the blade of your knife in the fire and wrap it in one of the clean rags in my kit. I have to sew up this wound."

"Yes, sir," Brent and Zachary said in unison.

Doc cleaned Jack's wound, cut his hair with Zachary's knife, and pulled the edges of the gash together. He poured whiskey over the gash and closed it with loose stitches before wrapping Jack's head with a clean rag. "Let's get you into the colonel's wagon. Brent, you and Zachary help him walk."

Between the three of them, they managed to get Jack into the wagon. "I expect you to stay on your bedroll, Jack. Prop your back up with pillows or blankets. Don't lie flat," Randolph ordered.

Jack put his hands on each side of his head and pressed. He closed his eyes and groaned. "What about my team? They need to be fed and watered."

"Brent will stay with you. He'll take care of your livestock. When you are able, Colonel Wilson will give you a horse from the herd. That headache isn't going away any time soon. I can give you some laudanum, but it would be best to wait."

Jack sighed and leaned back against the quilts. "Nah. I'll be fine."

****

"Silas is out there. Somewhere." Rebecca took Zachary's hand and pulled him down to sit beside her on a rotting log. The morning was young, but the rising sun promised to beat down on the emigrants. Wiping her hands on an apron, she glanced down and chuckled, causing Bolo to cock his head and ears at the sound. Aprons just didn't go well over pants.

Zachary stood in one movement and took her hand. "He is. Maybe he's gone for good. At least, that's what I hope. Come on, we need to join the others. Aaron might feel overwhelmed walking with two wagons. Besides, we need to tell him about Silas."

"I hope he is gone for good. I hope we never have to worry about him again, but he hasn't finished trying to fulfill his goal, to get me, to make me his. He wants Aaron back under his hate-filled control, too. Only one thing frightens me, and that is not being able to fulfill my

204

father's dream. That isn't totally true. He terrifies me." Rebecca jerked her hand from the comfort of Zachary's, which held hers as though it was made of the finest bone china.

"No, Rebecca, he won't. I will kill him and the two of us will build your dream, and mine, when we reach the Oregon Territory. That is a promise. My vow. As sure and heartfelt as the pledge you made to your father. Now, come on. We must tell your mother and Aaron."

Zachary put his arm around her ramrod-straight shoulders and led her toward the wagon. They met Sarah walking beside the oxen and stopped in front of her. "Mother, we're back. We need to talk to you."

Sarah reached for Rebecca and put her hands on her shoulders. "I heard Jack has been hurt. Is he going to be all right?"

"He will be fine. Just needs to rest for a few days. Have you heard anything else?" Her mother grew pale. Her hands dug into Rebecca's flesh.

"What are you not telling me? I know something is wrong. My intuition—the kind only a mother has—is bouncing from one extreme to the next, and each thought is worse than the one before."

Rebecca coughed and finally spoke. "Silas. Silas knocked Jack out and left him for dead. The horses are missing. He will show up one of these nights for me or Aaron or Zachary."

Sarah covered her mouth with an audible hiss. "Jack Farris is a gentle man! I can't even begin to say the words threatening to explode from my mouth! Can't even believe they're in my head or heart. I'm not a hating person, but I abhor Silas. I need to check on Jack. Doc will tell me what I need to do to help. Will you join me?"

"Not just yet. I want a few minutes alone to sort things out and write. It might help clear my head," Rebecca said, then climbed into the wagon. Bolo jumped in behind her.

Silas always shows up like a bad penny. Last night he tried to kill Jack. Almost worked. Silas stole his two horses and left the oxen on the barge. He's out there.

This journey is still one I would finish even if I knew what I know now. We've experienced storms, murder, landmarks, grief, and plenty of good events that will make for the telling of stories.

I want to marry Zachary Miller. I'm sure of it.

Chapter 23

Relentless Wind

Three weeks had passed since Silas tried to kill Jack. The wagons settled into a monotonous routine. No one had seen Silas. Rebecca's level of anxiety and fear diminished with each turn of the wheels, but she knew Silas would never simply ride away. That notion haunted her thoughts and stole her sleep, filling it with nightmares.

The harsh wind blew ruthlessly whistling across the land, growling over stones, and roaring through gorges in a continuous, nerve-wracking sound. Annie Murphy was the first to show signs of the madness that descended among the pioneers from the relentless howl. She scratched her face until rivulets of blood mixed with tears sliced through her dirty skin. She screeched and screamed at her husband, begging him to kill her. She pounded his chest with filthy fists. He sobbed, pulled her to him trying to calm her. In the span of a heartbeat, the sun struck metal and sent a flash of light between the young couple. Annie jerked the knife from Jacob's belt and stabbed herself in the heart.

Rebecca rushed to help. The moment she reached Annie's body, slumped at Jacob's feet, she knew help was a fleeting thought. Annie was dead. The tragic and bloody image would haunt her forever.

A circle of curious emigrants had gathered around when Annie started yelling and tearing at her clothes. Her behavior was unusual and out of character. She stabbed herself so quickly others nearby weren't prepared for the end. One man shouted, calling it a scene from hell. He was right.

How many more people would go crazy?

And still, the wind didn't cease.

The days of tall grass, colorful flowers, and frequent water sources seemed to be nothing more than a dream. Scrub brush and thorny yellow flowers were beginning to block out the beauty of the early days on the trail. The wind caused dust and dirt to thicken the air, coating everything. Dust devils were often seen dancing along the trail.

Colonel Wilson and Jacob Murphy buried Annie quickly while the wagons kept rolling.

Rebecca inched alongside the oxen with her head bowed, hand on the yoke. Bolo rode on the wagon seat watching everything. She noticed the people had spread out, forgoing the single-file pattern preferred by Colonel Wilson. Every living thing suffered in the wind. Worry combined with fear left her tense and shaken. Visibility was so poor Silas could sneak up and no one would hear him. Worst of all, her mother's lung condition worsened, aggravated by the wind, and forcing her to stay in the wagon. Doc Randolph assured them all would be well when they reached the mountains and hills as visible as hope on the horizon. Taking a moment, she climbed aboard the slow-moving wagon to check on her mother. "How are you?"

Sarah took a breath that resulted in a coughing fit–

hoarse, deep, and dry. She fell back against the pillows gasping. "I'll be fine. How far have we gone?" she whispered.

"Not far, the oxen can't move any faster. They are nervous and shake every time the wind changes directions. I pray it dies down. The northwest sky seems clear. I think Colonel Wilson is going to call it a day in an hour or two." Rebecca knelt beside Sarah and wiped her face with a cool damp rag.

"Have you seen Zachary? Doc said he's been working with the wranglers."

Rebecca shrugged. She missed Zachary and hoped he would be able to talk at the end of the day. He was the only person who would understand her fear. "I don't see him often. When I do, it's late and everyone is exhausted. He said the cattle and horses are skittish. Stampedes are one surprise away. The slightest things spook them. The animals can hear more in the wind than any human can."

****

No fires lit the night. Stars weren't lighting the night sky. The wind continued to blow. Zachary made his way to see Rebecca by the glow of lanterns inside the wagons. His stomach growled. He was in pain and craved rest. He needed to see her before he could settle in the grain wagon. He rapped on the wagon seat. "Rebecca. I made it." He shrugged his shoulders, tried to work out the kinks in his back, and twisted his neck. The knot between his shoulder blades felt as tight as a hanging rope at the end of its tether.

Rebecca opened the ties of the cover and crawled out carrying a rag-wrapped bundle. "I'm glad you made it. This isn't much. Colonel Wilson didn't allow fires tonight. Just a cold slice of bread, a handful of raisins, and some jerked beef."

Zachary reached to take the food and yelped with pain. "Thanks. This is fine. I wanted to see you before I bed down."

"What's wrong?"

"Just a tightness around my shoulders. I've been tenser than I thought. Being in the saddle for so long takes a toll. Not to mention the damn wind."

Rebecca began rubbing and massaging his shoulders, but the muscles weren't giving under any pressure.

"Take your shirt off. I'm going to get some drawing salve."

"You're what? Take my shirt off? What's gotten into you?"

"You've got tight muscles in your back. Now, off with the shirt." Rebecca climbed back inside, rustled around, then brought out a tin of something that smelled familiar. "Here we go. Now, sit up straight so I can apply this properly."

Zachary grimaced. The pain made it difficult to do as she asked but he did.

Rebecca opened the container and massaged the salve into his shoulders.

Within seconds, he relaxed. "Oh man. What's in that? Smells like wintergreen but what else?"

"Well, at least the dust hasn't affected your sense of smell," she replied with a chuckle. "Wintergreen mixed with willow bark and lard. Your muscles are knotted up like a rope some wild horse has drug around for days. Almost done, then you can put your shirt on."

Zachary rolled his shoulders and head and moaned with relief. "Works like a charm. You never did tell me how Sarah is."

"She's struggling to breathe. I pray the wind dies down. I'm grateful we stopped early today. The animals were hard to handle."

Rebecca moved in front of him, wiping her hands on her apron. Placing her hand against his unshaven cheek, she leaned over and kissed him. A brief feather touch of their lips. Zachary lifted her hand and kissed the palm. "Thank you, I feel better. You're exhausted. I know I am. I'm going to wash up and bed down. See you at breakfast. I've been keeping my eyes open. I haven't seen any sign of Silas or the horses he stole. He won't get to you."

Rebecca's relief was evident in her sigh. A quiet sense of calm filled the atmosphere.

"How did you know I'm worried about that?"

"Because I worry about it. Colonel Wilson wants to make it to Fort Laramie tomorrow. He thinks Silas may have made his way there. Even if he isn't there, he plans on having them watch for him." Zachary stood and pulled her close to him. He held her for a moment and whispered his love, then, bidding her goodnight, walked into the night.

****

Jacob Murphy found Brent at Colonel Wilson's wagon. "Brent, I need to talk to you about something."

"Sure. What is it? You should be resting. I'm sorry about Annie."

"When we get to Fort Laramie, I'm going to stay. Join up with the cavalry. I can't bear finishing this trek without Annie. I want to give you my wagon and team. Maybe you and Sally can get married sooner."

"Jacob, you need to think about this. It's a nice offer,

but make sure it's what you want. Talk to Colonel Wilson about it."

"My mind is made up. Please take the wagon and team. I want it to become part of someone's happiness. Like it's meant to be."

Brent reached to shake hands with Jacob but ended up pulling him into a bear hug. "All right. I accept. Thank you."

Chapter 24

Fort Laramie

Filthy, fatigued, and forlorn, the emigrants approached Fort Laramie relieved but disappointed to find the fortress smaller than expected. One by one, the wagons passed a handful of teepees surrounded by women scraping animal hides that were tightly stretched across frames. Strips of meat hung over poles, drying in the sun. Blood swarming with flies cast a stench that hung heavy in the air near the offal. Chaos seemed to be the norm among the traders, trappers, and mountain men inside the fort, yet they welcomed the travelers.

Rebecca stopped the team and moved into the circle. She untied the wagon cover. Bolo bounded out in a black and white blur. She held her hand over her eyes to block the sun. The river was near and would make chores easier.

"We should get Aaron some clothes that fit. He has outgrown everything." Sarah laughed when Bolo dashed out, but it turned into another bout of coughing. She sipped enough stale tepid water to calm the cough, and climbed out of the wagon.

"You're right about Aaron. I saw fires in the fort, so Colonel Wilson should allow us to build one. We can have a real bath." Rebecca unyoked the oxen and rubbed them down. She whistled for Bolo who rushed to her with his tongue hanging out and tail wagging.

"Where will we put the tub?" Sarah bent at the waist and twisted from side to side, stretching her muscles.

Rebecca heard Zachary's laugh. He and Colonel Wilson were coming their way. Her heart dove into her stomach, then catapulted back in place at the sight of his long limbs, lanky stride, and dimpled smile. Would she always be surprised at the impact he had on her? "We could either clear a space for the tub inside the wagon or set up our tent with the tub inside. What do you think?"

"The tent would be easier." Sarah turned to speak to Zachary and the colonel. "Good afternoon, gentlemen. Isn't it nice to feel as if we're not inside a springtime twister?"

Colonel Wilson removed his hat and slapped it against his thigh, releasing a cloud of dust. He spat in the dirt and wiped his mouth across the sleeve of his shirt. "Hope the wind stays down."

"Mother and I were just discussing a hot bath. Do you think it would be all right, Colonel?" Rebecca stood beside Zachary with her arm linked in his.

He coughed and spat another stream of the ever-present tobacco to the ground, leaving mud at his feet. "No need to pull out your tub. The soldiers have set aside spaces for bathing, both have several tubs, and people are heating water. One area for men. One for women. I suggest you ladies gather your things and head inside. Likely to get busy when I let the others know. Wranglers will care for your teams. Keep your good horses in the circle, Rebecca. Others will want them. We're stopping for two full days to rest the animals. Spread the word."

Rebecca squealed and clamped her hand over her

mouth. Turning, she grasped Sarah's hand. "I apologize, I'm over excited. A real bath. Oh, I don't know what to do first. Mother, if you gather our clothing and soap, I'll get Evie. Getting cleaned up will make her feel better. Zachary, please find Aaron. Will you go with him?" Her words tumbled like chickens being let out of a too small coop. She kissed Zachary on the cheek before turning and loping to Evie's wagon.

Hans and Evie were preparing a fire when Rebecca rushed to them. "Evie, get your things. We're off for a real bath in the fort. Hot water, soap, and tubs. Hurry, we want to get there before the colonel spreads the word. Hans, there is a building for men as well. Catch up with Zachary and Aaron."

"Slow down, Rebecca. You're jabbering like a magpie with a secret to tell. Did you say a bath?"

Evie laughed out loud, the first true bit of laughter since the baby died. A flash of guilt crossed her face, as though she didn't deserve to be happy about anything. Rebecca's heart cringed at the thoughts Evie might have to cause such guilt about the baby. But the loving grin Evie bestowed on Hans gave her hope that her friends would recover from their grief.

"Goodness, a real bath. I'll be right back," Evie said and hurried into the wagon.

Rebecca caught the tender look of Hans and the tears that filled his eyes as his gaze followed Evie. "It's the first time she's laughed like that since the baby, well, since he died."

"I know, I'm just as happy to see it as you are. Now, make her move a little faster."

The native women didn't speak. They held large blankets for the ladies lining up to enter the hut. Mud and straw bricks held the heat, making the space warm and humid. Steam rose from the tubs. Fires burned in the corners with cast-iron pots of water being constantly refilled and heated. Rebecca strode to the first woman and said hello. The woman didn't respond. Rebecca took the blanket and turned to the others hoping for an explanation. Her mother shrugged her shoulders. Evie covered her mouth to stifle a nervous giggle, but her shaking shoulders gave her away.

Using hand motions, the women encouraged them to undress and climb into the tubs. There was little privacy but being mesmerized by the thought of being truly clean for a change left any sense of modesty flying away in the wind. Within seconds, Rebecca, Sarah, and Evie were up to their chins in hot water. Talking wasn't needed. The baths relaxed their stiff muscles and cleansed them—body, and soul. The aroma of scented soap filled the air. The plop, plop, plop of splashing water and bursting soap bubbles mingled with sighs of contentment.

The native women motioned to a different set of tubs filled with tepid water. Ladles for rinsing hung from the sides of the vats.

Rebecca wondered if Zachary enjoyed his bath. Did he like the hot water, soap, and the feeling of being clean? She knew she would see him in a matter of minutes. Embarrassment settled heavily in her belly, confusing her. Why should she feel any sort of discomfort because they had just been in the baths? Rebecca shook away her thoughts with a chuckle and reached for the hairbrush in her bag, then brushed and braided her long locks.

A line of other women waited their turn. The

Garsons were at the front holding their leather valises as if they were filled with gold rather than clothing and soap. Ginny stood beside Edward Thatcher, holding his hand.

Rebecca stopped to speak to them. "Goodness, you have no idea what luxury this bath is. Enjoy the soak and the assistance. The women are so kind."

"I can't imagine that a wooden tub would qualify as luxurious. It will have to do. Lord knows a porcelain tub is superior to any other." Mrs. Garson smoothed her hands over the dirty apron covering her dress. The hem had been torn into shreds from thorny plants.

"I wouldn't know, Mrs. Garson, but it was the best bath I have ever had. Just enjoy it."

Zachary, Hans, and Aaron joined them. "Have a nice bath and shave, men." Zachary rubbed his hand over his smooth cheeks. "It sure is nice to not be covered in whiskers," he said with a chuckle.

"Indians. Helpful, you say? I would think they were barbaric." Mr. Garson tilted the lens of his monocle and wrinkled his nose at Zachary.

Zachary winked at her and bent his elbow for her to hold onto as they walked back to the wagons. "There was no danger. Just helpfulness. Rebecca, are you ladies ready to get back to the wagons? I hope you're ready to prepare a meal and start shaking the dust out of everything. Besides, I'm hungry."

Rebecca linked her arm through his. "You do smell better. Bolo will probably think you're a stranger and try to attack you."

"Not me. I have jerky in my pocket."

Zachary squeezed her hand and grinned when her eyebrows lifted and her nose wrinkled. "Surely not. You stuffed it in your pocket without being wrapped?"

"Why not? There's nothing else in there but my dirty handkerchief and my pocket-knife, the one I use to skin rabbits."

"You are insufferable. Don't you have any clean kerchiefs?"

Zachary roared with laughter. He put his hand on her shoulder and bent at the waist. "You should see your face. Of course, the jerky is wrapped. Thank you for the laugh. Now, I know never to put any food in my pocket without wrapping it first. Bolo doesn't care, though."

Rebecca laughed. "Get on with you. We have work to do."

Laughter and positive words floated clearly on the windless plains. The promise of rest offered bursts of energy that hadn't been felt in weeks. Several women gathered around large fires to boil water for laundering. Other fires were built for cooking. As the weeks progressed, they had learned to share the necessary chores. Men pulled out their tools and grease buckets to repair wagons. Children ran around squealing, playing tag and running with abandon in the circle of wagons.

Rebecca helped Ginny prepare rabbit stew and corn pone flapjacks drizzled with butter and sorghum molasses, then served the meal while Sarah played with Ginny's toddler, Sean.

Aaron watched and waited his turn while Zachary and Edward Thatcher played checkers on an overturned barrel lid. The men put the game aside when Rebecca brought out double portions of food on deep spatter-ware plates. "There's more where that came from. Eat up."

Zachary took the plate. "Smells great. Being clean and comfortable has given me a big appetite."

"C'mon, Aaron, Mother has your plate. Ginny and I will be right back," Rebecca said and within moments sat beside Zachary with a wink. "It would be nice to have a leisurely walk. Mother and Ginny plan on doing some mending. Doc Randolph will be checking on Mother after he has supper with the colonel. Ginny, I'll take food to the Garsons, so you and Ed can have a break and enjoy your meal."

"I told them I would bring their supper after we had ours, but your kindness is much appreciated." When she finished eating, Ginny stood and prepared plates for Mr. and Mrs. Garson. "The one on top is for Mr. Garson, he doesn't like anything on his corn pone. Thank you."

After they'd delivered the Garsons' dinner, Rebecca took Zachary's hand, brought it to her lips, and kissed the palm. "Are we allowed to walk away from the fort? The colonel didn't say."

"He said to stay close, but there isn't any reason why we can't go down to the river. I saw the perfect place for us to be alone. We don't get that chance much these days."

"I admit this is nice, but I'm glad Bolo is with us. He makes me feel safer." Rebecca glanced at the dog walking beside her.

"Bolo is a good dog, but I can keep you safe." Zachary stopped and knelt on one knee to pet Bolo.

Rebecca sucked in a deep breath and slapped her palm to her chest. Seeing Zachary on one knee forced the breath from her lungs. The beating of her heart escalated. Was he going to propose? What would she say if he did? *He's talking about Bolo, not marriage,* she chided herself mentally and took a deep breath "He's the best dog, not just a good one. I trust you, too."

****

Zachary stood up and took Rebecca's hand, leading her toward the trees. His nerves jumped like grasshoppers in a tin can, thinking about the big question on his mind. *What if she says no?* Surely, she wouldn't do that. He stuck his free hand into his pocket to make sure the necklace was still there.

Several layers of old leaves sat atop a bed of sandy soil beneath the trees. Rebecca unfolded the quilt she carried and settled on it with a sigh. "This is so nice. The sweet but pungent smell reminds me of a fluffed feather mattress." She took her knife from her bag, reached up, and cut two branches from the strange trees. "I wonder what kind of trees these are. They are short, but full."

Zachary sat beside her and put his arm across her shoulders. "It's nicer than I imagined it would be. Almost like we're alone in the world. We'll have to ask someone at the fort what they are. I've never seen any like them."

She leaned into his arm and pointed to the west. "I know we're going to be climbing those distant mountains before long. I'll take rocks and steep climbs over the wind. My aunt wrote that this will be the part of the journey when wagons are most apt to break axles and wheels."

"I imagine the best thing to do is to make sure everything is well greased and in good working order to begin with." Zachary wasn't sure why Rebecca sounded worried.

She nestled deeper into his chest. "Will you help me check my wagons?"

"No need to even ask. You know I will." Zachary kissed Rebecca's forehead, then lifted her chin with two fingers and kissed her on the mouth until he felt her shoulders soften and her arms wrap around him. They needed more time, had more to say and more to do before they reached the Oregon Territory.

****

June 28, 1845

This has been my favorite day on the trail. We arrived at Fort Laramie. I was shocked at the number of tipis outside the gates. The women were hanging strips of meat over wooden risers. Inside the fort everything was fast moving. We had real baths waiting for us. What an unexpected blessing. Zachary and I went for a walk. It was the first time in weeks we could relax together.

Rebecca stopped writing and closed her eyes. The memory of Zachary on one knee today combined with the sight of the chiseled muscles in his arms and chest when she tended his shoulders yesterday made her palms sweat. She rubbed them on her skirt.

I thought Zachary was going to propose today and, for a moment, panicked. Not sure if I'm relieved or disappointed that he didn't. I keep thinking Silas is around every corner. Ginny and Edward are marrying tomorrow.

Chapter 25

A Wedding at the Fort

Few days on the trail began with the charged atmosphere of joy and expectation waving like windswept grain among the travelers. This last day at Fort Laramie began as common and boring and routine as every other one, but there would be a wedding at supper time. Edward Thatcher and the widow, Ginny Granger, were getting married. Excitement and jubilation reigned among the pioneers.

Rebecca joined Ginny as she stoked the fire that morning. "Let me prepare breakfast. This is your day. Take time to prepare your wagon."

"My wagon?" Ginny cocked her head at Rebecca. Puzzled lines traced her forehead.

"It is our gift to you. The wagon and the team. You've been staying in it anyway. You need something to begin your new lives when we finally reach the Oregon Territory."

Rebecca hid a smile as Ginny fanned her cheeks, her face as red as a summertime beet at the mention of preparing the wagon. Everyone knew she and Edward would consummate the union.

"Thank you. You all have been so kind and helpful to me and Sean since Mr. Granger died. The wagon and team is a gift beyond measure. I doubt if I will ever be able to thank you and Sarah for all you've done. Not just for us, but for anyone needing help."

Rebecca put her hand on Ginny's shoulder and squeezed. "I think sharing and working together is the only way to make a trek like this a success, don't you?"

"Of course, the last thing I expected was to become widowed and then marry again on the trail. Mrs. Garson said she would give me a dress to be wed in. Can you imagine how special, how fancy it will be? I've never worn anything but homespun."

Rebecca folded a cloth and removed the Dutch oven filled with biscuits from the coals, inhaled the aroma and sighed. "You will be lovely. There's no need to feel less special because your circumstances differ. Mrs. Garson has proven to be more capable and accepting as the trip progresses. Tonight, you will stand tall and meet your new husband in a beautiful dress."

"I'm starving this morning and I smell biscuits." Zachary interrupted the conversation between Rebecca and Ginny.

Rebecca grinned and shoved a tin plate toward him. "Good morning to you, too. Just the usual, biscuits with butter and jam. Go ahead and help yourself."

After breakfast, Rebecca found Jeb running around with childlike abandon hitting a ball with a stick. He and several other children were caught up in different activities. "Jeb, I need you and your friends to make grass bundles today. Round everyone up and, please, include Sean. I know he's too young for your liking, but his mother is getting married tonight and she has a lot to do. Bolo will protect all of you. Take him with you."

"Sure, Miss Rebecca. I can have it done in no time.

Should we have a contest to win a hard candy? Everyone will do what I tell them to do. I'm the boss of them." Jeb linked his fingers through the straps of his suspenders, rose on his toes and rocked back and forth. He grinned at Rebecca, pulled a piece of grass from his pocket, and stuck it in his mouth.

"You have a lot of attitude for a five-year-old boy, but I like it. I know I can count on you to do your part. Do you think it's nice to consider yourself the boss? Out here we must work together. I think it would be a good idea to let everyone have a piece of sugar, don't you?" Rebecca tousled Jeb's hair, leaving a wayward cowlick sticking skyward.

"Well, yeah, I guess so." Jeb managed to act sheepish, but the dimpled grin he offered melted Rebecca's heart and made her wonder about the children she and Zachary might one day share. She hoped for a stubborn, independent boy like Jeb. Or a stubborn and independent girl like Sadie.

With a whistle from Jeb and barks from Bolo, children came running like ants from a disturbed bed. Jeb snapped orders and took Sean's hand. The longest grasses were pulled and wrapped with twine to dry on the wagon bows. Each bundle, made with laughter and child's play, would provide an animal with a small meal in the coming days

****

Mrs. Garson greeted Ginny with a genuine welcoming smile. Something she had rarely seen. "Hurry, I have something to show you. I'm excited. It's about time we had a break from this endless trek west. Take Edward and Mr. Garson their food. I'll be waiting in the wagon."

"Yes, ma'am. I imagine they're hungry." Ginny moved around back to find the men drinking coffee while waiting for her to bring breakfast.

"Let me take that." Edward reached for the plates. He caressed her hand when he took the food and winked at her before lifting the edge of the bandana cloth and inhaling the aroma. "Smells good."

Ginny's face heated up. She raised her hands and put them on her cheeks hoping to hide the redness caused by nervousness and embarrassment. "There is more to eat if you want it. I will be with Mrs. Garson."

Edward handed Mr. Garson a plate, set his down, then covered Ginny's hands with his own. "There is nothing to worry about. It is an acceptable thing to marry again. After breakfast I'll need to get the wagon ready and check on the oxen."

"Wait." Ginny took Edward's hand. "I have something to tell you. Rebecca and Sarah gave us their second wagon as a wedding gift. With the team. It's so kind." She swallowed a sob and wiped tears from her face with the back of her hand. Kindness wasn't something she had much of growing up.

Ginny watched disbelief then gratitude cover Edward's face. He placed her hand against his chest where his heart beat fast and strong. "Sometimes I think things couldn't get better, but they do," he croaked, the squeak of his tone reminding her of a boy getting his "man voice."

"We are blessed. Now, I need to see what Mrs. Garson needs."

Mrs. Garson sat in her rocking chair, holding two folded packages tied with ribbon. Her eyes sparkled and lit up her face. She moved her hands in every direction while she spoke. "Come here, come here. I must show you these dresses."

"Thank you, ma'am. To be getting married on the trail in a real dress is all so exciting and a bit scary. I am forever grateful for your thoughtfulness."

Mrs. Garson held a dress in each hand. "Please, choose one."

Ginny had no idea how to choose. Even the wrappings were fine. Because blue was her favorite color, she took the one with sky-blue ribbon and untied the bow. Mesmerized, she watched the ends of the ribbon flutter to the floor. The dress inside was pale yellow dotted with embroidered bluebells embraced by a spring-green sash.

"Do you like it?"

Ginny blinked back tears and wiped both hands on her apron before touching the garment. "It is so pretty and soft."

"The dress and sash are silk. Maybe you should open the other one. You might like it better."

Ginny took the other package from Mrs. Garson. "I can't imagine anything being more beautiful."

"Open it, my dear."

The second package was wrapped in white silk tied with a red ribbon. Inside was a white brocade dress embellished with pink and red roses on the collar and cuffs. A pink ribbon wrapped the waist, and tiny pearl buttons closed the front. Ginny gasped. "It is too much, too beautiful. You don't have to do this."

"I know I don't have to. But you and Edward have helped us so much. Let me help you. It is my honor. Now let's try it on." Mrs. Garson picked the dress up by the shoulder seams, unfolded it, and shook the wrinkles out revealing a full skirt falling in pleats and pooling on the floor. She waited patiently while Ginny stripped down to her coarse chemise, then lowered the dress over her head. "It is stunning, don't you think?"

Ginny covered her mouth to catch the sobs in her throat. How did she ever find herself in such a fine dress? "Yes. It is. I choose this one. I will never be able to thank you enough."

"You will be radiant tonight when you marry. I want you to have the other dress as well. It will provide you with something nice when we reach the end of this wretched journey. Now, let's get you out of that dress so you can do your chores."

"Yes, ma'am. I have much to do to prepare to leave Fort Laramie in the morning. I'll bake more bread and meat and catch up on the wash. I'll also need to make Sean a few more shirts, he's growing too fast. Edward will be sure the oxen are brushed, fed, and have secure shoes. He also said something about repairing the wagons." Ginny rambled as thoughts of things to be done pushed aside the magic of the moment.

Mrs. Garson turned away from Ginny and began securing her brushes and creams in the chest strapped to a wagon bow and, with a single hand motion, dismissed her.

The women spent the day washing and cooking. Being prepared was more important than play or anticipating Ginny's wedding. Even Ginny was busy with laundry. But she made a cake to serve her new husband the next day. A gift she could provide from her own hands. Rebecca had told her not to cook for the Garsons. She and Sarah were cooking two days of meals for their wagons and the Garsons.

Late in the afternoon Rebecca and Sarah led Ginny to the bath house in the fort. "What are you doing? I can't go. I still have work to do for Mrs. Garson."

"No, you don't. Everything is well cared for." Mrs. Garson joined the group and held up a large soft blanket. "I've arranged a private, muscle-soothing bath for you."

Ginny couldn't hold back the tears of thanksgiving she had for these three women who had accepted her. "I've never felt deserving of such attention or had such thoughtful friends. I want to thank you for your compassion, both when I became a widow and today when I will wed again. Sean needs a father. I need, well, I need a caregiver."

"Get in the tub. Stay as long as you like. I have left perfume, creams, and powders by the blanket for you to use as you wish. Sarah will stay. Rebecca has to get back to the children." Mrs. Garson dismissed the other women, turned, and left the room.

****

Every member of the wagon train gathered near Colonel Wilson's wagon. Campfires behind him cast his shadow toward the gathering crowd.

Pastor Hendricks waited next to Edward and Sean, who held a crown of wilting, woven wildflowers for his mother. Edward put his arm around Sean and pulled him close.

Gasps and clapping from the back of the crowd had every eye watching for the bride. Ginny Granger's simple beauty surprised many. She walked forward between Mr. and Mrs. Garson dressed in the white brocade dress. Her usually mousy brown hair shone in the moonlight and fell to the middle of her back in a cascade of curls tied with a white ribbon. Her cheeks were red. She walked with her eyes cast toward the ground.

Ginny glanced up and saw the love on Edward's face and the protective way he wrapped his arm around Sean and swallowed the tears building in her heart. Reaching her spot, she crouched to hug Sean and wiped his boyish tears.

"Ma, I made you a crown, but you already have ribbon. Do you still want mine?"

"Oh, I want your crown more than anything I've ever wanted. Would you like to put it on me?" She shed tears of sorrow remembering her husband and grateful tears of expectation and anticipation of a promising future with Edward. Wiping her face, she let Sean crown her like a queen. She glanced at Edward. He swallowed hard and blinked fast when she raised her eyes and lifted the corners of her mouth at him. Each tear she shed was a testament to love.

****

After the words were spoken, a feast took place followed by dancing. Every emigrant crowded around the board planks set up for food inviting them to eat until they were satisfied. Relaxed conversations took place from one group to the next. Rebecca gathered the children around to give them the promised candy. Her heart swelled with every hug from small arms. The pure emotion of children was one thing she cherished more than any other. A small awareness of sadness flitted through her heart when she realized she had never been able to establish bonds with children until leaving on this long journey.

Bolo distracted her when he took off at a dead run baying and barking at something. *Probably a rabbit, but what if ...*

Zachary came to her and put his hand on her back. He held his guitar with the other hand. "Don't worry. It's not likely to be Silas. Even if it was, he wouldn't come near us tonight with so much going on."

Rebecca leaned into him. "I know. I know."

"Have to go. Time for the dancing to begin. Save yours for me." Zachary leaned down, bowed, and kissed Rebecca on the forehead. Just as he turned to leave, Bolo bounded back with a bloody rabbit in his mouth. He dropped it to the ground, barked, and wagged his tail so fast he lost his balance.

Rebecca picked up the rabbit and patted her leg. "Bolo, come. Let's take this rabbit to Aaron."

The dancing, spirited and joyous, was a rare reminder that life on the trail didn't have to be constant fatigue, worry, and heartache. After a few dances, the newlyweds stole away to their wagon. When the evening ended, Rebecca gathered her journal and pen and took a few moments to reflect on the events.

July 1845

What a special day. We've been able to bathe, rest, restock, cook ahead of time, mend things, and get some clothes that fit Aaron. That boy is growing. The highlight was the wedding of Ginny Granger and Edward Thatcher. I know she still misses her husband, but there is surely a strong bond between them.

Mrs. Garson surprised everyone when she gave Ginny two nice dresses. One for the wedding and one to save for the day we arrive at the end of the trail. The wedding was beautiful in every way. Mother and I gave them the second wagon and team. Aaron will continue to stay with us in ours.

****

The next morning as the wagons lined up to leave the fort, Colonel Wilson called a meeting. Everyone gathered around. "Folks, it saddens me to inform you that Jacob has decided to stay on here and sign up with the Cavalry. He gave his wagon and team to Brent so he and Sally can marry soon. I know we'll miss him, but losing Annie like he did has led him to a change of course."

The close-knit group mumbled and shook their heads. Another moment of sadness had wedged its way into their community.

Brent and Sally moved beside the colonel. Brent cleared his throat and spoke. "We are so thankful for Jacob's act of kindness. It will never be forgotten. I don't know where he is this morning, but I know we will all miss him, just as we miss Annie."

"That's it for now, folks. Let's get rolling." Colonel Wilson mounted his horse.

Jacob Murphy watched from the side of the barracks. He wept. For Annie and for dreams that died.

Chapter 26

Lightening the Load

Time on the trail measured itself in placing one weary, painful step in front of the other, driving on as wind whistled through every bend. Dust devils whirled and skipped and taunted every living thing. Stones littered the ground causing possessions in the wagons to shift. Children fell, skinning their knees. Oxen and horses threw shoes. They stopped only for nooning and night. Keeping the animals healthy became more important than anything. The pioneers were forced to make do and plan for diminishing supplies. Mountains seemed nearer. Evenings became cooler.

Rebecca walked away from the wagon with Bolo at her heels. She needed time alone. Knowing the second half of the trip would be more dangerous, tension grew in the air. She continued to have a premonition that Silas would return and cause more trouble. She crossed her arms over her chest and shivered. It stood to reason that he could be ahead of them on the trail because he wasn't bound to a wagon train. He could travel faster and lighter. A shrill whistle brought her out of her troubling thoughts and into the present.

Colonel Wilson held his hand in the air. He bellowed for everyone to stop and ordered them to come to the front of the line. When everyone had gathered, he climbed onto the seat of his wagon. "Folks, things are becoming more dangerous. We've stopped early so you can rid yourselves of any heavy things you don't need. Get rid of furniture, stoves, or books that add weight to your load. You'll be able to replace them at the end of the trail. Nothing is too precious or sentimental. Don't make me use force. I will climb in your wagon and throw it out for you if necessary. Check your food supplies and plan for the remainder of the trek. The most taxing part of the journey is ahead of us. After we cross the South Pass, we'll travel through even more wind and unrelenting dust storms. I want several of you to form two or three hunting parties. Venison would be nice. Now get busy unloading."

Whispers and weeping filled the air. Women wailed about losing the family china. Men complained about losing tools they imagined they would need in the new land.

Mr. Garson must have figured he shouldn't be expected to abide by every dictate of the colonel because he complained the loudest. "Colonel Wilson, you must know I can't do without my books. I need them for my new office. What kind of solicitor leaves their books behind, what kind of client would trust a solicitor without books on every wall and table?"

"Yes, you can, Garson. I know the big books every solicitor owns are repetitive. Go through them and figure out what you need." Colonel Wilson shot back. He grinned at Garson whose shocked expression made him turn away to hide his laughter, then turned on his heel and walked back to his horse.

"This is a perfect opportunity for us to hide the gems

in a better place," Rebecca whispered to her mother. "We can make space for them in the seat. I can pull a board up without anyone suspecting anything. I'll get them from the barrel of meal if you'll remove the ones from the skirt hem."

"That's not a bad idea. Do you think we have anything we need to get rid of? I'm only asking because your father was especially careful about not overloading the wagons. I remember Emma sending a letter telling us not to bring anything heavy or not on the list."

"I have some books, but only a few of my favorites. The family Bible you brought and my favorite book of Shakespeare's Sonnets plus the tale of the Lewis and Clark Expedition. The wagon we gave to Edward and Ginny is loaded with supplies for the general store, but there isn't anything that would put a strain on the oxen and neither of them have many personal possessions."

Sarah removed a skirt from the chest and began to unstitch the hem. A handful of gems and a few coins fell into her lap. "I'll wrap these in a handkerchief and sew it shut. You've never completely told me what Silas said that made you believe he knew we had the stones in Bolo's collar. What did he say?"

Rebecca flipped her braid over her shoulder and bit her lip. She didn't like to even think about Silas, much less talk about him. The sound of his name in her mouth turned to bilious acid. "He confronted me about how protective I was of Bolo and his collar. I tried to tell him it was nothing, but he persisted and tried to get ahold of it. That's when Bolo bit him."

"I've wondered." Sarah closed the chest. "These two chests are heavy. Maybe we should leave one behind. Maybe even both. Our clothing and linens could be wrapped in muslin. Come to think of it there, would be more room for Aaron if we got rid of them. Emma might be upset if I left Mother's chest behind. What do you think?"

"I believe Aunt Emma would understand. She knows the difficulty of the trail. She didn't add a twelve-year-old growing boy to her possessions." Rebecca turned away and wiped a tear from her eye. She loved Aaron and wanted to protect him, but her grandmother's chest was filled with memories. The rose scent of homemade soap. Scraps of fabric being saved for a quilt. Diaries of raw-edged paper. Sketches. Everything in that chest reminded her of home.

Sarah sat on the wagon bed and rubbed her hand over the smooth wood of her mother's cedar chest. "You're right, Emma will understand. We'll choose the things that have the most meaning or usefulness, then leave the chests behind. Let's sort through them now while we've stopped to lighten our loads. I believe we could save the quilt scraps and spread them out to become protection for the things we wrap in muslin. What about the diaries? Mother kept them since she was a girl. Books are heavy."

"The diaries are bound in hard covers. We could go through each one and select the most poignant or important entries then carefully cut them from the cover. That way we would be able to have the treasure without as much weight. I can't bear the thought of getting rid of them completely. The reason I keep journals is because I watched you write in your own."

Sarah picked up a diary, ran her hand over the cover, opened it to a random page, and read about the day her father proposed to her mother.

Rebecca reached for the book. "It's entries like this, so full of hope, we must save. Each diary has the start and end date on the cover. We can probably find entries we want to save by focusing on the dates. What do you think?"

"You're right. I think we should get help removing the chests before we begin work on the diaries. I hear Aaron. He can help us."

Later, Rebecca and her mother sat on the two empty chests they were going to leave behind. Stew bubbled over the campfire. The journey was almost halfway complete.

"I wonder what will happen with these? A part of me hopes that some of the Indians find them and take them back to their villages. I imagine they will just dry out and fall apart." Rebecca rubbed her hand over the sleek polished wood. She heard Sarah sniffing and couldn't make eye contact with her because she didn't want to cry. Bolo sensed sadness and nosed his way under Rebecca's arm. She scratched his ears.

Sarah pulled a handkerchief with lilacs embroidered on it from her sleeve and wiped her tears then her nose. "We'll never know, will we? This entire trek is centered around sacrifice."

****

Zachary walked up behind Rebecca and put his hands over her eyes. "Guess who?"

Rebecca laughed. "How would I know? Just some cowboy, most likely."

"Your cowboy, but I have news you won't like."

Rebecca turned away from rubbing Glory and Patriot down with rags. "What is it?"

"Colonel Wilson is sending me and Brent on a

scouting trip tomorrow. He wants us to take Aaron and start teaching him more about tracking and things."

"You're right, I don't like it. I will miss you. Do you think Aaron is old enough? After all, his mother is dead, and his murderous father could be lurking around any corner." The fear that choked her clutched at her heart and squeezed until it almost quit beating. She had never been one to be afraid of anything. She was usually more understanding and accepting.

Zachary leaned down and kissed her on the nose. "He's old enough. I imagine he will enjoy it. Before you know it, he'll be thirteen. That's practically a man. The Colonel thinks it will show him we trust him and think he is a young man of worth. Aaron said something to one of the wranglers about feeling like he was tied to the apron strings of you and Sarah. I know he doesn't really feel that way. You just need to understand how a boy grows."

"He helps us so much. I guess he feels even more lost with Edward and Ginny living in the other wagon."

"He just needs more time with men. That's all. Just be alert and stay safe. This damn trail isn't a place to let down your guard."

Rebecca stood and wrapped her arms around Zachary's waist. "Will you be here for breakfast in the morning? I'll make a big batch of food for the three of you. Can we manage a walk tonight?"

"Of course. I need to gather some things and choose a sturdy packhorse from the herd. Reminds me, is Aaron's little mare sturdy enough to be ridden more than usual? I know he takes care of her. Wish everyone cared as much for their animals."

"He loves that horse. She's his last link to his

mother. Let him take her, I think it will mean a great deal."

He pulled her close for a kiss that left her wanting more time alone with him.

****

Aaron came running up with his arms outstretched. "Guess what! I'm going on a scouting expedition with Brent and Zachary tomorrow. Colonel Wilson said I'm old enough. I even get to take Misty. It's the best thing that has ever happened to me."

Rebecca grinned at Aaron. She realized he had grown several inches since they left Independence. "I heard. Is Misty ready? It would probably be a good idea to have Jack check out her hooves and change her shoes if necessary."

"What's wrong? Why are the chests out of the wagon? Is someone sick?" Aaron's voice dropped and took on a somber tone.

Rebecca stood up and put her arm around his shoulders. "Everything is fine. We're just lightening the load like Colonel Wilson said. We've taken the clothes and other things from the chests and covered them in muslin to make a mattress for you. Check it out. You'll only get to sleep on it one night before the scouting trip. I imagine it will get lumpier as we travel on, but it's better than the hard floor."

"Oh, that's nice. Thanks. I need to pack an extra set of clothes. Brent gave me one of his slickers. I'm going to give Misty some peppermint tonight. She loves it. When will the stew be ready? It smells good." Aaron talked so fast the words ran together.

"It's ready now if you want some. Zachary and I are going for a walk after supper. Do you want to wait and eat with him? He's just checking on Red and a packhorse. He'll be back soon."

"Yeah, I'll wait. I need to go see my horse." Aaron turned and headed to where the horses were tied.

****

Zachary took Rebecca's hand and pulled her up into a dance without music. "Time for our walk. Which direction do you choose?"

Rebecca giggled, spun in a circle, and stopped. She pointed west. "That way, I guess."

They walked hand in hand without talking for several minutes. Their growing relationship comforted Rebecca. She had a flash of a memory about Evie and Hans when they first started courting. Evie thought she had to be talking all the time. Rebecca finally broke the silence. "What exactly does the colonel want you to find?"

"The best way over the mountains. The way that will be easiest on the animals and the wagons. Plus, good water sources. He said it will be dry and dusty. It's where we need to be the strongest. After that, it's more plains and mountains then the Dalles and Columbia, which we will have to float across. Just a few more long weeks, then we'll be home." Zachary stopped, took a deep breath, brought Rebecca close to him and pressed her head to his chest.

"Home. Has a nice ring to it. I can imagine having a nice spread with flowing water and plenty of pasture for the livestock." Rebecca stretched her arms out wide, then leaned into his embrace. "Your heartbeat is strong," she whispered.

Zachary caressed her hair, tucking some wayward strands behind her ears. "It's strong because it beats for you. I'm happy and I love you. Come on, let's take this walk."

Rebecca matched Zachary's stride as he turned and led her farther away from the campsite. "Mother and I cleared out the two chests in the wagon today. It was one of the hardest things I've ever done. One belonged to my grandmother and was supposed to be mine when I married. I understand the need to lighten loads, but that doesn't make it easy. We did make Aaron happy."

"How did that make him happy?"

Rebecca covered her mouth and chuckled. "He likes the idea of being able to sleep on a mattress of folded clothes sewn between sheets of muslin. I reminded him he would only be able to enjoy it one night before he would be off sleeping on the hard ground with you and Brent. It really is good for him that he gets to go along with you. How long will you be gone? I don't mean to sound like a fainting violet, but I am nervous about you being gone. I still get frightened. Worrying is not a part of my usual personality, but thinking about Silas sometimes overwhelms me. I know I'm capable of taking care of myself, but he scares me."

"Colonel Wilson has ordered the wranglers and his crew to be on the watch for Silas. Your wagon will stay behind the chuck wagon. Not just for protection, but because Doc Randolph still insists on Sarah being out of the trail dust as much as possible."

"I know. Maybe I am just starting to miss you before you've even left."

They stopped at a small bluff and sat beneath a tree with grass growing thick and fragrant. Silence engulfed them in a comfort usually reserved for partners who had lived a lifetime together. Rebecca sighed and squeezed

Zachary's hand.

He took her in his arms and kissed her with a passion he hadn't ever expressed before. Rebecca matched the fervor of his kiss.

Chapter 27

South Pass

Rebecca lay awake in the dark confines of the wagon. This morning Zachary would be leaving on a scouting trip with Brent and Aaron. She didn't know how long they'd be gone, but she planned on preparing a large breakfast and filling their saddlebags with dried beef and fruit. She eased out of her bed and found Aaron already up and the fire lit.

"Good morning, Rebecca."

"What are you doing up? I almost always beat you out of the wagon? I need to get busy. Wouldn't want you to leave without sustenance." She ruffled Aaron's hair, leaving the cowlick on the back of his head sticking straight up.

Aaron spit on his hand and tried to get the wayward bit to lie down. "I have coffee going for you. I don't know how to cook, but Zachary said he will teach me how to fix trail food."

"I'm sure both Zachary and Brent can teach you a great deal about scouting and surviving on the trail." Rebecca poked at the wood of the fire to make it hotter and put the skillet over the flames. "Will you gather the bacon and a few potatoes for me? Oh, there is a small package for you in the wagon."

Aaron muttered and moved to the wagon. He picked up the package and scratched his head. He squeezed it, smelled it, and smoothed wrinkles from the paper before opening it. A short gasp had him tearing at the wrapping. His excited whoop of surprise assured Rebecca he liked the buckskin pants, a heavy wool shirt, and a pair of thick knitted socks nestled together.

"Where did you find these clothes? I never expected anything so special. I'm so lucky!" he exclaimed, then rushed to gather the supplies Rebecca needed plus a small bag of oatmeal, a pitcher of milk, sugar, and butter. "I thought oatmeal sounded good. Ma always used to say that oatmeal would stick to the gut."

Rebecca laughed and gave him a hug, then took the supplies from Aaron. "I'm glad you like the clothes. They belonged to my brother and might be a little big, but you can use your braces to keep them up. Now, let's have oatmeal plus biscuits and bacon. How about sorghum with your biscuits this morning?"

"Well, I am hungry. I bet Zachary and Brent are too."

Rebecca set to cooking, determined to satisfy the scouts as they left for a tedious and dangerous trail through the pass. "Go try the clothes on while I'm cooking."

Zachary walked up and kissed her on the cheek. "Good morning. Something smells mighty good. Where's Aaron? I figured he would be chomping at the bit."

"He is. I gave him some clothes that belonged to my brother. He's changing."

Aaron strode over to them. He tried to hide his excitement, but it didn't work. He rocked back on his heels and tucked his hands in the pockets of the britches. "I got warm clothes. Rebecca gave them to me this morning. They're perfect for the scouting trip. What do you think?"

"I think they're perfect. Are you ready for this? You seem to have Misty and your supplies ready. Your new clothes will serve you well. Do you have your knife? You'll need it. We'll head out as soon as we eat and double check our supplies."

"I'm ready all right. I have everything I need, including grain for Misty and my knife. Colonel Wilson said I couldn't take a rifle, but both of you will have one. Is Brent going to eat here?"

"Nah. Brent is having breakfast with Sally. Can't blame him, can we? Let's eat and get going." Zachary reached for Rebecca and pulled her to him.

Rebecca laughed, stood on tiptoes, and kissed Zachary. "Mind your manners. And your hands. I'm cooking. You could get burned."

****

Two hours later, the scouts reined their horses to the northwest, leaving the wagon train out of sight. The foothills of the mountains they'd be crossing in the coming weeks were green with short thorny bushes growing among the rocks. Wildflowers dotted the ground. A free-flowing stream fell from a rock face and twisted toward an outcropping of tall trees with narrow trunks and leaves shaped like needles.

Zachary reached for a limb and pulled the leaves off. He lifted them to his nose and inhaled the refreshing scent. "Aaron, come over here and smell the leaves of these trees. They smell clean. Do you think Rebecca would like to have some?"

Aaron smelled the pine needles and pulled them off several limbs then took a handkerchief from his pocket to wrap them in. "I know she will. She'll probably figure out a way to make medicine or soap."

Brent guffawed and snorted. "Damn, Zachary, you haven't been gone but a couple of hours and you're already missing Rebecca."

"Damn right, I miss her. You can't tell me you aren't missing Sally."

Brent mumbled something and pulled a folded map from his pocket. He held it up in front of him, comparing the drawings with the terrain. "Guess you're right. Colonel Wilson and I traveled the pass last year, but we think there is a better way to get through it. There's a path around here that will make the trek easier, though still difficult at times. We'll need to find areas that won't tear the wagons up. Whichever path we choose needs to have forage and water. Let's move on."

Turning east they passed through a prairie of lush grasses patched with sporadic areas of dirt dotted with cactus. The landscape mesmerized them. The mountains in the distance loomed higher than imagined, their beauty indescribable. The colors ranged from brown to red to purple to gray, with the tops of the tallest ones covered in snow.

Aaron pulled Misty to a stop. "I've never seen anything so pretty. I bet we'll find that pass soon."

"Well, I don't know about finding it. Nothin' we can do but keep riding" Brent clucked his tongue, urging his horse into a trot. Zachary and Aaron spurred their horses to catch up.

Several hours later, a clear flowing river came into view. Trees lined the banks on the south side. Zachary leaned into the saddle to stretch his back. "Hard to imagine it will be more spacious and plentiful in the Oregon Territory. Rebecca's aunt and uncle went out there last year. They have nothing but grand things to say." He dismounted and stooped to fill his canteen and let Red drink. "This is a good place to eat and rest the horses."

"I can't wait to get there." Aaron jumped from Misty and pulled three biscuits from his saddlebag.

"Slow down there. Make your food last. We'll follow this river. See if it could be wide enough and long enough for the wagons to pass through. Colonel Wilson said we would probably find it within a day or two."

After they'd eaten and rested, they remounted and got back on the trail. The three men rode abreast. The pass was so broad there were no discernable boundaries.

Zachary stood in his stirrups and whistled. "It is vast."

"It's too quiet out here. I miss the noise of the wagon train. How far away from them do you think we are?" Aaron watched everything within sight.

"What are you looking for?" Zachary asked.

"Oh, nothin'."

Zachary reached across to squeeze Aaron's shoulder. "He's not out here. No telling where he is, but he's not near us."

"Why do you think that?"

"You're searching for your no-good-for-nothing Pa. You're afraid of finding him."

"I'm mostly afraid of him finding Rebecca. I know he would do something to hurt her. He's bad." Aaron's voice tightened.

"Don't forget the colonel is there along with other

men and women who will be watching. You probably don't realize it, but most people believe your pa killed your ma. I know you do. I do. Rebecca does. Remember what he did to Jack Farris? He left him for dead." Zachary leaned over and pressed Aaron's shoulder again. Secretly, the fear of Silas finding Rebecca haunted him.

Brent rode over. "What's going on over here? Aaron, you all right?"

"I'm fine. Just kind of worried, but Zachary said everything would work out. He's right."

"Yeah. Catch me." Zachary kicked Red into a gallop.

Aaron kicked Misty and caught up with Zachary. He pumped his fist in the air. "Got you."

Brent rode up to them shaking his head. "We should take care of our horses. No need to run them in."

"Yes, sir." Aaron ducked his head and sucked in a breath. "My ma loved this little mare, it's my job to take care of her and here I am, running her for no reason other than a game of chase."

Zachary laughed so hard he almost fell out of the saddle. "He's just playing you."

Brent grinned at Aaron. "Zachary's right, I'm messing with you, but we do need to take care of the horses. We'll ride another two hours, then stop for the night."

At the end of the day, they had ridden eight hours. Brent chose a spot beneath a stand of trees with plenty of water and forage. "Time to call it a day. Rub your horses down and hobble them near the stream. Aaron, how about building a fire? Zachary, shoot a rabbit for supper or we'll have to settle for biscuits and jerked meat."

Within moments, a sizzling rabbit on a spit roasted

over the roaring fire. A sense of peace surrounded the area. Zachary picked up his guitar and strummed the strings. The makeshift peaceful melody relaxed them.

Brent wiped his fingers on his pants and leaned against his saddle. "I don't much think we're on the right track here. Tomorrow we'll head west and find the passage. Any thoughts?"

"I noticed the rocks were heavier and often blocked parts of the trail we were on earlier. I had to guide Red around some of them. The big rocks are dangerous, and the small pebbles could work their way into horseshoes. Last thing we need is lame horses or oxen teams. Aaron, you're quiet." Zachary propped his guitar on a fallen log.

"I'm fine. I don't know what signs you mean or anything about the pass other than it being wide. I want to be helpful."

"Aaron, you're along to learn. Hell, I'm learning. Colonel Wilson believes you could be a good scout. He wants you to experience new things. You've had a rough time. What with your ma and pa and all." Zachary's voice was tight with the emotion he felt for the young man. Sarah and Rebecca had decided to take the boy in as their own. He didn't know if he would have been as brave as Aaron.

Brent pulled a sack of tobacco and papers from his shirt. He rolled a cigarette and lit it with a stick from the fire. He sucked in the smoke and exhaled. "Sometimes we face struggles in life. I was orphaned when I was twelve. Didn't have any brothers or sisters. They all died before I was old enough to remember them. Colonel Wilson passed through when I was working for the blacksmith. He took me in and raised me on the trail with him. I owe him my life. And now I'm going to marry

Sally."

"Yeah, my brothers and sister died. That's when Pa got mean. We lost our farm and everything on it." Aaron swallowed hard and covered his eyes.

Zachary edged closer to the boy. "I know things have been tough. Wish I could help you more. You will always have a home with Rebecca and Sarah, even me."

Aaron wiped his nose on his sleeve.

****

"I'm going to check the horses." Brent covered his mouth in a strangled cough, stood, and walked away before his emotions took control. *Damn, that poor boy's been through more than I ever did.*

The horses were skittish, but they grazed. Brent climbed up onto a fallen tree and admired the horizon. An almost full moon and too many stars to count left him awestruck. He didn't see anything alarming, but he trusted horses. "I brought the horses closer to the fire. Something is spooking them."

"Any ideas?" Zachary walked to Red and replaced his hobbles before petting him and rubbing his neck.

"Nah. I didn't see or hear anything. Might just be because we're away from the wagons. Where's Aaron?"

"On the other side of that tree. He'll be back soon. Time to bed down." Zachary yawned.

****

The synchronized plaintive yipping and howling of coyotes combined with Zachary's and Brent's snores awakened Aaron. He hadn't heard coyotes often. Never had they sounded so close and dangerous. He got up from his bedroll, took an apple from his saddle bag, and cut it in half.

Misty nickered and pawed the ground. "Hungry?

249

Today we're going to set out in search of the pass again."

Aaron talked to her, held half of the apple in an open palm, and stuffed the other half in his mouth. "I think we will find the right place soon. I need to watch Brent carefully so I can learn. I would like to be a scout when I get older."

Zachary walked over and patted him on the shoulder. "I heard what you said to the horse. You're right about Brent. He's crossed this land more than once. This will likely be his last trek. He and Sally will settle down when we reach the new land. Now, we need to stoke the fire and make some coffee."

Brent poured his coffee and blew on it to cool it off as quickly as possible. The sky was pink and light in the east. "Sun's gonna' be up soon. We need to get back on the trail. Today we'll ride in a zigzag pattern to cover more territory and get a better feel of the land. Probably ride that way for several days."

Aaron spoke up. "Misty is saddled and ready. I've fed the horses. Just need to put some things on the pack saddle." He was surprised at the level of pride rising in his chest when he realized he was not only welcomed but appreciated as well. He had been a frightened boy for months. In a single day he had shucked off his boyish fear and grown into a young man.

The horses drank their fill from the free-flowing stream near the camp while the men filled their canteens. Zachary cupped his hands together and filled them with water. He drank from his fists then splashed his face. "This is some of the sweetest water I've ever tasted. Cold, too. It will be good for the wagon teams and folks."

Brent pulled a strip of red cloth from his saddlebag and tied it to a tree near the stream. "I need to mark the best spots so I can tell Colonel Wilson what our findings are and suggest the best route for the wagons."

"How will we be able to find the best spots after we go back? I mean, besides the cloth markers?" Aaron asked.

"I have a journal. I'm putting descriptions and directions in it so I can remember everything. The markers are also a way for the colonel to see where we've been if they get in the pass before we get back to them." Brent answered.

"Will we run across these markers on our way back?"

Zachary reined Red closer to Aaron. "I expect we'll see these sights again. Brent is careful about where he leaves the markers."

"How long do you think it will take us to find the best way through this pass?"

"No way to tell yet. I don't have the experience Brent does. He's been here before, and I think he can find the best way. As I understand it, the discovery of this pass was made by someone else a few years ago." Zachary whistled.

Brent rode closer. "What do you need?"

"Tell me more about the pass. How will we know if we find the best place?"

Aaron shifted in the saddle and leaned closer to Brent.

"Some mountain men discovered it. The pass has become important to wagon trains in the past couple of years. It's faster and has water and forage. I heard the best parts are on the west side. We'll find out. I don't think we have to ride the complete pass, just get a good measure."

"Is that why we're going in a zigzag?" Aaron asked.

"We cover more territory that way. I imagine we'll only have to be out here a few more days before we meet up with the wagons." Brent pulled a bandana from his pocket and wiped his face.

"Just going to get us back to Rebecca and Sally sooner." Zachary laughed out loud at his own joke.

Aaron chuckled at his love-struck companions. "I don't have no girlfriend, but I will be glad to get back to some good food."

****

The quiet comfort of being with friends was a blessing. Brent continued to lead the way with Zachary and Aaron beside him. It was cooler in the pass, but not cold. Birds called, some screeching, some sweet sounds. White clouds reminded him of the fluffy batting in quilts. The changing colors of the mountains in the distance made him think about his mother. He wished he could remember what she looked like. Having companions on a scouting trip was different. He hadn't been sure he would like it, but he did.

On their third day, the mountains held a majesty not found in rainbows. They loomed in purples, the deep green of the trees, golden sunrises and sunsets, wildflowers showing off in combined colors of purple and blue, bushes with thorns and yellow flowers, and cacti dotted the land. "When I came this way with Colonel Wilson last year, the cactus plants bloomed immediately after a rain shower. I didn't even know they had flowers," Brent said.

Aaron rode Misty nose to nose beside Brent's horse. "What colors were they?" he asked, his excited tone reflecting curiosity.

"They were bright. Vivid. I've never seen anything like it. Deep pink, sunshine yellow, orange, and white. The colors made me think of my mother. She would have loved them. I don't remember much about her, but I do recall that she loved flowers."

"Yeah, my ma loved flowers, too." Aaron's voice cracked.

Brent turned in the saddle to see the way they came. "According to the sun, it's about ten o'clock. If we see any cactus blossoms, we'll pluck a few for Sally and Rebecca, but mind the thorns. They're small and deceptive. I think this would be a good place to cross over to the other side. I see a body of water ahead.

"Halt. I see something over there. Near the water. Let's check it out. Be alert. Aaron, stay close." Brent's voice deepened and took on a serious tone. He stopped once in a while to tie a piece of cloth to a tree or brush. They dismounted and led their horses toward whatever was on the ground. The closer they got, the more agitated the horses became.

Zachary pointed to the sky. "Vultures are circling whatever's out there. That's what's scaring the horses."

"It's a horse. Still breathing and kicking. Let me check it out first. Zachary, stay with Aaron." Brent ordered. He handed his reins to Zachary and walked over to the wounded animal.

Zachary and Aaron tied the horses to a tree. Something was clearly wrong. Brent had rocked back on his heels when he reached the animal. This was more than just a dying horse.

"What's going on?" Zachary asked.

Brent held up his hand and motioned for them to come over. Shock and rage colored his tone. "It's Jack's horse. One Silas stole. The damn SOB left it to die with a broken leg and still in the pack saddle. Move on, I have to shoot him."

Aaron rushed to Brent and put a hand on his arm, forcing the rifle down. "No. I have to shoot him. My pa left him to suffer and die. It's only right that I put him out of his misery."

Zachary and Brent shared an understanding glance. Their eyes flashed in anger.

Zachary pulled his rifle from the scabbard and handed it to Aaron. "You're right. This decision is a sign you're beginning to mature as a young man. Do you know where the best place is to shoot an injured animal?"

Aaron took the rifle and stepped forward. "Yeah. In the head." He knelt beside the horse, pulled its head onto his lap, dripped water from his canteen into its mouth, and whispered to it. "I'm really sorry you had to suffer so much because of my pa."

He gave the black horse one last stroke, swiped a tear off his cheek, and stood. The rifle report echoed through the pass.

Brent unbuckled the pack saddle and tugged and pulled to get it off the horse. "We might need this sometime. I'll see if there's anything left."

Zachary gritted his teeth. "The bastard wouldn't leave anything of value."

Aaron held up a piece of paper that had fluttered out of the pack. "What about this? It's a map of the wagons. Maybe the drawing of mountains is these that we're close to. Pa couldn't read much, but he could draw maps and figure out how to get places."

Brent jerked the map from Aaron's hand and scratched his head. "Why would he make a map of the wagons? This drawing makes me wonder if Silas has been following us from a distance. I can't figure out how he could do that without someone noticing."

Brent knelt to check prints at the ground around the horse. "There's another set of hoof prints and boot heel marks surround the horse. They show that whoever this man is, probably Silas, kicked the ground, walked around the injured horse, remounted the other horse, and set off in the direction of the wagon train."

They covered the horse with rocks to protect it from predators. "You did good." Zachary put his arm across Aaron's slumped shoulders.

"I think we should head back soon. Maybe day after tomorrow. This place has a clear stream and forage. Not to mention that we've decided to follow the pass on the west side. Hopefully, we'll catch up to them soon." Brent tied a strip of cloth to a tree where the doomed horse had fallen. He scribbled a message on the map and impaled it on a branch.

They rode for several hours without saying a word. Each lost in his own thoughts until Brent called for a halt. The horses were brushed and hobbled. The scouts ate a cold meal with coffee. Nobody had the stomach for cooking or talking. Aaron was the first to bed down.

"I can feel the crawl of that yellow-bellied serpent twisting in my gut. Silas is out there somewhere. He won't give up his unholy quest to take Aaron and Rebecca," Zachary whispered.

"Yeah. Silas is a cruel man with something up his sleeve. Something no good. Something deadly. We're going to keep on doing what we came to do and stay aware." Brent poured water over the fire he had built. The logs fizzled for an instant, then burned brighter.

****

Silas and the mountain man watched from the far side of a plateau as Zachary, Brent, and Aaron bedded down. "I'll get my son. I'll kill those men. They probably turned him against me. I'll get Rebecca. It's time for me to get what is mine. I hired on with those women, got nothin' to speak of for my hard work."

The mountain man snorted, picked up a jug of whiskey, and sucked up a mouthful. He ran the back of his hand over his mouth. "Man, I think you've got a streak of evil running up your yellow-bellied back. Hard work, you say? I wonder if you just spout words. Are you willing to fight if need be?"

"Hell, yeah. I killed my wife to make this happen. I want to have money lining my pockets and those Pierce women have plenty of it. I believe they have valuables with them. Money and jewelry. If they don't have it in the wagon, they'll have it at the end of the trail."

"Was that your plan all along? To kill your wife?"

"Nah. We had a dirt farm, barely kept us fed. Lung sickness came through, three of my children passed and the wife got sick, but she lived and was left weak. My boy became quiet and didn't want to have anything to do with anyone. We lost everything. Luck came along when we got hired to take care of the second wagon that belong to those women. I listened to folks talking about the land of promise. Didn't take me long to figure out I wanted to start over in the Oregon Territory with land and money. Having the Pierce girl as my wife is just a bonus." Silas laughed and spit in the fire.

"Yeah. Don't forget the whiskey you promised me. In a day or two I'll make my way to the wagon train. I'll get that girl and bring her to you. I might want more than whiskey for my trouble."

Silas chuckled deeply. "Yeah, be careful. Rebecca has a wild-eyed dog that will do anything to protect her. He took a chunk out of me. Kill that creature and you'll get more whiskey."

The mountain man grunted, unrolled a matted bear skin, and lay down.

Chapter 28

Uneasy Feelings

Rebecca was ready for Zachary to get back. She lagged behind when the women walked together to relieve themselves. Something wasn't right. She felt it in the pit of her stomach where acid boiled like a witch's cauldron bubbling and burning up the back of her throat. She coughed. The air, thick and humid, made it hard to breathe. Bolo walked beside her, whining at the slightest change or noise. She could get some time to relax and think if she went for a ride. *This is ridiculous. You've never been afraid of anything. Now, you're worrying about nothing. You need to get back to being brave and sure. Zachary would say the same thing.*

Evie waited for her to catch up. "What's wrong? You're pale."

Rebecca grasped her hand. "I don't know. My stomach is off. I haven't been resting. I feel unsettled, like something is going to happen. Don't say anything to anyone, especially Mother. I have enough worries about her. Even Bolo is acting strange. I hope Zachary gets back today. Colonel Wilson thinks they will get back soon. I'm chattering on, forgive me."

Evie squeezed Rebecca's hand. "You can talk to me. Always. Maybe we're just uncomfortable because we're facing another difficult part of our journey. I often wish we could go back in time. Back when Hans and I lived above Mrs. Woodham's boarding house. We lived in one room and were happy. Day after day, we shared our dreams including our hopes for children. I wouldn't have lost the baby if we hadn't been on this trail. Hans tells me we can have more children. He's trying to cheer me up. Truth is, I think he needs more cheering up than I do." Evie pulled a handkerchief from her apron and buried her face in her hands. A torrent of tears wet the embroidered daisies.

Rebecca curled her arm around her friend's shoulders. "You will have more children. I just know that must be true. It doesn't mean you'll forget the baby. None of us will forget him. He was born during a full moon, that must be a good sign. Not because the baby died, but as a promise for your future. I've thought of you and the baby during every bright night since."

Evie wiped her eyes and rubbed her fingers on her apron. "I wonder how many more trials we'll have to endure before we finish this wretched journey. I'm weary."

"We'll surely face more hurdles. Zachary said we'll cross through some desolate areas and mountains after we go through the pass. I wonder when they will return. I worry about Silas showing up. Even though it seems unlikely. I've never been afraid of anything, but I am afraid of him." Evie's chuckle eased the specter of sadness and pain aching in Rebecca's soul.

"Yes, I know you and I'm surprised you've become more mellow. You were always moving at a full gallop. Always afraid you would miss something exciting. Maybe Zachary has something to do with that."

Rebecca jabbed her elbow into Evie's side and giggled. "Maybe Zachary tempers my lack of ladylike behavior. He makes me feel like I have a partner. He doesn't expect me to change who I am."

"Oh, I know. I became a different person when Hans and I were betrothed and married. I can't imagine my life without him now. We worked together and became a team. I think you and Zachary will fit together, like pieces of a puzzle, when we reach the new land. I hope you don't lose the person you are now. Don't lose your sense of adventure or your dream."

Rebecca whispered, "I will always be who I am, just with Zachary. He knows about my dreams and the vow to my pa. We even want the same things."

Even though it wasn't night, a single star could be seen. "That star, I think it's the North Star, makes me think of my mother. She never tired of gazing at the night sky. I expect we need to get back to the wagons. Colonel Wilson will have some of the wranglers out trying to find us. He's so protective. I pretend to act like it offends me, but I like it." Evie smiled.

"Yeah, I know. Mother often watches the stars. She once mentioned having special memories of them," Rebecca replied.

The friends walked in comfortable silence knowing friendship didn't require anything more than love. Splitting off, they went to their own wagons to prepare for the day.

Rebecca untied the liners that separated the outer wagon canvas from the interior and shook them out. Dust flew. She sneezed several times. Sarah chuckled behind her "God bless you. And you're worried about me."

Rebecca laughed and turned, holding a panel of the

muslin liners in her fist. Her mother continued to have coughing spells that racked her body. Doc Randolph ordered the liners to be dusted several times a day. "If I don't do what Doc ordered, he'll have my hide."

Sarah wrapped the ties of her apron around her waist and knotted them in front. "I'll prepare the wagon if you'll get me another cup of coffee and a slice of bread. I put some water over the fire to heat so we can wash up. Not that it will do much good. I feel better since we've reached cooler weather. I saw you and Evie talking. Is everything well?"

"I guess things are fine. She and Hans are trying to move forward. Grief still haunts them. I've been feeling unsettled, probably because Zachary and Aaron aren't here. Sally misses Brent."

Her mother brought the bucket of hot water to the front of the wagon. She wet a corner of her apron in it and washed her face. "You didn't sleep well last night, and you crawled out early this morning. What's bothering you?"

"I don't know. Nothing I can put my finger on. You know me. Sometimes I overthink things. I'll be glad when we get started this morning, it will mean seeing Zachary sooner." Rebecca pulled her hair to the side, braided it, and pinned it in place hoping it would stay. She never could get her hair to stay where she wanted it.

Sarah stepped down. "I do hope the scouting team returns soon. Is Edward going to walk with the second wagon team today or will we be tying them to the back of our wagon?"

"I think we need to tie them together. Edward mentioned helping Mr. Garson with something and Ginny is always busy with Mrs. Garson." Rebecca shook her head. Mrs. Garson's incessant and frivolous demands sometimes seemed outrageous.

Colonel Wilson whistled to get the attention of the travelers. The men walked closer so they could hear what he had to say. The women and children continued to prepare for another long day on the trail. Everyone was reaching the point of utter fatigue.

Wilson stood on an empty barrel. "In a few hours we'll enter the South Pass. It's wide and about twenty miles long. There is water on both sides. The scouts are searching for areas with healthy forage for the livestock. Watch for rocks. Brent and I traveled the South Pass last year. We think there is a better way than the one we took. He's putting strips of cloth on trees and bushes to mark their path. At some point we'll see where Brent has decided is the best path. If you see any of the markers holler out. Wagons, roll."

Wilson stepped off the barrel and mounted his horse in one smooth movement. He kicked his horse into a canter and rode to the end of the line before turning back to the front.

Later in the afternoon, Rebecca saddled Glory and left for a ride. She wanted to write, think, and figure out how much longer it would be before they reached the destination every member of the wagon train was focused on. Sometimes she couldn't remember the day of the week. Bolo trotted alongside her with his tongue hanging out, making it seem like he was smiling. The mountains seemed so far away. Everything seemed out of proportion in this untamed yet beautiful land. She stopped at a place in sight of the wagons. "Bolo, I think we might be at the place where the South Pass begins. The mountains are up ahead, but it's hard to figure out how far away they are. I guess this is a good place to rest. What do you think?"

Goodness, I'm asking a dog questions. She reached over to scratch Bolo's ears.

Rocks of all shapes and sizes surrounded the banks of a stream. Rebecca took the blanket she had tied to the saddle and laid it on a grassy spot. She drank from a canteen and pulled a dried apple from the saddle bag. Within a few breaths, she felt lighter. Better. Her mind was clear again. The sounds of nature relaxed her.

A rock caught her eye. Among hundreds of rocks this one was long and narrow and flat and had a streak of something blue down the length of it. She picked it up trying to figure out what was embedded in the rock. *I wonder if this is a gem?* She tucked it away in her bag and prepared to write. A moment of intense sadness overwhelmed her when she saw the message from her father. *Oh, how I miss him!*

I think Pa would like Zachary. I hope he's proud of me. Zachary should return from the scouting trip soon. Hopefully today. Something is eating at me. Nothing I can put my finger on. Probably missing Zachary is all. Colonel Wilson has said the South Pass is large and that it climbs, but we won't notice it because it's subtle. I bet it will be beautiful. We'll be able to see where we've traveled.

****

The mountain man hunkered down behind an outcropping of rocks. Silas was right. The girl was a pretty thing. The dark bay horse was the finest he ever saw, and the dog made him wish he had one to travel with. Tomorrow he would show up at the wagon train. An innocent man on his way to Fort Laramie to trade pelts.

****

The scouts rode in at supper time. Rebecca had to laugh at that. *It's just like Zachary to show up for a meal.* She walked to Colonel Wilson's wagon to be greeted with a bear hug from Aaron and a kiss from Zachary.

"I'm glad you're home."

Colonel Wilson stood with Brent. "Did you find a better route? Anything out of the ordinary?"

"I marked a route. We should have plenty of forage and water. It's more of a zigzag than we took last year. We did find something disturbing." Brent leaned in closer to the colonel. "We found a horse dying of a broken leg near a water source. It belonged to Jack. That bastard Silas left it to die still in the pack saddle. Aaron said since his pa left it to die, he should be the one to shoot it. We were proud of him."

Rebecca sucked in a shocked breath and felt the blood drain from her limbs. She grabbed Zachary's arm, squeezing so hard he pulled away, then put his arm around her waist. "What did he say about Silas?"

"Listen, we found one of Jack's horses dying of a broken leg. Silas wasn't there. We never saw him. Rebecca, we're going to be watching for him."

"Please take me back to my mother. I'm glad you're back. Will you stay under our wagon tonight? Silas is close. I can feel it."

"I won't leave you. I won't leave Aaron." Zachary promised as he walked with her to the wagon, making sure she was safely inside with Bolo.

Chapter 29

A Visitor

The mountain man, Fisher, rode into the camp leading a pack mule. He acknowledged folks who watched him with confusion and wariness on their faces. Everyone was busy working on the wagons, taking care of their animals, cooking, or filling water containers. He remembered the contentment of being with people and family. His was gone. He left home and never went back.

The man Silas described as Colonel Wilson stopped him. He tossed a used plug of tobacco to the ground and replaced it. "Stop right there. Who are you and what are you doing at my wagon train?"

"My name is Fisher. I'm on my way to Fort Laramie to trade pelts. My old mule is feeling poorly, and I hoped I could find someone here who could check on her. I wondered if I could travel with you for a few days to rest the animals."

"We're traveling away from Fort Laramie." Wilson turned his head and spit a stream of brown tobacco out.

"Yeah, I know. I figure I could make up the time when my mule is better."

"I reckon you can ride with us for a day or two. Follow me. I'll take you down to Jack Farris. He's our farrier and probably knows more about animals than anyone on this train."

"Thank you, sir."

"I've brought this man to you because he has a sick mule. His name is Fisher. Told him you would figure out what's wrong," Wilson said when they met up with Jack.

Jack shook Fisher's hand. "Can I give you some coffee? Maybe a tin of beans before I look at your animals."

Fisher couldn't believe how well he was being accepted. A flash of guilt had him thinking about not going through with taking the Pierce girl. The thought of whiskey stopped that. "Sounds good. I'm hungry enough to eat anything. You wouldn't have any whiskey would you?"

"Nah, I don't keep that stuff around. Don't want the temptation. Tell me about your mule. She's definitely acting tired and weak."

"She's getting old. Been with me since she was just a filly. Lately she isn't grazing well. She doesn't lift her head much. Is it all right if I go ahead and take the pack off her and give her some water from that stream? My horse is a young gelding. Full of piss and vinegar."

"Yeah, she could use water. One of her legs feels hot. I'll put a poultice on it, feed her mush from grain, and give her new shoes. Your horse could probably use new shoes, too." Jack stood in front of the mule, stroking her face and scratching her ears. He moved to her sides and ran his hands down her withers to her hooves, then offered her a handful of grain. She took it without hesitation but chewed carefully.

"I got a rabbit this morning. I can cook it." *Damn, this was going to be too easy. I'll figure out a way to meet the Pierce girl. If she's as nice as everyone else, taking her to Silas will be a piece of cake.*

"Rabbit sounds good. I can pan-fry a few potatoes."

Fisher took the rabbit from his pack and cleaned it. "Do you want me to put my stuff under the wagon seat? I can hang the pelts on my good horse when we travel."

"Store your things in my wagon. I don't sleep in it. We'll do something with your pelts, but it's best to rest both of your animals. Get two buckets of grain from the wagon near the front. You'll have to let Colonel Wilson know I need it. I don't have a horse anymore. Mine were stolen. I walk everywhere." Jack handed Fisher two buckets.

"A horse thief? The worse sort of man. I'll be back about the time supper's ready." Fisher set out. He was friendly with anyone he met. No need to let others think he was here to upset anyone.

He saw Colonel Wilson walking toward two women and a man standing near a wagon. One of the women was the one he would trade off for whiskey. The man was one of the scouts. He and the girl were standing with their arms around each other. They were talking about having to shoot one of the horses Silas stole. "Excuse me, Colonel. Jack sent me to get some grain for my horse and mule. I'm sorry to interrupt."

"No problem. Fisher, this is Zachary Miller, Rebecca Pierce, and her mother Sarah. Fisher's going to walk with us for a day or two to rest his animals."

He reached to shake hands with Zachary. "Nice to meet you. I need to get back to Jack with the grain."

He smelled the rabbit before he got to Jack's wagon. His mouth watered and his stomach grumbled. He decided to enjoy having someone to talk to and forget about everything else.

Two days later Fisher followed Rebecca when she went for a ride. He followed her but he didn't have a plan. He watched when she tied her horse to a bush and settled on an outcropping of rocks. *Wonder why she didn't bring the dog?* "Miss Rebecca, it's good to see you. I was out enjoying the nice weather. Have you ever seen such a blue sky?"

"It is a nice day. Sometimes I like to get away but not too far. How is your mule?"

"She's doing better. Jack seems to be good with animals. I was going down to the river to check some traps. The more pelts I have at Fort Laramie the better I'll do with trading."

"He certainly is gifted. What kind of traps do you use? I've wondered about that. My brother used to set traps for rabbits with string around a stick or something."

Fisher knew his opportunity just walked up to him. "Would you like to walk with me to check them? It isn't far."

****

Rebecca made sure Glory was secure. "Yes, I think that would be interesting."

She and Fisher made their way around several rocks.

He pointed. "Just over there around the edge of the water."

When she bent over to see the traps, Fisher came up behind her, put his hand over her mouth, and pulled her arms behind her back. "Just come with me. I won't hurt you. Someone's waiting to see you."

Silas. Rebecca tried to kick Fisher. She struggled to break his grip on her. She wanted to scream, but her voice had disappeared behind Fisher's fist.

Her muscles weakened. Fighting wouldn't help.

They walked across the stream in a shallow place. Silas waited behind some trees on the other side. He walked out. Triumph and hate settled on his face. "Rebecca, it's about time we meet again. You know, I saw my son and Zachary with that scout in the South Pass. I knew when I met Fisher, he was my answer. I made a deal with him. You. For two jugs of whiskey. Go get her horse and I will tell you where the whiskey is."

"Sorry, Miss Rebecca." Fisher went to get Glory.

Rebecca had never been too scared to move. She stood as still as a tree on a hot summer day with no wind.

Silas twirled a rope around one hand, laughed, and leered at her "Guess you didn't expect this. Now, turn around. Figure you need to be tied up. I wasn't giving up till I had you. Your uppity friends can't help you now."

Rebecca stepped back and widened her stance. She braced on one side, kicked out at Silas, and hit him in the stomach, but he didn't fall. "You won't take me without a fight."

"You goddam bitch. I will take you and you'll like it. You fight me again I'll leave you gutted and raped for your boyfriend to find." Silas roared, drew his arm back, and punched her in the face.

Rebecca yelped, stumbled, fell, and hit her head. When she sat up Silas was rearing back to kick her. She raised her eyes. Silas glared at her with such rage-filled hate that shards of sharp fear made her stomach roll and spill bile. Her heart was beating so wildly she clutched her chest. The pain in her head escalated so fast she grabbed it with both hands to squeeze it together. Blood ran from her nose; she couldn't stop it. Moaning in pain and fear, she curled into herself. Silas kicked her in the side, laughed, and turned away.

Fisher came back with Glory. Silas waved his hand toward the creek. "You'll find the whiskey behind the two largest rocks in that creek. Now, get lost."

Fisher turned and walked away.

"What are you doing? You know Zachary and Colonel Wilson will have every man on the train searching for me." Rebecca's voice was little more than a weak whisper. She tried to give it power. She swallowed the bile burning her throat and spit out a mouthful of blood.

"Your boyfriend won't be able to find us. I planned it all out." Silas jerked her up and tied her hands behind her back. He manhandled her to the horses.

"Get in the saddle."

"I can't." Rebecca shook inside and out.

"I'll help you. Just stand still."

"And what if I don't." Rebecca faked bravery and countered.

"You don't want to know. Try anything and I'll kill your horse." Silas picked her up and threw her onto the saddle. He put her feet in the stirrups and took the reins.

"Like you killed the horse you stole from Jack. The one you left to die of a broken leg. Your son shot it for you."

Silas growled. He mounted his horse and pulled Glory's reins tight and far enough that he could tie them to his saddle horn. He threw his head back and laughed. "Hold on."

Rebecca gripped the back of her saddle with her bound hands. She had to press in with her thighs to keep from losing her balance. Her head hurt so bad she was afraid she would pass out. *What has he got in mind? Where is he taking me? How can I get out of this?*

Time lost all meaning. After a while, Rebecca began to twist the ropes on her hands. This way. That way. Tug. This way. That way. Tug. Just like her brother taught her. She swallowed a squeal of hope when she felt the knot loosen.

Silas turned to make sure she was upright, his expression smug and satisfied that she seemed to be doing her best to stay in the saddle. Rebecca kept her head bowed and continued to work out the knots binding her hands.

"We'll stop in a while to rest the horses. And…whatever else comes to mind." Silas laughed.

Rebecca's heart stopped, skipped, and started beating again. Fear gave her an extra boost of strength to finish getting out of the ropes. She had to free her hands, or she wouldn't stand a chance.

When Silas stopped, he tied his horse to a tree then ambled over to Glory. "Well, now, time for you to get out of that saddle. Let me help you."

"I don't need your help. I can get down. Out of my way." Rebecca leaned to the side pretending to wiggle her boot out of the right stirrup. She made sure her hands still seemed to be tied from where Silas stood. Lifting her leg, she pulled the knife from her boot, jumped off the horse and lunged for Silas with her knife. She stabbed him near the shoulder, but he wrestled the knife from her grip. Without a second thought, she jerked it out of his hand. Blood ran off her hand onto the ground, but she held it toward him unwavering. "I know how to use this thing. I will. I don't think you have what it takes to out-guess me."

Silas roared. "You hateful bitch. I'll kill you and Zachary."

A lightning bolt of fear shot through Rebecca. Fear for Zachary. Not for herself. She lunged again this time stabbing him in the belly. She watched him stagger to his horse, gather enough strength to pull himself up in the saddle, and ride away leaning over the horse's neck.

"Coward." Rebecca wrapped her hand in her skirt and stumbled toward the sound of water, then dropped to the ground.

Chapter 30

Rebecca's Return

Fisher ran as fast as he could back to the wagons. He rushed to Colonel Wilson. "Sir. You gotta help me. Silas has Rebecca. I tried to get her back. I'll take you there."

Colonel Wilson bellowed orders for his horse and two wranglers to come with him. Before they rode off, he told Fisher to stay near the front of the train, but Zachary came in riding double with Rebecca and leading Glory.

"Colonel, Silas got to her! We need to get her to Doc! "

Rebecca's face was covered in dried blood, her hand was wrapped in part of a shawl, and the front of her dress was stained with blood. "What happened?"

Her head bobbed up and down like she had no control of it. She moaned and kept her hands over her eyes.

"We have to get her to Doc Randolph." Zachary's voice cracked. He rubbed his eyes.

The doctor shoved his way through the crowd. "Make way, make way."

Zachary dismounted and helped Rebecca down. He laid her on the ground and knelt beside her. He pushed hair away from her eyes. "We're home."

Rebecca turned her face away from the sun.

"What happened?" Doc knelt on the other side of Rebecca.

"Silas got to her. Her hand is cut bad. Tied her to her horse. She's in and out. Her head hurts. She can't stand the sun." Zachary buried his face in his hands.

"Colonel, get Rebecca to their wagon. I'll gather my supplies. Zachary, run ahead and give Sarah a heads-up. Help her make a place on the mattress," Doc ordered.

A wrangler pulled the Pierce wagon out of line. The others kept rolling. Sarah straightened the feather mattress and filled a bucket with fresh water. She and Zachary waited until Colonel Wilson came into view, carrying Rebecca like a baby. Zachary helped him put her in the wagon.

"What all did he do to her?" Sarah asked. Tears coursed down her cheeks.

Rebecca stirred at Sarah's voice. She struggled to sit up and talk. Sarah brushed the hair off her daughter's face. "Hush. Hush. Don't try to talk yet. Let's get you settled."

Bolo bounded into the wagon. He licked Rebecca's face and hand before curling up beside her. Rebecca wrapped her arm around the dog and moved closer to him.

Doc Randolph urged Sarah to start a fire and boil some water.

Zachary offered to build the fire.

"No. I need your help now. I have to ask you questions while I examine her. Tell me what happened. Be specific. Tell me what happened to her and how long she's been in and out."

Zachary cleared his throat. "I don't know how much

time passed before I found her, only about two hours since I came this way. She told me Silas made a deal with that mountain man, Fisher, to kidnap her for him. For whiskey! They rode for a while, but she doesn't know how long. Rebecca said she loosened the rope on her wrists and surprised Silas with her knife and stabbed him." A closed-mouth, one-corner smirk crossed Zachary's face.

"Silas?" Doc asked, his voice incredulous.

"Yeah."

Doc grunted. "Rebecca has a deep cut on her left hand. Any idea how that happened?"

"Silas jerked the knife out of her hand, but she managed to get it back and cut herself in the process. She was passed out by a stream when I found her."

****

"I have the hot water. Is she going to be all right?" Sarah climbed into the wagon and settled on a three-legged stool beside Rebecca. She felt Rebecca's forehead with the back of her hand. No fever. *What happened out there?*

"She'll be fine. Make sure she doesn't stay asleep. The wounds on her wrists and hands must be kept clean and bandaged. Don't want any infections. When she's awake, give her sips of tea with peppermint. It'll help keep her stomach settled, so she doesn't throw up. Doesn't she have a history of headaches?"

"Headaches? Yes, not so much anymore." A new round of tears and absolute anger built in her chest, threatening to choke her. Sarah coughed and sobbed. She yanked a handkerchief from her sleeve to wipe her eyes and nose. *Silas did this? I'll kill him. And Fisher? Why would he do such a thing to someone he never met?*

Sarah shook her head in disbelief, then pushed the thoughts away. She couldn't concentrate on anything but Rebecca right now.

"Okay. Zachary, you can tell the colonel she's stable enough for us to get rolling."

Zachary left to do as Doc bid. He gave Sarah a few more instructions on keeping Rebecca still and calm, then followed.

Aaron climbed onto the wagon seat and peeked in the front. He took off his hat and entered. "How is she? I'm sorry. It's all my fault."

Sarah reached across Rebecca and patted a space on the floor, inviting Aaron to sit. "It is not your fault. It is the fault of your pa. Zachary told us what happened. This whole thing has been an ordeal for everyone."

"The worst thing is Rebecca." Aaron's voice dropped to a whisper. Sorrow, fear, and anger flashed in his eyes. He rubbed his chest where his heart lay and vowed to never see his pa or talk to him again. "Do you think evil can pass from father to son?"

"Rebecca will be fine. I'm thankful everyone is safely back. I don't know how to answer your question. I guess evil could pass if a boy is raised in it. But you weren't raised that way. Your mother took good care of you, and she was a gentle soul."

"I'm glad Ma wasn't here to see what he did to Rebecca. I thought about shooting Pa. She wouldn't have wanted me to do that."

Sarah wished her throat wasn't swollen shut. She squeezed Aaron's hand and coughed to rid herself of the lump clogging her airways. "Rebecca and I have been talking, and we want you to live with us when we reach the end of the trail."

Aaron buried his face in his hands and sobbed. Tears escaped between his fingers and wet the front of his shirt. "I, uh, I, I don't know what to say. Why are you telling me now?" he croaked.

Sarah mustered a smile for the distraught boy. "Seems like the best time. We just want you to know that we care about you, no matter what," she said while smoothing Rebecca's hair behind her ears.

Rebeca groaned. "Could I have some water and a cold cloth?"

"You're awake." Sarah and Aaron spoke at the same time.

Aaron rushed to get a cloth while Sarah held the water to Rebecca's lips. "Doc said you could only have sips."

****

Rebecca sipped, then pushed the cup away. She took the cloth Aaron offered, folded it, and placed it over her eyes. "This is nice." *Damn, Silas. He left me bloodied and bruised, but not broken. Never broken. Mother and I won this battle. We will win any other battles that cross our paths.*

Evie rushed to the wagon, climbed inside and bent over, clutching her sides. "What happened? Lord, have mercy, I can't run like I used to."

"Evie, settle in. We'll tell you the story later. Rebecca is going to be fine, but she has a horrible headache."

Rebecca grasped Evie's hand and squeezed it.

Relieved sobs shook Evie's entire frame. "Good, that's good."

****

Fisher cringed when Colonel Wilson ordered him to

ride beside him.

"I don't have the time or luxury of talking to you about what happened in private. Tell me the whole damn story. Including the part about kidnapping Rebecca for Silas."

Fisher wiped his hand on his pants. "Well, sir, I am ashamed. I ran across Silas a few days back when I was trapping in the pass. He told me he would give me two jugs of whiskey if I brought him the Pierce girl. I didn't know she would be so nice."

"How could you do such a thing to anyone? Nice or not." Colonel Wilson moved his tobacco from one side of his mouth to the other.

"I felt bad and was riding fast to get back to her. That's when I ran across the scout, Zachary. Damned if the whiskey Silas gave me hadn't been watered down and tasted like horse piss."

"Enough about the whiskey. What happened to Rebecca?"

Fisher tried to comb his matted beard with greasy fingers. "I ain't sure about everything. He sent me on my way. I saw him punch her. That's when I rode for help. Didn't make it in time."

"You are going to go back to your horse and mule. Rest them like Jack said and leave this horse with him. I have a letter for you to deliver to the commanding officer at Fort Laramie informing him about Silas and your role in this mess. Apologize to Sarah and Rebecca on the way out. You'll live with this the rest of your life." Wilson took a packet of letters from his vest pocket and handed it to him. Without another word, or so much as a handshake, he turned his horse and left.

Fisher walked toward the Pierce wagon. The closer

he got, the slower he went. He didn't know what he would say to Sarah and Rebecca. An apology wasn't enough for what he did. He knocked on the wagon seat and waited.

Aaron stuck his head out. "Fisher?"

Fisher jerked his fur hat from his head and twisted it in his hands. "I've come to apologize to Sarah and Rebecca before I get my animals. Jack is waiting. Might I see the ladies?"

"Rebecca is asleep, but I'll get Sarah. Stay here." Aaron ducked beneath the wagon cover.

Sarah stepped onto the wagon seat and climbed down. Her hands clenched and unclenched, undoubtedly with the need to slap him in the face. She pursed her lips and sucked in a deep breath. "Mr. Fisher, what can I do for you?"

"Well, ma'am, I'm here to apologize for what happened to Rebecca and for believing Silas. I was wrong and will never get over what I did."

"Mr. Fisher, you couldn't have known about Silas. You didn't know us. I imagine Silas told you terrible things about us. I was angry at you, I still am. It will take a long time for me reach forgiveness, but I will try." Sarah's voice cracked.

"How can you ever forgive me?"

"We are forgiving people, Mr. Fisher. I would like you to consider taking on the mantle of forgiveness. Be fair to the people you trade with. I need to return to Rebecca. Godspeed." Sarah turned back and entered the wagon.

Fisher found Jack putting another poultice on his old mule. "How is she?"

"I ain't sure she's going to make it. She'll get to Fort

Laramie, but you'll need to get another pack animal when you get there."

"I had a run-in with Silas. You'll hear more about it when you catch up to Colonel Wilson. I brung Rebecca to Silas in trade for whiskey. I had second thoughts. He hurt her. Zachary found her and brought her back. I don't want to talk about it no more."

Jack stood beside his horse. "Silas? You don't want to talk about it. I get that. Maybe you should talk about it."

"Colonel Wilson said for you to give me my pelts and head back to the wagons. I'll rest my animals a few more days."

"I'll leave medicine for your mule. Both animals have new shoes. It don't take no genius to know Silas took advantage of you."

Chapter 31

Back on Track

Rebecca grew tired of being cooped up. She appreciated the concern everyone showed with kind words, food, and taking care of chores, but kindness began to smother her. Curious, she picked up the hand mirror and held it with the back lying face up in her lap. When she finally glanced at her image, the reflection shocked her. Her left eye was swollen. She squinted one eye, then the other, testing her vision. The bruising must have diminished because it resembled a purple and yellow sunset, and the fresh bruising was black and blue. She hadn't seen it when the cuts and colors were fresh. The unchecked anger behind Silas's fist remained obvious. Her body ached. The bandage on her hand was too tight. She unwrapped it and wiggled her fingers.

"What are you doing?" Doc Randolph entered through the back flap.

"Loosening the bandage. It was too tight. I wanted to check my hand. My own knife cut me when Silas grabbed it."

Doc made a noise deep in his throat. "Zachary told us. Give me your hand, I'll fix the bandage. How are the headaches?"

"Better."

"Good. Take a break and get outside. No lifting or strenuous work. Wear a bonnet."

"How's Aaron?" Rebecca wasn't sure she wanted to know how Aaron was coping but she asked anyway. He had suffered the most. He was so young.

"He's keeping to himself. Spending most of his time with the horses and oxen. Talks to them all the time. It seems to give him peace. He will eventually come to terms with all that happened. Bolo stays with him."

Rebecca reached for a bonnet. "I'll find Zachary. Maybe we can help Mother with something."

"No heavy lifting. No hard work." Doc reiterated.

"I feel fine." Rebecca grinned and saluted her physician.

"You aren't fine. Not yet. But you will be. Find Zachary, he'll keep you in line."

Rebecca pulled the brim of her bonnet low to block the sun. She found Zachary at Colonel Wilson's wagon. She stopped to pet Red. He nickered and rested his head on her shoulder. The sun warmed her. The fresh air filled her lungs, allowing her to relax. "Good morning."

Zachary put the guide stick on the wagon seat, turned and grasped her hands. "I'm glad to have you here but does Doc know you're outside?"

"He does. I promised not to do much. Would you help me groom Glory and Patriot?"

He held her face between his hands and tilted her chin up. "I've been taking care of the horses. The bruising is disappearing."

Rebecca lifted the front of her bonnet. "It is. Kind of. I saw it earlier."

"You're beautiful. I've given thanks time and again because you are here with me."

Rebecca linked arms with him. "I don't know what I would do without you. I've been wondering about the South Pass. Did you find a path? I want to talk about that. I don't want to discuss what happened. I only want to speak about how I can keep the vow to my pa and about the future."

"I believe our future is going to be better than we can imagine. I want to stand by you. We're both strong." Zachary stopped and pulled her to him then bent to kiss her.

Rebecca wrapped her arms around him and kissed him. She was done holding back and wouldn't allow the expectations of society to rule her actions.

"I need to get you back." Zachary put his arm around her waist and walked with her.

Rebecca sighed. "It's surprising how tired I am. I never imagined I could be so exhausted."

"It will improve if you listen to Doc. You have more than physical injuries to heal. You were betrayed by Fisher and attacked by Silas. We can hash it all out when you're ready, just don't rush it."

After a short rest, Rebecca decided salt pork would be good to season the beans Ginny had soaking. She stooped and lifted the lid of the corn meal barrel and dug through the contents. Bypassing the treasured cups and handkerchief with money tied inside, she grabbed the salt pork and sliced enough for the pot of beans.

Sarah leaned back against the wagon seat and folded the clothes she was mending. "I think I'll ask Aaron to put my rocking chair by the fire tonight."

"I imagine it will do you good to get fresh air. I'll take this to Ginny." Rebecca climbed out of the wagon, stopped, and took a deep breath.

****

Aaron met Edward Thatcher near the wagons when they halted that afternoon and circled up. They led the teams to the edge of a stream where the oxen drank their fill.

"Is Ginny going to come to the wagon when she finishes her chores? Sarah wants to be with Rebecca. They probably ain't interested in cooking. I can help with the fires but I ain't much of a cook." Aaron scratched an ox behind the ears.

Edward grinned. "She's right behind me. She won't mind cooking a little more, but she would appreciate you building the fire."

"Do you think she will fix biscuits?"

Edward wiggled his eyebrows. "She made some for breakfast. Likely there are some left over. She's got a pot of beans soaking. I reckon we'll be having beans and biscuits tonight."

"I'll gather some wood. I hope Rebecca is up to eating. Doc is worried. I can tell." Aaron's voice cracked. He hated the way his emotions ruled him.

Go on ahead. I'll check on Ginny and Sean."

Aaron walked away with a long-legged, purposeful stride toward a group of trees. *I'll get as much wood as I can carry and go back for more later. We need to tie some to the wagon.*

Later that evening, Colonel Wilson ordered several men to gather at the front of the line. Aaron joined them and listened to what the colonel had to say.

"We're heading into South Pass tomorrow. Brent tied strips of red cloth on trees and bushes. Watch for them. We'll be climbing, but it won't feel like it. Remind others to check their teams' hooves for stones or loose shoes. Get fur coverings from Jack for oxen if they don't have iron shoes. Groom them when we circle up. Pad the yokes. Your wagon teams are still the most important things you possess."

The men moved about, sharing news. Excitement about the new milestone was measured with back-patting, laughter, and guarded concern about the effects climbing might have on the teams and the wagons.

The travelers were light-hearted. Landmarks on the trail marked more than the passage of time. They were evidence that the things they dreamed of when they talked about the end. The ever-present hope they carried drew closer. The cooler air and signs of time passing energized the pioneers. Laughter and spirited conversations carried on the wind.

The next morning, Zachary joined Aaron while he was yoking the oxen. "Have you cleaned their hooves?"

Aaron took a pick from his pocket, twirled it, waved it at Zachary, and grinned. "Yep, I checked. They're healthy."

"I'm not sure which path Colonel Wilson will choose." Zachary stepped closer and threw his arm across Aaron's shoulder.

Aaron dug the toe of his shoe in the dirt. "I will stay in the wagon with Rebecca. She don't need to be reminded, and I don't want to."

Zachary pulled him close for a moment. "You'll be all right. But that's a great idea."

****

Rebecca walked with her mother, moving forward despite a persistent headache. One step at a time. Tugging at the ribbons of her bonnet, she huffed and squinted beneath the brim. "The sun makes my head hurt, and I have to wear this detested bonnet. I don't know which is worse."

"I imagine Doc Randolph would tell you to wear the bonnet or stay in the wagon. It is nice out here. Pretty. Is this near the place where Zachary found you?"

"I don't remember. I don't know how much time passed until Zachary found me." Rebecca clucked her tongue. The oxen increased their speed.

"How is Aaron?" Sarah asked.

"Fine, I think. He and Zachary are closer. Which is good."

"My prayers always include Aaron."

"I believe he loves us." Rebecca's stomach growled. She laughed and was relieved humor could still be found in the simple things.

Sarah's voice dropped to a whisper. "He cares about us and knows we care for him, but he misses his mother. He feels guilty."

"He's lost both parents and his siblings. There must be a part of him that worries about losing everyone in his life. Silas cared once." Rebecca adjusted the strap of her bag, causing the journal to shift. Funny how something so ordinary, something that was as much a part of her as breathing, could remind her of the strength her parents passed on to her. She had been through more than most ever would. She refused to allow the pain she felt or anything else get in the way of making her dream, the one she shared with her father, come to pass.

Rebecca noticed Aaron heading toward them and waved. "Are you hungry? We planned on bread, cheese, and raisins for lunch."

Aaron grinned and walked faster. "Yep. We're stopping for two hours to fill our barrels and water the livestock."

"You get water. I'll help Mother." Rebecca massaged her temples and whispered an ordinary prayer. She stopped the oxen, loosened the yoke, and rubbed their shoulders.

"Just over that rise is where Zachary found you at the bank of that stream." Aaron took two wooden buckets from their hooks then stood close to her. "I'm going to ride in the wagon with you while we pass through this area."

"You don't have to do that, you know. I'll be fine."

"Maybe. But you're as close to a sister as I'll ever have. I'm ashamed of my pa's actions, and I promise he'll never get near you again. Not if I can help it."

Before Rebecca could respond, he walked off toward the water.

Sarah carried a basket of food over. "I saw Aaron walking toward the stream. I have jam for the bread. Little Sean will like that. Will Zachary be joining us?"

"I'm sure he'll be here. He's been checking on me every chance he gets. I, for one, am happy to have jam with my bread. You'll likely need another jar for Sean. That boy loves his sweet stuff."

A whistled melody and Bolo's happy yipping made its way to Rebecca. "That has to be Zachary."

She turned as he came into sight with Bolo bouncing around his feet. Relief and a surprising surge of gratitude overwhelmed her. *You're alive. You're loved. You're not alone. You're on a path to fulfill a dream.*

"Hello, ladies." Zachary grinned and stepped close to Rebecca, who attempted to make Bolo stop jumping on her.

"What have you done to my dog? He's wild."

287

Rebecca stood on tiptoe, kissed Zachary on the cheek, and bent down to hug Bolo, who rolled over, flashing his belly for all the world to see.

"Everyone is hungry. Where's Aaron? I thought he would be here." Zachary straightened the quilt and sat down, patting a space, inviting her to sit with him.

Rebecca leaned into Zachary and bumped his shoulder. "He's getting water. He still gets upset when he thinks about his pa. Can't blame him. As soon as Sean and Aaron get here, we'll eat. Aaron said he would ride inside the wagon if we go near where Silas tried to kidnap me. I'll do the same." The thought of Silas and his ugly intentions sent a sharp stabbing pain through her head. She sucked in a breath and tugged on the ribbons of her bonnet.

"Colonel Wilson has to mark the place where you were attacked on his map. He must report anything out of the ordinary at the end of the journey." Zachary grabbed a biscuit from Sarah as she laid out the food.

"Who does the colonel report to?" Rebecca asked.

"I don't rightly know. I reckon someone in the land office."

Rebecca sighed and rubbed her temples which throbbed madly. "I had hoped to get past all of this without any more questions or fussing. I would just as soon forget it. Guess I'll do whatever is necessary."

Chapter 32

Jackrabbit Stew

Zachary rode to Rebecca, dismounted, put his arm around her waist, and walked beside her. "It's good to see you getting out and about more."

Rebecca touched her still-tender cheek with her fingertips. "The fresh air and the routine are nice. I want to set a good example for Aaron. He's been through so much, yet he still plans for a new life. This morning he was laughing and talking about building a house and barn when we finish this wretched trip. I saw a sketch he drew of a round corral with a split-rail fence."

"I'm thankful both of you are safe. Maybe being young works in Aaron's favor. I know for sure he's a hard worker. Smart, too. Do you think he would draw more for us?"

"I'm sure he will."

Zachary stretched. "Reckon I need to check on things with the colonel. There's Aaron coming back with the water."

Zachary patted Aaron on the shoulder. "See you both later."

Rebecca exhaled, surprised at how relieved she felt when she was safe. She hadn't realized how tense she had been until the tightness in her shoulders and back disappeared. "We're passing that place."

"I know. I don't want to see it. Hope no one thinks I'm acting like a scared kid." Aaron coughed.

"No one thinks that. I told Zachary about your drawing. He wants you to draw the barn next."

"Really?" Aaron grinned and turned to a clean page.

"I heard one of the poorest parts of the journey is just after the pass. I wonder if that's the truth? What do you think from your time here scouting with Brent and Zachary?"

"Yeah, there was plenty of food and water along here, but we didn't see the whole pass. Nor did we go further. Brent said this part of the journey has a lot to offer, though, so we should be able to stock up before we hit the rough spots. Misty's bored. Want to go for a ride later?"

"I imagine Glory and Patriot would appreciate a change of scenery. Zachary and Mother are worried about my headaches. I won't let them keep me from doing the things I like. I think this journey is testing me and making me stronger." Rebecca untied the bonnet and tossed it aside.

"The pass is nice. You'll like the colors. We saw big rabbits with longer ears than I ever seen and huge hind legs. Brent called them jackrabbits." Aaron held his fingers in a V-shape and wiggled them over his head. "Probably taste good in a stew pot with a couple of potatoes. Do we have any onions?"

Rebecca began laughing and couldn't stop. She snorted, clapped her hand over her mouth, and waved her fingers mimicking Aaron. "We probably have an onion. It will be good in stew." She huffed, holding her aching sides. *Been too long since we've laughed like that. Good for both of us.*

Bolo commenced howling.

"What's happening?" Sarah climbed up.

Zachary stuck his head in the back just as Sarah started in from the front. "What is so blasted funny? You 'bout scared the life out of me."

Rebecca could only imagine what he thought about her and Aaron wagging their fingers over their heads and wiggling their noses. "Jackrabbit stew," she and Aaron quipped simultaneously and began laughing again.

Sarah grinned, crawled in with them and retrieved an onion and potatoes from a box tucked at the back.

Zachary shook his head. "Jackrabbit stew? Guess I need to kill a rabbit. Anyone want to come along?"

"We do." Rebecca and Aaron said at the same time which set them to laughing again.

"I'll saddle the horses. Seems like Patriot could handle a ride."

"I'll meet you outside." Rebecca had thought she would never laugh or be unafraid again. She was ready for a ride. She could see once again that it would be possible to keep her vow.

Carefree moments on the trail happened so seldom they became memorable. Rebecca rode Glory leading the way into the middle of the pass at a gentle canter. She patted the journal in her bag, making a mental note to write later. Zachary and Aaron rode by her at full gallop.

She laughed, gave Glory a kick, and passed them. Patriot raced beside Glory, matching her stride.

They stopped and shared dried apples. Bolo lay at Rebecca's feet, panting and wagging his tail.

Zachary dismounted and loosened his bridle. "I swear to God, Rebecca, you are so damned competitive.

Where did you learn that? Most young ladies don't care about anything but sewing and cooking and raising kids."

"You should know by now that I'm not a lady. You should also know I don't know how to sew. It's nice out here. How long will it take to get through the pass?" Rebecca turned in a complete circle with her arms outstretched. She wanted to take in the scenery, not to mention the gratitude she gave up to prayer. A few days ago when Silas attacked her, the same area felt like hell. Once again, adventure and thoughts of new beginnings stirred in her soul. She had grown tired and forgotten to remember the dream.

Zachary moved closer to her and kissed her on the forehead. "It's good to see determination instead of indifference and pain in your eyes."

"Yeah." Rebecca stood next to Glory and waited.

Bolo's ears stood up. He stopped, cocked his head, dropped to a crawl, listened to something only he could hear, and rushed to a small stand of bushes. He barked, bounced, and brought a long-eared, big-footed rabbit to Rebecca. He dropped the creature at Glory's feet.

"I once heard that a rabbit's foot could bring a man good luck. I'm thirteen, mighty near being a man, these feet will bring me plenty of luck." Aaron held the bloody rabbit up, leaned down and scratched Bolo behind the ears.

Rebecca grinned at Zachary and Aaron. "Lots of luck. A word of advice, my brother used to put the cut end of whatever he wanted to keep over a flame just long enough to sear it and make sure it was dry. The first time he skinned a rabbit he set out to have a lucky piece of that thing. He was impatient and didn't consider searing the end of it. That was one of his bloodiest and messiest mistakes. He never did it again."

Aaron laughed. "Reckon I'll have to remember that."

The three friends rode abreast with Bolo bounding in front of them, then running to the side and behind the horses.

****

Rebecca and Zachary rode to the wagon while Aaron carried the rabbit to the stream to clean it. Coming back to the fire, he held the carcass up high in one hand and the two hind feet in the other. His grin was silly and brighter than the fire Sarah started. The smell of coffee, onions, and potatoes boiling had his stomach protesting its hunger. Loudly.

"Smells good."

Sarah laughed, reached up and attempted to force a cowlick into place on top of his head. "Rebecca's brother, Joseph, had a cowlick as stubborn as yours." A vivid memory invaded her mind, forcing her to catch a breath.

Aaron spit on his palm and smoothed down the wayward patch of hair. "Won't do much good. It'll pop right up again. My ma said I was born with it. How long before that stew is ready? I'm starving."

Sarah shook her head and put the rabbit into the pot. "You're always starving. About an hour or so. Gotta let that rabbit cook a while, so it'll be tender." She handed him a slab of cheese and an apple. "This will hold you over."

Aaron took the snack and wandered off to play with Bolo.

Once the meat tenderized to meet her approval,

Sarah leaned over the fire and spooned up four servings. "It's ready. Aaron, you and Zachary have been watching that pot boil. I'll fix you boys some. Rebecca is probably just as hungry."

The four of them sat in a circle with the bowls on their laps. The only sound for a few minutes was moans of gratitude and some rude slurping.

Zachary mopped his empty bowl with a biscuit. "That's the best stuff I think I've ever had. Is there any more?

Aaron piped in. "Yeah, is there more? I killed it. Shouldn't I have more?"

Rebecca laughed so hard she couldn't hold a spoon.

"All of you are being silly. Yes, there is more. We won't have leftovers tomorrow." Sarah refilled the bowls and let loose with a most unladylike snorting laugh,

It didn't take long for the word about the new kind of rabbit stew to make its way around the camp of emigrants, and several men left to hunt.

****

Later that evening, Rebecca pulled her journal out of her bag and wrote…

I have no idea what today is. What an extraordinary day! We went for a ride. Aaron went on and on about something called jackrabbit stew. I've never seen such a big rabbit. Aaron saved its feet for luck. I had to laugh and told him about the time Joseph went hunting, but he didn't know he was supposed to sear the ends to keep them from bleeding all over his clothes. Mother was so mad at him. The stew was delicious. We used one of our precious onions and two potatoes in it. Word got around and most of the men set out to go hunting. Every jackrabbit in this part of the world is going to run and hide.

Chapter 33

False Bottom

"Garson, pull your wagon over, it's riding low on the rear axle." Colonel Wilson ordered. He waved the other wagons forward.

Mr. Garson pulled his team to the side. He climbed down, crossing his arms over his chest. "What is the meaning of this, Colonel? You have no right to pull my wagon out of line."

Wilson stood toe-to-toe and eyeball-to-eyeball with Garson. "I have every right. I noticed your wagon is settling low to the ground and your team is pulling harder. Wonder what's causing that? I reckon I know. Unyoke your team, let them graze. A wrangler will bring fresh oxen from the herd."

"Thatcher and his wife can do it. I don't do physical work unless it is absolutely necessary. You forget, sir, that I am a gentleman solicitor, and my wife is a lady."

"Thatcher is helping Sarah Pierce today. You need to unpack this wagon. The wrangler will help with the heavier things. Things you probably should have left behind in the first place. I figured you didn't lighten your load."

Mr. Garson stole a glance at Mrs. Garson, who sat on the wagon seat tugging on a pair of gloves and opening a parasol. "You are ill, my dear. Perhaps Colonel Wilson should let us move on and check the wagon later."

"I feel queasy today. Colonel, may I rest as my husband has suggested?"

Wilson rocked back on the heels of his boots and spewed a stream of tobacco juice in the vicinity of Garson. "You can rest with Sarah Pierce."

Mrs. Garson huffed. "I'm sure I don't know what you mean. Pardon me while I get a shawl."

Mrs. Garson's attempted smile was more like a grimace, tight-lipped and straight across. Her eyes were narrowed and as dark and angry as a spring storm.

"If there is anything else you wish to take with you gather it now. Time to get started, Garson."

"I don't know how or where to begin. What needs to be removed? Perhaps, we should simply rearrange the contents." Mr. Garson tugged on the lapels of his jacket bringing the edges close and buttoning it.

"Start from the back and move forward." Colonel Wilson took a stack of quilts and tossed them out of the wagon. A colorful patchwork pile of disarray landed in a heap, followed by a tapestry carpet bag. He removed damp clothes hanging from the bows of the wagon and draped them over the tongue. A hand-painted ewer and bowl tipped over, crashed, and shattered into more pieces than could be counted. A twinge of guilt sliced through him. *Dammit, my temper is getting the best of me. This was probably special.*

"This will be your fault, Colonel. My wife's grandmother painted that set."

Wilson climbed on the wagon seat and peered inside. "I'm sorry about breaking the bowl and pitcher, but it ain't my fault. It was an accident. Damn you, Garson, you're pushing my last nerve. If I was you, I'd get that feather mattress out of there, then work on the food supplies. I reckon we can figure out what's causing this problem."

"Shouldn't that wrangler be here by now?" Mr. Garson wiped his face and hands with a white embroidered handkerchief bearing his initials.

"He had to get another team."

"This is absurd. Why couldn't you simply replace the teams later?"

"Get me a pry bar." Colonel Wilson ordered.

"I don't know what a pry bar is. Ed Thatcher takes care of the tools."

"It's in the toolbox on the side of the wagon. I can't believe you don't know where the tools are." Wilson roared.

"Is this it?" Garson held the tool with only his thumb and index finger touching it.

Wilson jerked the pry bar from Garson's hand and commenced pulling up boards until he saw the proof he expected to find. "It ain't a damn snake. You didn't leave your law books on the side of the trail or in Independence. Get busy removing the boards and get to the damn books, you're going to leave them now."

He chose six of the heavy gold-leaf-edged, embossed leather books for Garson to keep and tossed the rest out. The gilt-edged pages reflected the sun as they ripped from the bindings and blew away in the wind. He would never tell anyone, but it bothered him to destroy books of any kind. He read every night. Mostly from the Bible.

"Do you know how expensive those books are? Do

you know how long it takes to become a solicitor?"

"Nope and I don't care. I left you six of the books. I reckon you know more about it than I do, but your oxen suffer with every turn of the wheels. That makes it my business. I'm leading you and a hundred others. Here comes the wrangler with a fresh team. I'm telling the boy not to let you put those books back. He'll make sure the old team gets back to the herd. Get an axe and cut these boards into firewood," he ordered, then mounted his horse and rode away at a steady lope.

****

Mr. Garson grunted and picked up the quilts. The sight of the ewer and bowl in shatters forced him to blink a few times. "What is your name? It can't be Wrangler."

"No, sir. My name is Jessie Kelley. I hired on with Colonel Wilson because I want to have land and earn a living." Jessie ran his fingers through his unruly red hair.

"How old are you, young man?"

"Sixteen."

"That's a nice age, but I believe you have to be eighteen to get land. Colonel Wilson knows. I wonder if you would help me gather up the largest pieces of the ewer and bowl that was broken? My wife will be heartbroken. I can try to salvage some pieces for her."

Jessie squatted down to gather some of the shards. "This must have been beautiful."

"It was. My wife's grandmother hand painted it for our wedding. She knew lilacs were her favorite. I hope we can display some of the pieces in our new home or office. Forgive me for rambling. We need to get things done and join the rest of our group."

"What is your job, Mr. Garson? You seem important."

"Thank you. I am a solicitor. Choosing to leave New York for such a place as Oregon was against my better judgment at first. A firm in the new territory asked me to join them. According to them, there is a need for the rule of law. To be honest, I'm not sure I would have left without the promise of a lucrative position."

"That sounds vital. I always wanted to be a businessman. Farming will be my lot. I got off a ship in New York and tried to find work, but that was almost impossible. One day I found a pamphlet about the new Oregon Territory. I took the few things I had and sold them to buy a horse. Then, I headed for Independence. I met Colonel Wilson almost as soon as I arrived. He fed me and arranged a place to stay."

Mr. Garson put his hand on Jessie's shoulder. "Young man, you can get an education and become a solicitor or businessman if you wish. We can talk more about your future. I will ask Colonel Wilson if he can spare you a few times a week. He and I don't see eye-to-eye, but I know he's fair to those who work hard. How much education have you had?"

"I quit at grade eight to come to America. My teacher told me I was one of her brightest students, especially in problem solving and reading."

"Take one of those books on the ground. It doesn't matter which one, we'll be reading from it. They're law books. I will introduce you to a new kind of life if you want to try."

"Thank you. Are you sure? Why are you throwing books on the side of the trail?"

"I had the books hidden in the bottom of my wagon. Colonel Wilson noticed it riding low and the team laboring. He ordered me to throw them out. He has no idea about the worth between the pages. Yes, I am sure about working with you if you are willing. You have initiative, which is a positive trait."

****

"Thank you, sir." Jessie tied the worn-out oxen to the back of the wagon and joined Mr. Garson at the front. It had been so long since he smiled with meaning. He wasn't prepared for the shock of it stretching across his face causing his eyes to crinkle at the corners. He had great expectations when he walked off the ship onto American soil. The future he expected soon became tangled in hope that died day after day. He couldn't land a job anywhere except the ones no one would take unless they were desperate. Irish immigrants were not welcome, and they were desperate.

Chapter 34

Westward Proof

Colonel Wilson called a noon halt and ordered Zachary to pass the word they would stop for less than an hour. "Tell the folks the days will be shorter and cooler as we progress and to catch up on any chores that need to be done."

Zachary raised his hand in a less than snappy salute. "Yes, sir. Will we stop for the night earlier than usual?"

"As long as we make progress, we can continue to stop after ten or fifteen miles, depending on conditions. Why? Do you have some place to be? Is someone waiting on you?" Colonel Wilson scrubbed his beard and caught a belly laugh in his hand.

"Now, boss, don't be putting words in my mouth." Zachary threw the reins across Red's neck, mounted, and rode down the wagon line. His favorite part of relaying messages to other pioneers was sharing experiences, laughter, joys, sorrows, and concerns. He hadn't set out to be the person entrusted to be a listening ear, but the job suited him.

He rode to the back of the line, dismounted and walked alongside Jack. "I'm checking on things for the colonel. He wants me to remind everyone that the weather and other conditions will be changing soon. He wants everyone to be prepared."

"Good to see you. Gets lonely back here sometimes." Jack took off his hat and wiped his face with a bandana, then pointed to the shimmer of a stream rounding a cairn of stones. "See that? You're going to see proof we have crossed into the West."

"Proof?"

"You wouldn't believe me if I told you. Be patient." Jack slapped Zachary on the shoulder and laughed.

"Reckon I have to trust you. Time to tell our friends that Colonel Wilson is going to push harder. Join me for nooning with Rebecca and Sarah?"

"Sounds nice. At the Pierce wagon?"

Zachary mounted Red. "See you in a bit."

The emigrants knew rest time would be shorter. The rushing water of a fast-moving stream whispered and rose in crescendos like music. Families gathered to fill their barrels. Livestock pawed at the water, splashing their bellies, and slurping their fill.

They heard a nicker and turned to see Jack riding in. Zachary stood to greet him. "Welcome. Food's not hot, but your belly will be full."

"Anything's better than a tin of beans and hard tack." Jack wiped his hands on the front of his pants and sat down.

"It's good to see you." Rebecca handed Jack a steaming cup of coffee.

Jack took the cup, wrapped a hand around it, blew on it, and switched hands. "Heat feels good. My hands get achy. You still having headaches?"

"Yes, it seems fatigue and nerves bring them on. How about you? You once told me you sometimes suffer because of the blows Silas gave you. He has ruined and hurt too many people."

"Yeah. I get 'em. Probably shouldn't ask this, but do you worry about Silas showing up? Damned if he don't still haunt me," Jack growled. He took a long draw of coffee from the cup.

Rebecca put a hand on her chest. "I hate to think about Silas. Truth is, the idea of that man does more than cause my head to throb. It forces my heart to stall before beating so fast it feels like an axe slicing through my chest. I can't shake the feeling he will come after Aaron and me."

Zachary leaned over and put his arm around her waist. "We all worry. I figure in this case it will keep us alert. Silas is a snake."

"He's a snake to be sure. A poisonous one. I'll take more coffee." Jack handed Zachary his cup.

****

Aaron overheard the talk about his pa. He hadn't told anyone how thinking about everything that happened because of his pa shamed him. He worried that others thought he would turn evil. *What scares me most is the way he goes after Rebecca. I don't care what he does to me. It don't matter none. I wish he was dead. I figure I should have shot him in the past. I had a chance to do that."*

Rebecca must have sensed he was upset because she reached for his hand. "Listen to me. None of us blames you for what your father has done or even for what he might do. You've told us he wasn't mean until your family lost your brothers and sister and the farm. I think losing everything made him feel useless and turned his heart to stone. Maybe even replaced love with hate. You have a new family. We love you. We will keep you safe."

"Thanks for caring about me. I want to tell Jack about his horse. Have you told him?" he asked Zachary.

"No, I haven't. I think you should tell him." Zachary motioned for Jack to come closer.

"Aaron, are you all right?"

"Yeah, I'm fine. I need to tell you something. When we were scouting the Pass we found a dying horse. Zachary said it was yours. One of the horses my pa stole from you. It had a broken leg and was left there to die. Pa didn't even put it out of its misery. I shot it. We covered him with rocks. I'm sorry Pa was so cruel."

Jack put an arm over Aaron's shoulder. "I'm glad you told me. I can stop wondering about him. He was getting old. His name was Titan. I think now's as good a time as any for me to show you something just over that rise. It's an easy walk and I figure it would give us a boost."

"I hope this is what you've been teasing me about," Zachary said to Jack and held out a hand for Rebecca.

"It is. Everyone ready? We need something better to talk about." Jack led the way to the fast-moving stream.

Rebecca stood on the bank. She put her hands on her hips. "What are we supposed to be seeing?"

Jack chuckled. "Just watch, you'll see."

Aaron walked closer to the edge of the water.

Rebecca turned to Aaron. "Do you see anything?"

Aaron shook his head. "Something ain't right, but I can't figure it out."

Zachary stroked his chin and tilted his head from one side to the other. "I don't believe what I'm seeing. Must be an illusion. The water is going in a different direction."

Jack doubled over and roared with laughter. "Yep,

you're right. It's here where the water starts flowing west. Not east like we're used to seeing. Colonel Wilson calls it the Continental Divide. It's proof we're heading in the right direction."

****

The sky was clear except for an explosion of stars showing off their bright lives. They offered more light than most moons.

It had been a good day. Rebecca wanted to sleep outside. She brought out bedding for a pallet, a lantern, and her journal. Being alone in the vast wilderness sometimes offered blessings few people would ever experience. Despite fatigue, headaches, fear, and unknown hurdles, she welcomed the adventure.

"Are you all right? I noticed you were out here." Rebecca welcomed her mother when she sat beside her.

"I'm fine. Besides, the stars are putting on a show. They are truly remarkable. Zachary came by to let me know we'll be taking the less treacherous route when we leave tomorrow. It adds a week, but it will be safer for everyone, including the animals."

Sarah draped an arm over Rebecca's shoulder and took her hand and pointed to a specific star. "It is nice tonight. Do you remember the first night of this journey you remarked how beautiful the stars were? I told you I would tell you about my stars one day. This seems like a good time."

"I remember."

"The first time I met your father I was at a barn raising for a farmer who lost his in a fire. The whole community gathered around that family. Most of the women brought food. When it grew dark, someone started playing a fiddle. Your father asked me to dance.

I didn't even know his name. I danced, though. Later that night, as everyone left, he asked me to stay. I agreed even though my parents weren't happy. Robert stood beside me and pointed to that star. The same one you were pointing at. He said we would one day find ourselves searching for it because it would be our guide. He even suggested we would be married. I told him good night and all but ran home. We married within weeks. That's the story of why stars make me happy." Sarah sighed and didn't bother to stop the tears that fell onto the bodice of her dress.

"Why haven't you ever told me this?" Rebecca sniffled, pulled a handkerchief from her bag, and wiped her tears away.

"Because it was something your father and I shared. Something that belonged only to us. It's time for that memory to be shared in our family. I want future generations to know about this part of our history," Sarah said. "Don't stay out too late. We have an early morning and long day tomorrow."

"I'll be in soon; it's cool out here." Rebecca pulled the quilt around her shoulders, leaned back, and tried to memorize the stars. She squinted into the night sky and traced the shapes and patterns with her finger.

Chapter 35

Fog

The muffled report of Colonel Wilson's rifle awakened Rebecca. She untied the cover and peeked out. She lit a lantern and realized only the things in the direct path of the lamp could be seen. Fog hugged the ground, defying the light to diminish its power. The animals were restless and milled about the confines of the circled wagons. Bolo jumped from the wagon seat and nudged her hand with his nose. She scratched his ears. "It's fine. I promise. Mother and Aaron must think it's still the middle of the night."

Her father once told her about this kind of fog. Said it was like a wall without any support beams.

Rebecca woke her mother and Aaron. "Take care getting out of the wagon. There's a dense fog on the ground. I can't see much, even with the lantern. Everything sounds like it's underwater or trapped beneath something. I'll get the coffee going."

Daily routines had been established weeks earlier. The same thing morning after morning. Lighting fires, heating water, preparing breakfast, and hitching up the teams. There was something comforting about habits, but she was short-tempered on this dark, dreary morning.

Rebecca recognized the fuzzy forms of Colonel

Wilson, Brent, and Zachary standing near the front of the lead wagon. *I won't have much time with Zachary. Maybe at supper.* Sometimes she frightened herself when all she could think about was Zachary and beginning their life together. At least she thought they would have a life together even though nothing had officially been said or done to make her believe her future was in the arms of Zachary Miller. She used to say she could do anything a man could do and be better at it. She still could, but it was becoming clearer that she wanted Zachary as a partner. Not just on the trail, but in life.

Aaron climbed down from the wagon seat. "This is scary. I don't remember seeing fog like this."

Rebecca handed him a buttered biscuit sweetened with a spoonful of honey.

"Thanks."

Rebecca took a sip of coffee. "My father once told me about this kind of fog. He was just a boy and got lost. When the fog lifted, he figured he had walked a mile or more in the wrong direction. From that day on, he stayed close to home when clouds hugged the ground. He had a bright white streak through his hair that day. I've heard being afraid sometimes does that."

"That's scary. What color was his hair to begin with?"

"Dark brown. I remember hearing about a young surveyor who was marking some land and saw a cave and wanted to explore. I think it was in Tennessee. Anyway, he dropped his torch and was afraid of falling into the dark abyss. After three days, some of his friends found the cave opening and called out for him. He followed the sounds of their voices and the light from the torches they held. When he came out his hair was all white."

"What caused their hair to turn white."

"I'm not sure. Probably because they were scared. We should ask Doc Randolph tonight when he comes to check on my mother."

****

Zachary bumped Brent's elbow as he handed him a cup of coffee. Brent spilled some on his hand. He waved his hand around and blew on it. "Damn, that's hot. Can't see enough to get this cup to my mouth. Can't even get a good breath. Feels like I'm drowning."

"Sorry about that. It's going to be slow going until this god-awful fog lifts. I've never seen such a thick, smothering haze. I figure Colonel Wilson will hold the wagons here for a while. Red is skittish. I need to check on him and get him saddled. I'll meet you over here soon." Zachary led Red to Colonel Wilson's wagon.

"Ride down the line. Tell everyone we're heading out late but be prepared to leave. After that, move on."

Zachary pulled himself up into the saddle. "Yes, sir."

The fog lifted about midday and the travelers were able to push a little harder the rest of the day to make up a bit of time and distance.

****

Doc Randolph met Sarah by the fire. He leaned in and kissed her cheek. "Good evening. You seem to be feeling better. I don't know how you manage to always be so beautiful on this never-ending trail, but you do."

"You're so kind. Fair warning to you. Rebecca and Aaron are up to something, they've waited all day to talk to you. I don't know what it is, but something about the fog has them perplexed."

"There's no telling what those two have on their minds. They come up with the strangest things. Here they are." Doc shook his head, laughed, and waved at Rebecca and Aaron.

"Aaron and I have a question for you. The heavy fog made me think about something that happened to my father when he was a young boy. He got lost in some like this. When it lifted, he realized he was lost and far from home. His hair had a white streak in it. It was dark brown before that."

Aaron interrupted. "Tell him about the man who got lost in a cave."

"I read about a man who crawled into the entrance of a cave to explore. It's said he wouldn't leave because he was afraid to move. He dropped his torch into water far below him. When his friends found him his hair had turned white."

What are they getting at? "What do you need to know? I'm not sure if I have an answer for you, but I'll try."

Aaron turned to Rebecca. "We wonder…we want to know…well, can being really scared cause a person's hair to turn white?"

Doc Randolph stroked his chin and thought about the question. "I think it could possibly be because we all react differently to things that frighten us. I suspect people who face something which frightens them to the point they can't control their fear, may produce changes in their brains, and that causes a retreat away from the threat. Maybe that causes the change."

"But if being scared causes hair to go white, why didn't mine change colors? I've been afraid lots of times.

Especially when my pa got so mean. Am I different?" Aaron asked.

Sarah caressed Aaron's cheek with the palm of her hand. "I believe your hair didn't change because deep down you knew you were safe and loved by your mother and us. We know your father killed your mother, abducted Rebecca, and tried to kill Jack. Those things have impacted our lives. We'll never forget them, but we are able to move forward."

Aaron turned away from the others. "My pa is still out there. He won't stop doing whatever he sets his mind to. That is what upsets and scares me the most."

****

Rebecca wasn't tired. Thoughts of Silas caused the familiar twinges in her temples. Her heart rate increased. She sorted through her bag, taking stock of the newest treasures tucked into the corners. Sharpening a pencil with a knife, she opened her journal. Leafing through the pages always calmed her no matter what. She wanted to write.

The days are running together. But I wonder, why doesn't everyone who is frightened by something or someone who hurts them have white hair? Aaron and I both suffered at the hands of Silas. In different ways, but we both knew we were safe when it was finished.

Chapter 36

Loss on the Snake River

The weary travelers reached Three Island Crossing. Brent had reported the water between the islands was shallow enough to cross, but deep enough in some areas to experience rapids and get into the wagons. Most of the wagons had been caulked with tar or in some cases, lard, to help keep water out of them.

Men stood on seats and wheels to get their first glimpse of the Snake River. Mumbles of concern hidden by bravado vibrated in the air.

"Don't seem so bad to me."

"Ain't nothin' to worry 'bout."

Rebecca and Aaron watched the wranglers handling the herd in the river. "You know, they call this Three Island Crossing. Sounds like a game of checkers. You want red or black?"

Rebecca rubbed her hands together mimicking a sinister figure she had seen at a traveling show. She started laughing like a lady and finished sounding like a drunk man guffawing at a bawdy joke.

Aaron shook his head and grinned. "I think you need coffee, maybe with a splash of whiskey."

Rebecca knew Aaron didn't mean anything about the whiskey. She knew he wasn't thinking about how

Silas used whiskey to lure Fisher into kidnapping her. She knew he wasn't thinking about how the mention of whiskey triggered the horrible headaches that made her head threaten to explode. She circled her temples with the first two fingers of each hand. "Since when do I use whiskey in anything?"

"What's wrong? You've gone white. It's another headache, isn't it? I'm so sorry." Aaron pulled a handkerchief from his pocket, wet it in cool water, and handed it to her. "I'm an idiot to even mention something from the kidnapping. Damn my pa. Damn him to hell."

The tears in his voice sent an ache through her heart. "It's okay, Aaron." Rebecca draped the handkerchief across her eyes. She was seeing stars and knew they would turn to double-edged daggers if she didn't lie down and drink a cup of willow bark tea. "Will you check the teams? Make sure there is enough tar on the bottom of the wagon beds and the water barrels. I must lie down."

"I'll take care of everything. Let me help you. Is this headache the kind that makes you faint?" Aaron's voice went from normal to an almost nervous screech. He took her arm to help steady her.

She stumbled. The headaches blinded her. Sunlight, any light, was intolerable. She covered her eyes and slipped into the comfort of the feather mattress.

Sometime later the wagon rocked as someone climbed inside.

"Rebecca, wake up. We'll begin fording the river soon." Rebecca felt her mother's fingers stroke her forehead, then cheeks.

Rebecca rubbed her eyes and opened them in tiny increments one by one. She moved slowly, testing herself. "I'm better. The headache isn't as severe, more like a lingering pain. Has Aaron done everything?"

"He has. He said to tell you to stay in the wagon if you need to. Listen, Colonel Wilson said the Snake River can be dangerous even when it's low. We need to be aware of undercurrents and sand bars. This feels ominous." Sarah's voice trembled. The hand she held over Rebecca's shook. "I don't know how much more danger we can take."

Rebecca took her mother's hand. "We can handle it. Zachary said Colonel Wilson suggested the horses be ridden across. He's afraid they would panic if they were tied up. I need some willow bark tea. Would you like a cup?"

"Tea sounds perfect, but I'll make it. I think peppermint and honey would be nice. Do you want some in yours?" Sarah eyes searched hers for the telltale signs of a worsening headache. She didn't clench her fists or rub her stomach until her mother left the wagon, but Rebecca couldn't control the rising nausea when she changed positions. The headache pounded in protest. She threw up in the chamber pot and lay back with a groan. She couldn't focus.

Her mother came back into the wagon with tea. "Rebecca! You can't do this. Not this time. Drink this. I'll ask Aaron to get Zachary. I can handle our team. Bolo will stay back here with you."

The sound of Zachary's voice comforted her. He would know what to do.

"Rebecca, I'm here. Colonel Wilson said I could stay near your wagon unless he needs me somewhere else. I'll be right here with you. I'll lead Patriot, and Aaron will lead Glory. You stay in the wagon, but beware, the movement might make your stomach roll more. Isn't there something stronger than willow bark and peppermint you can take for the headache?"

Tears escaped from the corners of Rebecca's eyes. She couldn't stop the flood of them. "I feel useless. I can do this. You know I can."

Zachary helped her sit up. "I know you can, but not this time. Besides, Colonel Wilson is having two wranglers cross with the wagons instead of the herd in case they're needed. Do you think it would hurt if you took some laudanum? Maybe just a small dose?"

"The laudanum is in that wooden box by the pitcher. Will you also bring me a peppermint? They're in my bag." Rebecca pulled a handkerchief from her pocket and blew her nose, causing her head to pound to the point she feared losing her hearing. She threw up again. She tried to apologize to Zachary, but the words escaped as painful whispers.

He brought her the medicine, a peppermint, and two wet cloths. "I thought you might want to wash your face and have a cloth to put over your eyes. I don't believe you'll suffer from these terrible headaches once we get to the Oregon Territory. We won't have to worry about the things that bother us out here. We'll be busy living our dream."

"I choose to believe I can live without headaches in Oregon, but I wish I could get rid of them now. Doc Randolph says stress causes them." Rebecca measured a small dose of laudanum in a spoon and swallowed it. The bitterness caused her to shake her head. Funny how a simple reflex could cause more pain.

Zachary leaned over and kissed her on the forehead. "I'll tell him about this one. I'm sure he'll come ride with

316

y'all. You rest now." He tucked the quilt around her and left.

Lethargy cocooned Rebecca in warmth as the medicine took effect, but not so much that she didn't hear the fear and guilt in Aaron's voice when he asked Zachary how she was.

"I was joking and said the word 'whiskey.' It made her remember."

Compassion echoed in Zachary's tone. "I'm sure there's more to her headaches than that. Rebecca trusts you with the wagon and the animals. She took some laudanum and finished the tea. I expect she'll be asleep in a few minutes. I hope so. I need to get back to the colonel and ask if Doc Randolph can come ride with you."

****

Colonel Wilson had reached the point of dread when he told the folks about the dangers of crossing. He prayed none of them turned a deaf ear. Not this time. Fording the Snake River at Three Island Crossing was one of the most treacherous parts of the trip. Even when the water was low, it was deceptive. He stayed in his wagon to smoke part of a cigar. Wasn't much left of this one.

He climbed on top of a barrel, whistled, put a plug of tobacco in his cheek, and got the attention of the folks. It didn't take long for most of them to turn his way. "Mornin', folks, you're probably tired of hearing me talk about the hazards on this trail. The threat is real. The Snake River is a mean old harlot. Even though the water is low there will be shifting sand bars that can hold the wheels of a wagon in a tight grip or the damn stuff can suck animals, people, or wagons down if it's quicksand. There's also going to be places where the water is turbulent and rapid.

"Ride your saddle horses. Being tied to the wagon could drown them. At some point we will likely need to bind several wagons and teams together to keep them from drifting or being swept away. All of you, whether you're on a horse or on a wagon seat, should have a rope at the ready.

"Brent's been across. He thinks we can make it to the other side without too much trouble. We'll cross the first and second island, then turn upriver. The animals might have to swim at this point. There will be food and water on the north side when we get there. We'll lay by for two days. Questions?"

None of the emigrants had a question. They were afraid but tried not to show it. Men cleared their throats and coughed. Women smoothed their hair and tied their bonnet ribbons tighter. Children remained silent.

"Let's roll." Colonel Wilson nudged his horse into the cold water, leading the way for the others. The river was less than a foot deep and calm. He reined away, turned the horse, and watched the first few wagons pass. The animals and folks had calmed down. *They need to have their wits about them. Animals follow calm people. People follow calm people.*

Brent rode up beside Wilson and tipped his hat. "Sir, there's a large sandbar about twenty yards ahead. Have the folks veer to the left in ten yards. I'll wait there to lead them past it. Things are clear after that except for patches of swift water between the islands. It's not too bad. Zachary can ride down the line."

"I'll tell everyone. Rebecca is ill. One of those headaches. I want Zachary close to their wagon."

"Damn. Who's working with their horses?" Brent

took his hat off and laid it across the saddle horn. He pushed his fingers through his hair, leaving it standing on end.

"Aaron and a wrangler I pulled from the herd." Wilson tugged his hat down and turned his horse in the direction of the Pierce wagon.

****

Zachary rode ahead of Sarah's wagon to meet him when Wilson approached, then turned around to relay the colonel's message. "Brent brought an update. He said there's a sandbar a few yards ahead. He'll wait and guide the wagons away from it. Might want Aaron to ride at the head of the oxen when we veer to the side. Has Rebecca stirred?"

"No, she's still asleep. I imagine she'll declare herself fit to ride when she awakens. I've been praying these headaches stop. She isn't going to like it when I tell her Doc said she must stay in the wagon until we reach the other side."

Zachary chuckled. "You're right, she won't like it one bit. I'll be thankful when she realizes Silas isn't hiding behind every rock. All we can do is love and support her. I'll tell Aaron and the wrangler about the changes before I move along to see if I can be of service to someone else. You must be strong. For her." Zachary leaned across Red's neck and squeezed Sarah's hand. He tipped his hat and reined around.

****

The wagon jerked, forcing Rebecca awake. Dizziness and the splintering headache kept her from sitting up. Something else woke her. Horses? Oxen? Shouting? Splashing? She heard Zachary telling Aaron to stay with the lead oxen. She scooted closer to the wagon seat. "Mother? What is wrong?"

Sarah pulled the flap of the canvas to the side and climbed into the back. "Rebecca, what are you doing? You should be lying down."

Rebecca kept her eyes shut tight. She held her head between her palms. "Who's on the wagon with you? What is wrong? The animals are upset. I heard Glory. I need to check on the horses."

She felt her mother's hands on her shoulders. "The horses are fine. A little frightened of the water, I think. Doc Randolph is with me, and you have been ordered by him to stay in here. Zachary is going to help me put a few things up higher. Just in case water gets inside."

Rebecca focused on the words. "What do you mean? Water in the wagon? Where is Zachary?"

Zachary climbed in. "I'm here. There's nothing to worry about. We're crossing from the first island to the second one. The animals are hesitant. Brent said we most likely wouldn't get water in the wagon. He just wants us to stay prepared."

Rebecca dropped her chin to her chest and rubbed both eyes with the tips of her fingers. The throbbing worsened. *These headaches are likely to keep me from doing what I love. They may even make Zachary regret falling in love with me. Should I talk to him about it? I will not saddle him with a sick woman. What if I can't keep my vow? What would I do?* "I need to lie down. Mother, will you make some tea with five drops of laudanum?"

"I will. Zachary, can you sit with her for a few more minutes?"

Her fears eased when Zachary took her hand and kissed her palm. He wiped her face with a cool rag and put pillows around her. "I love you. We'll lay by for two days on the north side. That should help you."

Rebecca groaned and squeezed his hand.

Sarah returned with a cup of beef broth laced with willow bark, honey, and laudanum. She helped Rebecca wrap her fingers around the cup. "Sip this while I freshen the bedding."

Rebecca couldn't believe how heavy the cup seemed. She spilled some on her bodice. "Mother, I…I spilled."

Sarah took the cup and held it to Rebecca's quivering lips. "I'm beyond thankful Doc is riding with us so I can stay with you unless I'm needed out there. Don't worry about such small things as spilling."

****

Crossing the unpredictable Snake River between islands seemed easy enough, but it was as deceptive as a snake-oil salesman. Within a few yards, Brent's horse lost her footing in a spot of fast swirling water and fell. Brent jumped out of the saddle and helped get the animal out of the tornado-like eddy.

"Come on, girl. Let's get you away from this mess." He held the reins near her head and moved like thick cold molasses through rapids up to his waist. When he reached calmer water, he took a while to catch his breath and let his horse settle.

Zachary rode over to help him. "Anything I can do? There doesn't seem to be any more of the rapids in the next few yards. Want me to lead the wagons for a while?"

"Yeah, go ahead. I need to check Jezebel's legs and make sure she's not hurt." Brent bent over and squeezed the moisture dripping out of his pant legs.

"Take care. Anything else?"

"Nah. Thanks."

The river acted like a lady the rest of the way to the second island.

****

Colonel Wilson rode to check on Jack, whose wagon was the last to reach the second island. "How're you doing? You and your team are worn out."

"We are all tired. I don't think they will live through swimming upriver when we head north. I'm thinking about ditching some of my supplies. Smithing tools are heavy."

Wilson took his hat off, hooked it on the saddle horn, and rubbed his face between both hands. "What if I bring in eight more oxen and let a wrangler take yours to the herd? We'll be hitting the Blue Mountains soon and will likely need your skills more than ever. I expect we'll lose wheels, axles, and teams. Can you spare any tools?"

"Yeah, I have two or three of some and I reckon a few of the other men might have similar tools. We could check."

"That will work." Wilson whistled loud and long.

"You need something, boss?" A young wrangler reined in close to the colonel's horse.

"Yeah, take these four oxen to the herd and bring back eight more with yokes. Jack has to wait here while he rests. When you come back, help him drive the team upriver. His oxen were heaving and exhausted from pulling too heavy a load. Ask around about the tools some of the men brought with them, specifically smithing tools. Jack may have to leave some of his behind."

"Yes, sir." The wrangler tipped his hat to the colonel and Jack.

"I'll get back now." Wilson reined Buck around to catch up with the others.

Colonel Wilson stood in his stirrups and whistled as he approached the weary group. "Listen up, folks. Before we head upriver, I want you to tie your wagons together as securely as possible. Run the ropes along each side of your wagon and stabilize them on the next one. Put six wagons in a row and tie your teams to the one in front of you. We'll move forward with one group at a time. When the group in front of yours are about one hundred yards ahead, move in. There will be places where the water will be rapid and other places that are deep enough the teams will have to swim. Be prepared. I'll give you an hour to get ready. Questions?" He held a hand over his eyes while he waited to find out if anyone had questions.

Ed Thatcher waved. "Colonel, who will show us how to tie the wagons together?"

Wilson shrugged his shoulders all the way to his ears. "That would be me. You're in that first group so you can learn and help others. We'll start by tying mine and Red O'Reilly's chuck wagon to Doc Randolph's, Sarah, and Rebecca's. Yours will be fifth, followed by the Garsons."

****

"Yes, sir." Ed was usually the one who had to wait on the Garsons. Today would be his chance to prove he was as capable as any man to help. He had grown fond of the Garsons, but most of the time felt like he was invisible. Ginny had said the same thing one night.

"Ginny, where are you?"

"I'm here, in our wagon."

Ed opened the back cover. "I have some news. Colonel Wilson is having the wagons and teams tied together before we go into the river again. He's going to show me how to do it and let me help others."

"Why are the wagons being tied together? Seems dangerous."

"It's supposed to be safer for us and the animals. He said we may hit some rapids and deeper water. Where is Sean going to be?" He didn't want Ginny to know he was worried.

"It's good that you're helping the colonel. Don't you worry about Sean. He's going to be on the seat next to me. I'm even thinking about tying him to me in some fashion. Would that be too dangerous?" Ginny's voice cracked, betraying the brave face she'd offered Ed a moment ago.

"That boy ain't going to let you out of arm's reach. He'll be right beside you. He's old enough to understand danger, isn't he? He'll soon be three years old."

"I think he'll be fine. I just worry. Besides he's been around Jeb Slaton too much. That boy is a bad example. He's funny, though. See if I've put things up high enough. I heard the water could get in the wagon beds. Is that true?"

Ed kissed Ginny on the cheek. "Everything's fine. I'm not too worried about water getting in. I need to get back to the colonel. We'll be fifth in line. I'll be back when it's time to tie our wagon to Rebecca's."

****

The first group of six wagons splashed into the Snake River for the precarious third part of the journey. Colonel Wilson, Brent, and Zachary rode three abreast, leading the way. Nobody knew what to expect of the trip upriver, but they knew a land with feed, water, and rest lay ahead. A collective sigh of relief sounded when the wagons touched solid ground. The men watched as the second group drew near and the third entered the water.

A man shouted. A woman screamed. Colonel Wilson whirled around and rode into the water to see what was happening. It was the quiet couple, Mr. and Mrs. Lawson.

"Help us. We must be untied from this group!" They were reaching for something in the water, something that frightened them. *They have a young daughter.* He spurred Buck to move as fast as he could.

Colonel Wilson rode alongside the wagon. "What is it? What's wrong? I can't stop the teams, they would drown."

The couple sobbed. After a few long seconds the man pulled his wife closer to his side. Tears and snot mixed and marred his face. "Sir. Our daughter, Sadie…"

Mrs. Lawson covered her face and screamed a long, loud NO. "This isn't true! I'll check the back of the wagon again. Sadie's probably hiding under her quilt. She likes to play hiding games."

Colonel Wilson leaned out of the saddle and jumped onto the wagon. He grasped Mr. Lawson's hand. "Can you tell me what happened to Sadie?"

"Our Sadie was holding the cow's rope from the wagon seat. When the water became faster the cow slipped and pulled Sadie off. I yelled at her to let go of the rope. She said, 'No, Pa. I have her.' The last time I saw her she was floating downstream. She wasn't moving. I wanted to jump off and go for her, but I knew in my heart she was gone. All because of her pet cow. We must find her."

"I will have someone find her. In the meantime, I must keep the wagons moving. Please understand. When we are on the other side, we will honor your Sadie."

Silent tears, the worst kind, the kind without hope, coursed down the faces of the grief-stricken parents. They had their arms around one another, holding each other up. He spit in the river, cursing its spite.

Zachary and Brent met Colonel Wilson at the riverbank when he returned.

Wilson took off his hat and slapped it against his thigh. "The Lawson girl, Sadie, was holding the cow's rope and was dragged into the river when it slipped. The last time Mr. Lawson saw his girl she was floating downriver. Zachary, I want you to find her little body. She was only seven years old. We need to bring her back to her family. Word's goin' to get around fast. Brent, keep the folks moving."

Zachary nodded in response to the order and rode over to the Pierce's wagon.

Chapter 37

Burial and Betrothal

Zachary couldn't speak. He needed a quilt. Something to wrap the girl's body in. It surprised him to see Rebecca on the wagon seat. *She must be feeling better.* "You seem to be better. That's good. Listen, I need to borrow a quilt."

"You're going to find little Sadie, aren't you? That poor family. I feel better, but my heart hurts. Sadie and Jeb used to fuss about who should be in charge. I think they finally decided he would be in charge of the boys, and she would be in charge of the girls." Rebecca's voice trembled with sadness.

Sarah came from the back of the wagon carrying a heavy quilt. "I heard you. You keep that baby warm until you can give her back to her parents."

Zachary rode slowly searching for Sadie in every direction. The tiny thread of hope he clung to evaporated like morning dew on a hot day when he saw the pink calico dress floating in a tangle of branches. Sadie had been trapped. She drowned, but still held onto the rope around the neck of her cow. A part of Zachary was thankful sweet Sadie and her pet had died together. He would want to be with Red.

It didn't take long to retrieve Sadie's body. He

covered her face with the soaked bonnet he knew she was proud of, and wrapped the quilt around her small body. Balancing her across his lap proved to be more difficult than he imagined. He tied her to his waist. Damned if he would let her stay in the water anymore.

The river churned under Red, forcing him to swim most of the way upriver. Zachary talked nonstop to keep his horse calm. "I remember when Hans carried Evie and the baby. He said they grew heavier with each step. He said Evie was so cold she shook like a fall leaf holding onto a branch before losing its fight. Our losses and damages have struck through the quick of our hearts. Rebecca is improving. I think. I hope. I'll fight for that woman."

Red nickered and lunged forward when his hooves gained traction in the sandy river bottom. Zachary reined him to the bank and dismounted with Sadie in his arms. He began walking toward the girl's parents, who stood watching and waiting to hold their baby girl. He couldn't see their faces, but knew their fear was confirmed when he walked toward them. Colonel Wilson and Doc Randolph anchored them like heavy bookends.

Sadie's father walked toward him with outstretched arms and slumped shoulders. His face was splotched and red.

Zachary placed Sadie in her father's arms. "She was still holding onto the rope of her cow. It was tangled in the same brush she was."

"Thank you. She loved that old cow. This must have been hard for you. Mrs. Lawson and I want you to be with us when we lay our girl to rest. We haven't dug a grave. I reckon Brent and some other men have started taking care of that chore by now." Mr. Lawson swayed.

His knees buckled. He fell, and pulled the body of his daughter so close there was no space between the two of them.

Zachary put his hand over Mr. Lawson's shoulder. "I will be honored to stand with you. Is there anything else I can do?"

Mr. Lawson glanced up, touched the bonnet covering Sadie's face, scratched his beard, and shook his head.

****

Brent and Ed Thatcher leaned on shovel handles when the grave was deep enough to protect its precious gift…or package…or *something.*

But not life.

Mrs. Lawson inched forward then bent over the open grave. She laid a pink blanket in the bottom and put a worn-out rag doll on top of it. "Her name is Melon. I don't know why Sadie named her that. She's never gone to bed without her."

Friends of the family and fellow travelers gathered around. Some cleared their throats. Some cried openly. Some stood holding the hands of their own children as tightly as possible.

Young Jeb released his mother's hand and walked to the edge of the grave. He sucked up tears and snot and dropped a ball into the grave. It rolled over to Melon. "I think Sadie needs to have my red ball to play with in Heaven."

Mr. Lawson pulled Jeb close in a hug they both understood. "Thank you, Jeb."

Mr. Lawson put the rope Sadie had held in the grave. He and Zachary placed her in the crypt beside the doll and Jeb's ball.

Someone whispered the twenty-third psalm. Brent and Ed slowly returned the dirt to the burial place when everyone turned away.

****

Zachary and Rebecca sat beside the campfire. The firelight shadowed sadness and brought the sharp edges of grief and despair in exaggerated angles to their faces. They held hands and leaned into each other for the support only they could offer to one another. Bolo lay curled up snoring between them.

Rebecca stood and tugged his hands. "Let's check the horses. They had a rough day. Especially Red."

Stepping inside the circle where the horses were tied, they stopped beside Red. He nickered and put his big head on Zachary's arm. "I know. I know. It isn't supposed to be this sad, is it? I don't think this journey can take much more sadness."

Rebecca knew he wasn't talking to Red. She sighed and nestled her head into the comforting space between his neck and shoulder. "Yes. It's sad. Especially for the Lawsons. The one sure thing we've learned is that we can handle anything if we're together. We love each other. Sometimes it doesn't feel like enough, but it is. I've had more than enough time to think lately. I realized I was in danger of giving up when I was sick. On us and my dream. I decided I am too strong to dwell on the things or people who wanted to cause harm or interfere with our happiness, dreams, or the promise I made to my pa."

He kissed her on the head and stroked her hair. "Love is enough. I never doubted you would return to me strong, confident, and sure of what you want. Not just the promise but the future. I do love you. I know you feel the same way."

Rebecca turned and wrapped her arms around this man she loved. She turned her face up for the kiss she wanted. He didn't kiss her, instead he fumbled for something in his pocket. Pulling out a handkerchief he unwrapped a ruby necklace and draped it across his palm. The pendant flashed in the firelight.

"Rebecca, will you...will you marry me? Will you be my partner in every way? My wife?"

Rebecca stepped away and saw nervousness and fear in his eyes. Her heart clutched for one beat, then took off like a horse headed to the barn. Goosebumps popped out on her arms. She shivered. She placed a shaking palm against his chest and grabbed his free hand with her other one. When she opened her mouth, she could barely form the word. There was no sound. She laughed out loud. "Yes. Yes. I'll marry you. Of course, I will."

"Thank you. I knew you'd say yes. Turn around and let me put this on you." He put his arms across her shoulders.

Rebecca did as he asked and lifted her hair. "Knew I'd say yes, huh?" She laughed, spun around to face him, and received his kiss full of promise.

He continued to hold her hand. "I am relieved. I wouldn't have asked if I didn't know you would accept. I told you once that I would never leave you. I won't. I'll make sure we work together to build a home."

"We're getting closer to home. Everything will come together. For now, let's just sit and gaze at the stars. The moon is full." Rebecca slid the ruby pendant along the length of the chain and pulled Zachary's face to hers for another kiss.

He traced the chain around her neck with one finger

and choked the words out. "My mother handed me this necklace the day I rode out. She said to use it for trade if necessary or give it to the woman I fell in love with. I can't remember ever seeing her without it. It was my grandmother's and her mother's. She'll be glad to know I found someone to love."

"When should we tell my mother and Aaron? I don't want to tell them tonight."

"Tomorrow will be soon enough." He pulled her in for another kiss.

Everything was peaceful and quiet when Rebecca returned to the wagon a while later. Her heart continued to beat as fast as the blurred wings of a hummingbird. She hugged herself and danced in a circle. Settling on a rock near the embers of the fire, she pulled her journal and a pencil from her bag.

August 16, 1845 (I think) What a remarkable day this has been. As a group, we've been afraid and grief-stricken. I ended today on the very top of the world despite everything. Young Sadie Lawson was pulled off the wagon seat by her pet cow. Both drowned. Only seven years old. She and Jeb were good friends. Burying such a small girl was heart wrenching. I'll make sure to watch out for her parents.

Zachary and I were able to spend time alone. He asked me to marry him. Marry him! I said yes. Right now, I'm wearing a ruby necklace that belonged to his mother and grandmother. It seems like a lifetime ago when I left Independence with nothing more important to me than keeping the vow to my pa. I can still keep it. I will.

I'm tired.

Chapter 38

A New Announcement

Rebecca awakened and stretched. She heard her mother humming and Aaron talking to Bolo. The smell of the first pot of coffee of the day added an extra edge to the happy energy flowing through her. She reached for the ruby necklace beneath her chemise and held the mirror up. She gasped. The faceted gem sparkled even in the dim wagon. Last night she hadn't seen it except in Zachary's hand. More than ready to begin this new day, she dressed quickly and stepped out of the wagon.

"Good morning. Isn't it a beautiful day? A good day for getting things in order." Rebecca poured a cup of coffee, and reached down to scratch Bolo's ears hoping her mother wouldn't notice her shaking hands.

"Something's got you in a good mood." Sarah wiped her hands on an apron.

"I guess it's just the sunny day and the lay-by. There's a lot to do. No hurry, though. Biscuits smell good. I'm hungry." Rebecca checked on the biscuits and removed them from the fire.

Sarah put a crock of butter and fresh milk on the board balanced over two buckets. "We have honey if anyone wants it. I'm surprised Zachary hasn't shown up yet. Do you know what's keeping him?"

"What? Zachary? He'll be here soon." Heat crawled up her chest and settled on her face. Rebecca knew she was red as a ripe summer tomato. The cloth she held to keep from getting burned slipped. She lost her hold on the skillet and some biscuits fell into the dirt. Juggling the hot cast iron, she managed to get another grip before she dropped the whole thing. *Why on this earth am I nervous about telling mother and Aaron I accepted Zachary's proposal? I'm happy to be marrying Zachary.*

Rebecca caught her mother's grin. She suspected something.

Bolo yipped and wagged his tail, announcing Zachary's arrival. Rebecca suddenly felt shy. "Good morning, biscuits are ready. Hope you're hungry. You ready for this?" she whispered when he got near enough to hear her.

Zachary bent and kissed her on the cheek, flashed his double dimples, and chuckled deep in his throat. He cupped her face in his hand. "Of course, I'm ready. How about you?"

"I got nervous and almost dropped the biscuits. Lost a few actually. Ready as I'll ever be. I think Mother and Aaron will be happy." Rebecca pulled the necklace from inside her blouse and laid it over the bodice. She took Zachary's hand, squeezed it, and sat on a log.

"I'm starving." Aaron took the biscuits and stuck one in his mouth before setting them on the board to lather them with butter and honey.

Rebecca leaned across her mother to get butter. "Excuse me."

"Wait. What is this?" Sarah took the pendant in her hand. The early morning sun caught the ruby's facets, sending red prisms across the pan of biscuits.

Rebecca leaned into Zachary and held his hand in her lap. "Zachary asked me to marry him last night. I said yes."

Sarah covered her mouth with a hand. Her eyes filled with tears. "I figured this was coming. I am thrilled. Tell me about the beautiful necklace."

Zachary tried to speak, but his voice sounded like a sick bullfrog. He cleared his throat. "It was my mother's and my grandmother's before her. I think it first belonged to my great-grandmother. Ma gave it to me and told me to give it to the girl I fell in love with. I knew on leaving day that would be Rebecca."

Sarah stood and paced for a moment. She stopped and put her hands on her hips. "When is the ceremony? Where? On the trail or when we arrive? What will you wear? We must make plans."

"Goodness, we haven't had a chance to talk about any of that yet. We don't want everyone to know right away because of the sadness associated with Sadie's death. We'll tell the colonel, Evie, Hans, Brent, and Sally tomorrow. Brent and Sally are getting married tonight. Remember?"

Zachary pulled Rebecca up, gathered her close, and danced around the breakfast board. "No hurry. We have the rest of our lives. Not to mention the rest of this trip."

Aaron walked over, stood between Rebecca and Zachary, and draped his arms over their shoulders. "'Bout time."

They spent the day preparing for the rest of the trip. The mountains and another dangerous river crossing lay ahead. Contrasting emotions fought for attention—the heavy cloud of sadness and grief for the Lawson family and joy for the wedding of Brent and Sally.

Small groups of women gathered to cook food for a few days. Several meals were made for the Lawsons. Sarah volunteered to deliver them. Just before nooning, Sarah and Rebecca walked to the wagon. "Mrs. Lawson, we've brought food for you and Mr. Lawson."

Mrs. Lawson came out, still wearing the clothes she had on the day before. Her hair wasn't combed. The grief she carried pulled her shoulders down. She walked as if her legs weighed as much as an ox. "Pardon me, I haven't cleaned up. You said you needed to see me."

Sarah tucked her arm beneath Mrs. Lawson's elbow and led her to a stool. "Please sit. We just left some of the other ladies and have enough food for several days. You probably don't feel like cooking or eating. It's important for you and Mr. Lawson to keep up your strength. Is there anything you need help with? We're going to be washing clothes and bedding, would you like us to do yours?"

"Bedding? Would you take Sadie's? It needs to be washed and stored away."

Rebecca handed a small container of honey to Mrs. Lawson. "We'll be happy to do Sadie's bedding. I brought this honey because I know how much she loved honey with corn cakes."

Mrs. Lawson took the jar from Rebecca. "Thank you."

Later, Rebecca took most of the children out to gather grass bundles. She knew they needed to talk about Sadie. When they were about a hundred yards out, she had them sit in a circle and handed them pieces of twine for the bundles. "How is everyone today? Yesterday was sad. Does anyone want to say anything about Sadie?"

For a long moment silence was the only sound in the

grassy area. Rebecca watched the children.

Jeb was the first one to speak, his voice meek and shaky. "I am sad about Sadie. She was my friend. I wonder why she held onto that rope. All because of a cow."

"I don't know, Jeb. I think she loved that old cow too much to let it go alone. I know everyone is sad. Especially Mr. and Mrs. Lawson. Maybe we should gather extra grass for them. They know how much Sadie liked doing this. What do you think?"

Every one of the children stood and let Jeb lead them. He was their only boss now.

****

Celebrations provided opportunities for weary travelers to enjoy a break from day-to-day life. Food and laughter would be shared. Weddings signaled hope.

Rebecca dressed in a dark skirt and simple white blouse for Sally's wedding. She wore the necklace outside of her blouse, expecting questions to come her way. Excited, she had a hard time not shouting her news to the world. *Tomorrow.* Tonight was for Brent and Sally. She and Zachary walked hand in hand to the Hendrickses' wagon. "I bet it will be hard for Pastor Hendricks to lead a wedding service for his own daughter."

Zachary squeezed her hand. "Nah, he loves Brent and knows Sally's happy."

Just as dusk settled along the banks of the river, Pastor Hendricks stood before Sally and Brent. He held his favorite Bible in front of his heart and repeated the vows. His voice cracked. He swallowed once, twice, three times before whispering the words, "I now pronounce you husband and wife."

Shouts and clapping added to the happiness of the moment. Rebecca rushed to Sally. She hugged her and took both of her hands in hers. "Congratulations! You and Brent are going to be so happy. I'll leave you to greet everyone. Your mother and sisters are waiting to see you and Brent."

"Come over there with us. Mother made a nice stew from the rabbits Brent shot and corn cakes. Very pretty necklace. I've never seen you wear it before. Is it special?" Sally lifted one eyebrow like she had a secret waiting to be exposed.

"It is special." Rebecca pulled the pendant along the chain.

"Really? It resembles the one Zachary showed Brent and me one day when he was talking about asking you to marry him." Sally grinned.

Rebecca gently punched Sally in the shoulder. "Oh, did he? Yeah, you're right. He asked last night. Of course, I said yes. We weren't going to tell anyone except my mother and Aaron until tomorrow. We didn't want anything to interfere with your happiness."

Sally giggled. "I'm surprised it took as long as it did. That man is as hooked as a moon-struck calf. Truly, though, you're both very lucky to have each other. Have you made any plans yet?"

"We haven't even talked about plans except the ones we have for the land when we get to the Oregon Territory. I think we should wait to get married until we finish this journey. My uncle is going to obtain land for Mother and me. We can't do it ourselves because we're women. I'm overjoyed to be the future wife of Zachary Miller. What about you and Brent? Have you talked about your plans?"

Sally shrugged. "Our plans are just about making it to the end of this trail. We want to have a farm with some cattle, sheep, and mules. Maybe children. The best decision Brent has made for us is that he's not going to sign on as a scout for Colonel Wilson again. What a relief that has been for me. In the meantime, we're going to stay in the wagon Jacob gave us when Annie died. It will be our home for the rest of the journey and when we get to our land. We're headed that way now. I'll see you tomorrow."

Chapter 39

News Sharing

Colonel Wilson rode along the wagon line informing everyone they were heading out just after nooning. He stopped to talk to Sarah and Rebecca. "Y'all have any more coffee?"

Rebecca patted Buck's neck and then gave the colonel some coffee. "You have something on your mind? I noticed you were visiting along the way."

"Well, I say, what's that around your neck? Sure is pretty. Zachary's in a good mood, too." His blue eyes twinkled, and creases climbed up the sides of them when he smiled. He was always full of joy.

Rebecca held the pendant for a moment. "Zachary asked me to marry him. I said yes. We don't have any definite plans, except that we're going to wait until we reach Oregon Territory to marry. Mother sure is happy. She's been on pins and needles. I'm going to tell Evie and Hans this morning. Did you have something to tell us?"

The colonel spit a stream of tobacco to the ground. "I decided we're going to leave after nooning. We need to make some time. Every hour counts."

"Yes, sir."

Rebecca walked to Evie's wagon. "Good morning,

do you have time for a short walk?"

"Sure. Is anything wrong?" Evie took Rebecca's hand and tucked it in the crook of her arm.

"Nothing's wrong. Everything's right. I have something to show you." Rebecca stopped and turned to her friend. She pulled the necklace from her blouse and showed it off.

Evie gasped, covered her mouth, and leaned in to see the pendant. "It's beautiful. Is it a ruby? Tell me all about it. Not just the necklace."

"Let's walk. It's a really nice day. Zachary took me aside the night before Brent and Sally got married. He said he wanted to talk about something. He took something wrapped in a bandana out of his pocket, unwrapped it, and draped it over my hand. Goodness, Evie, it caught the moonlight and red prisms bounced around us. I know my mouth was gaping open. Then, he asked me to marry him."

"That is so romantic. I've been wondering if he was ever going to ask. Tell me about the necklace. It isn't just any red bauble."

"It's a family heirloom, belonged to his grandmother, and probably his great-grandmother. Zachary said he never saw his mother without it around her neck. His mother must be a sweet woman. She gave this to him the day he rode off to join the wagon train. She told him to give it to the woman he loves or to use it for trade."

"We should share our noon meal and tell Hans unless Zachary has told him. Either way we need to celebrate before we leave today."

"Yeah, we'll celebrate with cold biscuits and dried fruit." Rebecca laughed the way she did in the past. With heart, humor, and honesty. Without worry or fear.

"Stop a minute. I have something to tell you. I was going to wait, but why not? I'm with child again. This baby will be born in Oregon Territory. I'll take care of myself and not push any limits. I was scared at first, now I'm just ecstatic."

Rebecca squealed. "Really! I am so excited. We both have good news to share. Nooning will be extra special. I'll make sure you get some buttermilk. Have you told anyone else?"

Evie giggled and hugged Rebecca. "Just you. We'll tell Zachary then. We won't keep it a secret. It seems our last few weeks will be busy, but full of joy. Come on, let's get back to our wagons and get things done. I love you, my dear friend. It is good to see you happy."

****

Rebecca and Sarah sat on the floor of the wagon to take stock of the remaining supplies. They moved the flour and meal barrels around to even out the weight in the center and on the sides. The side of bacon was still fresh, and they had enough for a little more than two months. Rebecca rewrapped it in a clean sheet of muslin and hung it from the hook attached to the middle bow.

"I'll check the supplies in my medicine box. I think if I move it to the front left, it will allow us more room to roll up our mattress in the daytime. You could put our clothes on the opposite side. Aaron's things would be on that side. We keep the cooking things under the wagon seat anyway. What do you think?"

Sarah didn't answer.

"Mother. Did you hear me?"

"What? Yes. Yes, I heard you. I found these among my clothes."

Rebecca saw her mother holding some papers by the top edges like they were delicate treasures that might disappear. "These are the pages we tore out of the journals my mother kept. Remember when we had to leave the hope chests behind to lighten our load?"

"I remember. Let's read some of the pages together. Just for a few minutes."

Sarah handed Rebecca a page. "Your grandmother loved to tell this story about how your grandfather asked her to marry him. She said he walked her home and stood there wringing his hat in his hand and hemming and hawing around trying to talk. She said his words turned into tongue-twisted garble. He finally got around to telling her he didn't have much. Just some land, a one-room cabin, a cow, two horses, a mule, some chickens, a pig, and a really big garden with fertile soil, and an orchard of fruit trees his father planted. She said he started in talking about how special the dirt was. He finally asked her to marry him and threw up right where he stood. She said yes and handed him her handkerchief."

Rebecca laughed. "I wish I could have met them. I think I would have laughed a lot."

"They were happy. Probably happier than anyone I've ever known except maybe your father and me. They had struggles like everyone. You and Zachary will have times of plenty and times of want just like every married couple. But you'll be happy and content."

"We're hoping we can get adjoining land and have more space for raising horses and cattle. We'll need pasture. Remember the drawing Aaron made of a split rail fence? We've decided to do that. There's so much to think about." Rebecca leaned back, closed her eyes, and held the precious pages close to her heart, wondering what her grandparents would think of Zachary.

Sarah gathered some cooking supplies. "I think I'll put a pot of beans with a slice of fatback in a pot to soak for supper. Maybe make corncakes tonight. We have biscuits left over from breakfast we can have for nooning. It won't be much, but we can fill up."

"Sounds good to me. I'm going to check on the teams and horses." Rebecca put things back in place and made sure everything was secured.

****

Hans and Zachary returned from hunting with two prairie chickens and rabbits. Zachary handed the rabbits he carried to Hans and slapped him on the back. "See you tonight."

He loped over to Rebecca. "Guess you've heard Evie's news. Hans told me. He's so happy his feet aren't touching the ground. Hans has invited us to celebrate at supper tonight. Said Evie will save the rabbit pelts for the new baby."

"I'm going to check on the animals. Feel like joining me?" Rebecca kissed him on the cheek.

"Wish I could. Colonel Wilson needs me and Brent for something. I'll see you soon. I love you, Rebecca Pierce."

"I love you, too. What does the colonel want?"

"I'm not sure. I'll let you know." Zachary leaned over and kissed her on the forehead, then left.

****

Zachary and Brent met Colonel Wilson at his wagon. He waited with a map laid over a table and anchored in place with rocks on each corner. "Sorry to bother both of you. I know you've got other things on your mind. This is important."

Brent grunted and poured a cup of coffee. "Yeah, what is it?"

"We're about a month out from Flagstaff Hill. That's where we'll get our first glimpse of the Blue Mountains. From there it's about two weeks to the Dalles. We'll have to cut trees to make barges to cross the river; it's dangerous. I don't know how long that will take. After we cross the Dalles, we're only another two weeks out from the end of the journey. Things will be rough. I need to know how the folks are as far as food and warm clothes are concerned. Ask around." Wilson leaned over the map and pulled a stubby gnawed pencil out of his pocket.

Zachary and Brent stood on each side of the colonel. "This is where we are now. This is Flagstaff Hill, these are the Blue Mountains, and this is the Dalles." He punched the pencil on the map. "This is the Columbia River Gorge. And this is the end of the trail."

"What are you asking us to do?" Brent figured he knew the answer. *Dammit, what's Sally going to say?*

"In a week's time I want the two of you to head out toward Flagstaff Hill and scout it for me. We'll meet up with you around that area. Leave markers on the trail. Sorry about this, Brent. Truly, I am."

"Yes, sir. Zachary and I will talk to Rebecca and Sally later today."

Zachary stopped Brent before they reached Rebecca's wagon. "I've got something to tell you. Last night Rebecca agreed to be my wife when we get to the Oregon Territory."

"Congratulations! You're a lucky man. Sorry about the orders, bad timing."

"Guess we better tell our ladies." Zachary shook Brent's hand.

****

Despite good news and a hearty meal, a pall hung around the fire. There was little conversation but the sounds of enjoying a meal were enough to settle everyone.

Rebecca finished her food. "That stew was good, and the beans were perfect, and here we sit feeling sorry for ourselves because Brent and Zachary are going to scout ahead for us. It's their job. But we're blessed. My mother is doing better. Aaron is growing into a fine young man. Brent and Sally are married. Evie and Hans are going to have a baby. And Zachary and I are going to get married. Let's celebrate tonight. Zachary, will you get some music going so we can dance? We should take food to Mr. and Mrs. Lawson after we clean up."

Chapter 40

Shooting Stars and Rabbit's Feet

Several mornings later, Zachary and Brent left when the sun was only a promise in the eastern sky. Colonel Wilson expected them to find the route with adequate water to Flagstaff Hill and meet back at the wagons for the remaining miles to the landmark.

They followed a narrow tributary of the Snake River. Sagebrush dotted the landscape. Some clumps were ankle high while others stood as tall as a grown man. The leaves were light green, and the branches thin, but the air smelled like a simmering spice. "There's been plenty of rain out here. Things are still green, even if it is just the sagebrush."

Zachary leaned forward and patted Red's neck. "Will the livestock survive on this stuff? It seems sparse and not much in the way of branches."

"They'll eat it. The oxen and mules won't care. Horses don't like it, but it will serve. The branches make good firewood. Water might be a problem unless the rains fell further north and west. I hope there will be plenty as we get closer to the Blue Mountains. I figure Colonel Wilson has everyone conserving water. We'll probably find water where the sage is thickest and tallest."

They followed the creek for several more hours, leaving red cloths around some brush nearest to the river's edge to guide the colonel.

"Reckon now's a good time to settle for the night." Brent pointed to a group of tall sagebrush.

Zachary led the horses to drink. His thoughts turned to Rebecca. *Wonder what she's up to? Probably the same thing we are. Taking care of the animals, eating, drinking coffee, and searching the stars.*

Brent had coffee brewing and leftover biscuits warming over the fire.

Zachary walked back and hobbled the horses near a grassy area. "Coffee sure smells good."

Brent handed him a cup. "It's biscuits and jerky for supper. I did heat the biscuits. Not that it will make much difference."

"Don't matter. Our bellies will be full. Wonder what our girls are doing? Bet you miss Sally."

"Yeah, probably about as much as you miss Rebecca. Something new grows in your heart when you find the perfect woman to love, don't it?" Brent handed Zachary a biscuit.

"I don't even have the words for how special it feels and how scared it makes me. What if I'm not good enough?"

Brent huffed. "Oh, hell. You're more than good enough. You've protected her from Silas. You've regained her trust. You're sharing the same dream. Sally has made our little wagon into a home. That kind of thing is what amazes me. Women can do things men don't even know need doing."

"That's likely true. I've seen the women on this trail rise above every kind of trial and keep moving." Zachary reclined back on his saddle to see the stars. He knew Rebecca was watching the same ones.

Brent pointed to the west. "There goes a shooting star. Sally said they're lucky."

Zachary watched the tail end of the star as it dived over the horizon. "Hope Rebecca saw that. She loves them. Told me her pa said they were guiding lights sent from Heaven. Wonder if there's any truth to that?"

"Yeah. I want to stay up a few minutes longer." Brent settled next to his saddle and pulled his hat lower on his head.

****

Rebecca waltzed with herself to music only she could hear. A shooting star stopped her. She crossed her heart and said a prayer for safety, health, and a bright future.

The sounds in the camp were as familiar as her own voice. Men sharpening axes and knives against a whetstone made whooshing sounds. Women putting children down for the night and preparing for the next day. Children complaining and dropping off to sleep. Animals grazing and settling in for another night. Spent firewood collapsing in the ashes. It was Rebecca's favorite time of day.

She curled up under a warm quilt beneath the stars. Sleep came quickly.

****

Colonel Wilson spotted the first red cloth tied high on a limb of sagebrush when the train stopped for nooning. "We'll stop for an extra hour so everyone can fill their water barrels and other containers. We will be coming up on areas with little to no water before we get to Flagstaff Hill. You might want to take some of the time to wash up. It's as good a time as any."

It had been a while since Rebecca used the sledge her pa made to haul water. She untied it from under the wagon and asked Aaron to hitch one of the horses to it. He put their barrels, the Thatchers', and the Garsons' along with available pitchers, buckets, and canteens on the sled.

He and Ed Thatcher walked down to the water's edge to fill everything.

Ed walked with him in front of Misty. "How are you feeling about reaching the last of the journey? Ginny's beside herself. She's busy mending, knitting, and sewing some kind of thing for Sean. Every night she checks on the food stores and plans the next day's meals. Like there's much to plan."

"We're about the same. Except Rebecca misses Zachary. I heard her asking her ma what kind of things she would need to set up housekeeping. Must mean she's ready to get married. Sarah is trying to finish something she's sewing for her sister. I stay busy making sure our tools are in working order, gathering wood, and hunting when I can. I just want to do my part. Sarah and Rebecca didn't have to take me in, but they did. I'm grateful."

"They certainly are caring and giving. Good Christian examples. I thank God for them in my prayers every day. Here we are. Better get this water back. Colonel Wilson might have something else for us to do. Have you checked your oxen's and horse's hooves? I usually do mine before we bed down."

"I'll do it after I milk the cow. I hear her bellowing for attention. Wish I had time to go hunting. I would love to have a good stew. Sarah is the best cook ever."

Ed slapped Aaron on the back and laughed out loud.

"Tell you what, let's go hunting tomorrow. It will be a nice ride away from the wagons. And the possibility of a good meal doesn't hurt either."

Aaron shook Ed's hand. "Deal."

****

Aaron and Ed left before daylight. "Wouldn't it be nice if we flush out a deer? We could share it with everyone." Aaron held his rifle across his lap.

"Yes, it would. I'll feel lucky if we get a couple of rabbits and prairie chickens. Did you know Ginny saves the bones to boil for broth? I would toss them out to the dogs. She uses every part of an animal when we get lucky enough to get fresh meat."

Nearing a stand of trees close to the water's edge, they dismounted and tethered the horses before going in different directions.

Aaron settled behind a rock to wait, in a sense of quiet awareness, confident he'd be able to take food back. Time passed breath by breath. A rustle in the bushes caught his attention. He saw a young stag watching him. Aaron slowly lifted his rifle and fired, surprised he felt remorse when the animal fell with a thud.

The report of Ed's rifle matched his own.

Aaron met Ed coming out of the brush. He held two jackrabbits. "I got a deer, a young stag. We will have enough to share with everyone."

Ed held up the rabbits. "Ginny will have a nice stew made with these. She'll probably want to save one of the feet for Sean. Reckon Jeb will want one. He'll have ideas for the others. You know that boy."

Aaron laughed. "Yeah, Rebecca always has stories to tell about Jeb."

They skinned and dressed the animals before catching up with the wagons. The news of their luck erupted in jubilation.

Ginny salted the rabbits and put them in a pot to soak.

Colonel Wilson asked Red O'Reilly to salt the venison and cut it up into portions for each family.

That night, the enticing aroma of roasting meat and bubbling stews filled the air. The sounds of laughter, singing, and gathering lifted heavy moods. This was the kind of night every person thought life on the trail would be like.

Rebecca heard her name and turned to see Jeb running to her. "Hey, I heard Ed, I mean Mr. Thatcher, killed two rabbits. What did he do with the feet? I figure I need one for good luck and one for Obed. He's too young to need luck. What about the rest of the feet? Any plans for them?"

"Well, I don't know. You should talk to Mr. Thatcher. He's just over there. I bet he will make sure you and Obed each get one."

In record time Jeb ran back to her.

"Guess what? He gave me and Obed two of the big back feet. I think he's keeping one for his little boy. He said he would ask you for recommends about who gets the rest of them. See you tomorrow." Jeb ran off without another glance.

Chapter 41

Scouting Report

The next morning during breakfast preparations, Zachary and Brent rode in and stopped at Colonel Wilson's wagon.

"Any news for me?" Wilson set his cup down and poured coffee for the scouts.

Brent took the coffee and answered, "Thanks. Not really. The trail is clear. Forage is mostly scrub, but there's plenty of it. Water is plentiful if we stay close to a tributary. There's been recent rains. It's a hot and dry stretch. The animals will need extra rest. So will we, I imagine. Even though we're closer and can see the Blue Mountains, it frustrates me that we're still so far away."

"Good to know. Just what I figured. Tomorrow morning, I will have a meeting with the men to give them a heads-up about the coming conditions. Might as well grab some breakfast. There's a couple of young ladies waiting for you."

"Yes, sir." Brent elbowed Zachary.

****

Rebecca and Sally ran to Colonel Wilson's wagon when they got the news their men had returned and were there.

Sally picked up her skirts, ran, and jumped straight

into Brent's arms. He kissed her and walked back to their wagon for breakfast. "I'm famished. Hope you have something to eat."

"How about a few slices of venison with your biscuits?"

"Venison? Sounds good." Brent grinned and took Sally's hand.

"Aaron killed it. He and Ed went hunting. Came back successful."

Rebecca wrapped her arm around Zachary as they went their way. "See you later, Sally. It's true. Aaron shot a stag yesterday. We had a great supper last night. I saved you some. Ed got two jackrabbits. I think Jeb managed to cajole a rabbit's foot for you."

Zachary laughed. "That boy is something else. I wouldn't mind having one like him someday."

Rebecca laughed and tip-toed to kiss him. "You get the discipline job."

"I bet you're better at that than I am."

When they arrived at their destination, Rebecca announced, "We have a hungry scout joining us for breakfast this morning. Could we spare some venison and biscuits?"

Aaron came from grooming Misty. He grinned from ear to ear. "Welcome back, Zachary."

"So, I hear you shot a stag yesterday." Zachary took the venison-stuffed biscuit Sarah offered.

"Sure did. One young enough to still be tender."

Zachary took a big bite, chewed, and swallowed. "Man, this is good. Was it the first deer you've shot?"

"Nah, I killed two others before we lost the farm. This one felt like the most important and appreciated one, though."

Rebecca kissed Zachary on the cheek. "You should have been here last night when it was freshly roasted. Never doubt yourself, Aaron. Meat is greatly appreciated."

"Did you make it to Flagstaff Hill?" Aaron asked.

"We didn't make it all the way. Colonel Wilson is having a meeting with the men before we head out tomorrow morning. I think you should come with me."

Aaron grinned. "Really?"

"Yeah. When we stop tonight we have to make sure the wagon teams and horses are sound. There isn't much for the animals to graze on out there. Mostly sage. We're lucky to still have some grain in the wagons. We will have to limit it. Water is available at first but slacks off. There are holes in the ground we need to watch for. Brent said they belong to gophers or some such critter and can break an animal's leg if they fall into one. The brush and branches can be used for firewood. Smells good, too."

"Smells good? Like what?" Rebecca asked.

"I don't really know. Reminded me of something my mother cooked with. When she comes this way next year, I bet she'll try to use it to season things. Might not work, but she'll try. How about some time alone tonight, my dear Rebecca?"

"Without a doubt. We'll get away for a while. Hope the stars are bright."

"They'll be out. They always shine for you." Zachary pulled Rebecca in for a quick kiss, promising more later.

****

After supper, Zachary and Rebecca walked away from the wagons. They settled on a rock surrounded by tufts of brush. The stars winked at them from their own galaxy.

"Everyone wants to know when we're getting married. I told them after we arrive in Oregon. The people that matter think that's the best idea. Mother has told me that her gift to us will be her share of the land my uncle obtains. She has no desire to live away from town. Her dream is to help Aunt Emma. And, get this, she even hinted that she and Doc may wed at some point. Can you believe it?"

"That's good news all the way around. Is Sarah serious about the land? Do you think your uncle will try to get both plots beside each other? That's just like we dream about. Doesn't surprise me about her and Doc. How do you feel about it?" Zachary twined his fingers through Rebecca's and pulled her hand to his heart, then to his mouth for a kiss.

"She's serious for sure. What will we do with that much land? I'm not at all surprised about Doc. I've actually prayed the two of them would find happiness together. Sometimes prayers get answered."

Zachary wrapped an arm over her shoulder. "I've thought about building a one-room cabin for me and Aaron while we build a barn, our cabin, and fencing like Aaron drew. Then, Aaron could live in the first cabin. We'll need to clear the land. Brent said it's forested. The trees will provide wood. I also dream of having a garden, a pasture for hay, and plenty of water. What about you, what do you want?"

"I've thought about many of the same things you have. I've also thought about a Christmas wedding. What do you think of that?" Rebecca snuggled into his side.

"I had hoped to get married sooner, but Christmas sounds very nice. By then we should be well under way with a cabin. It's almost unreal to be this close to being at the end. The end and the beginning at the same time."

Rebecca pointed to the night sky. "A shooting star! That means good luck. I saw one when you and Brent were scouting. I wished on it."

"The first night we were gone?"

"Yeah."

"I think we saw the same star."

Rebecca turned her face up and kissed Zachary before he could kiss her.

****

Colonel Wilson called for attention before leading the wagons out for the day. "It gets hot out there during the day and is colder at night. The animals will need more rest. We'll stop for twenty minutes every two hours. During that time, give your animals just enough water to wash the dust out of their mouths. The scouts said we will have access to water along the way if the tributary holds out, but we'll probably have to boil any we get from the creek. Doc will decide that. Any questions?"

Aaron raised a tentative hand and waited for the colonel to acknowledge him.

"Aaron? Good to have you with us."

Aaron swallowed hard and straightened his shoulders. "Sir, can you tell us how much grain is left?"

Colonel Wilson moved the tobacco from one side of his mouth to the other and spit a wide arc of the brown juice to the dry ground. He mounted Buck. "We're down to about half a wagon of grain. I'll be watching how much we have and doling it out as I see fit. I think we have enough to get over the Blues if we're careful. Okay, let's roll."

One by one the wagons rolled along, grass crunching under the wheels.

****

Ten days later, the folks reached Flagstaff Hill, disappointed the "hill" was no more than a rise in elevation. Still hot, dusty, and dry. The wagons stretched across the land so everyone could catch their first glimpse of the Blue Mountains in the distance. Even at a ten-day drive, it was easy to imagine trees, grass, water, and cooler temperatures.

Rebecca held her hand over her eyes to shield them from the sun. "Just think. In a few days we'll be able to heat water to bathe. I feel like a garden plot could be planted on me. Wiping down just isn't enough."

Sarah sighed. "I am looking forward to being able to make coffee and tea without measuring the water. And, of course, to bathing and doing laundry."

Chapter 42

Seeing the Blues

Colonel Wilson called a meeting one evening. The weather was cool enough that women wore shawls, men wore jackets, and children were dressed in flannel. When he climbed on an overturned barrel, conversations dropped. Those gathered cleared their throats, murmured, and gave children orders to be quiet. The colonel pulled a bag of tobacco from his vest and took out enough for a chew. He spit once, took the used chew from the pocket in his cheek, tossed it aside, and added the new one. "I know it isn't often I call everyone together. From here on out, we will all have more jobs to do. We'll start crossing the Blues tomorrow and the going will be rocky and steep. There's a strong possibility you men will have to cut down trees to make a path. We'll use oxen from the herd to pull logs down the mountain to build rafts for floating the Columbia.

"When we reach the Columbia, there may be barges and rafts with native guides or workers from the Hudson Bay Company. The barges are the safest, but they can be costly. Some of you may want to use them. Folks, the Columbia is rough. The gorge is little else than rapid white water and rocks and may turn out to be the most dangerous part of the trip.

"You older boys will walk ahead and move rocks and other things that block the path. I don't know how long it will take to get over the mountains. Maybe three days. Ladies, I recommend making hardtack and jerky. You also might want to cook something tonight that lasts a few days and get together to figure out what food provisions we have as a group. Early tomorrow I'm sending Brent, Zachary, Aaron, and Ed out to hunt.

"Jeb, your job is to stay out of trouble and help Rebecca with the children when their mothers are busy. Let your animals graze when we're working on the trees. Even if the only option is brush. Questions?" The expressions of fear on people's faces caused his heart to squeeze for a few precious beats.

Mr. Garson raised his hand. "Will I be required to cut down trees and build rafts?"

Wilson spit. "Of course, you will. You're a man. You have gloves. Every person on this train will help. Especially in these last days."

Jeb raised his hand. "I could teach Mr. Garson to cut down a tree. I watched my pa."

A roar of laughter filled the air. Mrs. Slaton shushed Jeb and gave him the narrow-eyed, tight-lipped glare only mothers used to convey orders.

Wilson grinned at Jeb. "I'm sure you could, but I think we need your help with the other children more than anything."

****

Early the next morning before anyone awakened, the hunters left, each pair going in a different direction.

Rebecca heard Zachary leave. She shivered and crawled from beneath the quilt and chose to dress in britches and a flannel shirt. The fire started with a roar when a gust of wind stirred it. The flames were bright orange, red, and blue at the base. She stood close and warmed her hands. Walking down to the edge of a free-flowing stream, she filled the coffee pot and Dutch oven. The creek wasn't large enough for bathing but did allow for cooking and filling water barrels. *I'll bring the animals down for a cool drink before heading out this morning.* Sarah stood warming her hands over the fire when Rebecca returned. "Good morning, I have fresh water for coffee."

"Good morning. It's cold. I'll make extra biscuits and corncakes tonight. We're getting low on flour and cornmeal. We have very little bacon, but I think there's enough for breakfast. I pray the men bring back fresh meat."

Rebecca took a rope, three-legged stool, and bucket from the side of the wagon. Bolo bounced around her, reminding her of a jack-in-the-box toy she once had. Walking around to the cow, she sat down and started milking. "Morning, girl. I'm going to treat you and the others to a walk down to the stream for fresh water. How about that?"

She dipped a cup into the bucket of milk and gave it to Bolo, who lapped it up like he was starving. The cow ducked her head, allowing Rebecca to tie a rope around her neck. Glory, Patriot, and the four oxen waited for her by the wagon like they did every morning. She led them out, tied them together, and walked to the stream.

Sarah sat eating a biscuit when Rebecca returned. "Breakfast is ready. I've given us a slice of venison. I wrapped the rest for you to bring to Evie. She needs to eat as much meat as possible while she carries the baby."

"That's nice. I'll take it to her after I yoke the team.

I want to give the animals a small measure of grain before we start today. The mountains will be hard on them. The oats we brought are almost gone. Brent said there will probably be grass in the mountains."

"I'm not very excited about these last days. Doc doesn't want me to help too much. He's afraid the elevation and changes in temperature will cause more damage to my lungs."

"How is Doc? I haven't seen much of him lately."

"He's been checking on everyone to make sure they're ready for the Columbia Gorge. He asked me and some other women for scraps of fabric to make bandages. I gave him our most threadbare aprons and skirts. How is your supply of medicine?"

"I think it's enough. I know I have enough peppermint and chamomile tea. I haven't had to use much willow bark. Plenty of laudanum. I'm more concerned about salves and ointments." Rebecca glanced toward Colonel Wilson's wagon. He seemed worried, and that concerned her.

"Colonel Wilson is ready." Sarah climbed on the wagon seat, tied her bonnet, and pulled on a pair of gloves.

****

Zachary and Aaron caught up to the wagons around midmorning and stopped to talk to Colonel Wilson. "We're back with good news," he said, holding up three rabbits and a prairie chicken. "Hope Brent and Ed are as lucky."

"Nice hunt. Give Hans and Evie a rabbit." Colonel Wilson breathed a sigh of relief.

Brent and Ed came in with another rabbit, which meant several soups could be made to share in the camp.

****

Jack Farris walked along the line, checking the hooves of every ox, mule, horse, and cow. Some he'd have to take back to his wagon to receive new shoes or hoof care. He stopped to chat with the colonel. "I'll stop long enough to get these tasks done. May take all night. I'll catch up."

"Take care of the wagon teams first. If anyone needs to stay behind with you, let me know. I'll see to it that someone drives them down to you."

"Yes, sir."

****

Colonel Wilson walked back and forth checking on everyone and everything. Something was needling him. He couldn't put his finger on it. Maybe it was the dangers ahead. Nerves. The Blue Mountains and the Columbia were real hazards. He removed his hat and slapped it against his thigh. Dust flew. "We need the path up these mountains to be about six feet wide. You men cutting down the trees, leave them on the side for the folks who will be scraping bark and trimming branches. Save the larger ones for firewood. Tomorrow, the wranglers with oxen will drag the fallen trees behind the last wagon. Your reward is almost in sight."

The sound of axes and saws cutting away echoed through the crisp air. A victorious shout followed every tree that fell. Wood planers whooshed along the tree, removing bark, and small axes removed branches, setting a clear rhythm in motion.

Wilson took a planer and tomahawk from his saddlebags. "I'm here to help."

Mr. Slaton stopped chopping and leaned against the handle of his axe. "Colonel, I think this is what it'll be like when we clear our own land and build homes. Getting good practice."

****

Sarah tried to mend a skirt while the wagon bounced. "Doc told me Colonel Wilson is going to stay in Oregon. He's tired after doing these treks. I figure he wants to find happiness and a new home just as much as the rest of us."

"Maybe it isn't such a good idea to sew on a bumpy wagon." Rebecca grinned at her mother when she pricked her finger and gasped.

Chapter 43

Final Preparations

Several days later the wagon train reached the Dalles. They had lashed rafts together with double-strength rope. Cracks and holes were filled with tar. Oars and paddles were whittled out of crooked trunks around campfires at night.

Mr. Slaton leaned against a wagon wheel, rolled a cigarette, and lit it. "Tell us, Colonel, what happens when we reach the point these rafts go in the Columbia?"

Wilson scrubbed at his beard and combed his fingers through his hair. He stopped to re-tie the leather thong keeping his hair in place. He spit twice. "I guess this is as good a time as any to talk about the final leg. It's going to be dangerous. I hope to find enough native guides to steer us across. As I've said before, it's the safest. It's good planning to have our own rafts, but we might be able to trade them for passage. If you choose to steer your own, I recommend that you follow a raft with a guide. They know that damn river. Another thing we haven't talked much about.

"There will be decisions to make about your wagons and livestock. The animals will have to go by a path along the banks of the Columbia. Matter of fact, it might be best if you choose to sell or give your animals to villagers near the Dalles. Wagons will either have to be left behind or broken down and lashed to the rafts."

Zachary stood to get Colonel Wilson's attention. "Brent and I have talked about this. He thinks we should take only what we can carry on the rafts. It's up to us to make the best choices for ourselves. I haven't talked to Rebecca and Sarah about this yet."

Most of the men stopped whittling and carving and laid their knives down. For a few seconds, the only sound was breathing until whispered conversations and concerns took over the peace of the campfire.

Wilson held up his hand. "Include your families. Brent, Zachary, Red, Jack, and the wranglers will take the long land route to the end. The rest of you will go by raft unless you choose to go by land.

"Go. Talk to your families. Don't take anything on the raft that isn't necessary. Zachary, tell Rebecca to bring her medical supplies. There will be other supplies available later. Take provisions. It's good to have trinkets, shirts, and other things to trade for steerage. Have your wives and older children carry what they want in a bundle. Talk to them about leaving or selling the wagons and teams. I understand wanting to keep your animals, but hard decisions must be made."

****

Zachary and Brent walked away from Colonel Wilson's wagon.

"Sally sure won't like it when I tell her I'll be going by the land route. I worry about her on the raft. She'll want to be with her family. I understand that. Maybe I can arrange for another man to help them out."

"I understand. Ed and Ginny will be with my family. Aaron should be able to help. He's getting stronger and surer of himself. Rebecca is going to worry about Glory and Patriot, but I figure she'll sell the oxen and cow. Hopefully, they'll use a guide. I wish everyone would. What do you think?"

Brent stopped, turned, and made eye contact with Zachary. "The land route is brutal. We and our beasts start out almost too tired to put one foot in front of the other. It's hot, has very little forage, and access to water is almost impossible in most places. The inclines are steep. Animals have trouble getting a foothold. Going down is worse. The rocks trip them. They can't get good traction because it's straight down. There's a lot of sand. It's better in the long run if we keep moving. I think it's easier on the animals. For us, the same problems. We won't be able to hunt. Sometimes a man will go ahead and set rabbit traps. I reckon we'll lose some animals and maybe men. Last year we almost lost two wranglers. On the bright side, when you come out on the other side, you'll be so close to home you can see it.

"This year, I have Sally to think of. You have Rebecca. Make sure you bring plenty of hardtack and jerky or pemmican. As much as you can carry and some to share. Have Rebecca give you medicine if she can spare it. Especially salve for torn up feet and willow bark for pain. And extra socks if you can find some." Brent stopped talking and watched Sally at their wagon.

Zachary blew out a breath and chuckled. "The first thing Rebecca will ask is if Bolo will stay with her or go with me. I'll make sure he stays with her. Thanks for sharing. I'll ask about medicine and the other things. See you tomorrow morning."

"She's going to worry about those horses."

Zachary shook his head. "She will. She sure will.

Glory and Patriot are the horses she and her father set their stock on for the ranch they dreamed about in Oregon."

****

Rebecca waited for Zachary. Her instincts told her the meeting with the men had been serious. The simmering anger she often stuffed because women weren't included in major decisions heated to a rolling boil. She recognized the familiar sound of Zachary's low whistle and spun around before he stopped. "About time. What's so important it took so long?"

Zachary held up a palm. "Whoa, what's that all about?"

Rebecca lifted her chin. "I'm tired of being ignored when serious business is discussed just because I'm a woman. I do more than most men on this train. I know that we're fixing to go straight into danger. Now, tell me."

Zachary took a step back. "I suppose I understand how you could feel left out. Especially since you lead your family. I'll get Sarah and Aaron. Ed's getting Ginny. I'll fill you in when everyone is here. We have hard decisions to make."

Rebecca realized she was being unreasonable and turned to wait for the others. "I'm sorry. Guess I'm just tired and worried. But Zachary, understand this—I won't stop being who I am. Not for anybody. I'll stoke the fire and boil water for coffee."

Zachary stepped closer and wrapped his arms around her. "It will be fine. I promise." He turned her to face him. "And I don't want you to change at all," he whispered and covered her lips in a tender gesture.

Rebecca leaned into Zachary's strength. "I know."

But, will it be fine? What if Zachary doesn't make it? The horses? Mother? Will I make it?
****

The small group gathered around the fire. They stood together, silent, and somber. Rebecca held hands with Zachary. Sarah and Aaron stood behind him. Sally leaned into Brent. Ginny stood in front of Ed holding his hand by her side.

Brent stepped away from Sally. "Find a place to sit."

When everyone was comfortable, Brent kissed Sally on the cheek and cleared his throat. "We need to make tough choices tonight. Tomorrow or day after, some of us will be crossing the Columbia. The wagons can't go on the rafts fully assembled. Colonel Wilson suggests everyone sell their wagons or leave them. Some of you might choose to take yours apart and put them on the rafts. That isn't recommended. Sally and I have decided to try and sell ours. Consider selling your oxen and milk cows. They're tired and wouldn't do well on the trail.

"Several of us men will be taking livestock down a trail running near the river. The area is rocky, sandy, and very dangerous. Forage and water are scarce. Colonel Wilson is sending Zachary, Red O'Reilly, Jack Farris, a few wranglers, and me. Other wranglers will be helping with the rafts." Brent waited. He could see questions and concerns on the faces of his friends. Tears filled Sally's eyes. He watched her shake her head and wipe the moisture from her cheeks..

Rebecca started to stand but sat back down. "I have a question. How do the animals that have to go on the trail fare? I still have a few head of cattle, two yoke of oxen, and four horses in the herd. Glory and Patriot will have to go this way won't they? I worry most about

369

them."

"Well, it is difficult. We might lose a few head of oxen, especially those that have been pulling heavy wagons all these months. I figure your horses will do well because they're healthy and young. I don't really have an answer for you besides that. By the way, Bolo stays with you.

"Another thing, Colonel Wilson asked me to tell everyone he hopes you choose to hire an Indian guide or someone from the Hudson Bay Company to help with the rafts. They know the river. If you choose to use your own raft, see about following another one with a guide on board or hire one for yours. Some Indians will take you for something in trade. They like getting animals, especially horses. Their women like sewing things, cloth, lace, trinkets, and other odds and ends. Check your possessions to see what you can spare."

Aaron stood. "How is it decided who goes on the rafts? Does the colonel do that?"

"He will make suggestions. He wants all of you to stay together. The Irish kid, Jessie, will stay with the Garsons and two other families. Beyond that, I don't know. Don't take anything you don't need, like tools, furniture, or things like that if you can help it. If you have something precious to you that is easy to carry, wrap it in oilcloth and put it in a bag or bundle with your clothes. Rebecca, he wants you to bring your medicine box. Anything else?"

"What do you mean by a bundle?" Aaron asked.

"It's just items you tie up in a quilt or something. Some folks have small cases they can use. You'll be fine. Colonel Wilson wants you on the raft because you're strong enough to help. Any other questions?"

Ginny Thatcher stepped forward. "What did you mean when you said we might want to take our wagons apart?"

"Well, it means you can take the wheels off and leave them or stow them on the raft. It's more dangerous but can be done. Remember this, if you sell your wagons, some of your belongings, and your wagon teams, you'll have some money to replace them with. Not much, but enough to get you started. Like I said, Sally and I are selling the wagon and team."

Quiet conversations and suggestions took a few minutes.

Brent let them talk, then continued, "It's time we all get back to our wagons and prepare for the next stage of the trip. I wish you all well. One other thing, Zachary mentioned to me the other day that this group was close and willing to help each other without giving it a thought. He's right. That's how I know we'll be fine, and we will succeed on our new land."

Chapter 44

Rafts on the Columbia

Rebecca didn't sleep that night. She took out her journal.

Date unknown

Tomorrow we'll sell the wagon, team, and the cow. It makes me sad. Mother, Aaron, the Thatchers, and I will take a few meager possessions on a raft to go down the Columbia. I think this is the only time I've been scared of anything except Silas. Zachary and Brent will join some other men to take the horses and other livestock along a dangerous land route. The animals can't go on rafts. Bolo gets to go with us.

I've heard someone almost always drowns on the wretched river. We will use a guide.

How far is home from the end of the river?

She packed and repacked two dresses, her journal, the pages she kept from her grandmother's diary, along with a teacup and saucer. The most important things were between the dresses. She wrapped everything in a quilt, then oilcloth. When satisfied everything would be safe, she bound the bundle with rope. She then checked how much meal and coffee they had left.

Sarah pulled her beloved comb from her hair and wrapped it in a handkerchief. She took some of the money from the meal barrel, tied it inside a chemise and rolled it up. The rest she secured in a cloth and pinned it to the inside of her dress. She put those things she considered most important in the tablecloth she'd made for Emma, then wrapped it all in two dresses, a quilt, and oilcloth. "It seems strange that everything I've ever owned is being replaced by this small bundle."

"I know. Aaron, what have you packed?" Rebecca sat cross-legged on the floor.

"I don't have much. I've packed the extra clothes you gave me, my book of sketches, some hardtack, and a rabbit's foot. It's wrapped like yours. Listen, I promise I'll do all I can to keep you safe and help you build your new lives. You've given me more than any boy deserves."

Rebecca reached across the narrow wagon and hugged Aaron. "You are our family, Aaron. We do have enough meal for corncakes to go with the last of the coffee in the morning. How about we try to sleep for a few minutes?"

Bolo whined. He came between Rebecca and Aaron, turned around three times, lay down, put his head on his paws, and sighed.

****

Early the next morning as the sun began to announce its presence, Rebecca built a fire. She pulled her shawl close and tried to figure out if the way her entire body shivered was due to the colder weather or dread. Zachary would be leaving. *Lord, I know I'm stubborn and proud, but I ask that you walk with Zachary and the men on that trail. I don't pray as much as I should, and I try not to overthink you—though I fail—and I ask forgiveness. Keep us all safe and bring us home to this new land.*

Amen.

The crack of twigs interrupted her prayers. Aaron came to her carrying corn meal and coffee. "Good morning. Have you seen Zachary yet? I saw Brent and Sally. He was dressed to travel."

"Zachary hasn't been here yet, but I expect he'll show up soon. He stayed with the horses last night. He'll be here when the coffee boils."

Sarah climbed out of the wagon. "I found some sugar to go in the corncakes."

"I smell coffee. Did I hear something about sugar?" Zachary walked into the circle and put his arms around Rebecca, then pulled her in for a quick kiss.

Rebecca laughed and tugged on the collar of his shirt. "You hungry? We're using the last of our meal and coffee. Maybe we can send you off with a full belly."

"I'm starving as usual. I'll be joining Brent and the others at the herd soon." Zachary held her trembling hand, a hint of concern in his eyes. He pulled her to the other side of the wagon with him.

When they were out of sight Rebecca's knees weakened. She leaned into him to keep from falling. She was scared. Shards of fear stabbed her heart, breaking it as easily as a rock would shatter fine china. "You'll be taking Glory, Patriot, and Misty when you go, won't you?"

"Yeah."

"Come back to me, Zachary Miller. Bring my horses and come back."

"I will. How could I leave you alone to live our dream? I love you and know our life will be perfect. Now, let's go get breakfast." Zachary lifted the ruby necklace and kissed Rebecca deeply, his kiss assuring her how much he loved her.

"I think I might be able to eat. Wait! I forgot to give you something. While cleaning out my bag, I found some dirty, almost melted peppermints at the bottom. Will you give the horses one when you lead them away from me?" Rebecca's last words almost strangled her. She cleared her throat, swallowed hard, and handed Zachary a bag with the peppermints and fur hoof protectors for the horses.

A heavy, somber mood cloaked the members around the fires. Everyone in the small circle knew the time they would be on the overland trail would draw to a close. Their destination lay close, finally within reach. After they sold their belongings and animals. After they found a guide. After they challenged the Columbia River.

A shrill whistle interrupted them. Brent motioned for Zachary to meet him. When he stood to leave, Rebecca rose with him, kissed him on the cheek, and climbed into the wagon.

****

They found a group of people wanting to buy whatever they could from the travelers. A line formed at the rafts. "Rebecca, go secure us a place in line for a raft. I see Colonel Wilson over there. Aaron will help me with the wagon and animals. I'm certain it will be easy to sell the wagon and animals."

"Colonel Wilson wants us on the same raft as him. He's probably got someone. I'll check. Let me know if you need any help with the oxen and cow." Rebecca patted the side of her thigh, and Bolo came to her. She petted him on the head and scratched his ears.

"Sounds good. Bolo knows something is going on. He won't leave you, but you should put him on a leash."

Rebecca didn't trust herself to speak, she nodded, and walked to Colonel Wilson, leading Bolo.

****

Wilson stood with his hands on his hips motioning to a man dressed in buckskin and pointing to a line of rafts tied to stakes in the riverbank. People from the wagon train circled around him.

"Sir, my name is Colonel Wilson. I need four or more rafts to ferry folks down the river as safely as possible. How many can each raft hold? How much is the charge?"

"Pleased to meet you. Name's Campbell. Price depends on how many are on each raft. No more than ten on the large rafts. How many you needin', did you say?"

"I need at least four. The folks have sold all they could. One couple will be loading their broken-down wagon, it's the only one we'll be hauling. Mrs. Lawson can't walk anymore. Grief over her daughter's death has 'bout killed her. She's all but stopped living. The first raft will carry eight, the second one nine. After that, I'll make decisions. There will be at least two able-bodied men on each raft. It would be best if you give instructions to everyone at once."

"Sounds like a fair plan."

Rebecca stepped in beside the colonel. "Colonel, is there anything I can do?"

"Good morning. I think it's all worked out. Mr. Campbell here is going to provide at least four rafts. Where's Aaron and your mother?"

"They're selling the wagon and animals. I couldn't stand being there for that. Zachary left before sunrise with the men on the trail." Rebecca reached down to scratch Bolo's ears.

Colonel Wilson whistled for everyone to come to him when he saw Sarah and Aaron coming their way. He spit and spoke. "We're going to be heading down the river on the rafts supplied by Mr. Campbell. All of you have given me what you can to pay; others have put in more to make sure we all have a space. There can be no more than ten on a raft. The first one has eight, the second has ten right now. The Lawsons will be on the third one. He will remove the wheels before the raft sets out. Mrs. Lawson has to travel in the wagon as you know. Listen carefully to the rules."

Mr. Campbell stepped forward. He tipped his hat at the gathering. "Mornin'. We'll need to start down the river as soon as we load. Rules are simple. I have a guide at the front and back. Men may be needed to help with other oars. I want everyone sitting and evenly spaced. I have added hand rings to hold onto. Use them. Some of the river is smooth, most is rough, rocky, and dangerous. The falls are loud. You'll get wet. You, girl with the dog, keep him tied to you. Don't let him run loose. Keep your belongings in front of you. Won't take too long."

Rebecca bit her tongue to keep from saying something she would regret to Mr. Campbell. *How dare he even think Bolo would cause problems or that she couldn't handle him!*

Colonel Wilson moved to the first raft. "I'll be on this raft with Rebecca, Sarah, Aaron, Doc, Ed, Sean, and Ginny. The next one will be the Hendricks family, the Garsons, and Jessie Kelley. Third will be the Lawsons, the Slatons and Hans and Evie. The rest of you will be on the fourth raft. Get ready."

****

Ginny stood in front of Rebecca wringing a

handkerchief into a shredded rag. Tears ran down her cheeks and sobs choked her. "I'm so scared. You remember about my sister."

"I do. I think we're all afraid. You just focus on holding Sean. The guides know the river. And the men can help if need be." Rebecca's voice shook. She bent over and hugged Ginny.

The strangers who left Independence had since become family during the journey hugged, prayed, and wished each other well before loading onto the rafts.

****

Mr. Campbell spoke to the group. "The guides will tell you where to sit when you get on. Some of them don't speak English, but they can direct you with hand signals. You men might be needed to assist in the rough areas."

Rebecca, Sarah, Ginny, and Sean boarded first. The guides put Ginny with Sean on her lap in the center. They showed her the ring to hold onto. Rebecca and Sarah flanked her. Ed sat behind Ginny. Aaron and Doc settled next to Sarah and Rebecca with Aaron in front of Sarah and the colonel behind Rebecca. Ropes ran from ring to ring in front of them. Their bundles were tied to larger rings.

The guides took their places fore and aft. When the raft pushed off, every member of the group sucked in deep breaths.

"Ma, you're squeezing me too hard," Sean cried.

"I'm sorry, son." Ginny loosened her hold.

The rafts slipped into the deceptively calm river. Black basalt cliffs towered above them, inspiring awe and fear at the same time. Rebecca wondered how deep into the river the cliffs went, then shook her head to keep from imagining too much about the danger below the surface. The rocks clinging to the cliffs had sharp points that resembled the forks of the devil himself. Where were the forests? Where were the lush pastures? Where were the bubbly brooks she dreamed about?

Without warning, the raft took a downward dive, splashing and soaking everyone with cold water, then jerking up over a section of frothy and rapid white water. Rocks littered the river. Some were too large to see around, others seemed small. The guides moved among the whirlpools and rocks with ease until the river raged, trying to devour them.

"Oars! Push away from rocks on your side." The front guide ordered Colonel Wilson and Ed to move to the sides and help. They lurched up, got their footing, and put oars into the angry, willful river.

The biggest boulder she had ever seen loomed directly in front of them. *Lord, protect us. Why isn't he steering to the side? Why is he heading straight for it?* Waves crashed across the floor of the raft, soaking everyone. Sean didn't cry but turned his face to Ginny and squeezed into her as close as he could. Rebecca took Ginny's hand, hoping to reassure her, but had to pull away when her hand became numb from the force of Ginny's grip.

Just when it seemed certain they would crash into the boulder, the guide reached out and pushed the front of the raft away with his oar while the other guide, the colonel, and Ed worked to turn the raft. *They made it!* The river remained rough and dangerous but lost the battle that time.

When the raft made a sharp turn, the noise they'd heard in the distance became a deafening roar unlike anything Rebecca had ever heard. *Like a roll of thunder that refused to cease.*

Colonel Wilson latched his oar in the ring and anchored himself with a wide stance in front of his folks. "That roaring sound you hear are the falls. We'll pass them soon. After that the river will act more like a lady. She'll still be mad and unpredictable as hell, but we'll be almost to the end. The biggest danger are the whirlpools. Stay alert."

Rebecca cupped her hands around her mouth and shouted. "How much longer do we have on the river?"

"Not long. I don't rightly know. The others have hit the river by now. We'll be off the river about thirty minutes apart." Colonel Wilson took his oar and moved to the side in case he was needed.

Wonder replaced and suspended fear for an unimaginable moment when the falls came into sight. They tumbled down the side of the cliff beneath a shroud of clouds and ended in a flood of churning white water. Rebecca startled at the beautiful, majestic, and frightening sight. *How will I describe this wonder in my journal or to others?*

The outer side of the raft caught the edge of a whirlpool, and the motion almost pulled them into the eddy. The guides ordered the colonel and Ed to work the oars from one side and the others to lean away from the pull of danger.

Ginny fainted and let go of the ring. Her hold on Sean wasn't strong enough to keep him close and he began to slide away.

"Aaron, grab him. I'll get Ginny!" Rebecca shouted over the noise of the river and the men manning the oars. She tied herself to Ginny and slapped her cheeks, trying to wake her.

"I've got Sean. He's safe." Aaron's teeth chattered so hard he could barely speak. Rebecca sent him a reassuring nod. "You did good, Aaron. You're growing into a man people can count on."

His look filled her heart with pride.

Ginny groaned. "What happened? Sean? Where's Sean?"

"You fainted for a moment. Aaron has Sean. He's fine. You're fine. We got away from the whirlpool. Soon we'll be off this raft and on dry ground. You are safe. Sean and Ed are safe."

Rebecca scooted over when Ed came to sit with them. He sat behind Ginny and pulled her to him, wrapped his arms around his family, and prayed aloud for safety.

When the water calmed and he wasn't needed at the oars any longer, Colonel Wilson turned to face them. "The land you've dreamed of is in sight. In a few minutes you'll be stepping off this raft onto your new homeland. There isn't much here, but we can build fires and find something to eat. I reckon many of you tucked some hardtack and jerky into your bundles. When everyone is back together I'll talk about where we go from here."

Chapter 45

The New Land

When the raft reached the edge of the river, the guides stepped off and pulled it closer, stood side by side on the shore and waited for the settlers to disembark.

Aaron stood first, pumped his fist in the air and let out a loud whoop of relief. He hugged Rebecca and Sarah. Everyone laughed and gathered their belongings. One at a time, they followed Colonel Wilson off the raft. Sarah stopped and pressed a coin in each guide's hand. They thanked the guides and walked several yards away from the shoreline.

As a group they collapsed, caught their breath, and looked around. The long trail had finally reached a stopping point.

Ed started a fire. Ginny had packed tea, a small pot, and several cups so everyone could have something hot to drink. Sean took off running, then stopped to pluck flowers and play in a mud puddle. The unbridled joy of the toddler erased the tensions left by the Columbia River.

Exhausted but finding comfort in the playful antics of the child, Rebecca let Bolo off the leash to play. She unwrapped her bundle, put the quilt on the ground and motioned for her mother to join her. "Come sit with me.

The next raft will be here soon with some of the others."

Rebecca glanced to the south, knowing Emma and George waited in a small community they called Journey's End. "It's hard to believe the trek is coming to an end. I wonder when the men who took the animals along the land route will get here. I hope soon. I miss Zachary, to be sure."

"He'll be along. If they don't get back before we head out, he knows where to find us."

****

The second raft came ashore safely. Colonel Wilson met them. "Right on time. The first group has settled in that batch of trees to the south. Ginny has a fire and water for tea going. Head on over there."

"When will we be going to the fort?" Mr. Garson asked.

"Tomorrow. We rest now. I thought you were going to the community where the Pierces are headed? They won't be going to the fort, but they could if they want to wait an extra day. You need to talk to them. For now, I suggest you gather around the fire and get warm. Your wife is shaking, and her teeth are chattering." Colonel Wilson motioned to the fire.

Sally Henry came to the colonel. She put her hand on his arm. "Any news from the others who went by land?"

"Not yet. Talk to Rebecca. I gave her what little news I could. All will be fine. You'll see."

Dusk painted the western sky in slashes of red and orange when the last raft arrived. When it landed safely, Colonel Wilson checked on others. He walked with Hans and Evie. "Any problems?"

"Only one. We hit some rapids and the wagon Mrs.

Lawson was in started falling over. We got her out and wrapped her up before the wagon went into the water. It was close. I hope ending this journey gives her the inner strength to start a new life. Grief is a strange thing. Doc thinks she will recover. I sure feel sorry for the Lawsons since they lost little Sadie. They didn't have much, but they're grateful to be alive. You should probably pay them a visit."

"Is Evie holding up?"

"Yes, sir. She's fine. We're ready to get settled and have this baby. I think it's a boy."

Colonel Wilson patted Hans on the shoulder and laughed. "A boy. Hope it happens for you. Rebecca's waiting for you and Evie. We still haven't heard from the men who took the animals. I think she's nervous about it."

Wilson stood and watched over the men, women, and children he had led across the country. Almost two thousand miles. A mixture of relief, pride, joy, and utter fatigue filled his heart. He wondered if this was the way a mother hen felt when she had all her chicks safely together. He raised his hands and whistled.

"Listen up. We've made it. Rest tonight and tomorrow. If you want to go on to Fort Vancouver or one of the small communities, you're only a few hours' walk away I know you're hungry. Share whatever you might have. For now, bed down before you fall down."

Rebecca stood. "Thank you, Colonel. We all know we wouldn't be here without you. Our new lives are just around the corner. Join us over here for tea and hardtack."

Every person stood and applauded the colonel.

Chapter 46

Homecoming

Rebecca watched the sun rise on the second morning. Funny how it seemed so bright two thousand miles away from home. She lay on the quilt and slid the ruby pendant along its chain. *Zachary, where are you? Will you make it before we walk away from this place? Hurry, please hurry.*

When her mother roused, Rebecca turned to her. "Today is the day. Tonight, we will be with Aunt Emma. Aaron is up. He's busy sketching. He has a fire going. Bless him."

"I want to clean up as much as possible. I'll change into a fresh dress and chemise. Will you change into a dress?"

Rebecca threw back her head, clapped her hands, and laughed. "Of course. Who knows what Aunt Emma would say if I showed up in buckskin. What do you think, Bolo?" Bolo sat in front of her, cocking his head from side to side.

There was no tea or coffee. Breakfast consisted of jerky and hardtack washed down with water.

Several women gathered to go out for private moments. A mixture of happiness, relief, and expectation created a relieved mood among the women as they washed their hair and bathed in the cold Columbia water.

Rebecca stepped out from behind a group of her friends, held her skirt out and twirled around. "I've been keeping my blue dress aside to wear today. It's the one I had on when I met Zachary at the first dance. I hope he and the others get back before we reach the end."

The ladies gasped when Ginny changed into the yellow dress Mrs. Garson gave her on her wedding day. Her face turned red.

"You're beautiful, Ginny." Mrs. Garson took Ginny's hand and squeezed it.

Sarah smoothed the skirt of her navy-blue dress with the white collar and cuffs. "I agree with Mrs. Garson. You are beautiful. I think we're all pretty."

****

Colonel Wilson gathered everyone up. "Mornin'. I need to know which way you all are headed. I'm going to Fort Vancouver for a few days to turn in the paperwork from our journey. After that, I'll be going to Journey's End. I plan on opening an office as a solicitor."

Everyone murmured in disbelief. Rebecca grinned. Mr. Garson crossed his arms over his chest and heaved a sound of derision.

"It's true. I am a trained solicitor. An educated man. When my wife died, I decided to go west. Ended up running the wagons for three years to get the need for adventure out of my system. I'm ready to settle down."

"We're going to a town north of the fort. We want to start over where nobody knows us. I think that's best for my wife. She sat up this morning and moved her legs. I think she's going to recover. The colonel will help us get a wagon and team. Until he brings that to us, we'll stay here." Mr. Lawson choked up as he finished his explanation.

Rebecca went to Mr. Lawson and hugged him. "We'll leave you a quilt and some food. I think my buckskin pants will fit you. I have an extra dress I can leave for your wife."

Those who could spare things gave them to the Lawsons.

The Slatons decided they'd go south to Journey's End. Jeb and Obed ran around chasing each other and throwing a stick for Bolo.

The Garsons and Colonel Wilson would travel to Fort Vancouver first but planned to settle in Journey's End later. Everyone else was going to Journey's End. They had heard about Sarah's sister and felt comfortable they'd at least know someone when they got to town.

At noon, everyone began the walk into their new lives.

"I can't wait to see Emma. My goodness, I wonder if she's changed. I have. I wonder what she'll think of Doc. She'll be thrilled about you and Zachary." Sarah reached back and tucked her special comb tighter in her hair.

"I wonder if she'll like my necklace. Do you think Uncle George has obtained any land in our names? I do hope so. I want to start raising horses as soon as possible. I sure hope Zachary gets back before we get there. Hans and Evie will have a new home before the baby comes. Everything we've been talking about for more than a year is actually happening. I do get sad thinking about Pa and Joseph. Can you imagine what our future might hold?"

Four hours into the last part of the trek, Rebecca

heard the gallop of horses. She stopped and turned to see Zachary and Brent coming and leading Glory, Patriot, and Misty. "Sally, Sally!"

Rebecca and Sally took off running as fast as they could to meet the men they loved.

Rebecca all but pulled Zachary out of the saddle and jumped in his arms. "You're back. With my horses. Thank you, Lord!"

"I am back. I'll never leave you again. That trail was harsh. I think if we had stopped, the animals would have given up. We had to keep them moving. I'll tell you all about it when we get settled and fed. How far are we from town?"

"I don't know. It doesn't matter. We're close. I wonder if they know we're coming? Where are the others?"

"They went on to Fort Vancouver."

The next hours seemed to move as fast as the shooting stars Rebecca and Zachary watched for every night.

Suddenly, Sarah squealed, pulled up her skirts, and ran screaming toward a wagon in the distance. "Emma! Emma! We're here."

Emma jumped from the wagon and ran to her sister.

Sarah and Emma cried and hugged and cried and hugged some more. "We've known you were close for days. My goodness, is that Rebecca running to us with her skirts flying? Of course, it is."

Rebecca slammed into her aunt so hard she almost knocked her over. "Aunt Emma! We're finally here. I have so much to tell you. Why are you out here? Where is Uncle George?"

"I brought food and lemonade out to greet you and

your friends. I know you're tired and hungry. Uncle George is with the wagon and some of our friends. You're beautiful and you've grown into a woman. I have missed you so much." Emma gazed past Rebecca and Sarah. "Where are Robert and Joseph? I hope they're well."

Sarah and Rebecca reached out for each other.

"They are both dead. Joseph was killed in an accident six months before we left. Robert died of lung problems a short time before we left. It was a difficult decision for us to go ahead and make the trip. But here we are." Sarah pulled a handkerchief from her sleeve and blew her nose.

Emma rested her head on her sister's shoulder. "I wasn't there for you. I am so sorry for that. Please, come with me and refresh yourselves. Tell your friends there is plenty."

Zachary joined Rebecca. He tipped his hat. "Ma'am. My name is Zachary Miller. I gather from the scene I just witnessed that you are Emma."

"I am. Sarah's sister. Won't you all come join me at the wagon. I have some food and cool drinks for you. I know you are tired."

Rebecca took Zachary's hand. "Aunt Emma, Zachary and I are betrothed. We want to raise horses, cattle, and have a farm."

Emma beamed. "Well, if that doesn't take the cake. Congratulations. You just might want to know what your Uncle George arranged, young lady. What's that necklace you keep playing with?"

"Zachary gave it to me. It belonged to his mother." Rebecca didn't know why her face flushed and grew hot enough to start a fire.

Winona Bennett Cross

"It's pretty. When are you going to get married?"

"We aren't sure. Maybe Christmas or the spring."

Emma grinned and clapped her hands. "That's long enough to make you a nice dress. What do you think we should make it out of, Sarah?"

Jeb bounced over to Emma. "Ma'am, do you have any cookies? My baby brother, Obed, wants to know."

Emma laughed. "Well, it just so happens that I do. Cookies and cake. Cool milk just for little ones. You may call me Miss Emma. What can I call you?"

"Jeb. Just Jeb."

"That one's a trickster." Emma laughed.

"That he is," Rebecca said.

Everyone laughed and followed Emma.

****

Three days later Zachary and Rebecca stood on a bluff taking in the beauty of their land just as the sun set. Lush with trees, a cool running stream, and a clearing perfect for a house and barn, the property was perfect for raising horses and hopefully one day, children. They leaned into one another and laughed.

Rebecca pointed to an appealing spot. It had a small clearing and a border of trees near the stream. "That's the perfect place to build our home. What do you think?"

"I think any place will be home if you're with me." Zachary pulled Rebecca to him and hugged her so tight she didn't want him to ever let go.

Rebecca's uncle had procured two lots. One for Sarah and another for Rebecca. Sarah gave hers to Zachary as a wedding gift.

The two held hands and lifted their arms in a victorious salute. Each one of them held a deed in their entwined hands. Sealing their dream with a kiss, they sat

390

down to figure things out and drew plans for their home with sticks in the dirt.

Hobbled nearby, Glory, Patriot, Misty, and Red grazed while Bolo ran around in circles barking at anything that moved.

A word about the author…

Winona Bennett Cross lives in Durant, Oklahoma with her husband. She has two sons, one daughter-in-law, two teenaged granddaughters and a cat.

Winona is a retired Labor and Delivery nurse and nursing educator.

She believes dreams can come true.

She is a member of RWA, CROW, OKRWG, and OWFI.

Winona enjoys hearing from readers and can be reached at:

nona143writer@yahoo.com

https://winonabennettcross.com